Prologue

1693, Central Lapland

Aslak stumbled, a sign of exhaustion. He never missed his footing otherwise. The old man kept a firm hold on the package he was carrying. He rolled forward, head over heels. A clump of heather broke the force of his fall. A lemming darted out. Aslak got to his feet. Glancing back, he estimated his advance on his pursuers. The baying was louder now. There was little time left. He continued his silent race. His deep-set eyes burned brightly. His gaunt features and jutting cheekbones gave him a mysterious, hieratic air. He ran on, sure-footed now, trusting to instinct, working his body hard. He smiled and quickened his breathing, feeling fleet and light, sharp-eyed, infallible. He knew he would not fall now. Knew, too, that he would not survive this mild and gentle night. They had been tracking him for a long while. It had to end.

He took in every detail of his surroundings, the high plateau, the ancient commotion transfixed in the rocks, the sinuous lakeshore describing the outline of a bear's head, the rounded summits of the distant mountains, bare of vegetation. He could just make out the forms of the sleeping reindeer, a rushing stream. He stopped, barely out of breath. Here. Aslak stood solemnly, clutching the package, gazing at the scene: the stream tumbling into the lake, reindeer tracks threading east across the mountain, where the sun's gleam heralded the last dawn before the long winter night. He saw a small island in one corner of the lake and made his way towards it, cutting through the dense thickets of dwarf birch with his knife. The islet was covered in heather and scrub. The barking was louder still. Aslak pulled off his boots and tossed birch branches onto the mud, leaving no tracks as he crossed the marshes to the rocky island. He clambered up, pulled aside a section of heather and buried the package under its roots. He retraced his steps and ran on. He was no longer afraid.

The dogs tore after him, closer than ever. Soon, the men would emerge over the summit of the hill. Aslak gazed one last time at the lake, the mountain stream, the islet. The sun's rays marbled the clouds with bright streaks of purple and orange. Aslak ran and knew his legs would carry him no further. The dogs were upon him. The growling mastiffs formed a circle but left him untouched. He stood motionless. It was over. The men were there, panting and pouring sweat. They looked evil, but their eyes were filled with dread. Their tunics were torn, their foot-gear sodden. They leaned heavily on their sticks, waiting. One man stepped forward. Aslak looked at him. He knew. He had understood. He had seen this before. The man avoided the Laplander's gaze. He walked around, behind Aslak.

A violent blow shattered the old nomad's cheek and jawbone. Aslak fought for breath. Blood spurted. He dropped to his knees. The cudgel was raised for a second strike. He swayed in shock, though he had tried to brace himself. A thin man arrived on the scene, and the attacker's gesture froze. He lowered the cudgel to his side and stepped back. The thin, wiry man was dressed all in black. He shot an icy glare at Aslak and the man with the cudgel, who recoiled further, glancing away.

'Search him.'

Two men stepped forward, relieved that the silence had been broken. They tore the Laplander's cloak from his back.

'No sense in resisting, savage devil.'

Aslak said nothing. He did not resist, but still the men were

FORTY DAYS
WITHOUT
SHADOW

Olivier Truc

Translated by Louise Rogers LaLaurie

TRAPDOOR

First published in Great Britain in 2014 by Trapdoor
This paperback edition published in 2014 by Trapdoor

Copyright © Olivier Truc 2014
Translation copyright © Louise Rogers LaLaurie 2014

A CIP catalogue record for this book
is available from the British Library.

ISBN 978-1-84744-586-5

Typeset in Bembo by M Rules
Printed and bound in Great Britain by
Clays Ltd, St Ives plc

Papers used by Trapdoor are from well-managed forests
and other responsible sources.

MIX
Paper from
responsible sources
FSC   FSC® C104740
www.fsc.org

Trapdoor
An imprint of
Little, Brown Book Group
100 Victoria Embankment
London EC4Y 0DY

An Hachette UK Company
www.hachette.co.uk

www.littlebrown.co.uk

terrified. His pain was overwhelming. He was pouring blood. The men pulled him this way and that, forced him to drop his reindeer-skin leggings, pulled off his boots and his four-cornered hat. One of them hurled it into the distance, taking care to spit on it first. The other took Aslak's knife, its handle crafted in antler and birch-wood.

'Where have you hidden it?'

The wind rose, blowing across the tundra. It did him good to feel it.

'Where, vile demon?' shouted the man in black, his voice full of menace.

Even his companions took a step back. The man in black began a silent prayer. The wind dropped and the first mosquitoes appeared. The sun secured its foothold on the flank of the mountain. Aslak's head lolled painfully. He hardly felt the fresh blow of the cudgel, half shattering his temple.

The pain woke him. Near-unbearable pain. As if his head would burst. The sun was high, now. The stench was all around him. Men, women and children were bending over him. Their teeth were rotten. They were in rags. They looked murderous, reeking of fear and ignorance. He lay stretched out on the ground. Flies had replaced the mosquitoes, clustering at his gaping wounds.

The small crowd parted and the man in black stepped forward. Pastor Noraeus.

'Where is it?'

Aslak felt feverish. His filthy tunic was soaked in blood. The smell of it dulled his senses. A woman spat at him. Children laughed. The pastor slapped the child nearest him. Aslak thought of his own son, how he had tried to cure the boy's sickness by invoking the gods. The gods of his own people, the Sami. The children hid behind their mother.

'Where have you left it?'

A man in a sky-blue shirt stepped forward and whispered in the pastor's ear. The pastor gave no reaction, then jerked his head. The man in blue held out his hand to Aslak. Two others caught him under the arms, heaving him to his feet. The Laplander gave a sharp cry, his face a mask of pain. The men dragged him to the low wooden house used for village business.

'See these vile icons?' The Lutheran pastor began his interrogation. 'Do you recognise them?'

Aslak was barely able to breathe. The pain beat against his skull. The heat rose. His wounds itched appallingly, seething with flies. His torn cheek swarmed with life. Villagers piled into the room. The heat became suffocating.

'The swine is riddled with maggots, already,' said one of the men, grimacing in digust. His spittle stung Aslak's skin like a dagger-point.

'Enough!' shouted the pastor. 'You will be judged, Sami devil!' He thumped the thick pine-log table, calling for silence.

These country people sickened Noraeus. All he wanted was to get back to Uppsala as quickly as possible.

'Silence, all of you! Show some respect for your God and king!' His dark gaze fell on the icons of the Sami gods, and the image of Tor. 'Lapp, have these icons ever brought you the slightest good?'

Aslak's eyes were half closed. He pictured the lakes of his childhood, the mountains he had roamed so often, the dense tundra he loved to explore, the dwarf birch trees whose wood he had learned to carve.

'Sami!'

Aslak's eyes remained closed. He swayed slightly.

'They brought healing,' he whispered, his breath rattling. 'Better than your God.'

A murmur ran around the room.

'Silence!' The pastor's voice thundered. 'Where is the hiding place? Where is it? Say it, or you burn, cursed demon. Speak, damn you. Speak!'

'To the fire! Burn him!' yelled a woman holding a baby to her wan, flaccid breast.

Other women took up the refrain.

'Burn him! Burn him!'

The pastor was sweating. He wanted this over with. The stink, the proximity of the swarthy devil with his blood-soaked face, the vile, brutalised peasants – all had become intolerable to him. A trial sent by the Lord God himself. He would be sure to remind the bishop in Uppsala of his zealous service to the Lord here in the virgin territories of Lapland, when no other pastor was prepared to set foot. But for now, enough was enough.

'Sami,' he pronounced, raising his voice and his finger for silence. 'You have lived a life of sin, clinging obstinately to your pagan superstitions.'

Silence fell, but the tension was stifling. The pastor drew a thick, illuminated Bible towards him and pointed at the accusing words:

'He that sacrificeth unto any god, save unto the Lord only, he shall be utterly destroyed!' His thunderous voice filled the company with terror.

A thick-set peasant woman with a red, congested face sighed heavily and fainted, overcome by the heat. Aslak crumpled to the floor.

'This soothsayer, this pedlar of lies shall die, for he has preached apostasy, denying the true doctrines of Yahweh, your Lord God.'

The men and women fell to their knees, muttering prayers. Children gazed around, wild-eyed with fear. Outside, the wind rose again, bringing oppressive gusts of warm air.

The pastor was silent now. Dogs barked. Then they, too, fell silent. Stench filled the village assembly room.

'Sentence has been confirmed by the royal courts in Stockholm. Sami, may divine and royal justice be done. Take him to the pyre. And damn his soul.'

Two filthy men took hold of Aslak and dragged him outside. The pyre stood ready, halfway between the lakeside and the ten or so wooden houses making up the village.

Aslak was bound fast to a thick pole that been brought upriver specially, from the coast – there were no trees tall and strong enough for the purpose here inland. The pastor stood stoically while the mosquitoes sucked at his blood.

No one noticed the arrival of a young man, down at the lake, his boat loaded with skins to trade. He saw what was taking place in the village and froze. He understood the tragedy unfolding before his eyes. He knew the man on the pyre. A member of a neighbouring clan.

One of the peasants set the pyre alight. The flames spread quickly, engulfing the branches. Aslak began to tremble and shake. He struggled to unstick the lid of his one good eye.

He saw the lake in front of him and the hill. He saw the silhouette of a young Sami man, standing as if transfixed. The flames licked at his body.

'He saved the others of his clan, let him save himself now!' grinned a man blind in one eye, and missing a hand.

The pastor struck him hard.

'Do not blaspheme!' he hollered, and hit the man a second time.

The peasant scuttled off, his one hand pressed to his head. 'Sami, Sami, burn in hell!' he yelled as he ran. 'Cursed demon!'

A child began to cry.

Suddenly, the Laplander gave a piercing shriek. He was raving now, gripped by the flames, uttering bestial moans and cries. The wailing of a man no longer human. The cry sank into a hideous rattle, then rose again in a new register, a new dimension, beyond pain. A kind of harmony, utterly alien and unexpected, born of suffering, but clear as crystal to anyone capable of listening through the torment.

'Curse him! The demon is chanting to his gods!' cried a frightened villager, pressing his hands to his ears. The pastor stood by, impassive, searching the Laplander's face as if, in the heat of the fire, the man might suddenly reveal the whereabouts of the thing he had been sent to find.

Aslak's cry petrified the young Sami in his boat. Afraid but fascinated, he recognised the guttural chant of a *joïk*, a Sami song. He was the only one present who could understand the words, fragmented now, tumbling out fast. With his dying breath, the condemned man was doing his duty, passing on what he knew.

Then the singing ceased. Silence fell. The young Sami was silent, too. He turned back the way he had come, his head ringing with the dead man's screams. His blood had turned to ice. There could be no mistake. He knew now what he must do. And after him, his son. And his son's son.

1

Monday, 10 January, present day

Polar night

9.30 a.m., Central Lapland

It was the most extraordinary day of the year, pregnant with the hopes of humanity. Tomorrow, the sun would be reborn. For forty days, the men and women of the *vidda* had survived, their souls huddled against the dark, deprived of the source of life.

The taint of original sin, thought Klemet Nango, police officer and man of reason. Why impose such suffering on ordinary human beings otherwise? Forty days without shadow, crawling like insects upon the face of the earth.

And what if the sun failed to show its face tomorrow? Klemet smiled to himself. He was a rational man after all, a police officer. Of course the sun would be reborn. The local daily paper had even proclaimed the hour of the lifting of the curse, in its morning edition. Now that was progress. How could his ancestors have coped without the *Finnmark Dagblad* to inform them of the return of the sun at winter's end? Perhaps they never knew what it was to hope.

Tomorrow, from 11.14 to 11.41 a.m., Klemet would be a man

again, casting his own shadow by the light of the sun. And the day after that, he would hold on to his shadow for forty-two minutes more. Things happened fast once the sun was minded to return.

The mountains would stand proud once more, sculpted in sharp relief. Sunlight would pour into the depths of the valleys, bringing their sleeping vistas back to life, awakening the quiet, solemn vastness of the semi-desert covering the high plateaux of central Sápmi – the region's traditional name.

For now, the sun was a mere glimmer of hope, reflected orange and pink in the clouds scudding above the blue-tinted snow on the mountain tops.

As always, gazing at the spectacle of the landscape, Klemet thought of his uncle Nils Ante, renowned as one of the most gifted *joïk* singers in the region. A *joïk* singer and a poet: the hypnotic rise and fall of his uncle's chanting told of the wonders and mysteries of their Arctic world.

Nils Ante's mesmerising *joïks* had been the lullabies of Klemet's childhood, magical tales worth all the storybooks read by Norwegian children, safe at home. Klemet had had no need of books. He had Uncle Nils Ante. But Klemet had never been a good singer, and mere words, he had decided as a child, could not describe nature as he saw it, all around him.

'Klemet?'

Sometimes, as now on patrol in the vast, empty plateau of the *vidda*, Klemet allowed himself a brief, nostalgic pause for thought. But he said nothing. Awed by the memory of his uncle's *joïks*, he was incapable of poetry.

'Klemet? Can you take my picture? With the clouds behind.'

His young colleague brandished a camera, retrieved from a pocket in her navy-blue snowsuit.

'Honestly, Nina, is this really a good time?'

'Is this really a good time to stand there daydreaming?' she retorted, holding out the camera.

Klemet grunted. Nina was always ready with an answer, the sort of reply that generally occurred to him when it was too late. He pulled off his mittens. Might as well get it over with. The clouds had thinned and the cold bit harder still. The temperature was close to minus 27°C.

Nina removed her sealskin and fox-fur chapka, shaking her blonde hair loose. She sat astride her snowmobile with her back to the speckled pink and yellow clouds, and aimed a broad smile at the lens. She wasn't stunningly beautiful, but she was charming and attractive. She had big, expressive blue eyes that betrayed every nuance of emotion – a trait Klemet often found useful. He took the photograph slightly off-centre, on principle. Nina had joined the Reindeer Police three months ago, and this was her first patrol. Until now, she had sat behind a desk at the station in Kiruna, the local headquarters over on the Swedish side, and after that in Kautokeino, here in Norway.

Irritated by his colleague's constant requests to have her picture taken, Klemet always made sure he poked a fingertip into the corner of the photograph. Every time Nina showed him the result, she would smile and explain sweetly, without fail, that he should be careful to keep his fingers to the side, out of the way. As if he was ten years old. Her tone irritated him beyond words. He had given up with the finger thing, found something else instead.

A light breeze was blowing – instant torture in this cold. Klemet glanced at the GPS on his snowmobile, a reflex. He knew the mountains by heart.

'Let's go.'

Klemet climbed onto his snowmobile and set off, followed by Nina. At the bottom of the hill, he followed the bed of an invisible stream, frozen solid under the snow. He ducked sideways, avoiding the low branches of the birch trees, then turned to make sure Nina was still following. But, he was forced to admit, she had already mastered her machine to near-perfection. They rode on for another hour and a half, threading through the hills and valleys. The gradient steepened as they approached the summit of Ragesvarri. Klemet stood up astride his snowmobile and accelerated. Nina followed. Two minutes later they pulled up, drinking in the complete silence.

Klemet removed his helmet, worn over his *chapka*, and took out his binoculars. Standing on the step plate of his snowmobile, one knee resting on the seat, he scanned the surrounding landscape, peering at the hilltop ridges, looking for moving specks on the snow. Then he took out his thermos and offered Nina a coffee. She struggled forwards, up to her thighs in the dry, powdery snow. Klemet's eyes glittered mischievously, but he held back a smile. Revenge for the endless photos.

'Looks quiet enough, doesn't it?' asked Nina, between gulps of coffee.

'Seems that way, yes. But Johann Henrik told me his herd had begun to disperse. His reindeer are already short of food. And if they cross the river Aslak will blow his top, if I know him, which I do – stubborn as a rock.'

'Aslak? The one who still lives in a tent? Do you think their herds will mix?'

'Reckon they already have.'

Klemet's mobile rang. He took a moment to wedge it inside the earflap of his chapka.

'Reindeer Police, Klemet Nango.'

Klemet listened for some time, cradling his coffee cup in both hands, grunting occasionally between sips.

'Yep, we'll be there in a few hours. Or maybe tomorrow. And you're sure there's no sign of him?'

He swallowed another mouthful of coffee, listening to the reply, then ended the call.

'So finally, Mattis's reindeer are the first to go walkabout. Again. That was Johann Henrik. Says he saw thirty of them on his land. They must have made it across the river. Let's go take a look.'

2

5.30 a.m., Kautokeino

The museum's entrance was broken wide open. Snow swirled through the gaping double doors. On the floor, shattered glass mingled with flakes already freezing hard in the icy wind, lit by a shaft of light from a snowmobile outside.

The driver lunged forwards clumsily, weighed down by his heavy snowsuit. He rubbed his cheeks hard, struggling to contain his mounting apprehension.

Helmut Juhl and his wife had come to this forgotten corner of the Norwegian Far North in the pre-tourist era. In Kautokeino their fascination for Sami culture, and their talent as jewellery-makers, had found a place to flourish.

Patiently over the years, the couple had created one of the most remarkable sites in the country. Little by little, a group of ten asymmetrical buildings had sprung up, clustered one against the other, on the hillside overlooking the valley. Helmut unhooked a torch from the lobby wall and began the painful process of taking stock. His 'forbidden city', as some dubbed it, had shocked a few of the local aesthetes and Sami culture-vultures, while arousing suspicion among Sami artisans. Helmut had learned their silver-smithing techniques and become one of the region's leading experts. By creating an ambitious, dedicated exhibition space, he had restored the status of this and other ancient, nomadic arts from across Europe and Asia. Helmut knew he had won the first battle when Isak Mikku Sara, chief of the Vuorje *siida*, a powerful clan west of Karasjok, had brought him his own childhood cradle, carved in birchwood, so that it could be displayed in the pavilion devoted to traditional Sami lifestyles. Now, he had one of the finest collections in northern Europe.

Helmut crossed the second room, a spacious gallery devoted to collections from central Asia. The silver jewellery and pots were all there. Everything seemed in order.

The silence was broken by the distant, unmistakable crunch of boots over broken glass. The footsteps had to be coming from the lobby. He paused to listen. The faint sound echoed through the galleries. Helmut held his breath, listening hard. Almost without thinking, he reached for an Afghan knife hanging on the wall, and extinguished his torch.

'Helmut!'

Someone was calling him by name. He breathed a sigh of relief.

'Here! In the Afghan gallery!'

He replaced the knife. Seconds later he saw a thickly swaddled silhouette struggling towards him. The local reporter, Tomas Mikkelsen, rotund in his tightly stretched snowsuit.

'Tomas. Good God, what are you doing here?'

'Berit called me. She saw a scooter heading off about half an hour ago.'

Helmut moved on through the museum galleries. He was perplexed. Nothing seemed to be missing. Perhaps some drunken kid had shattered the front door? He reached the last gallery, known as the 'white room', arrayed with Sami art treasures – the finest jewellery in gleaming silver, beautifully worked and chased. Then Helmut saw the door to the museum's reserve collection and stores. It stood open, with the handle wrenched off. Someone had struggled to open it. His stomach clenched tight.

Seconds later, the neon strip lights flickered into life, flooding the space with raw, white light. The huge room was lined with storage boxes, numbered and arranged on shelves. A series of worn deal tables occupied the central area. Everything was in perfect order. So far, so good. Helmut looked again at the first shelf. Two boxes held figurines of camels, carved from horn in a workshop in Kandahar. All present and correct. But the shelf above was empty. His stomach clenched tighter still. That shelf could not be empty. The casket had disappeared.

The reporter spotted the German curator's horrified look.

'What's missing?'

Helmut's mouth had fallen open in shock.

'Helmut, what's missing?'

The museum director stared at Tomas, clenched his jaw and swallowed hard. 'The drum.' He stammered the words.

'Fuck.'

3

11.30 a.m., Central Sápmi

Nina crouched low on her snowmobile, the accelerator handle turned fully forward. Dwarf birch twigs lashed her visor. The powerful machine climbed the steep slope with ease. A thick layer of snow softened the relief, making progress easier. Mattis's trailer nestled in a dip halfway up a second, gentler hill. She reached it just a few seconds after Klemet. It never ceased to amaze her that the reindeer breeders were able to survive in these mobile shelters for weeks on end, in the depths of winter, in temperatures as low as minus 35°C, sometimes even minus 40, in complete isolation, dozens of kilometres from the nearest village. The wind had risen now, blasting unimpeded across the bare, empty mountains, but Mattis's trailer stood in a relatively sheltered spot just below the summit. Nina removed her helmet, adjusted her chapka and took a closer look at the trailer. Part caravan, part shipping container, but smaller. Smoke issued from a tin stove-pipe. The trailer was white, mounted on broad runners allowing it to be towed through the snow. The sides were reinforced with metal sheets. It was ugly, but aesthetic appeal counted for little out here in the tundra.

Nina looked around at the clutter outside the shelter: the breeder's snowmobile; a rudimentary workbench for cutting wood, with an axe planted in a log; jerrycans and plastic containers; two metal storage boxes loaded onto a snowmobile trailer; lengths of plastic-coated rope scattered everywhere; even the skin and head of a reindeer tossed in front of the trailer, its blood staining the snow. The animal's viscera were strewn about in a mess of torn rubbish bags, doubtless the work of a hungry fox. Nina stepped through the narrow doorway behind Klemet, who had entered without knocking.

Mattis sat up slowly, rubbing his cheeks.

'*Bores.*' Klemet greeted him in the traditional way. As usual, he had taken advantage of the reliable mobile signal at the nearby lake to call ahead and give Mattis advance warning of their visit.

Nina stepped forward in turn and bowed slightly towards Mattis.

'Hello. Nina Nansen. I'm new to the Reindeer Police: Patrol P9, with Klemet.'

Mattis extended a greasy hand. Nina shook it and smiled. She looked around, struck by the mess and filth. The trailer was sparsely furnished. Shelves along the left-hand wall were loaded with tins of food and plastic containers filled with different-coloured liquids. Utensils, leather straps and traditional Sami knives hung from nails. The shelves were actually quite tidy, Nina thought. These items were obviously important. There was a set of bunk beds.

A wood-burning stove and a fitted bench-seat stood against the right-hand wall. A long, narrow table occupied the space between the bench and the bunk beds. The top bunk was piled with plastic sacks overflowing with clothes and more tins of food. Ropes, blankets, a snowmobile suit, a large reindeer-skin cloak, several pairs of gloves and a chapka formed an untidy, dirty jumble. Mattis had been lying on the lower bunk, half submerged in a thick sleeping bag laid over a bed of reindeer skins. The sleeping bag was covered with frayed blankets, stained with food and grease marks.

A large cooking pot stood warming on the stove, on a low heat. Another pot stood at Mattis's feet, full of melting snow.

Two sets of reindeer-skin leggings and several pairs of grubby socks had been hung up to dry on a line strung across the width of the trailer, together with two pieces of reindeer hide, scraped clean of their fur. Two pairs of thick winter shoes could be seen poking out from under the shelves.

Nina gazed around, her eyes wide. She would have liked to photograph the scene, but didn't dare ask. The shelter was dirty, repellent. But fascinating. She was venturing into unknown territory, beyond her comprehension. How could people live like this here in Norway, in her own country? The scene reminded her of a TV documentary she had seen once, about a Roma encampment in Romania. All that was missing was a cluster of half-naked children. She felt uneasy, without really knowing why.

Klemet seemed perfectly at home. But then this was his country. He knew all about this – the other face of Scandinavia. Klemet had explained that Mattis did not live here all year round, he had a small homestead, too. Still, could this really be Norway? In Nina's home village, in the south, the fishermen kept cabins scarcely any bigger than this, on stilts out over the water. They used them to store their boats and nets. Nina had hidden there sometimes as a child, watching the big fishing boats as they came into the village harbour – the boats her mother had forbidden her to go near. Men were the bringers of sin, her mother said. Her mother saw sin everywhere.

But the fishermen's cabins were not squalid, like this. Then again, the trailer wasn't really squalid either, Nina thought after a moment. No, the trailer reeked of misery and distress.

Nina's mother would have known how to succour this lost soul. She always had been a decisive judge of character, capable of distinguishing good from evil. Nina wondered if Klemet was thinking the same thoughts as her. Perhaps her colleague was immune to it all by now. Perhaps he thought conditions like this were perfectly normal up here.

Mattis glanced uncertainly from one police officer to the other. He avoided making eye contact.

'You gave me a fright when you called just now,' he ventured, addressing Klemet who had taken a seat opposite him on the bench. 'You said "police". Scared me half to death. You should have said "Reindeer Police".'

Klemet chuckled and took a set of cups from his rucksack.

'S'right, though, isn't it?' Mattis went on. 'Get a call from the police, you might be in any sort of trouble. Get a call from the Reindeer Police, you know it's nothing serious. Right? Eh, Klemet?'

Klemet seemed pleased to have scored a point with his call. He took out a plastic bottle full of transparent liquid.

'Ah, no way!' exclaimed Mattis. 'You won't get me on that rot-gut liquor of yours ...'

'It's water this time,' Klemet reassured him.

Mattis relaxed. He began to sing softly, opening his arms, addressing Nina, a hypnotic, halting, sometimes guttural chant. Nina understood nothing, but recognised what was probably a *joïk* of welcome to strangers. Klemet listened and smiled.

Nina was about to sit on the end of the bench. It was covered in stains, like everything else.

'Fetch the pot over to the table, before you sit down,' said Mattis.

Nina glared at him. He had made no effort to get to his feet.

'Of course,' she smiled. 'You look tired. Your song was beautiful.'

Mattis showed signs of drunkenness, Nina could see that. She hated to see people in that state. It made her feel very uncomfortable. She removed her chapka, looking for somewhere clean to leave it, then picked up the pot and carried it over to the table with good enough grace. Immediately, Mattis plunged his fork into the stew and pulled out a chunk of meat. He began to chew, the broth trickling unchecked down his sleeping bag, from which he had barely extricated himself.

'My uncle was a great *joïk* singer, too,' said Klemet.

'That's true. Your uncle Nils Ante. He was good *joïker*.'

'He could improvise a chant just like that, on the spot, about a place, a person, something he'd seen, something that had touched him. Even when he spoke, his voice had that chanting quality. I used to notice how his eyes sparkled when he was about to sing.'

'And what's he do now, your uncle?'

'He's old. He doesn't sing any more.'

Klemet poked a knife into the pot and pulled out a piece of meat, transferring it to his mess tin. Nina watched, but didn't join him. He was used to dealing with the breeders. You had to take your time with them, he said. She wasn't sure Mattis was allowed to slaughter a reindeer for food, as he clearly had. Klemet was already bending over the stewpot again, apparently in no hurry to get down to business. He spotted a length of shank.

'May I?' he asked Mattis.

The breeder replied with a jerk of his chin in the direction of the pot, while fishing out a tobacco pouch. Klemet's mobile rang just as he was preparing to snap the reindeer shank with a blow from the handle of his dagger.

'Dammit!' he groaned.

He stared for a moment at the slender bone, as if expecting it to reply. A few shreds of meat clung to it, trickling with salty broth. Irritated by the intrusion, he turned to look at Mattis. The reindeer herder was putting the finishing touches to a hand-rolled cigarette. Droplets of broth glistened on his chin. A tiny shred of meat had stuck in his beard. Klemet made a face, still holding the bone and the dagger. Between ringtones, the only sound was the furious Siberian wind that had chilled the Finnmark for the past two days. As if thirty degrees below zero wasn't enough.

Mattis took advantage of the lull in conversation to pull a three-litre plastic container out from underneath his bunk. He heaved it up onto the table and filled his cup.

The mobile was still ringing. Even in the depths of the *vidda*, there were places within range of a signal.

The ringtone ceased. Klemet looked at the screen but said nothing. Nina stared at him, insistently. Finally, her partner passed her the telephone. Nina read the name.

'I'll call him back later,' was all Klemet said.

Evidently, reindeer breeders were quick to turn jumpy and short-tempered when their herds began to mingle.

Mattis pushed the plastic container across the table to Klemet.

'No thanks.'

Mattis looked at Nina, who shook her head and thanked him with a smile. Mattis drained half his cup and winced, narrowing his eyes. Klemet picked up the shank bone again, snapping it clean in two. He held out one half to Nina. There was no smile of thanks this time. Nina had made herself comfortable, stretched out on the bench, her snowsuit gaping open at the front. The trailer was almost warm.

'Want some?'

'No,' she replied drily. Here it came again. Klemet's favourite joke.

Slowly, her colleague raised the bone to his mouth, staring at her all the while. He sucked out a piece of marrow, slurping noisily, then wiped his mouth on his sleeve, winked at Mattis and turned to Nina with a twinkle in his eye.

'Know what they call this? Sami Viagra.'

Mattis looked uncertainly at the two police officers, until Klemet burst out laughing.

Nina stared at him. Yes, she had heard that one at least twice already, during their four days on patrol. Now it was Mattis's turn to laugh, a manic laugh that caught Nina by surprise. He took the other piece of bone and sucked out the marrow, with obvious relish.

'Heh heh! Sami Viagra!'

Unable to contain himself now, Mattis threw his head back and roared with laughter, his mouth wide open, offering a broad panorama of his remaining, stumpy teeth. Bits of meat jumped around in his mouth. Nina began to wonder what on earth she was doing here, but kept her feelings to herself. She knew Klemet was playing her up and hoped he would know when to stop. She knew she was still too much of a novice in the breeders' world to tell Mattis what she was really thinking.

Mattis held the dripping shank bone out to her, drooling from the corner of his mouth.

'Go on, try it! Sami Viagra!'

And he burst out laughing again, not without shooting a quick glance at Klemet. He launched into a new *joïk*, clapping in time, staring in Nina's direction, though he seemed to be looking straight through her. Klemet seemed to be enjoying the show. He wiped the corner of an eye and looked at Mattis, smiling.

Still on the end of the bench, Nina tucked her knees under her chin and folded her arms across her shins. Her sulky pose. The snowsuit made the manoeuvre difficult and uncomfortable. She frowned, then gratified Mattis with a diplomatic smile of refusal. Women were a rare sight in these parts, it seemed.

'Well, that's set me up for the day, anyhow,' Klemet insisted, with a wicked glance in her direction. Mattis roared with laughter once again, slapping his thighs.

'She's a beauty, though, isn't she?' He hiccuped.

Klemet stood up suddenly and helped himself to a ladleful of broth. Clearly, the joke was over. Mattis's laughter stopped short. Nina unfolded herself and poured coffee, refusing a cup of reindeer broth. Mattis glanced at her out of the corner of his eye, leering at the young woman, the hint of her breasts in the outline of her dark-blue sweater. Then he shot another quick glance at Klemet and lowered his eyes.

Nina felt exposed and out of place. The lecherous reindeer herder disgusted her, but she knew that, more than anything, he deserved her pity.

'Well then, Mattis, your animals have got over to the other side of the river. You know they're with Johann Henrik's herd? That was him calling just now. For the second time today.'

Mattis was surprised by Klemet's sudden change of tone. He looked nervously at the police officer, then at Nina, first her face, then her breasts.

'Oh?' he said innocently. He rubbed the nape of his neck, glancing sideways at Klemet.

The mobile rang again. Klemet picked it up, his gaze still fixed on Mattis, and cut the connection straight away. This time, the screen announced a call from police headquarters in Kautokeino. They could wait, too.

'So?' asked Klemet.

Nina looked at Mattis. He had his people's prominent, high cheekbones, a deeply lined face and quite a well-developed beard. Whenever he was about to speak, he would wince sharply and narrow his eyes, his lower lip gripping his top lip, before opening his eyes and mouth wide. She felt uncomfortable in this man's presence, but riveted, too. There was no one like him in her little village on the shores of the fjord, two thousand kilometres to the south.

'Dunno,' said Mattis.

Klemet opened his bag and took out a set of 1/50,000 maps of the region. He pushed the cooking pot to one side and the empty bean cans full of cigarette butts. Mattis drained his cup, winced again, then filled it back up to the top.

'Look, we're here. That's the river, there's the lake you pass when you head north for the migration. At the moment, Johann Henrik has his reindeer here, and here, in the woods.'

'Oh yeah?' Mattis yawned.

'And yours have got across the river.'

'The river . . .'

Mattis giggled, hiccuped, then straightened his face.

'Well, the thing is, see, my reindeer, they don't know how to read the lines on the map.'

'Mattis, you know perfectly well what I mean. Your reindeer shouldn't be on that side of the river. You know there'll be all hell to pay in the spring when you have to separate your herd from Johann Henrik's. You'll get into a dispute, like before. You know what hard work it is separating the reindeer.'

'And watching the herd all alone, in the middle of winter, out in the tundra, that's not hard work, eh?'

'Can you show me your winter pasture on the map?' asked Nina.

Her knowledge of reindeer herding was theoretical for the moment – acquired during her brief training in Kiruna. As a little girl, she had often looked after the sheep her mother reared. That had been more for fun, really – the sheep were left to themselves at the far end of the fjord. Being a herder wasn't work where she came from, more of an idle pastime. It was incredible to think the Sami

23

herders would spend all night watching their reindeer, in an icy gale. She needed hard, quantifiable facts, to try to make sense of their lives.

Mattis yawned again, rubbed his eyes and drank a mouthful of spirit. He ignored Nina's question.

'And why's Johann Henrik complaining?' he said, looking at Klemet. 'He just needs to push his reindeer back towards the hill. He's got people, he has.'

'Mattis,' said Nina, 'I asked you to show me your winter pasture on the map.' The young policewoman spoke calmly and quietly. She couldn't begin to imagine that Mattis had ignored her on purpose.

'Yes, he's got people,' Klemet replied. 'But still, you're on his land. That's how it is, you're responsible for your herd.'

'Well, it's not me that drew them, those boundaries,' objected Mattis. 'It's the blasted bureaucrats at the Reindeer Administration, with their pretty coloured crayons and their rulers, in their centrally heated offices.' He drank another gulp, without wincing this time. He was annoyed now. 'And me, I was out almost all night watching the herd. D'you think I do that for fun?'

'Mattis, please can you show me where your pasture is, here on the map?' Nina's voice was still calm.

'Haven't you got anyone who can help you?' asked Klemet.

'Help me? Who?'

'Aslak does, sometimes.'

'Well, not this time, it's been a rotten winter for everyone. He's probably still cross at me. And the reindeer haven't got enough to eat. They can't break the ice to get at the lichen. And I've had just about enough, I have. And I haven't got the money for the dry feed. So my reindeer, they go where they can to get food. They eat the moss off the tree trunks, in the woods. What can I do about it?' He took a longer swig of the drink. 'I'll go take a look later.' He drained the cup and yawned elaborately. 'And the little Miss – does she want me to tell her fortune?'

'The little Miss would like you to show her where your winter pasture is, on the map.'

'Klemet'll tell you. No fortune-telling then? Well, I'm going to get some shut-eye.'

Without further ado, Mattis shifted around on his bunk and lay down in his sleeping bag. Klemet rolled his eyes and signalled to Nina that it was time to go.

Outside, he took a look at Mattis's snowmobile, touched the engine and stared at it for a moment.

'Klemet, why wouldn't Mattis answer me?'

'Oh, you know, it's a man's world out here. They're not used to seeing a woman out in the tundra in the middle of winter, still less one in uniform. They don't know how to handle it.'

'Hm. And you do, of course?'

'What's that supposed to mean?'

'Nothing,' said Nina. 'Nothing. So what about this winter pasture? Your pal in there said you'd show me how far it extends.'

Snow was falling again, despite the bitter cold. Klemet spread the map on the seat of his snowmobile and showed Nina the pasture.

'But then, if his reindeer need woodland right now, he could take the herd north-west. There's a much bigger wood there, and it's in the middle of his zone, a long way away from Johann Henrik.'

'Perhaps . . . Or perhaps they've already been there. And perhaps most of his herd is still there. We can go and take a look, if you like,' said Klemet. 'And after that, we'll call on Johann Henrik.'

They climbed aboard their snowmobiles. A few minutes later, Klemet stopped in the middle of the frozen lake, taking advantage of the signal to call his voicemail. The first message was from Johann Henrik, who sounded exasperated. The second, from headquarters in Kautokeino, was briefer still. Patrol P9 was to return to base immediately. Johann Henrik would have to wait.

4

12 noon, Kautokeino

Karl Olsen had left the engine running on his pick-up. A few kilometres outside Kautokeino, the lay-by was empty apart from an abandoned trailer in front of the reindeer enclosure, unused at this time of year. It could not be seen from the road. He poured another cup of coffee, drank it scalding hot and looked around. Soon he would have to start checking the equipment. He pushed his cap back, high on his forehead. Above the brown leather peak, the green crown bore the logo of a large fertiliser company. He scratched his head slowly, squinting. Yes, he would need a lot of barley this year. He wanted to try tomatoes under polytunnels, too. There were EU subsidies up for grabs. Not for the local market, of course, but tourists always went for kind of thing: genuine Lapland tomatoes. He grinned to himself.

The theft had been headline news at 9 a.m., and it was still top of the midday bulletin.

'This was the first traditional Sami drum to be returned to Sami territory as part of a permanent collection,' explained the German museum curator on the pick-up's radio. 'The drums were used by shamans. This one was tremendously important for the local population. It's a tragedy for them. For years, people have been fighting to get the drums returned to their ancestral lands.'

Karl Olsen sneered as he listened to the interview.

'"Their ancestral lands . . . " Damned Kraut. Fine one to talk about ancestral lands.'

His coffee had gone cold, and he tipped the dregs out of the window. Nothing new since this morning, then. He poured himself another small cup.

A few minutes later, a sky-blue Volvo parked next to Olsen's Korean pick-up. A slim man with a moustache got out and settled himself into Olsen's passenger seat.

'Coffee?'

'Thanks,' said the new arrival, pulling off his knitted hat. 'So what've you got? Make it quick, I haven't got much time.'

'This business about the drum?'

'Yes. Everyone's on edge.'

'You know, Rolf, I knew your father well. A really decent man. I think he liked me, too.'

'Yes. And?'

'How long have you been in the force, now, lad?'

'Seventeen years. What's this about? Call me up here to listen to my life story, did you?'

'And it's been, what, three years since you came back home to Kautokeino?'

'A bit longer than that, as you well know.'

'Listen, kid, this business with the drum is a pain in the arse.'

'Yes, of course it is. So?'

'Everyone's going to get worked up about it, see.'

'Everyone's already worked up about it.'

'Yeah, yeah. I just heard that idiot Kraut: "a tragedy, a tragedy".' The elderly farmer rolled his Rs, imitating the museum director's accent. Rolf Brattsen was no fan of the German curator, either. The man was too preoccupied with the blasted Lapps, not enough with the true Norwegians.

Karl Olsen turned a little further towards the policeman. He cursed the stiffness in his neck which forced him to twist his whole body to look at the person next to him. He peered sideways at Brattsen.

'Listen, Rolf. I'm going to tell it like it is. Because that's the way I am. I say what's on my mind. You know me. You know I'm a member of the Progress Party. And you know what the party thinks about the Lapps and all their nonsense.'

The policeman said nothing.

'I know what you're thinking, Rolf. But I know what your father thought, too. And your father and I, we thought the same way. Your father was a good Norwegian, you know that? Eh? And you, you're a good Norwegian too, lad. Aren't you, though? Eh, lad?'

Tired of twisting around, the farmer leaned forward to tilt the rear-view mirror. Now he could look Brattsen in the eye without straining his neck and back.

'So listen. I know you're a good kid. Your father was a good man. We gave the Commies a run for their money back in the day, he and I. You know all about that. Well, the Lapps are no different. Bloody Communists, the lot of them. All their nonsense about land rights. Me, I know about the land. And the land chooses its own master. It belongs to whoever takes good care of it, no one else. You understand me? I look after my land. And they'll all be waking up now thanks to that damned drum. "My drum, my land," the whole blasted mess. It's no good to us once they start. It'll bring all the shit stirrers up from Oslo, too. We don't need the suits up here, eh? We're better off among our own kind. Better off still without the Lapps, too, that's a fact.'

The farmer paused to tip his cold coffee out of the window and pour another cup, steaming from the flask.

'Well, you don't have much to say for yourself, lad. Just like your father. Oh, he was good man. Absolutely straight up and down. Trustworthy, you know. Ha! Those Commies. We gave them what for. You look like him, you know? He'd be proud of you, lad.'

'Look here, Karl,' said Brattsen, suddenly, 'I don't like the fucking Lapps any more than you. And I don't like the fucking Ruskies sniffing around here either, or the fucking Pakistanis overrunning our country. But I'm a policeman, OK?'

'Steady on there, lad.' Olsen smiled indulgently, pleased with the turn the conversation was taking at last. 'Of course you're a police-man, and a good one at that. I just wanted you to know you're not alone. It won't pay them to do too much thinking, that lot. And me, I reckon it won't do any harm if the Lapps never get their drum back. It'll give them ideas otherwise. They've already got their own police force . . .'

'The Reindeer Police? Some crack squad, they are. Can't even think straight, half of them. Bunch of fake cops.'

Brattsen had dropped his guard now.

'Right this minute,' he went on, 'the Kautokeino contingent are over at that tramp Mattis's place. Idiot spends all his time chanting and drinking when he should be watching his herd.'

'Is that where they are?' Olsen struggled to turn in his seat, then checked himself. 'Talk about a degenerate drunk. He's your man. Well, it's the inbreeding, isn't it, though? You knew Mattis's father?'

'That crazed old guy people said was a shaman?'

'That's what people said, lad. Fact is, Mattis's father was his uncle. His mother's own brother, you get me?'

Rolf Brattsen shook his head. 'Got to get back to the station,' he said. 'I didn't know you and my father knew each other that well.' For the first time, he turned to look closely at Olsen. 'He never talked about you.'

Olsen stared straight ahead.

'Get back to your work, son.' He looked away. 'Never forget who your real people are. And don't be in any hurry to get that drum back. It'll only stir the hornet's nest. Blasted Lapp Communists.'

5

4.30 p.m., Kautokeino

Klemet Nango and Nina Nansen entered the town from the south-east. They took the 'motorway' as it was called in winter, riding up the broad, frozen river that passed through the middle of Kauto-keino, and stopping at the police station right in the centre. The public entrance was next to Vinmonopolet, the State-run liquor store, whose clients frequently veered in through the wrong door.

The sun had long since sunk back from its zenith just below the horizon, but a faint blue glow remained. Klemet and Nina left their snowmobiles in the parking lot, carried the storage boxes between them, one by one, to the garage and headed up to the first-floor offices.

'Perfect timing, the meeting's just starting in the Sheriff's office,' said the station secretary, passing them on the stairs. 'I'm rushed off my feet. This drum business.'

'What drum?'

'Haven't you heard? You'll see,' said the secretary, brandishing a wad of papers. 'Back in a minute.'

Nina and Klemet dropped their equipment at the lockers and went to the meeting room. They were greeted by Superintendent Tor Jensen, known to all as the 'Sheriff' thanks to his habit of rolling his shoulders and sporting a leather cowboy hat when he wasn't on duty.

The Sheriff waited for them to take their seats. There were four other police officers in the room. Klemet noticed Deputy Superintendent Rolf Brattsen was absent.

'On the night of Sunday to Monday, a Sami drum was stolen from Helmut Juhl's place,' Tor Jensen began. 'As you know, this is a very special drum, the first to be returned to Lapland as part of a permanent collection. I'm not Sami, but this is very important for them, apparently. Important to you, is it, Klemet? You're the only Sami here.'

'I suppose, yes. Perhaps.' Klemet was embarrassed.

'There's been a great fuss about it, in any case. The Sami are saying their identity has been stolen all over again, they're being discriminated against, as always, etcetera . . . And Oslo isn't happy, of course, especially with a major UN conference on indigenous peoples about to start up here in three weeks, and the Sami being our very own dearly beloved indigenous people, as you well know. Taught you all about that at police academy, did they, Nina? Be surprised if they did. Well, our Oslo friends are getting tetchy. They like being teacher's pet and top of the class at the UN, especially where the handouts are concerned, and they don't want their knuckles rapped over a stupid business about a drum.'

'Do we have any idea who's responsible?' asked Nina.

'None,' replied the Sheriff.

'Are there any leads, or theories?' she asked.

'Begin at the beginning. We'll get on to that in a minute.'

The secretary entered the room and distributed five stapled sheets of paper to everyone present.

'So the drum was in a sealed case,' the Sheriff continued. 'A private collector had sent it to the museum just recently. The drum has disappeared with the case. Apparently nothing else was taken. There was a break-in. The thieves broke through two doors. The main glass door was shattered to pieces (photograph number one). And then the door to the archives, photo number two, which was forced. We don't know how. There's a plan of the museum premises. That's your lot. See what you can do.'

Klemet leafed quickly though the sheets of paper. Thin pickings indeed. A rushed job.

'Remember: political pressure big-time from Oslo, but also the Sami politicos here. Not forgetting the Far Right who are trying to score points off the Sami, laying it on thick, too. You guys can get over to the museum and investigate.' He indicated the other officers in the room. 'Klemet and Nina, you'll be reinforcing the street patrols in town. Things are quite lively, it seems.'

'And the leads, any theories?' asked Nina, with a sweet smile. For the second time today, her questions had been ignored and it was starting to annoy her.

The Sheriff looked at her for a moment in silence.

'All we know is that a woman living next to the museum . . . ' he glanced at the slim report, 'Berit Kutsi, heard a snowmobile in the night. Nothing unusual in that, what with the breeders coming in and out at all hours, but it's unusual in that location. The tracks were obliterated by the snowstorm. Oh, and Rolf is in charge of the investigation. I want to see everyone report back tomorrow morning.'

'Klemet, how are things out in the *vidda*?' asked the Sheriff, when the others had gone.

'Getting a little tense. It's been a bad winter. It's very hard for the small-time breeders. I think we'll be seeing an escalation of fights and disputes.'

'Klemet – we don't need any major trouble, with this conference just around the corner. You get my meaning.'

Klemet frowned. 'Try telling that to the reindeer.'

'And you try telling that to the breeders. Do your job. Meanwhile, take Nina into town. In a professional capacity, you understand.'

'Got any new jokes, Sheriff?'

'I know you, Klemet.'

Klemet and Nina rode a few hundred metres on their snowmobiles along the Alta road, as far as the crossroads. Everyone referred to Kautokeino's main intersection as 'the crossroads'. The Alta road came in from the north, along the riverbank, leaving town in the direction of Finland and Kiruna in Sweden. The big trucks used it as a direct link between southern and northern Norway. It had the advantage of running in a straight line: the route crossed two national borders, but it was better than the interminable road around the Norwegian fjords. Perpendicular to it, another route led to the supermarket car park and, in the opposite direction, to the road serving the industrial estate. Beyond that, it circled the imposing wooden church, visible from all over the town.

A group of about ten people occupied the middle section of the crossroads. Most wore traditional Sami costume, the rich colours silhouetted against the snow in the twilight. Two elderly women carried a banner that had clearly been made in a hurry and was barely legible, its letters seeping into the cloth: 'Give us back our drum.' Succinct and to the point, thought Klemet. Another group clustered around a brazier. It was a little warmer now, only about minus 20°C. But a light breeze made the cold bite hard.

Klemet and Nina left their vehicles in the parking area, near the brazier. There was very little traffic. As usual. A woman apparently in her late fifties turned to them and offered coffee.

'Well, Berit, what are you doing here?' asked Klemet.

He and Berit Kutsi had known one another since childhood. Her fine, smooth skin lay close over the contours of her face, stretched smooth across her high, prominent cheekbones, creasing only when she smiled. She radiated goodness and empathy, and her kind expression was accentuated by the slight downward slant of her eyes.

Klemet knew all the protesters, in fact. They were Sami, but none was a reindeer breeder apart from Olaf, the youngest present. He was talking to the driver of a car, bending over its open window. The other herders had no time for protests. They were out in the *vidda*, watching their reindeer or sleeping, catching up on a night's vigil in the cold. Like Mattis, no doubt, at that very moment. Trying to forget that in a few hours' time they would have to go back out into the biting cold and wind, pile on the layers of clothes, ignore their hangover, fire up the snowmobile and set off alone across the tundra, hoping to avoid an accident. More than once, a herder had been found frozen to death near his snowmobile after hitting a rock, invisible under the thick snow. Reindeer breeding was justly famous as the most dangerous job in the Far North.

'Well now, what a pretty girl!' smiled Berit, teasing Klemet gently, as she always had. 'Watch out for him, dear,' she added, for Nina's benefit. 'Klemet's a charmer, one for the ladies. You might not think so to look at him? Make sure he keeps his hands to himself!'

Nina glanced at Klemet with an embarrassed smile. He could see she was unused to the outspokenness of northerners. It did not sit easily with the natural reserve of southern Scandinavians. 'Berit, you say you heard a snowmobile in front of the museum?'

'Well, I've already told Rolf everything. When I heard the scooter, I thought it was a breeder coming in from the north side of the valley. From the other side of the hill where the cultural centre is,' she noted, for Nina's benefit. 'There are some herds over that way. But the snowmobile stopped in the front of the Juhl Centre, which never happens in the dead of night, and the engine kept running, just ticking over.'

'What time was that?'

'About five o'clock this morning, perhaps, or earlier. I often wake up around then and I go back to sleep. But the noise of the engine woke me up when it drove off again.'

'Did you see the snowmobile, or the rider?' asked Nina.

'Just for a moment, the headlights lit up my bedroom as bright as day. I was dazzled, so I couldn't see the rider. Not from the front, anyway. But when he rode off, I saw from behind that he was wearing an orange-coloured boiler suit, like a construction worker.'

That was little enough to go on. Contrary to the Sheriff's pre-conceptions, Klemet wasn't particularly traumatised by the theft of the drum. Except that it was a criminal act, of course. Klemet had never been a very orthodox Sami, for a host of reasons. And he didn't like

34

rummaging through those too often. Even less so in front of non-Sami.

Berit had returned to the side of the crossroads, joining another group of protesters blocking the road leading to the church.

Olaf Renson walked over. In his late forties, he was still the youngest of the group. Nina noticed his proud, dynamic carriage, the determined set of his jaw, the sensual mouth and high, prominent cheekbones. His wavy, black, jaw-length hair was in striking contrast to Klemet's stiff, chestnut-brown crop.

'So! Here come the cops.' He spoke quickly. 'What do you want from us? Found the drum already, have you, Klemet? Good afternoon, miss . . .' He eyed Nina seductively.

'Hello,' said Nina with a polite smile. Klemet saw no point in extending a greeting of his own.

'Klemet, if there's a drop of Sami blood left in your veins, you must see that the theft of the drum is a scandal. A knife in the wound! We won't stand for it. It's an insult too far. You can understand that, Klemet, or have you forgotten your roots?'

'That's enough, Olaf, all right?'

'Did you ever see the drum?' asked Nina.

'No, I think it was going to be put on show in a few weeks.'

'Why is it so important?'

'It's the first one to be returned here to Sápmi,' said Olaf, glancing from Nina to Klemet and back. 'For decades, the Swedish, Danish and Norwegian pastors persecuted us, confiscating the shamans' drums and burning them. They were terrified of them. Just imagine – we used them to heal the sick and talk to the dead. They burned hundreds of drums. There are barely more than fifty left in museums, in Stockholm and elsewhere in Europe. One or two in private collections. But none here, with the Sami people. Unbelievable, isn't it? And then finally, the first drum ever to be returned is stolen. Sheer provocation!'

'Who stood to gain by it?' Nina asked.

'Who?'

Olaf lifted his chin and ran his hand through his hair.

'Who would want the drum to disappear? Who do you think? People who don't want the Sami to hold their heads high again, of course.'

Klemet stood watching Olaf in silence. The posturing irritated him. Renson was supposed to be a reindeer breeder, but he always found time to strut about on protests like this. He was a piece of work all right. A hard-nosed militant for the Sami cause since his teens, in the late 1970s. Back then, a number of Norwegian, Chilean, Australian and other companies had developed mines and dams in Lapland. One of them, a Chilean company called Mino Solo, had attracted fierce opposition for its unorthodox methods, leading to demonstrations for which Olaf Renson had provided a willing figurehead. He had forged a solid reputation as a militant and righter of wrongs, provoking more than a few pangs of conscience for Klemet.

Two trucks approached the crossroads. They were blocked by a couple of elderly Sami women, who stood in their path for a few brief seconds in a token show of defiance, before letting them through. The drivers – Swedish according to their plates – did not seem bothered. A line of cars had formed in the opposite direction. The driver of a green Volvo began to sound his horn. Others soon followed suit. The elderly ladies carried on as before, stopping for five seconds in front of each vehicle.

One of the trucks reached the middle of the crossroads. There were two people in the cabin. The Swedish driver seemed to be enjoying a joke, elbowing his passenger. Klemet recognised the second man as Mikkel, a local herder who worked for the wealthier reindeer breeders. The driver wound down his window and leaned his tatooed arm outside, despite the cold. Klemet heard him call to one of the elderly women: '*Hej hej!* Spose a fuck's out of the question, darlin'?'

Klemet was relieved to see she hadn't understood. The driver roared with laughter, high-fived his passenger and drove off. Klemet shook his head in disgust. He felt ashamed on behalf of the women.

Olaf returned to the other side of the crossroads and stood

proudly in front of the green Volvo, eyeing the driver without a word. He turned to look at Klemet, as if throwing down a challenge. Then, with a lordly wave, he let the driver pass.

Tomas Mikkelsen, the reporter, had arrived on the scene. He held a microphone up to Olaf, who glared at it, apparently outraged. Klemet could just about lip-read his words. Olaf gestured expansively, puffing out his chest, as he always did. Just as the interview was getting under way, a minibus drove up the road opposite the supermarket, honking its horn. Tomas held out his mike to catch the sound, background 'colour' for the 6 p.m. bulletin. A tall man stepped down from the bus, shouting. Klemet recognised the local pastor, a heavy-featured man with a luxuriant blond beard, looking for all the world like a vociferous lumberjack.

Klemet and Nina walked over.

'Clear out of my way immediately! What on earth's got into you all?' The pastor was incensed. Three elderly protesters stood politely to one side to let him through. He regained his composure. 'What's all this about, my friends?'

'It's the drum, Reverend,' said one of the men.

The pastor frowned.

'The drum, the drum ... Well, I can see that would be very upsetting, losing the drum. But you'll get it back, won't you? I suggest you get off home and stop blocking my road.'

Olaf reached the pastor at the same time as Klemet, Nina and Tomas Mikkelson, his microphone still recording.

'It's not your road, Pastor,' Olaf declared. 'And the drum isn't just any drum, you should know that better than anyone – your predecessors burned all the others.'

Surrounded by the small group, the pastor adopted a honeyed expression. But his lips were pinched tight. He was struggling to contain himself.

'Come, come, my children. That's all in the past, and well you know it, Olaf. You ought to know it, at any rate, rather than getting these good people worked up into a frenzy.'

'Worked up? The drum is our soul, our history ...'

37

The pastor's fury rang out once again.

'Your damned drum is the instrument of the devil! And you, the police, will be so kind as to keep the road to my church clear. I am expecting my flock.'

Klemet felt acutely uneasy in the man's presence. Like his own family, the pastor was a Laestadian, a member of one of the Lutheran Church's most hard-line sects.

'Olaf, you can carry on demonstrating, but stay off the road, is that clear?' Klemet ordered him.

'Ha! The collaborator shows his hand,' scoffed Olaf. 'Always on the side of authority, eh, Nango? Got the uniform to prove it. All right folks, let the reverend drum-burner through.'

The pastor shot a furious look at the protester.

'Time to be getting along, too, Reverend. Back to your church. And keep your comments to yourself in future.'

Nina had spoken. Everyone stared at her in astonishment. Olaf flashed a smile. But her attention was already focused on the cross-roads once more.

The line of cars was getting longer, and the chorus of horns louder. It was shopping time. Stuck in the jam, Karl Olsen sounded his horn, furiously. The farmer was red with rage. He shouted a warning to Berit Kutsi.

'For Christ's sake, Berit, get them to let me through.'

'I'll tell them to hurry up,' said Berit, recognising her employer.

'I thought you were supposed to be at work on the farm today?' Olsen asked her, drily.

He swore under his breath, accelerated hard and disappeared into the dark, loud with the din of car horns.

'What a charming man,' said Nina.

'Life is not always kind here,' said Berit. 'But kind hearts keep watch, and the breath of goodness is felt in the *vidda*. God's peace,' she added, in parting.

6

Tuesday 11 January

Sunrise: 11.14 a.m., sunset: 11.41 a.m
27 minutes of sunlight

8.30 a.m., Kautokeino

The events of the previous day had plunged Patrol P9 into turbulent, unfamiliar waters for the Reindeer Police. For Nina, the recent police academy graduate, the repercussions came as less of a shock than for Klemet: she had spent the past two years in Oslo, where politics and social issues were hotly debated in police circles. The scene at the crossroads proved to her that, despite appearances, tensions could run high in the region. She knew very little about Sami issues. A member of parliament for the populist Progress Party had expressed concern over the creation of a Sami court, dealing exclusively with Sami affairs. 'What next, a special court for Pakistanis?' he had declared. He had been fiercely criticised, but the outburst had gone unpunished. People were becoming immune to the excesses of the Progress Party.

The first visit of the morning was to Lars Jonsson, Kautokeino's brutish-looking pastor. The police car made its way slowly past the dozen or so Sami still occupying the crossroads and briefly blocking the path of each car, following the ritual established the day before.

Patrol P9 was no exception. Berit Kutsi stood aside after five seconds and waved to Nina and Klemet, who drove on down 'the pastor's road' and parked outside the immaculate wooden church, painted a deep, ox-blood red. The pastor was at work in the sacristy.

The Kautokeino police had shared out the interview duties. Deputy Superintendent Rolf Brattsen and his men were taking care of the usual Saturday-night suspects. The town's disaffected youth generally congregated at the pool table in the pub and often ended the evening in an alcoholic stupor during which any number of petty, idiotic misdemeanours were likely to be committed. Nothing serious, in Brattsen's view: dustbins overturned, neighbours kept awake, car or snowmobile races on the frozen river, pot-shots at the street lamps, girls given a bit of rough treatment, or forced into things. He would interview the local losers one by one and soon see if one of them had been showing off for the others at Juhl's place. Klemet and Nina would make the rounds of the others, the Sami 'politicos' as Brattsen dismissively called them. They would see the pastor, too, and the Progress Party representatives, together with any other potential suspects.

'Morning, Lars. We've come about the drum,' said Klemet.

Her partner did not like the reverend and it showed, Nina thought.

'Ah, the drum. Which I am now accused of burning, I imagine?' The pastor drew a long, deep breath. 'Bringing drums back here is a bad idea. And do you know why, Miss?' He addressed Nina, the newcomer, and gestured for them to sit down. 'Not because of the drum itself, but because of everything that goes with it. Drums are all about spirits walking abroad, trances and all the waywardness that accompanies them – the means the shamans use to achieve the trance state. I mean alcohol, Miss. Alcohol, and the ravages of alcohol,' growled the pastor, fiercely. 'And that I cannot accept.'

The two police officers said nothing for a moment. The pastor's eyes blazed and his jaw trembled.

'You see, it took decades to rescue the Sami from the spiral of evil. Only the grace of God and the rejection of their ancient beliefs saved them. They are all the better for it, believe me. They fear

40

God, and so it should be, henceforth and for ever. A drum marks the return of evil among us. Anarchy. The sufferings inflicted by alcohol. Broken families, the end of all we have struggled to build here over almost two centuries.'

Nina knew she was far too ignorant in these matters to argue with the pastor, but she noticed Klemet shifting irritably in his seat.

'I don't know many Sami who go in for shamanism these days,' he retorted.

The pastor shot him a furious look.

'What do you know, you of little faith? Since when have you shown any interest in the salvation of souls? Your family did, but you, Klemet? You spent more time tinkering with cars and going to parties in your youth than you did at church.'

'Reverend,' Nina interrupted him, 'we need to know who stands to gain by stealing the drum.'

'And burning it, I know what you're inferring! If I had it in my possession, I'd burn it right now, believe me!'

He quickly recovered his composure.

'Figuratively speaking, of course. I respect the culture of our Sami friends. Hm. Their culture, you see, not their ancient superstitions ...'

'But you talk about it in very disparaging terms,' Nina broke in.

'Disparaging? No, indeed. Don't misunderstand me. But I know what rumbles beneath. I know the lure of the forces of evil, I wage war against them. Our leader Laestadius understood how to save the Sami long before anyone, and better than anyone.' His barely contained rage broke the surface once again. 'We must show not the slightest weakness!'

'Lars, where were you on Sunday night?'

'Watch your tone, Klemet! You don't seriously think I stole the drum?'

The pastor was being altogether too familiar with her colleague, Nina thought. And patronising. She did not like it.

'Please just answer the question,' she ordered, no longer trying to keep things friendly. 'And remember you're addressing an officer of the police.'

41

The pastor smiled benevolently.

'After Sunday eucharist, I always spend the afternoon with my family – my wife and four daughters. We go for a long walk, and we take mulled cranberry juice and oat biscuits along with us. It's the only time in the week when we eat biscuits. My wife makes them in the morning. And in the evening we eat early – bread and butter and jam – after I've supervised the girls' homework. That's really about it. After supper, we read the Bible and we are early to bed. And that's how it was this Sunday, too. My wife and daughters will confirm that.'

'Do people seem disturbed by the presence of the drum here in Kautokeino?' Nina asked.

'Truly, I think they are. Some of my parishioners have spoken to me about it. They do not, perhaps, see the same dangers as I do and I cannot blame them for that. They are simple people, as is right, for God loves the pure in heart. I have reassured them, of course, as a pastor should always reassure his flock. But I see none of them capable of such a criminal act. My parishioners fear God and respect the law of men, I can vouch for that,' he concluded, defiantly.

Thugs weren't an obvious presence on the streets of Kautokeino. Policing was low-key – you just had to handle the right people, the right way. Unless it was reindeer business, of course, in which case the rules were quite different. There wasn't much of a drug problem, either. There were drugs about, of course, like everywhere else, but the traffickers were mostly passing truck drivers.

Rolf Brattsen knew where his regular suspects were to be found, when they weren't at school or at work. Or hanging around on the dole. They'd be practising their Sami hip-hop or some such ludicrous nonsense. The best thing, he told himself, would be to put one of them under arrest, fast. At least hold someone at the station for questioning. In the run-up to the UN conference, that was definitely his best course of action. Unlike the Reindeer Police, he operated in plain clothes. But that didn't change anything. Everyone saw him coming, knew who he was. That was the trouble with places where you'd spent too much time, he told himself. He thought about Karl Olsen's remark on the number of years he had spent in the force. And what had he got out of it? What had he achieved? In Kautokeino, Norwegians always lost out to the Lapps. The State was stymied by its guilty conscience over the indigenous population and their supposed mistreatment in the past. Mistreatment, for Christ's sake! The upshot was, everyone was too scared to strike hard when it mattered. I'm just here for show, Rolf Brattsen told himself. Reduced to going through the motions.

He stopped his car behind the theatre and was pleased to find three youngsters smoking and drinking beers. They showed no sign of running off when he got out of the vehicle.

Brattsen knew all three. He had already had them in on minor charges. That was how he operated. Make them feel you were keeping an eye on them. If they put a foot out of line, they'd be carted off to the station to cool down and sober up. Keep up the pressure. Never let them think they can get away with murder just because they're Lapps.

'Revising hard for our exams, are we?'

The youths carried on smoking their roll-ups. They looked at him, grinning. Unfazed, thought Brattsen.

'Good weekend?'

'Yep.' One of the youths ventured a reply. He was wearing canvas trainers, in spite of the cold.

'Few parties?'

'Yep.'

'Which party were you at on Sunday?'

'Sunday?'

The youth in trainers was wearing a Canada Goose jacket, like a lot of young people in the town. He seemed to be giving the question some thought.

'One you weren't invited to, whatever . . .' The show of bravado prompted a burst of laughter from his friends. But his expression was anxious. For a whole host of possible reasons, Brattsen thought to himself.

'Nice jacket you've got there,' he said.

The youth made no reply, dragging on his cigarette.

'Mind if I take a look?'

Brattsen examined the jacket and pulled on something sticking out of the sleeve. A feather. He looked at it carefully. Stared hard at the other youths, too, both of whom were now watching him nervously.

'Looks like a flight of wild geese came through here recently,' he said. 'Except it's not the migrating season. Is it, lads?'

The three youths stared at him, uncomprehending.

'What do you kids take me for, a complete novice? This jacket's fake. Fell off the back of a passing truck, did it?'

A long silence greeted his words.

'Can't hear you, sorry . . .'

'Well, there's no fooling you, Officer,' said the youth in the trainers, who had finished his cigarette and stood with his hands deep in his pockets.

'Dear, oh dear, Erik, you've really decided to mouth off today, haven't you? Where were you Sunday night, what time did you leave, and which way did you go home? What else was going on, on Sunday night? I want to know everything, now! Or I'll be shoving your black-market goose feathers right up your arse, one by one.'

Erik shot a quick glance at his friends.

'There was only one party Sunday, at Arne's, at the Youth Hostel.'

'Near Juhl's place. Well now. Why don't you tell me all about it back at the nice warm station, gentlemen?'

Patrol P9 left the church and climbed back into the car. Nina turned to her colleague.

'You seemed to be having a hard time with the pastor.'

Klemet looked at her for a moment, then put his index finger to his lip.

'Hush. Not now. You're going to spoil the most magical moment of the year.'

Nina stared at him in blank incomprehension. Klemet picked up the *Finnmark Dagblad* from the floor and showed her the back page. The weather information. She saw straightaway what he meant, and smiled. There was less than a quarter of an hour to go. Klemet drove fast, past the police station and out of Kautokeino, taking a track that wound to the top of a hill overlooking the town. Cars and snowmobiles were already parked. Some locals had spread reindeer skins on the ground and were settled with thermos flasks and sandwiches. Children ran about, shouting. Their mothers told them to be quiet. People were well covered with parkas, rugs, chapkas. Some were stamping their feet to keep warm. Everyone fixed their gaze on the horizon.

The magnificent gleam intensified, reflecting more and more brightly against the scattered clouds lingering in the distance. Nina was entranced. She looked at her watch. It was 11.13 a.m. Now, a bright, trembling halo of light blurred the point on the horizon at which everyone was gazing. Instinctively, Nina reached for her camera. Then she saw the emotion on her colleague's face and decided not to ask him to take her picture. She took a discreet photograph of Klemet instead and turned to enjoy the spectacle. The children had fallen quiet. The silence was as great as the moment itself.

Down in southern Norway, Nina had grown up knowing nothing about this phenomenon, but she sensed its physical, even spiritual power. Like Klemet, she leaned back against the side of the car to savour the first ray of sunshine. She turned to look at him. He was deep in thought, his eyes screwed up against the light. The sun seemed to struggle, keeping low on the horizon. Now, he stepped forward, turned and gazed intently at his shadow on the snow, as if seeing a magnificent work of art for the first time. The children began running around again. The adults clapped their hands together or jumped on the spot. The sun had kept its word. Everyone was reassured. Forty days casting no shadow by the light of the sun. The wait had not been in vain.

*

After sunrise – and sunset – Klemet and Nina went for lunch at the Villmarkssenter hotel, named for its remote location, out here in the backwoods. Kautokeino was a Sami town of around two thousand souls, far from the coast, in the Sápmi interior. From the hills over-looking the town, on both sides of the river, the views extended far and wide across the *vidda*, though not far enough to give a true impression of the size of the municipality, which covered an area roughly the size of a country like Lebanon. A further thousand or so people, many of them reindeer breeders, populated the rest of the vast area, living in small, isolated hamlets.

Patrol P9 chose the dish of the day: reindeer hash in brown sauce with cranberry jelly and mashed potato. Nina took a photograph of her plate before tucking in. She ate hungrily, asking a stream of questions about Sami cuisine. When she had finished, Klemet told her what had been on his mind since the beginning of the meal.

'Nina, don't try to stand up for me when we're interviewing people. It was OK in front of the pastor, but never do that with a breeder. Do you understand?'

'No, I don't understand. If someone fails to show proper respect to a police officer, they're not showing me respect either. I can't pre-tend not to hear.'

'That's not the point, Nina. The Sami have a very particular rela-tionship with authority, you'll see soon enough. It's very ... old school. People's individual status is important.'

Klemet hoped Nina would understand what he was getting at. But she stared at him expectantly, seeking further explanation. Mads, the proprietor, came over to serve coffee and sat down at their table.

'So how's business?' asked Klemet.

'Quiet ... pretty quiet. A Frenchman, a few truck drivers, an elderly couple – Danish tourists – the usual for the time of year. How's business with you?'

'Rather less quiet than usual for the time of year,' said Klemet, smiling. 'I haven't introduced you to Nina, my new colleague. She's from the south, near Stavanger.'

'Welcome, Nina! How do you like it here?'

'Very much, thank you. It's all new to me.'

'And you're off to a strange start, with this drum . . .'

'Yes, but that's not really our patch,' Nina corrected him. 'We're just helping out with the investigation. In fact, this afternoon, we have to go and take reports of some reindeer hit in a road accident in Masi. Ordinary Reindeer Police business comes first.'

'And Mattis's reindeer are all over the place,' said Klemet. 'We need to call his neighbours to find out where they are now. And, Nina, we'll call at the Reindeer Administration on our way back from Masi, too, to get the latest data on the state of his herd.'

'Still, the drum, what a business!' Mads persisted. 'People are talking about nothing else.'

'And what are people saying?' Klemet wanted to know.

'Oh, you know, rumours. They say it's the Russian mafia, or some of the older shamans . . . Load of old nonsense, in my opinion. Makes you wonder what was so special about this drum, anyway.'

'Indeed,' said Klemet, indicating it was time to go.

The sun's brief appearance was a distant memory by the time Patrol P9 returned to base, late in the afternoon. Nina had filled out a reindeer accident report for the first time. She was surprised to see the specially designed form, with a diagram of a reindeer. Whoever filed the report had to circle the parts that had been hit. They had brought back the animal's ears, too, and deposited them in the Reindeer Police freezer, with all the other pairs. Evidence from the scene of the accident. Proof, too, that the breeder had not applied for compensation twice for the same animal. At the Reindeer Administration offices, they had been treated to an extended presentation on the precise status of Mattis's herd. Fascinating stuff.

They were getting back into the car when Klemet's mobile rang. He listened and ended the call quickly. Nina was unprepared for his expression of shock.

'We're leaving right away. Mattis's trailer. He's been found dead. Just now.'

7

7.45 p.m., Central Sápmi

Klemet and Nina pulled up on their snowmobiles and left the headlights on full. She hesitated to move away from the warmth of the engine, feeling completely exhausted. They had made the journey back to Mattis's trailer in pitch darkness, taking extra care along the route. She looked at Klemet. Seemingly impervious to the cold and fatigue, he was already heading straight for the trailer, caught now in a halo of light from the headlamps of the police snowmobiles. Nina saw the same clutter they had left the previous morning. If anything, it looked even worse. Jerrycans, plastic containers, piles of wood, bits of rope, lay strewn about outside.

'Well now! Here come the Mounted Police.' A man stepped out from inside the trailer, wearing a thick snowsuit and chapka. His tone was not calculated to please. Nina couldn't see who it was at first. Then she recognised Rolf Brattsen.

There were traces of snowmobile tracks. Dry, powdery snow swirled in the shafts of light. Shadows shifted. The whole place looked unreal.

'Rounded up all your reindeer, did you? Found yourselves at a loose end?' taunted Brattsen.

It was clear he disliked Klemet, though Nina had no idea why.

'He's like that with everyone,' Klemet whispered, anticipating her question. He looked around, putting the unfriendly welcome to the back of his mind.

Brattsen continued. 'So, Chubby-chops, since when are the Reindeer Police playing with the big boys? What brings you to this neck of the woods?'

'Sheriff's orders,' said Klemet. 'A possible dispute between herders.'

'A dispute between herders. Ah yes! Drunken brawl would be more like it.'

'Chubby-chops?' Nina grinned at her colleague.

'Nina . . .'

'Yes?'

Klemet wasn't smiling.

'Just get on with the job.'

Nina smiled again, to Klemet's intense irritation. He decided to ignore her. 'It's quite sweet, actually.'

'Nina!'

'Only kidding.'

Klemet walked around the trailer. Two other police officers were going about their business on higher ground, further up the slope that sheltered the site from the east wind.

'Hi, Klem,' said one of the policemen.

'Hi.'

'Take a look, bet you've never seen anything like this.'

The body lay across a large, flat rock on which the snow had been partly cleared away.

'Dear God . . .'

Klemet recoiled. Behind him, Nina stood stock-still. The cold wind seemed to dull her senses, fortunately for her. Mattis lay on his back, his body blue with the cold, unless the livid hue of his skin was an effect of the headlamps, casting deep, unnerving shadows across his face. One of the other officers blew away the fine dusting of snow. Nina saw Mattis's wide-open eyes and the shocking act of mutilation, so completely at odds with the peaceful, magnificent landscape: his ears had been cut away. The raw flesh had already frozen solid. The holes marking the openings of the ear canals were half concealed by snow.

'We haven't found them,' said the officer, following his colleagues' gaze. 'The pathologist hasn't arrived yet, but we estimate the time of death at less than six hours ago. He was stabbed. You'll see inside the trailer, it's been turned upside down. Obviously been searched.'

He indicated Mattis's burned-out snowmobile.

'The smoke was what alerted us. Well, it was Johann Henrik, his nearest neighbour, in fact. We were lucky he saw it. He was the one who called us. He had tried to contact you, apparently.'

'It looks as if he might have been tortured,' said Nina. 'It's barbaric.'

'You two must be some of the last people to see him alive,' said Rolf Brattsen suddenly, coming up behind them. 'Make yourselves useful. Try to see if there's anything missing compared with what you can remember from yesterday.'

'It was a mess when we were here,' Nina remarked.

Brattsen spat into the snow and made no reply.

Nina gazed at the body, lingering on Mattis's face, his wide-open eyes and mouth. The expression he wore just before he was about to speak, she remembered. Had he been about to plead with his killer, when he was stabbed? What had he tried to say? His hands were clenched and twisted. Already, the holes left by his severed ears looked less horrifying by comparison.

'We're lucky with the cold and the snow,' said Klemet. 'It's stopped the bloodflow and the smell. The birds and foxes have held off. Usually, that's how we find the reindeer carcasses, with carrion birds circling overhead.'

'I didn't notice the dark rings under his eyes yesterday,' said Nina.

'Bruises – perhaps he took a beating,' ventured the other police officer. 'Or the cold. Don't know really. The body reacts strangely at times.'

Mattis's gaping mouth was missing some teeth, but no more than the day before.

'Mattis died as he lived,' said Klemet, looking at the body. 'Like a pauper. Death didn't even see fit to close his mouth. A poor bastard with a bad set of teeth, right to the end.'

Klemet looked at Mattis's eyes, too, and noticed the dark rings. Focusing closely on them, he bent down and examined the ear-holes.

'A clean cut,' he observed.

'We haven't looked under his clothing yet,' said the other police officer. 'But there's a knife-wound, apparently. Very powerful and accurately placed on the first strike, despite all the layers.'

Gently, Klemet touched the area around the ears, frozen hard in the snow. Again, he scanned the face and Mattis's deeply ringed eyes. He began walking back to the trailer.

'Get fingerprints!' Brattsen called out to the police officer taking photographs of the body and its surroundings. Then he walked over to Klemet, standing now at the entrance to the trailer.

'Hey, Chubby, no need to waste your time here, come to think of it. This isn't for you. Best get along and see to the old drunk's reindeer. They're going to cause a lot of bother for everyone, now there's no one to watch over them.'

Rolf fastened his crash helmet and set off cautiously on his snow-mobile, followed by another police officer. The camp was darker now. The only scooters left belonged to the scene-of-crime team and Patrol P9.

'What should we do, Klemet?' asked Nina. 'Are we going to take care of the reindeer?'

'Brattsen's not my superior,' grunted Klemet. 'We take orders from Kiruna, and the Sheriff, if I feel like it. Not from him. No way.'

'Yes, but the reindeer. He's right.'

'We'll go and see to them soon enough,' said Klemet, entering the trailer. 'We'll have to call up the other patrols. Can't do it all by ourselves. We'll call once we get back down to the lake.'

He sat in the same seat he had occupied the previous morning. The trailer looked in an even worse mess. The interior was brightly lit by a gas lamp. The clutter originally piled on the top bunk had been pulled to the floor or thrown out through the door. The same went for the sleeping bags and blankets on the bottom bunk, where Klemet and Nina had left Mattis preparing to sleep. Even the stove had been overturned. Either there had been a fight, or everything had been meticulously searched. Or both. Mattis's snowmobile had been set alight, but not the trailer. Why?

'Notice anything, Nina?'

She had copied her partner and sat in the same place as the day before, to get the same view of the scene.

'It's an even worse mess.'

She stared around the trailer, taking in every detail, then got up and took three steps forward.

'They don't seem to have touched this shelf.'

Some plastic containers and tins of food had been thrown to the floor, but the leather straps and pieces of wood were still tidily arranged. The finely engraved Sami knives, too, were all in place. Nonetheless, it was hard to tell if anything was missing.

Klemet followed her gaze.

'A breeder would never steal one of the knives,' he said. 'A Sami will steal a man's reindeer, but never the equipment needed for the sleds. You don't touch anything that could save a man's life out in the *vidda*. Or so my uncle Nils Ante taught me. That's a line the herders will never cross.'

Nina thought again of Mattis's severed ears and found it hard to countenance such barbarity in her own country. She pulled on a thin pair of gloves and took hold of the first knife, removing it from its sheath, then did the same with the other three. All were clean. She returned to the bench.

'Perhaps we should take fingerprints, all the same,' she said. 'Good grief, Klemet, I was told the Reindeer Police were mediators, anticipating disputes, preventing trouble. But trouble like this? Killings? And torture – the ears?'

'It's rare,' Klemet admitted. 'There have been cases of herders exchanging pot-shots, especially when drink is involved. But there's never been a death, at least not as a result of a direct killing. Not that I know of, anyway. And the ears . . .'

'Why did they do that?'

Klemet was silent for a moment.

'Theft.'

'What do you mean?'

'All the reindeer are marked on their ears. Both ears. As you know. And we need the marks from both ears to identify the owner. Reindeer thieves cut off the ears, so that the animal can't be traced to its owner. No proven owner, no reported theft.'

'And no reported theft, no inquiry,' said Nina.

'Or if there is an inquiry, it's over and done with very quickly,' he said.

'So this was an act of revenge? Mattis was stealing reindeer? He was being marked as a thief?'

Klemet frowned.

'There are thieves and thieves. He did a bit of rustling, if you like. But he was just a poor lost soul. I mean, look at the trailer, the dirt, the mess. And he was an alcoholic. Revenge? Perhaps. Times are hard for everyone at the moment. We'll have to go and talk to Johann Henrik. He's another hard case.'

'Do you think he could have done this?'

'Mattis was involved in disputes with all his neighbours. He didn't keep a close enough eye on his livestock. He was all alone. Aslak helped him out sometimes, but otherwise he was on his own. And no one gets far on their own, in the *vidda*.'

'How many neighbours did he have?'

Klemet opened his snowsuit and pulled out the 1/50,000 map of the area. He spread it on the table and pointed to the location of Mattis's trailer.

'Remember,' he said, sliding his finger across the map, 'this is the wood where Johann Henrik keeps his reindeer, and here's the river that Mattis's herd crossed. Mattis's pasture covers this part. And here's Johann Henrik, from here – the river – to this lake. Aslak is on the other side of the mountain. And another herder, Ailo. He's a Finnman.'

'The Finnman clan? I've heard about them,' said Nina. 'Even in Kiruna.'

Listing Mattis's nearest neighbours, Klemet reflected that fate had dealt the breeder a poor hand. A winter pasture hemmed in by those three was no recipe for a quiet life.

8

Wednesday 12 January

Sunrise: 10.53 a.m.; sunset: 12.02 p.m.
1 hour 9 minutes of sunlight

Central Sápmi

Four Reindeer Police patrols had been called in: from Karasjok and Alta in Norway, from Enontekiö on the Finnish side, even from Kiruna in Sweden. Klemet directed operations. Nina was the only woman present. The faint glow of the pre-dawn twilight allowed for an early start, in tolerable conditions.

It took ten police officers to round up Mattis's reindeer. A day had been set aside for the work. Luckily, the herd was not large, and the steep terrain all around had prevented the animals from straying too far. By prior agreement with the neighbouring breeders, the reindeer were guided in small groups to an enclosure about ten kilometres south-east of Mattis's trailer.

They began with the simplest task – identifying the head reindeer, easily recognisable by his age and antlers. He was down by the side of a lake, surrounded by the major part of the herd. From experience, Klemet knew that Mattis's reindeer could be nervous. It would not be easy to get close without the animals taking fright and bolting. He indicated to the other officers to contain them by approaching in a circle. The reindeer would not cross the invisible line closing in around them and began circling this way and that, as they always did when trapped. Klemet moved forward very slowly on his snowmobile, then left it a few metres from the jostling herd and continued on foot, holding his orange lasso. The reindeer moved away as he drew near, but continued their slow, circling dance, grunting and trampling the snow. Klemet glimpsed their huge, startled eyes in the shafts of light from the other snowmobiles. But still, they made no attempt to break out of the circle.

He prepared his lasso and tossed it in the direction of the head reindeer, but caught the antler of another animal. It struggled furiously. The rest of the herd began revolving around Klemet and the frantic reindeer, while the police moved around the herd. Two perfect, concentric circles. Soon, the sun would rise above the horizon for the second time that year. Klemet moved slowly towards the reindeer as it reared and tossed its antlers. He tightened the rope and brought it down to the ground, forcing the animal to kneel, then immobilised its head while he removed the lasso. Immediately, the reindeer bounded away to rejoin the herd. He repeated the operation twice over before finally catching the head reindeer. The animal was bigger but less energetic. And, crucially, more accustomed to this sort of treatment. Klemet paid out a good length of rope and drew the reindeer over to his snowmobile, then set off slowly. Docile now, the head reindeer walked quietly behind. Instinctively, the others followed suit, forming an elongated triangle behind their leader. The police officers surrounded the formation, driving forward the stragglers and strays. The Finnish patrol, who had brought a special trailer, were forced to catch two young reindeer who failed to follow the rest, and tie them aboard.

A few kilometres from the enclosure, four police officers moved on ahead to prepare for the arrival of the reindeer. They pulled back the barriers to form an opening and installed plastic-mesh fencing to either side, as high as a man's shoulder, forming a broad funnel that extended several dozen metres out from the entrance. Approaching the enclosure, some of the reindeer bringing up the rear became nervous again. The patrols accelerated hard on their snowmobiles to keep them in check. The four police officers stood motionless behind the mesh barriers. A sudden movement would draw attention to their presence, frightening the reindeer, which might turn around and bolt despite the scooters. Then the whole operation would have to begin again. The animals suspected nothing, and the four officers on foot ran heavily through the snow, bringing the mesh barriers together behind the last of the reindeer, to close them in. After that, the reindeer were ushered into a much bigger, adjoining corral.

And so the day progressed. The rest of the herd was scattered in five smaller groups. Each time, the officers reconnoitred the surrounding terrain, observed the animals' behaviour and identified the best approach for the snowmobiles, so that they could drive the reindeer ahead of them in the desired direction, looking out for side tracks that would have to be blocked, to prevent the herd from pouring off in the wrong direction. The day wore on. It was a race against time in the fading light, but with night-vision binoculars the officers carried on working. By mid-evening, the bulk of the herd had been secured in the main enclosure.

The ten officers gathered at the foot of the tall barriers, having chopped wood and dug a hole in the snow to light a fire. Nina was exhausted. She felt the creeping onset of the cold, but watched in fascination as the the heavens sprang to life. The Northern Lights seemed to reach out and take possession of the firmament. Faint, ghostly curtains of greenish light hung high above them, rippling slowly, always in the same direction. Everyone fell silent. The aurora gathered pace. Successive trails of light snaked across the sky, hesitant and slender. The slow dance spread wider, flickering and pulsing, a cavalcade beneath a cone of striated light convulsing in luminous waves.

Hot coffee was quickly prepared. The officers' thoughts turned again to Mattis. There were bound to be a few, isolated reindeer left, and others that had mingled with the neighbouring herds. They would be identified in the spring triage.

'What will happen to the animals now?' asked Nina.

'The men from the Reindeer Administration are coming tomorrow,' said Klemet. 'It's up to them now. They'll feed the herd and decide what to do with them.'

Mattis had no surviving family. No one close, anyway. The reindeer would almost certainly be sent for slaughter. Ironic, really, thought Klemet as he reflected, exhausted, on the scorn Mattis had heaped on the Administration employees shortly before his death. The animals looked half starved. Mattis's herd was known as one of the worst kept in the region. Again, Klemet pictured Mattis's corpse, his gaping mouth and missing teeth. The herd was in its owner's image.

Klemet sat in silence, blowing on his coffee, though it had long since gone cold. On high, the flickering mosaic set the kingdom of the dead ablaze with the fires of heaven.

9

Thursday 13 January

Sunrise: 10.41 a.m.; sunset: 12.15 p.m.
1 hour 34 minutes of sunlight

9 a.m., Kautokeino

It had been a short night's sleep for Klemet Nango and Nina Nansen. The Sheriff had called a 9 a.m. meeting at headquarters. Brattsen was there, too. Two flasks of coffee stood in the middle of the conference table. Everyone helped themselves. The Sheriff did not seem in a good mood. He said nothing for the moment, waiting until everyone was served. But Klemet knew him well enough to guess he had been on the receiving end of a stiff warning from Oslo.

Finally, the Sheriff rose impatiently from his seat.

'OK. We have a big problem.'

He stressed the word 'big'.

'Two important cases in the space of twenty-four hours. No problem hitting our performance targets this year,' he added drily. 'A robbery – and not just any robbery – followed by a murder. Exceptional, you'll agree. Oslo's in a panic over the conference, and with Mattis's ears cut off, I wouldn't mind betting the press will be here in droves, from Oslo, Stockholm, even further afield. Especially after the sex abuse stories two years back. So, what have you got?'

Brattsen was the first to speak.

'On the murder side, we've begun questioning the neighbours. Only Ailo Finnman for the moment. We still don't know the exact time of death. Finnman says he was here in Kautokeino. We're checking that. But there's the rest of the clan, too. Five of them are taking turns out in the *vidda* at the moment. He says he hadn't quarrelled with Mattis over the pasture, but he reckons it wouldn't have been long coming, given the way the lazy bastard looked after his animals. Finnman's phrase, you understand,' he added quickly, with a brief grin.

'When will you finish checking the other Finnman clan members?'

'Tonight, I hope. There are two herders out in the tundra. We won't see them before then.'

'Anyone else?'

'Johann Henrik and Aslak,' said Klemet, getting in before Brattsen could say anything else.

Brattsen shot him a cold stare. 'As Chubby here says,' he left a deliberate pause for effect, 'we need to speak to those two as well. We haven't been in touch yet.'

'Any clues?'

'No scooter tracks until we reached the scene. The fresh snowfall obliterated everything. But we may find some under the top covering of snow, which is fairly light. We're looking for fingerprints. The scooter was set alight. We're taking samples. We don't know whether the fire is linked to the murder or not. The machine might have burned before the murderer arrived. We just don't know. The ears suggest a revenge attack between herders. Makes perfect sense to me. But over to our local expert on that one,' he added, with heavy sarcasm.

Klemet acquiesced in silence.

'I find that theory hard to believe,' he said. 'Mattis seemed more and more depressed recently. He was in a state close to despair when we saw him before his death. I'd never seen him drink like that before.'

'Yes. Well, we're not talking ritual suicide here,' said the Sheriff. 'What else have you got?'

'We're going to check every reported case of reindeer theft over the past two years,' said Brattsen.

'I'm not sure there's much point in that,' Klemet interjected. 'In most cases, the breeders don't register an official complaint. They know it's pointless, and they prefer to settle their own scores, without the police.'

'Too right, Chubs. I'm not the only one who thinks the Reindeer Police are a waste of time.' Brattsen couldn't resist that one.

'Check back over the cases anyway,' ordered the Sheriff. 'Got to start somewhere. So, to sum up: we have a breeder apparently tortured to death. Why torture him? To exact revenge. Or get him to confess to something. Revenge for what? A theft? Or something else? Confess what? That he stole something? Reindeer, or something else entirely? What do we know about Mattis, anyway? Klemet, I want you to dig deeper, come up with some answers. And I want you to find the other two breeders, especially this Johann Henrik, the one involved in a dispute with Mattis. Apart from all that, anything new on the drum?'

'Huh! The Sami moo-box.' Brattsen grinned again.

Another officer spoke up.

'The drum was in a sealed case. It was a gift to the museum from a private collector. A Frenchman, apparently. We're trying to contact him. According to the museum director, no one so far had had the time or opportunity to photograph it. The museum wanted to get it treated first, prior to handling, and they were going to do that in the next couple of days. So no photos of the drum itself. Not here, at any rate. We don't know what the drawings on it showed.'

'Bloody unbelievable!' Brattsen burst out. 'This is the age of Google for Christ's sake. We can scan every fucking scrap of toilet paper behind a bush, from space, but there's not one picture of this damned drum, which is apparently so important? Not even for the insurance?'

'Agreed. That is surprising,' said the Sheriff.

'I could try to talk to the collector,' suggested Nina. 'I worked as an au pair in France. I could brush up my French.'

'Fine. What other leads do we have for the moment?'

'There was a drunken party at the hostel near Juhl's place on Sunday night. One of the kids' families runs the place. It finished late, but definitely not at five in the morning.'

'Berit didn't say anything about that,' Nina observed.

'Perhaps not, but it happened,' Brattsen insisted. 'None of the kids were involved in the robbery, it seems. Their stories match and, given what I've got on them, they're not likely to go telling fibs.' He gave the company a knowing smile. 'Apart from that, this might be something to do with an illegal trade in artefacts, stolen to order for another collector – these drums are pretty rare, after all.'

'Yep. Money in it for someone,' said the Sheriff. 'Nina, you can check that out with your Frenchman. Might be worth seeing if any other drums have been stolen.'

'Apart from by Swedish and Norwegian pastors, who've been at it for three centuries,' Klemet blurted out.

The Sheriff stared at him in surprise. The heartfelt comment was very unlike Klemet. He smiled, noticing Brattsen's weary sigh at the same time.

'But locally? Who stands to profit from the disappearance of the drum?'

'Well, we know the pastor wasn't too happy about its being here in the first place,' said Klemet. 'Thought it would raise the old demons, lure his flock away. Afraid of a reawakening of the old religion. Something like that.'

'Can you really see the pastor committing a theft like that?' asked the Sheriff.

'No more nor less than anyone else.'

'And what about Olaf?' Brattsen volunteered. 'The theft would suit him down to the ground. Gives him a pretext to get everyone worked up, regurgitate all his old grievances – human rights, land rights, any bloody rights. And just before a UN conference, too. What a happy coincidence. People like him dream of kicking us out of here. I heard him on the radio just now, all indignant and outraged. He said that in any case the drum had no place in a museum, that it belonged to the Sami people. The guy's queer in the head, a regular Commie. He manipulates everyone. He's the one who's done time, don't forget, for trying to blow up that pit-head in Sweden.'

'You know perfectly well that was never proved, and he was released after four days,' said Klemet. 'And you know as well as I do, Olaf represents a tiny minority.'

'Perhaps, but he still couldn't lie straight in bed. And *you* know as well as I do that he got mixed up with the IRA during the demonstrations against the Alta dam. No, I wouldn't put it past him to steal a drum, if he thought it would stir things up a bit. A good old-fashioned bit of Commie provocation.'

11.30 a.m., Kautokeino

Klemet and Nina stopped at the supermarket in Kautokeino to stock up on food before setting off on patrol once again. They had decided to start with a visit to Johann Henrik. He was Mattis's nearest neighbour and probably one of the last people to see him alive. After that, they would call on Aslak.

Shopping was an important part of life in the Reindeer Police. Patrols could take several days out in the tundra, bivouacking in trailers – or huts if you were lucky – in bitter cold, with long, exhausting hours riding snowmobiles. Meals were important, and officers took care and trouble over their preparation. Not haute cuisine (or seldom): hearty, sustaining food was essential, in case you had to skip a meal on a longer-than-expected excursion.

Klemet liked shopping. Selecting a bag of frozen potatoes invariably set him thinking. Nice with cutlets – he took another bag out of the freezer – and Béarnaise sauce, he would need a packet of that.

Perfect for this evening's meal, after two or three hours on the scooters. He wouldn't overcook the cutlets, no way, and he'd add a sprinkling of garlic to the potatoes. A hot tip from a colleague who holidayed regularly in Majorca.

'I'll cook tonight,' he announced, taking no chances.

'OK, great, thanks,' Nina replied. 'I admit, cooking's not my strong point.' She looked at the frozen-food bags piling up in the trolley and thought to herself that it probably wasn't Klemet's, either.

'But we take it in turns, on alternate days. That's the rule.'

They carried on around the store, dipping into the freezers, consulting one another each time. Klemet stocked up on sweet-tasting polar bread, and *mysost*, his favourite, soft-textured, caramelised whey cheese. Not forgetting the essential tubes of prawn- or roe-flavoured paste for breakfast. Breakfast was important, too. He began to feel hungry. And eager to set off. Hurriedly, he added coffee, sugar, chocolate, dried fruit, ketchup, pasta, a few packs of low-alcohol beer. He hesitated over dropping into Vinmonopolet for a bottle of three-star cognac, then thought better of it.

Next, they filled the scooters' tanks and the jerrycans. Nina did the honours at the petrol pump, while Klemet filled their water containers. Then he checked the straps on the snowmobile trailers, holding the storage boxes, jerrycans and water containers in place.

They took the frozen 'motorway' and climbed rapidly up the hill beyond the edge of the town, its summit bathed in dazzling light. Klemet had almost forgotten the sun had reappeared. It looked glorious. A good sign, he thought.

The brilliant glare on the snow made driving hazardous at times, especially for Nina, whose sun-goggles weren't up to the job. She trusted to Klemet, following in his tracks.

They reached their destination towards mid-afternoon. The sun had disappeared, but the light was still bright. Johann Henrik had been given advance warning of their arrival, by phone. At times of tension, as now, the breeders did not appreciate being taken by surprise. Henrik greeted them outside his trailer. Just as Klemet and Nina stepped off their machines, a young man – apparently Johann's son – mounted his scooter, wearing a chapka but no helmet. He nodded in their direction and accelerated hard, standing up, one knee folded on the broad saddle seat.

Johann Henrik wore a three- or four-day beard. A cigarette stub clung to the corner of his mouth He fetched a reindeer-skin poncho hanging outside the trailer, slipped it over his head without removing his cigarette and moved slowly towards the police officers. He greeted them, still with the cigarette between his lips. He had small, cunning eyes, a lopsided mouth and a narrow nose. His fur chapka was pushed back on his head, revealing strands of greasy hair. He had the deeply lined complexion of a man who has weathered many storms, and the expression of one who has seen too much.

Klemet watched the herder pulling on his poncho, and understood that he had no intention of inviting them into the trailer, hoping to keep the interview as brief as possible. True to form, evil-tempered and stubborn as ever. Johann Henrik had always respected authority – like all Sami breeders – but he did nothing to facilitate the work of the Reindeer Police. Again, like all the breeders. They preferred to settle their own scores in their own way.

'Where's your son going?' Klemet fired the opening question.

'The reindeer are nervous. Too much traffic about at the moment, what with you, and Mattis's death, and the herders taking the dry feed to the animals. It disturbs them. It's no good.'

He chewed the cigarette stub. 'So you want to know if I killed Mattis?'

'Basically, yes.'

The two men observed one another. Henrik looked at the police officer through narrowed eyes. Took his time relighting the end of his cigarette.

'Know what I think?' he went on, after a deep intake of smoke. 'Whoever set fire to the scooter did it to attract attention. To sound the alarm. So that the body wouldn't get eaten. That's what I think. So there, I've answered the question you haven't asked yet. Apart from that, I don't know anything.'

'You don't know anything else at all—'

'Nothing. Got any other questions?'

Klemet looked at him. He did not like Johann Henrik's attitude.

A light breeze was blowing, but it was enough to bite the skin off your face. Klemet did not feel the cold. Long ago, he had learned not to be cold. Since childhood, he had known how the cold could rob a man of his reason, awaken unspeakable terrors. Like the dark. He could not allow himself to feel the cold. A personal oath, sworn a long time ago. Another story. He tried not to think about it, but he could never break free entirely.

Henrik chewed on his cigarette, drawing on it more frequently now, to keep it from going out. He stood motionless, squinting, in his fur cloak. Nina felt excluded from their silent stand-off. Klemet could see that, but for the moment there was nothing he could do to bring in his young colleague.

The tension was palpable. Johann Henrik was a hard man, one of the old school of breeders who had known the time before snowmobiles, and quad bikes, and helicopters. The time when the herders watched over their animals on skis, in all weathers, spending hours rounding up their herds; now, the same task could be accomplished in minutes, aboard a snowmobile.

Out of consideration for Nina, Klemet decide not to prolong the confrontation, which was proving fruitless in any case.

'When did you last see Mattis?'

'Mattis? I could have done with seeing him a bit more often. His reindeer were always around and about, unlike him . . . '

Klemet said nothing, waiting for Johann Henrik to answer his question. Nina stood stoically by. She was a tough kid, thought Klemet. She didn't seem bothered by the cold. Her cheeks and the upturned tip of her nose were bright red, her eyelashes tinged with frost, but she stood her ground.

Johann Henrik took his cigarette stub between his thumb and forefinger, cradling it in the hollow of his palm. He spat into the snow, took another drag. But still he said nothing. He stood stubborn as a rock, his mouth half twisted to one side.

'Your reindeer OK?' asked Klemet, suddenly.

The breeder's mouth twisted further askew. Almost a nervous tic.

'Of course they're OK. What's that got to do with it?'

His mouth twisted again.

'Nothing. Nothing to do with it, I was only asking,' said Klemet. 'It'll be a hard task sorting out Mattis's reindeer. Bound to be a few left, scattered all over the district. Probably some in with your herd, too. All that, coupled with the murder inquiry now.'

'What does that have to do with my reindeer?'

'Oh, I'm not interested in your herd as such. Of course not. But I need to know how many more of Mattis's reindeer are alive and exactly what state they're in. All the signs point to a spot of rustling behind all this, wouldn't you say?'

'And people would kill a breeder for that?'

'You were shot at yourself, ten years ago.'

'That's not the same thing at all.'

'Well, that remains to be seen. We've rounded up most of Mattis's animals, at any rate. But we still need to inspect the neighbouring herds.'

Klemet let that hang for a moment, watching Johann Henrik's curled lip, still with the cigarette hanging, though it had gone out. Then he spoke again, as if passing sentence.

'Johann Henrik, we will have to round up your herd and count the animals.'

'The hell you will!' exclaimed Henrik, almost by reflex, and spat his cigarette butt into the snow. The blackened end landed within Klemet's shadow. Klemet moved aside so it lay in the lights of the snowmobiles. He cursed his superstitious nature, sometimes. It looked idiotic in a policeman. But he kept his shadow untainted.

He had decided to let Henrik stew for a while. 'Think about it. We'll stop by again later.'

'I didn't kill Mattis. What more do you need to know?'

Johann Henrik fidgeted beneath his fur cloak. The breeders hated anyone taking too close an interest in the numbers of their reindeer. It was like asking someone how much money they had in the bank. Henrik was caught in a trap, and he knew it.

'Only one way to find out whether you've got any of his reindeer,' said Klemet, just to be sure the breeder had got the message.

Henrik's mouth twisted again, a defiant leer. After more than half a century on the tundra, he was used to low cunning, more than the policeman could possibly imagine.

'The last time I saw Mattis, he worried me,' Klemet went on. 'I need to find out how he was doing. I know you had problems with him, but you knew him well, too.'

Johann Henrik seemed to be evaluating the proposition. Mattis was dead. And he had no desire to have his reindeer counted by the police. He had enough trouble already with the nit-pickers from the Reindeer Administration, haranguing him with their absurd quotas, sending him letters by recorded delivery.

'Mattis was at the end of his tether,' he said. 'If his ears hadn't been cut, I would have bet on suicide.'

Johann Henrik began rolling another cigarette. He had fallen silent again, taking his time.

'Aslak,' he said. He moistened the paper with his tongue, watching Klemet as he did so, his eyes lively with curiosity, testing the policeman's reaction. 'Aslak had Mattis right where he wanted him. You have no idea. Mattis worshipped him like a god. But heaven knows, he was terrified of him, too. Oh yes, terrified. It bothered me, every time I saw them together.'

'What do you mean, exactly, "terrified"?' Nina asked.

To her astonishment, Henrik looked her straight in the eye. He glanced at Klemet, finished rolling his cigarette, then turned to Nina again. 'You're new.'

It was an observation, not a question.

'Have you come across Aslak yet?'

'No,' said Nina, intrigued now.

'You'll find out all about him soon.'

Johann Henrik had lost his earlier, suspicious look. Apparently, the thought of Aslak affected him, too, however hard-boiled he appeared.

'Aslak is not like the rest. He lives far out on the tundra, with his reindeer and his wife. No one else lives like them today.'

Klemet said nothing, but nodded. He could feel Nina's eyes on him. He had never spoken to her about Aslak, though he had known him for a very long time. Nina seemed to sense something. Her curiosity was obviously aroused, but she was careful not to let it show in Henrik's presence. Klemet appreciated that.

Johann Henrik dragged on his cigarette and spoke again.

'Aslak frightened Mattis the same way he frightens everyone in the *vidda*. Me, I am not afraid of him, because I know. I've seen it. Aslak is half man, half beast. I saw him one day, on all fours, in among his herd. He's the last one on the *vidda* to castrate his reindeer with his teeth. Did you know that, Klemet?'

He turned again to Nina.

'You won't find a better wolf-hunter anywhere in the region. I saw it with my own eyes one day. He followed a wolf, one that had killed several of his reindeer. He tracked it for hours in the snow, to wear the animal out. He got rid of his gun, so that he wouldn't be weighed down by it. All he had was a big stick. When he caught up to it, the wolf threw itself at him. I was a long way off, on the other side of the valley, but I watched it all through my field glasses. How do you think he killed it? When the wolf pounced, with its jaws wide open, he thrust his fist forward and stuffed his hand down its gullet, right up to his elbow, and with the other hand he smashed its skull with the stick. Can you imagine? His arm right down the animal's throat!'

'How was he with Mattis?' asked Nina.

'You will understand, perhaps, when you meet Aslak. People are overawed by him. And Mattis was very impressionable. You know that Mattis's father, Anta, was a shaman? Klemet didn't tell you? A throwback to an earlier time. Strange. Anta kept himself to himself, but he was well respected. He's been dead a long while. Mattis grew up in that world. But he had no gift, no talent, nothing. The son of a shaman. But that won't get you far today. He was not respected, Mattis. I think that's why he drank. Well, that's what I say.'

Johann Henrik relit his cigarette. The wind had dropped. It was a little less cold. Klemet felt stiff, but his reindeer-skin boots kept the cold out. Nina's standard-issue police boots were less effective. She stamped on the spot to warm up. The conversation had lasted longer than planned. Johann Henrik had opened up, talking more freely now, but he still hadn't invited them into his trailer.

'Aslak liked Mattis, in his way. He used to spend time with Mattis's father before. They were close. And Aslak and Mattis are both exiles, each of a kind. Mattis was excluded by other people, and Aslak excluded himself. He helped Mattis with his reindeer sometimes.'

'But not recently?'

'When Mattis was drinking, he would retreat into himself. He didn't dare ask Aslak for help, he was ashamed for Aslak to see him in that state.'

'Did they ever quarrel?'

'How shall I put this – Mattis's quarrel was with the whole world. He had disagreements with everyone, at different times. Recently, he had been doing very little. I know Aslak was annoyed by that, and he made sure Mattis knew it. Mattis told me so last week. He was afraid. I don't think Aslak would ever have hurt him, but Mattis felt intimidated. Aslak would pass comment, and Mattis would imagine terrible things.'

'So why do you say we should be thinking about Aslak?'

'I say – I say . . . that there are things I don't know.'

'And the drum. Any ideas about that?' asked Klemet.

'The drum?'

Johann Henrik dragged on his cigarette, spat into the snow.

'We don't need any drum round here. That's all over now. Who wants to reawaken the past? That's just fancy dress for the tourists. You think I've got time to worry about some old drum? Name me one herder who has time for that all that crap.'

'Olaf is very committed to it.'

'The Spaniard? The man's a joke! There's no such thing as a part-time breeder, believe me. I wonder how he does it, really I do. And what would he want with this drum, if ever they find it again? Much good it did Mattis!'

'What do you mean?' asked Nina, in surprise.

'Mattis was fascinated by drums. With his father a shaman and all that. He was unhinged, Mattis. It was a kind of obsession with him. The power of the drums. The power of the shaman. All that stuff. When he should have been taking care of his reindeer.'

Swiftly, Henrik took a pair of field glasses out from under his fur cloak and scanned the valley. He tossed his cigarette away.

'I need to go.'

'Johann Henrik, where were you on Tuesday, during the day?'

The herder stared angrily at Klemet as he adjusted his reindeer-skin gloves.

'I was watching the reindeer with my son, all day. And with Mikkel and John, the Finnman herders. We tried to push Mattis's herd back. They were everywhere. That ought to do for an alibi, no?'

He spat into the snow, climbed aboard his snowmobile without waiting for a reply and accelerated hard. Seconds later, he was a mere dot in the valley.

10

Thursday 13 January

8 p.m., Kautokeino

The customer leaning on the zinc bar seemed no longer to notice the small man who had been gesturing at his side for some time now. He wasn't doing any harm, just gesturing. Nothing aggressive, although the smaller man did look exasperated from time to time, at the lack of response. Then he would burst out laughing all of a sudden, pounce on his beer glass, drink deep and start gesturing all over again next to the man at the bar, propped on his elbows.

The pub in Kautokeino occupied one room on the ground floor of a building right opposite a large chalet put up recently by a fundamentalist splinter group from the church. Some found their close proximity strange, to say the least, but ultra-religious types and hardened sinners needed one another, after all. The pub was furnished with ten mismatched tables, square and round, though together they created a certain stylistic unity. The same went for the chairs, all different. The thick log walls were hung with a curious mix of framed photos of cars from the 1950s and 1960s, images of Elvis and a handful of other rock legends, and paintings of Sami motifs: encampments of reindeer herders, reindeer and the Northern Lights. Antlers of every shape and size filled the space above the bar.

Overhead, red bulbs cast a dim light reflected in the melted snow that gleamed on the dark-red linoleum underfoot.

The pub hosted its usual clientele for a weekday evening – it was almost empty. Two tables were occupied. At one, three men sat hunched in worn-out snowsuits, silently draining their beer glasses. One sported an orange lasso looped across his chest and a chapka pushed back on his head, revealing a strand of hair plastered down with sweat. To judge by their outfits and exhausted air, the men were breeders back from a vigil not too far from town. At the other table sat a woman in traditional, colourful Sami dress, wearing the local headgear. The man at the bar noticed she drank no beer, just coffee. She seemed out of place, glancing frequently in the direction of the small, gesticulating man, as if keeping an eye on him.

The young waitress behind the bar spoke to her, in Sami.

'Berit, do you want a refill?'

Berit shook her head and lifted one hand in a gesture of thanks.

'Could you call your brother off, do you think? I wouldn't want him to frighten away our new customer.'

The customer put down his glass.

'He's not bothering me,' he said in Sami.

'You speak our language,' said the girl, in surprise. 'And Swedish too. But your accent isn't Swedish.'

'No, French. But I lived in Sweden for years.'

'Oh! French . . .'

The girl gave him a pretty smile.

'Another beer?'

'Yes, thanks.'

'We don't get many strangers here. Even fewer who can speak Sami.'

'I can believe that,' said the man, raising his glass to drink and taking a good look at the girl's prettily rounded figure.

She noticed and smiled again.

'On holiday?'

'Lena!' One of the three herders called out suddenly. 'Beer!'

Lena rolled her eyes and carried three beers over to the men. The one who had called out – the herder with the lasso – stared at her hard. Lena acted nonchalantly, avoiding his gaze. The Frenchman took it all in, watching impassively from the bar. No business of his.

André Racagnal was in his late fifties, but knew he looked younger. He was still well built, with swept-back brown hair and the deeply lined face of a man who has spent his life out of doors. He wore the tundra uniform of hiking pants with thigh pockets, plus a fleece jacket and scarf. On his left wrist, a silver identity chain bore an inscription engraved in thick letters. On his right, he wore a large watch on a steel bracelet.

Lena returned to her post behind the bar, smiling again for the Frenchman's benefit.

'So, are you on holiday?'

'No.'

Racagnal sipped his beer slowly. He took out a packet of cigarettes, shook one free and held it out to Lena.

'You can't smoke in here, but I can show you where,' she said, with a significant look. He narrowed his eyes, as if sizing her up. With an encouraging half-smile, he held out his arm, inviting her to lead the way.

'Lena!'

Another urgent shout from the bar room, behind them.

Lena rolled her eyes again. Racagnal found the affectation annoying, but the young girl's figure was mesmerising, all the same. He did not turn around, but carried on slowly sipping his beer.

Behind him, he heard one of the breeders raise his voice, thick with fatigue or drink. Apparently, the man disapproved of Lena's simpering with the 'stranger who thinks he's so mighty superior'. He heard Lena whisper something back.

'So what if he can speak Swedish? I don't give a damn ...'

Slowly, the Frenchman got down from his bar stool, took a last sip from his glass and placed his hands on the bar, fists clenched, in full view of the rest of the room. He stood motionless, still with his back turned to the trio of herders.

The little man had left off moving back and forth between Berit's table and the bar, and had been sitting quietly for a time. He now began to show signs of agitation. He moved back to the bar and addressed the Frenchman, grimacing as he spoke, his words forming broken sentences, tumbling out.

'So, so then I went in a car. I came back. In a car. You take me for a ride? Mine's got four wheels. Four. And I've got four fingers. See?'

He thrust his right hand in front of Racagnal's face. There were indeed four digits: his thumb and three fingers. He ran them along the counter, making the noise of a car engine, veering wildly between the glasses. Then he burst out laughing, slapped his thighs, turned to Berit, lifted his arms and applauded. He laughed loudly and clapped the Frenchman on the back. Racagnal didn't flinch. Took another sip of his beer. Berit got calmly to her feet, took the little man by the hand and led him back to her table. He quietened down once more, still smiling broadly.

'Lena, three beers and three *avkvavit*,' grumbled the breeder with the lasso, dragging out his words.

Lena took the drinks over, then returned to the bar and addressed the Frenchman.

'Follow me, I'll show you where you can smoke.'

She picked up her long, fur-collared coat and walked ahead of him between the tables, avoiding the dark looks from the breeder, who drank his chaser down in one.

Racagnal followed, glass in hand. At the far end of the bar room, a narrow corridor led to a second room, further along on the right. It was empty apart from a pool table. The girl pushed a door on the left-hand side of the corridor, opening onto a small covered space with a basic wooden roof, walled with panels that could be taken down in the summer. It was bitterly cold.

Racagnal offered Lena a cigarette, cradling her fleshy hands in his to light it, stroking them gently with one finger. Then he lit his own. Lena breathed out a cloud of smoke and smiled.

'Admirer of yours, back there?' he asked.

'Huh! He's an old friend.'

74

'A reindeer breeder?'

Lena laughed.

'Like everyone here. Or almost everyone. Or if you're not, then your family are breeders, which comes to the same thing. He's from one of the big families around here. The Finnman clan. They have thousands of reindeer out in the *vidda*.'

'Were you born here, Lena?'

'Yes. What about you, were you born in Paris?'

Racagnal was from Rouen, but he didn't want to disappoint.

'Yes, Paris. Ever been to Paris, Lena?'

'Oh! No. But I will go there one day.'

'How old are you, Lena?'

'I turned eighteen a few months ago. I started working in the pub the week after my birthday. You're not allowed to before that. What's your name?'

'André.'

Racagnal was beginning to feel the cold and wondered how he could cut short their exchange of small talk.

He wanted to screw her, that was all.

He looked at her thin lips. A shame, that. He preferred a full mouth. Memories of Africa. But the rest – what he had seen of her at the bar – was perfect. She looked older and more experienced than her eighteen years, but the local girls wore plenty of make-up from a young age – he had discovered that – making them look more grown-up than they were.

He was lifting a hand to the girl's face when the door to the smoking area was flung open. The Finnman boy stood swaying in the frame, his chapka askew, eyes glazed over. He was clearly drunk, and Racagnal knew he would have to proceed with care. He would have no trouble overpowering the boy, given the state he was in, but there were two others back in the bar. And though they were all small in stature, they had muscles of iron.

Finnman stood right in front of the Frenchman. Racagnal was a good head taller. The boy raised a hand to Lena, who cried out, but Racagnal blocked the gesture. Finnman took a swipe at his opponent with his free fist, but his thick snowsuit slowed him down. Racagnal easily avoided the blow and pushed the breeder away, hard. He fell back against the other two, who had appeared just at that moment, and all three collapsed to the floor. Lena began shouting at Finnman, but he was already back on his feet. He threw himself at Racagnal a second time, while Lena slipped away quickly through the door. This time, Finnman fell heavily into the powdery snow beyond the wooden terrace floor. He wiped it from his face and lunged forward clumsily, a third time. The Frenchman avoided him without difficulty, but the Sami came at him again.

The slow-motion brawl continued. Ducking and dodging the breeder's attacks, Racagnal dropped his guard and Finnman caught him on the chin. Another of the trio threw himself into the fray, delivering a sharp kick to the Frenchman's shin so that he stumbled forward in pain. The third breeder charged at him, tipping him backwards into the snow, softening his fall. Racagnal sprang to his feet and started punching back now. The little man from the bar room appeared in the doorway, gesticulating and shouting incoherently. He was pushed aside by a man whose voice filled the covered terrace.

'Mikkel, John, Ailo! That's enough!'

To André Racagnal's surprise, the three breeders straightened up and calmed down immediately.

'Wait for me in the bar.'

The three men left without a word.

The man introduced himself as Deputy Superintendent Rolf Brattsen. He seemed intrigued by Racagnal's presence in town.

'Everything all right?'

'Yes. People have a short fuse round here.'

'You're not local, I can see that. The Lapps are more hot-blooded than the Scandinavians. Or so they like to think. But they're not bad boys, really. Follow me back to the station, it's just near by, and I'll take a statement.'

'Oh, I won't file a complaint over that.'

'Perhaps, but I need a statement all the same.'

Racagnal had no intention of telling the policeman what he was doing in Kautokeino, but he couldn't afford to arouse police suspicion, either. The cop looked like an uncompromising character, but he'd get him off the scent quickly enough. Crossing the bar room, he noticed the three Sami, standing waiting in silence.

'Proud of yourselves? Get off home and sober up.' The policeman spoke as if he was addressing a bunch of kids. 'I'll see you all later.'

André Racagnal left the pub, looking intently in Lena's direction. The girl lifted one hand in a discreet wave. He immediately wished she hadn't. Brattsen had taken it all in.

They stepped out into the cold, crossed the road, passed in front of the supermarket and entered the police station, which was empty at this time of day. Brattsen showed the Frenchman into his office and settled himself behind his computer screen.

'Who were those three?' asked Racagnal.

'Ailo Finnman, the guy with the lasso, is the son of one of the big families around here. A breeder. Worth about two thousand head of reindeer. The other two, Mikkel and John, are herders who work for him, when there's work to do. The rest of the time, they work for local farmers, or do odd jobs. They've been out all day watching the herd. Been a few problems around here lately. Nothing serious.'

The Frenchman didn't invite any further information. Brattsen seemed disappointed.

'So, tell me everything. Briefly. Why you're here, and the rest.'

Racagnal told him he was a geologist, working for a French company prospecting in the area. He was staying at the Villmarkssenter, despite the fact that the new hotels were more luxurious. He was planning to spend a few weeks in town, he explained.

'We don't get many prospectors at this time of year,' said Brattsen. 'Mostly, they come in the summer when they can see the rocks. What can you do when everything is under snow?' He looked sceptical.

Racagnal didn't give a damn, but he would have to reassure him.

'I worked around here a lot, a long time ago. For several years. I know the region pretty well. In winter, the freeze gives us access to marshy areas that are inaccessible in summer. That's what I'm interested in now. And the interior of the *vidda* is dry, there's not so much snow, as you know. No, believe me, a good prospector can get plenty of very useful work done in winter.'

Racagnal could see Brattsen wasn't convinced, but he wasn't about to deliver a geology lecture. The man would never understand, in any case.

'What are you looking for?'

'Oh, the usual.' The geologist gave a fixed smile, indicating that the policeman was trespassing onto private territory. 'Same as everyone else, I imagine. I just hope I've got a better nose for it than my colleagues.'

'So, what, then?'

Damned cop. Racagnal straightened up.

'Listen, I'm not obliged to tell you anything, under the law. I've registered my application for an exploration permit with the council. All in order. I'm prospecting. If I find anything you'll know all about it soon enough.'

Racagnal hoped that would shut him up, but Brattsen clearly didn't appreciate the crash course in Norwegian law, from a foreigner.

'Where were you during the day on Tuesday?' he asked suddenly, staring intently at Racagnal.

11

Thursday 13 January

8 p.m., Central Sápmi

The afterglow of daylight had long since faded when Klemet and Nina reached the Reindeer Police hut. The cabin was cosier than the trailers used by the breeders. The police had others, too, scattered in the four corners of the region covered by the patrols. Some were proper little mountain chalets. This one was plain in the extreme, Nina noted. There were two compartments, one of which served as a kitchen. Klemet was taking charge of the latter, with a proprietorial air. They had unloaded the storage boxes and bags from the scooters and piled everything up in the small entrance area. She was new to the brigade, but experience had already taught her that any arrival at a new bivouac followed a pre-defined ritual. Beginning with heating the hut and preparing food.

She went back outside to fetch some dry firewood, stored under a shelter. This was important. The police took dry firewood on every mission out in the tundra, to maintain the permanent stocks at the shelters. A matter of life or death for yourself and others, if a patrol had to stop over in an emergency.

Nina had adjusted quickly to the essential rules in such a harsh environment. She came from the maritime south, but she had been raised in a village at the back of a deep fjord, where the isolation was almost as extreme. She tore some strips of bark from the surrounding birch trees to use as kindling and took them back indoors. The flames caught quickly. Nina filled a large cooking-pot with snow and placed it on the heat.

In the hut's living quarters, two sets of convertible bunk beds stood against opposite walls, separated by a long table. Nina propped one of the upper bunks back into position and threw her bag onto the bed below. She lit two candles on the table. She felt at ease now and, for the first time since they had been on patrol together, she found Klemet more accessible too. Her partner was mostly reserved. Not the talkative type. She regretted that: the people in Kiruna had told her Klemet was the most experienced Reindeer Policeman they had. And the only Sami on the force, surprisingly – something he had complained about to her before, and she could understand why. Knowing the language had to be an asset when dealing with reindeer breeders, who tended to talk business among themselves in their own tongue.

She watched Klemet busying himself in the kitchen. He seemed relaxed. She decided to seize the moment.

'Klemet,' she ventured, 'why does Brattsen call you Chubby? You're really not overweight. For a man of your age, I mean.'

She bit her lip, cursing her thoughtless slip, but compensated with her best, radiant smile. Klemet stopped stirring the potatoes and looked over at her. She kept up the smile, showing she meant no harm. He stirred the pan again, then looked at her a second time, saying nothing. Finally, he put her out of her misery.

'Don't worry about it, Nina, I don't mind. Plenty of puppy fat when I was a kid. Hence the name. It only bothers me now when a character like Brattsen uses it to wind me up.'

Nina smiled, but was happy to change the subject. She sat down. 'And why did Johann Henrik refer to Olaf as "the Spaniard"?'

Klemet laughed. 'Couldn't you tell?'

'Why? Because he has brown hair and eyes?'

'No, many Sami have brown hair and eyes. Notice anything else?'

She couldn't say.

'People call him the Spaniard because of the way he holds himself. All proud and upright, back arched, bum sticking out like a matador.'

Nina smiled at her mental picture of the protester and his seductive smile. She felt lost in this new world, still. Everyone here seemed to have known everyone else for ever. Graduating from the police academy in Oslo just a few months before, she had had no choice in where she was sent, like every grant-assisted student. The State paid for their studies, but they had to accept the first posting they were offered, and no complaints. Villages in the Arctic north were hardly top of everyone's list. So she had ended up here. Nina had never set foot in the region before. Like so many southern Scandinavians, she knew nothing about the thinly populated semi-wilderness of the Arctic.

'And his time in jail?'

'Olaf is Swedish. Passports and frontiers don't count for a whole lot up here, except if you're trying to get into Russia. People roam free. Everyone is of mixed blood. Well, most people. I'm Swedish, too, on my mother's side. Olaf lives in Kiruna most of the time. He's a member of Sámediggi – the Swedish Sami parliament. But as with a lot of breeders, his reindeer have pasture on both sides of the border. And in between Kautokeino and Kiruna there's a bit of Finland, too. Olaf was suspected of planting explosives on a minehead there in 1995, I think. They kept in him the cells for a bit, but they couldn't prove anything. Except that imprisoning a Sami militant always causes a stir. He was released after a few days. Made the most of it afterwards, of course. It helped him get elected. And he lets everyone know about it even now.'

'What about the IRA?'

'There were some IRA militants nosing around up here when all the protests were going on about the Alta dam, in the late 1970s. The police boarded a boat in a small port up by the Russian border. It was loaded with explosives and arms. Two guys were arrested. But the story was suppressed. We found out later that the two guys were IRA mules, and Olaf was their local contact. The IRA had offered to help blow up the dam, can you believe. But like I said, it was all hushed up, and Olaf was left in peace.'

'Tell me about the dam.'

'Well, I was a young police recruit. They wanted to build a hydroelectric dam between here and Alta. But it meant drowning a valley, a valley used by the Sami for their reindeer. There were protests. The eco-warriors got involved. They didn't give a toss about the Sami, though. They were all from Oslo. They wanted to protect Mother Nature. Well, everyone joined forces on the barricades.'

'What about you?'

'Me? Like I said, I was a young police recruit. It was just before I left for Stockholm. And I did what a young police recruit must.'

'But the dam project was unjust, wasn't it?'

Klemet hesitated, watching her cautiously. He knew they were both perfectly entitled to express an opinion, even as officers of the law. Still, this could get awkward. His colleague seemed sincere, though.

'To be honest, I could see the Samis' point of view. It was an attack on their way of life, and on the landscape. I would probably have stood with them, yes. But what could I do? I was a policeman.'

The big wood-burning stove was radiating heat now. Klemet began frying the meat, turning the potatoes in the pan from to time. Nina could feel her cheeks reddening. After almost an entire day out in the cold, they seemed to be radiating intense heat, too. She remembered Berit's friendly warning, but she felt entirely comfortable in her colleague's presence.

'Do you know all the breeders?' she asked.

'I know most of them, yes,' said Klemet, after a moment's silence. 'I should hope so, after ten years in the Reindeer Police.'

'But I mean, do you know them personally? Did you know them before that?'

Klemet flipped the meat in the pan, taking his time.

'A few.'

Blood from a stone, Nina thought. It was always the same, when the questions got too close.

'Aslak and Mattis?'

'Yes . . . Slightly. We lost touch for years. Especially Aslak.'

'You had been close?'

'Close . . . No, not close.'

'Were you a breeder, too?'

Klemet stopped attending to the food and looked up. 'No. My family was poor.'

Nina thought for a moment.

'Mattis was a breeder, and he didn't seem particularly wealthy to me.'

'But we weren't alcoholics. If Mattis had kept a clear head, he might have given up reindeer breeding years ago, like my grandfather had to because he couldn't make enough to feed his family. Mattis was like all those Sami who think they've failed somehow, if they aren't reindeer breeders.'

Nina said nothing. Klemet was a harsh judge, she thought. Perhaps he was jealous, just a little.

'OK, we can eat. And then we'll call the station.'

Nina understood he was drawing the discussion to a close.

'No one has a drinking problem where I come from,' she said. 'Everyone watched out for everyone else on the fjord. My mother was a devout believer. Evangelical. There were a lot of them in the village. Sometimes, when the boats came in, the fishermen would drink and cause trouble. My mother hated that. She and the other women, her friends, would keep watch until the boats left.'

'Alcohol always brings trouble,' said Klemet, carrying the dishes over to the table.

They ate in silence.

When they had cleared everything away, Klemet spread a map out on the table and replaced the candles. He put in a few calls to the local breeders, then contacted the Sheriff, activating the loudspeaker. He gave him a brief summary of their conversation with Johann Henrik. They would see Aslak tomorrow, at the earliest.

'I've been thinking,' said the Sheriff. 'Do you have any ideas about Mattis's scooter? Why burn it? And why not burn the trailer?'

'There might have been prints on the scooter ...' suggested Nina.

'But then, it would have made sense to burn the trailer, too,' Klemet cut in.

The station had found the French collector's details. He didn't speak much English. Nina would have to dust off her language skills.

'She should call him as soon as possible,' the Sheriff insisted. 'We're getting nowhere. Oslo are already on my back. And the press has caught the scent. There are a few journalists in town, setting everyone on edge. Brattsen's spoken to the two herders working for Finnman. They confirm that they spent Tuesday with him, out on the tundra. They were together the whole time, near Govggecorru. Too far to get to Mattis's trailer and back around the estimated time of death. So no help there.'

Nina could hear the Sheriff muttering to himself. She pictured him helping himself from his bowl of *salmiakki* – the overpowering, salty liquorice sweets he always kept in his office. He dispensed further instructions, his mouth apparently full.

'Klemet, you have got to see Aslak as soon as you can, tomorrow. He's the only one of Mattis's immediate neighbours we haven't seen. If he can't produce an alibi, you'll have to bring him in. No two ways about it. And if it isn't him, we really are in the shit.'

'Bring him in, bring him in ... Ask Brattsen. He'd love to bring him in. It's not really our job, you know that.'

'I know, but if you have to, you'll do it, Klemet. And what about the reindeer thefts over the past two years?'

'Haven't had time for that yet. In any case, we'd need to search back over ten years, twenty ... Reindeer rustling leads to vendettas. Blood feuds over generations. But I'll work on it tonight. With Nina. Any news on clues at the trailer?'

Klemet heard the Sheriff rustling the bowl of *salmiakki*. He smacked his tongue on another sweet.

'Dozens of fingerprints, of course. Including yours and Nina's.

84

Estimated time of death around two in the afternoon on Tuesday. And the burned-out scooter is definitely Mattis's. They tried to take a cast of the tracks under the top layer of snow, but nothing conclusive for the moment. And for your information, Olaf and his band of Sami elders are still occupying the crossroads. They've set up a camp with two trailers and tents. They're planning to spend the night. A proper village fête. But the pastor's calmed down.'

Klemet replaced his mobile on the table, went outside to put diesel in the generator, then fired up the engine. They could hardly hear it inside. Nina had taken out her laptop and set up the satellite connection. The hut morphed from cosy candlelit diner to operations HQ. Klemet put his mobile to charge next to Nina's, took out his own laptop and connected to the police intranet. He punched in the passwords, entered some search terms and quickly retrieved a long list of cases of reindeer theft. Sitting next to him, Nina followed his progress, unconvinced.

'Two hundred and thirty-five reports in two years. That seems a lot, doesn't it? Is it really such a problem around here?'

Klemet said nothing for a moment. He rubbed his chin, staring at the reports at the top of the list.

'Not to mention all the thefts we never get to hear about. You can easily multiply that by five, I'd say. It's always been a problem. That's why the Reindeer Police was created, in fact. Just after the war. The Sami breeders had had enough of Norwegians stealing their reindeer. People were left with nothing to eat after the Germans slashed and burned everything when they withdrew.'

'And today?'

'Well, the Norwegians still steal the Sami's animals. Usually in the autumn, when the reindeer are all fattened up on grass after the summer. Around September, before the migration to the winter pastures. That's when the meat is most tender. There are always Norwegians from down on the coast ready to take out a reindeer on the roadside. One for the freezer. But those aren't the thefts listed here. The Norwegians don't venture out into the tundra in the middle of winter. That's Sami territory.'

'It's strange, I can't imagine the Sami stealing reindeer. I didn't think they would quarrel among themselves. I thought they would show solidarity.'

Klemet frowned.

Nina went on: 'From what you say, we still have several hundred suspects among the other breeders, taking into account all the vendettas dating back over decades ...'

'In theory, yes. Not only vendettas, though. If two herds get mixed up, a breeder might decide to slaughter the new animals from his neighbour's herd. To save his own from starving. He just has to get rid of their ears, with the incised markings, and they can't be identified, so no one can file a complaint and no one can investigate either. That's the way it is, very often. But people don't like to talk about it, of course. And if you cream off a few reindeer from your neighbour's herd, no one gets too worked up about it. Your neighbour will do the same. In the spring, young calves that have lost their mothers get the same treatment. An unmarked calf picked up in the middle of the forest, well, it's finders keepers. Mostly, the breeders don't think of that as theft. Not as we define it, anyhow.'

'Was Mattis implicated in cases like that?'

'Mattis, and everyone else. Then it's a question of degree. There are people who'll take one or two reindeer, people who'll take ten, and people who double the size of their herd in a few years. The Finnman clan have a reputation for that, for example. Nothing's ever been proved. But that's what they're known for in the region. I'm going to start sorting through the list. You should call France before it's too late.'

Nina had spent nine months in France as an au pair, in the year before she joined the police. It was because of what had happened in France that she had decided on a career in the force. She had never told anyone, except the police superintendent who interviewed her when she applied and who had supported her application subsequently. Keeping the secret. Nina felt ashamed of the incident in France. She had a very clear idea of right and wrong. The remnants of her strict upbringing, courtesy of her mother. She knew that what had happened was bad. And yet she had been lured into it, unable to resist, against her better judgement. She had lost control. She was ashamed even at the memory of that loss of self-control. She felt disgust for the man involved, disgust at herself. Why hadn't she found the strength to refuse? Why hadn't he listened to her?

She looked at the telephone number. Paris. It had happened in Paris. She punched in the numbers, adjusting her earpieces. A man's voice answered after just a couple of seconds. When she opened her mouth to speak, she was surprised to find her French was still fluent.

'Bonjour, Monsieur, je m'appelle Nina Nansen.'

'Bonjour, Mademoiselle ...' The voice was polite, distinguished and quite young.

'I'm calling about a Sami drum you donated to the museum in Kautokeino.'

'The drum, yes, absolutely. Then you will want to speak to my father. The gift was his. I am Paul Mons, his son.'

'In that case, yes. Please.'

'Unfortunately, my father can't come to the telephone. He is bedridden and has difficulty talking. He is very weak. What can I do for you?'

'This is the Norwegian police. I'm calling because the drum was stolen on the night of Sunday to Monday, from Juhl's museum in Kautokeino.'

'Actually, I know. Your colleagues called the next day. They gave me to understand that someone who could speak French would call back. A very strange business. Have you found it?'

'No, sir. That's why I'd like to ask your father a few questions.'

'Well, if I can help you, I'll be happy to answer them. Otherwise, I will pass your questions on to my father.'

'The museum hadn't opened the sealed case, in fact. So we have no idea what the drum looks like. We'd like to know what was special about it. What might have interested anyone.'

'Can I call you back on this number in few minutes? I'll go and speak to my father.'

Nina ended the call and turned back to Klemet's screen. Her partner was scrolling through the files of registered reindeer thefts. According to police records, Mattis's name had come up three times in the past two years. Out of curiosity, Klemet had then searched the entire database of digitalised reports dating back to 1995. Twelve incidents had been reported. Of the twelve, nine were unresolved due to lack of evidence – par for the course in cases like this. The thefts were mostly small-scale. Most of the complaints had been registered by Mattis's direct neighbours: the Finnmans (they showed some nerve, thought Nina, given their reputation), and Johann Henrik in the case of two more serious thefts. None were from Aslak. Nina was not surprised. She hadn't met him yet, but a reluctance to involve the police fitted her mental picture of the man about whom she had heard so much.

Nina's mobile rang again shortly afterwards. Paul, the collector's son, had been able to ask his father a few questions. Apparently, he had received the drum directly from a Sami man, shortly before the war, during a visit to Lapland.

'My father took part in several expeditions at the time with the explorer Paul-Émile Victor, to Greenland and Lapland. That's why I am called Paul, in fact. My father's admiration for him has been lifelong and quite boundless. As I understand it, he promised Paul-Émile he would return the drum to Lapland when the time was right. He did not volunteer any further details. I sent it to the museum. According to my father, there was some sort of problem with the drum. But as I have said before, he is quite weak, and I don't like to trouble him with too many questions at once. I did not understand the exact nature of the problem. I shall have to call you another time, to tell you more. This is all I know for the moment.'

'Could you ask him who the Sami man was, and what was depicted on the drum?'

Nina ended the call. She had never heard of Paul-Émile Victor, but she was intrigued by Paul Mons's reference to the unidentified Sami man, and to a problem with the drum.

'Paul-Émile Victor? No idea,' said Klemet, when they resumed their conversation.

He sent a radio message to Aslak, letting him know they would call on him the next day. Aslak had no mobile phone and no landline, just an old radio set – NATO surplus. Klemet had no idea whether he was listening in and took it for granted that Aslak wouldn't answer in person. In truth, the call forced Klemet to prepare himself for tomorrow's visit. He didn't like meeting Aslak.

He got up to put more wood on the stove. The hut was thoroughly warm now. Through the small window, Klemet could see nothing but thick, black night. A faint, greenish light glimmered in the sky over to his left, but nothing extraordinary. Tomorrow would be clear and bright. The splendours of nature and the Northern Lights always put him in mind of his uncle. Uncle Nils Ante, who could describe the phenomenon in wonderful words, while he, Klemet, always felt clumsy and incapable. And not only when faced with the spectacle of the natural world, if he thought about it. He banished the aurora from his thoughts.

Nina was making instant coffee, her fresh features concentrated on the task, her long blonde ponytail dancing against her bulky sweater, which nonetheless revealed the outline of her breasts. She reminded Klemet of the tall, wholesome, uncomplicated girls he had so desired when he was a young man. But they had been far beyond his reach. He had felt so different. Awkward. Clumsy ... It always came back to that. Even here, in the hut, far from anywhere.

'Is everything OK, Nina? Do you feel all right?'

Nina turned, flashing her dazzling smile.

'Fine, thanks. Three sugars, as usual?'

'Three. Thanks. I mean, do you like it here?'

'Very much so.'

She poured the coffee into the brightly coloured plastic mugs.

'Actually, I don't know why there aren't more candidates for the North, fresh out of police academy. I really like it here.'

'That's good. It's good for us to get people from the South. Especially women. We don't have enough women up here.'

She smiled again but said nothing. Klemet felt like an idiot now. Infuriated to find himself behaving like his own, gauche, twenty-year-old self. He never hit on the right thing to say. Or too late, when someone else had already made off with the booty. He moved towards her, to collect his mug.

'Yes, there aren't many pretty girls like you around here. Are you planning to stay?'

Nina seemed impervious to her colleague's efforts. Damn it, thought Klemet. She kept smiling, stirring the powdered milk into her coffee.

'I feel good here. What I'm learning about the Sami, and the Norwegians, really interests me. I wouldn't at all mind staying a few years. I'll have to discuss it with my boyfriend, though.' The same beaming smile.

Jesus, thought Klemet. What a fucking idiot. Why had he brought the conversation round to this? Nina was oblivious, apparently, but that only annoyed him more. He remembered an old friend who could charm any girl he liked, whenever the time was right. Klemet had never known what to do. He was saved by a mobile ringtone. This time it was Nina's.

12

10 p.m., Kautokeino

André Racagnal managed to get out of the police station after about an hour. The Deputy Superintendent was a hard case. It was written all over his face. Stubborn and hard. Racagnal's blood had run cold when Brattsen asked him what he had been doing on Tuesday. He thought fast, running through the events of the day in his mind. But the policeman was after something else, it turned out. Brattsen had made the object of his inquiries clear: he was looking for leads on the reindeer breeder's murder. Racagnal was overcome with relief, but let nothing show. The policeman had suspected nothing. He resumed the detached, ironic, cynical tone he affected with everyone. But the policeman had insisted. It wasn't enough that Racagnal had a concrete alibi for the Tuesday afternoon in question. Brattsen had asked a load of questions about his work as a prospector.

There was a simple enough reason for Racagnal's absence from Kautokeino on Tuesday, the day of the Sami breeder's murder. He had made a round trip to Alta, an hour and a half north on the coast, to get his car serviced, and the vehicle had been stuck at the workshop because the garage owner had closed for a Progress Party march. The first demonstration in the area for a quarter of a century, and there he was, caught up in it all! A demonstration that 'couldn't

91

be missed', said the garage owner, who had taken his two mechanics along with him. Idiot. The man had felt it necessary to explain all about the demo to André – how the Norwegians were taking action because they had had enough of the Lapps getting on their high horses about their blasted drum, and because the stolen drum in Kautokeino had worked everyone into a fever of excitement, and the Lapps were so damn keen on proclaiming their rights, but they, the Norwegians, they had just as many rights, too, dammit, and if they kept on granting more rights to the Laplanders, they'd have to start granting them to the bloody Somalis too, and then where would we all be? Right, or not?

Stupid bastard, Racagnal thought. Personally, he couldn't give a damn about the Sami, the Norwegians, the Somali immigrants, or the drum. He couldn't give a toss about the whole damn lot of them. But he wanted his four-by-four. Worse still, the garage owner seemed convinced that the visitor from France, of all places, would be delighted to see that Norwegians were capable of taking to the streets and protesting, too. Fool.

Racagnal had used the time to buy equipment, said he would be back later, then spent the day making a tour of the pubs in Alta. Which didn't take long. He had started at the Nordlys hotel, then taken his taxi-driver's advice and wound up at the Han Steike pub and café, in the centre of town. Things had looked up around mid-afternoon when a group of giggling Norwegian schoolgirls came in. Racagnal sized them up and down in detail, taking care no one noticed. One of the girls caught his eye more than the others. A pageboy haircut neatly framing her face, the fringe falling into her eyes. She wasn't the prettiest, but of all of them she was the one who'd be ready and willing, with her fringe down to her eyes, so that she had to lift her chin to see out. As ready as they came. A real little minx. As a rule, he preferred girls with curly hair. But the little blonde with the fringe excited him.

Racagnal had cast an eye around the room. Ten or so customers were seated at tables, mostly drinking coffee. Three workers in fluorescent overalls were finishing their day with a beer at the bar. The schoolgirls were laughing out loud. The one with the fringe had taken out an exercise book. Several of them were doing their home-work. Too risky here, he thought. Racagnal concentrated on his glass, his prospecting mission. It didn't help. The girl's childlike face rose before him. The little soft-skinned minx. Racagnal closed his eyes. Thought about his last trip to the Congo. Tried to stay calm. The Congo. The little girls in Kivu. There for the asking. Not even that – people had brought them to him. Things were more com-plicated here.

The trip to Alta was two days ago now. The police had left him in peace since then. He had been able to focus on getting ready for the mission. He was staying at the Villmarkssenter, for years Kautokeino's only hotel. It was plain and simple, with a well-meaning host whose Danish wife liked to play the haughty chatelaine, but who drank and smoked, though only outside on the terrace, so as not to shock the guests. He had stayed there a long time ago, too.

Three more hotels had sprung up since the little airfield had been built, not long ago. The town's sudden expansion was fuelled by the mining companies' growing interest in the region. Around Kauto-keino and the interior of the Finnmark, mining companies were allowed to prospect only in the summer months – in theory – when the reindeer were hundreds of kilometres to the north, dispersed in their summer pastures along the coast. In winter, after the autumn migration, the reindeer were concentrated once again in the region between Kautokeino and Karasjok, feeding on lichen. The Sami did not allow any activity likely to disturb the animals or cause them to move into a neighbouring herder's territory. Rare exceptions were granted for non-intrusive prospecting, or activity that was limited to a very small area.

Racagnal had completed an application form, stating that he was carrying out a reconnaissance mission, mostly on foot, and very occasionally aboard a snowmobile within a clearly defined perim-eter, sticking to a marked trail. Things had been simpler in Kivu on that score, too. But Racagnal knew that if you wanted to work here, you had to follow the rules. Within reason, of course.

*

93

Klemet returned to his seat with his coffee while Nina took the call. He settled himself in front of his laptop and continued reading the reports of reindeer thefts. But the sight of Nina's lips talking into her mobile, the pretty outline of her sweater, set him thinking again.

Even now, after twenty-five years, he felt the same bitter regrets. So many wasted opportunities. And yet, as a young man, Klemet had been to the same parties as all the others, held in the same barns, or the same forest clearings. How many times had he hung around outside, or at the end of forest tracks, leaning nervously against his red, open-top Volvo P1800. He had installed a cassette deck on the dashboard. Roy Orbison's 'Pretty Woman'. But the girls never said yes – not to the quiet boy the others called Chubby, no matter how hard he tried to impress. Trouble was, if he stayed in the driver's seat, the near-side window didn't wind down completely, and he had to rest his elbow on top of it at an awkward angle, undermining any attempt to look cool and relaxed.

He had dreamed of owning a garage. He loved cars and engines. The purr of a finely tuned motor was a thing of wonder, approaching even the hypnotic beauty of one of Uncle Nils Ante's *joïks*. On Midsummer Eve, the decorated poles were set up and he would watch, elbow in the air, from behind the wheel of his P1800. But girls like Nina were never for him. Klemet didn't drink. He would lean against the hood of his Volvo, while the others enjoyed themselves. But he didn't mind. At the end of the evening, the girls were happy to see him, when their dates were dead drunk. Chubby was their reliable friend, a boy you could count on, the only one who stayed sober. Sometimes he would steal a kiss, never going too far; the girls knew he wouldn't, or that if they objected he would know enough to stop. He was a reassuring presence. And even if he felt frustrated, he was content with his lot. The stolen kisses excited him for days afterwards. When he joined the police, he had become more confident with women. It felt like confidence to him, at any rate. To others, his swaggering behaviour masked the awkwardness beneath.

Klemet remembered the day he had returned to Kautokeino after years away, sporting a police uniform. Remembered it like yesterday. He was still solidly built, but now he was fit, in good shape. People had looked at him differently, to his great satisfaction. The local women had given him more than kisses on the corner of the mouth, especially when he was out on patrol for days at a time, touring the farmsteads. No one called him Chubby. No one. Until Brattsen had showed up, and some kindly soul had told him about Klemet's moniker from years gone by. No one but Brattsen ever dared use the nickname, but he caught people exchanging glances, sometimes, when Brattsen was winding him up. That hurt.

Nina ended her call, after talking in French for some time. Klemet's reverie was interrupted.

'That was Paul. The Sami man who gave his father the drum worked as a guide for Paul-Émile Victor's expedition. Paul saw the drum very often in his father's study. He remembers there was a cross in the middle, and a straight line separating it into two sections. He doesn't remember the other symbols, apart from the reindeer.'

'Nothing exceptional then.' Klemet sighed. 'Most Sami drums have a cross in the middle. Usually, it symbolises the sun. The reindeer are very common, too. And the dividing line. It separates the world of the living from the world of the dead. I think so, anyway. That's what Uncle Nils Ante always said, if I remember rightly. We won't get far on that description.'

He ran his hand over the top of his head. A case like this was rare in the Reindeer Police. The theft of a priceless Sami drum, a murder, and practically no leads beyond the usual quarrels between the breeders. But there was always tension between breeders. Who stood to gain by Mattis's death? He couldn't say. His animals would be slaughtered by the Reindeer Adminstration, and they had been in poor shape, anyway. Who would take over his district? Could that provide a lead? He would check with the Administration. But he didn't hold out much hope. The parcelling out of territories was tightly controlled, too. There were strict administrative procedures to be followed.

'Paul says his father has kept a set of old papers from the expedition, in a trunk.'

Klemet thought further. Suddenly, he reached for his mobile and called the Sheriff. Tor Jensen answered almost immediately. It was late.

'Tor, you need to send Nina to France to make inquiries. We won't make any headway otherwise.'

Nina stared at her partner, wide-eyed. He hadn't even bothered to ask her opinion. She couldn't hear the Sheriff's response, but this wouldn't be an easy decision for a small station like theirs. Klemet ended the call, leaving her no time to object.

'The Sheriff's OK with that. Apparently, Oslo are giving him such a hard time, he thinks he'll have no trouble asking for an extended budget. Seems like a good idea to me. What do you think?'

'You might have asked me first.'

'Why, do you have a better plan? You need to go and take a look at those papers. We have nothing at all to go on at the moment. And tempers are rising. The Sheriff said there was a Progress Party demo in Alta on Tuesday. A demo against the Sami demo in Kautokeino.'

'You don't have to treat me like a kid!' Nina was angry now.

Klemet fell silent. He felt a bizarre sense of gratification at the thought that Nina was taking a hit for all the times he had sat waiting at the end of the party, waiting while girls like her kissed all the other guys. It didn't cross his mind that she hadn't even been born at the time.

'Unless you've got a better idea.' But he looked obstinate.

'Your idea's fine. But everyone treats me as if I'm invisible, somehow. You and your reindeer-breeder friends.'

'They're not my friends.'

'Oh really? You seem to be on the same wavelength, at any rate. Just tell me if you want me to make the coffee next time we interview a suspect. They have a special course for apprentice girl investigators at the police college, didn't you know? It's called "how to help your male colleagues solve cases that are too difficult for you all by yourself". They teach us how to make nice coffee, and smile, and play the innocent in interviews, so our colleagues' questions look really clever. Get it?'

Klemet's stubborn expression remained. He wanted to respond, but didn't know how. And what was more annoying still, he would think of a rejoinder just at the wrong time, and far too late. Nina was an annoying kid, really. He was thirty years her senior. He'd done his time in all the stations in the region, not to mention Stockholm, and here she was, putting him in his place. Plus all that talk of coffee was making him thirsty. Wretched kid, he thought again.

He got to his feet. Nina's fit of temper had subsided. He noted with satisfaction that she was not opposed to his Paris idea. He offered to make her a coffee. She accepted. Case closed.

Nina spoke next.

'Do you think the Sami nationalists could have stolen it?'

'Them, or the Progress Party. Everyone has an axe to grind when things flare up around here. You've got the local and national elections in less than a year, too.'

'What about Mattis and the reindeer thefts?'

'The most serious case he was involved in was ten years ago. Around the same time Johann Henrik was shot at. We had a succession of really hard winters, after really bad autumn weather, a bit like this year. Snowfall, and a melt, then another hard frost on top of that, so that you get a layer of ice. And then another melt, and so on, two or three times over, which is enough to build up the ice, so the reindeer can't break through to the ground lichen. That throws everything off kilter. The reindeer can starve by the hundred, by the thousand. Ten years ago, one family in a very exposed district lost thousands of head of livestock that way. They made up for it in part by rustling hundreds of reindeer from their neighbours' herds. Mattis was involved. He wasn't the ringleader, but he was accused of complicity in the crime. Spent a few months behind bars for his trouble.'

'But how could they steal the animals, if their ears were marked?'

'They recut the ears.'

'Recut?'

'Yes, they cut away the marked part of the ear, then incised what was left with their own mark.'

'Good grief.'

'Result – hundreds of reindeer with tiny ears. Some had been cut back so far they got infected. All the reindeer identified that way had to be slaughtered. Since then, even the size of the ears is strictly controlled. They can't be too small.'

Nina was astounded. She found it hard to believe that any Sami would be prepared to go that far. Like most Nordic people, she knew nothing about their way of life. She had accepted the quaint, folk-loric stereotypes without question, which came to the same thing.

'What about the other cases Mattis was involved in?'

'Bits and pieces. I've been wasting my time, I think. Mattis was a pitiful character. And I think most people around here saw him that way. A poor guy, down on his luck. Not a serious threat.'

'And people slice the ears off poor, unthreatening guys like him, here in lovely Lapland?'

Klemet said nothing. She was right. Something didn't fit. People didn't kill over a few stolen reindeer, either, especially not a small-time rustler like Mattis. There were worse culprits than him.

'Did Mattis live alone?'

'As far as I know. Aslak may know more about that. I don't think he was "in a relationship". You saw his trailer. A professional bachelor pad.'

'But wives don't live in the trailers, do they?'

'No. That's not what I meant. The wilderness shelters are men's territory. If a woman does go there, she probably isn't the breeder's wife, if you see what I mean. But the breeders mostly try to keep some semblance of order. Mattis had given up on that, too.'

'He made me feel very uncomfortable when I met him. He kept looking at my chest.'

Klemet fixed her firmly in the eye. An effort.

'Really? Did he?'

'And he kept leering at me.'

Klemet took a sudden interest in the tips of his fingers.

'Hm. You shouldn't let that bother you,' he said, at last. 'A man alone out on the tundra is bound to get excited at the sight of a pretty girl like you. It's only normal.'

'No. It isn't normal at all.'

Now Nina was the one with the stubborn expression. Klemet saw there was no point in insisting. And he had no idea where to look now. Fortunately for him, Nina picked up the thread of the discussion.

'So Mattis had no family?'

'His mother died a long time ago. His father died more recently. If he had any brothers or sisters, they don't live locally.'

'A very lonely man, in other words. A lonely, pathetic, penniless drunk, who had his ears sliced off for no apparent reason before being stabbed to death. All barely twenty-four hours after the theft of the drum. Notice anything strange?'

'Of course it's bloody strange!' Klemet felt angry and helpless. For the moment, they hadn't a single clue: no murder weapon, no useful fingerprints, no motive.

'And the drum?'

'What about the drum?'

'I don't know. I've been trying to find a possible connection. Johann Henrik said Mattis was obsessed with drums.'

'True. I've been turning that over in my mind, too. But what connection? We don't know anything about the drum yet. It was just an old drum. It was—'

He snapped his laptop shut, placing his hands on the lid. Nina waited for him to say something. He knew her intuition was right – there had to be a connection. He just didn't want things to become even more complicated than they already were. He had joined the Reindeer Police for an easy life, after all. He had come back to Kautokeino because he'd had his fill of bad business. Investigations in tiny villages on the coast, ravaged by alcohol, prostitution and trafficking. He'd had his fill of all that. Unaccompanied Saturday-night patrols, because budgets were tight. The feeling of dread every time you stepped outside the station. It had all contributed to a full-blown depression, a few years on medication. And he knew plenty of colleagues who had gone to the wall that way. How could Nina understand? He had no desire to talk about it. He had lost his nerve, spent months on sick leave. That was all there was to it. So yes, the Reindeer Police had meant peace and quiet, the open air, no bad business. None at all.

Klemet sighed heavily. He was about to say something, then decided against it. He couldn't afford to play the prima donna. The new directives from head office explicitly favoured the promotion of women officers – there were quotas to fill, and targets to meet: forty per cent of the top jobs to be occupied by women. Given the almost complete absence of women cops in the Far North, Nina was all set for the fast track, if she didn't make any mistakes.

'You may be right,' he said, at last.

13

Friday 14 January

Sunrise: 10.31 a.m.; sunset: 12.26 p.m.
1 hour 55 minutes of sunlight

7.30 a.m., Central Sápmi

Reindeer Police hut

Klemet woke early the following morning. Outside, all was darkness. The gusting wind buffeted the window, piling snow crystals against the pane. The stove had gone out. He shivered. His legs felt stiff and slightly numb in the warmth of his sleeping bag, but he didn't stay lying down for long. He wriggled out of his bag, pulled on his reindeer-skin shoes and stretched. Nina was still asleep on the opposite bunk, on the other side of the table. The first woman officer in the Reindeer Police. The brigade's shelters weren't designed to accommodate men and women together, but Nina hadn't seemed to mind the lack of privacy when they turned in the night before. Just as well. Klemet wouldn't have put up with any fussiness.

He stoked the stove with more wood and lit the fire. The noise woke Nina up. She greeted her colleague, dressed quickly while

Klemet made coffee in the kitchen, then stepped outside. Five minutes later she returned, freshly scrubbed with snow.

'It's quite nice when you get used to it,' she said, her cheeks glowing red.

Klemet put the coffee and breakfast on the table. He had folded away his sleeping bag while she was outside.

'You can finish your wash and brush-up here, if you like,' he said, pointing to the pan of hot water on the stove. 'I'll be back in five minutes.'

He stood for a moment on the small porch at the front of the hut, facing into the icy wind, staring out into the darkness, as if searching for something. He unfastened his snowsuit and pulled his arms out from the sleeves. He made himself do this at the start of every new day, while darkness reigned over the tundra. He didn't enjoy it, but he stuck to the ritual. He felt the cold grip his body, then took a deep breath and stepped out into the dark. He clapped his hands on his shoulders, then scooped the snow and scrubbed his face, torso, underarms and neck, dried himself with a towel and went back inside.

They sat and ate in silence.

'When will we go and see Aslak?' asked Nina.

'Soon.'

Klemet chewed his bread, spread with cod-roe paste.

'Aslak's one of a kind,' he said, without looking at her. 'He's well respected in the region. Feared, too. But people fear him because he's different. He hasn't gone the way of everyone else – bought a house, a fleet of snowmobiles, four-by-four cars. He doesn't work with helicopters. Some of them even hire Thai herders to watch the reindeer. None of that for Aslak. He's – well, he keeps to the old ways.'

'And that makes him unique?'

'People see him as a kind of image of the past. He makes them nostalgic, I think.'

'Does he make you feel nostalgic?'

Klemet didn't reply.

*

Klemet and Nina had been riding their snowmobiles for forty-five minutes when the incident occurred. A harmless incident, to all appearances, but one Nina wouldn't forget in a hurry.

As usual, Klemet was riding up front. It was still two hours to sunrise, but the gleam of daylight beyond the horizon was amplified by the thick snow, and it was bright enough to see without headlamps. Nina gripped the heated handlebars, lulled by the rich purr of the engine, responsive to the slightest turn of the wrist. Its warmth spread from her thighs throughout her body. They couldn't be far from Aslak's camp. Her helmet visor blocked the cold wind, though a tiny wisp found its way in through a crack, irritating her like a persistent, buzzing fly. Her thoughts wandered, mulling over the descriptions of Aslak. They painted a strange portrait of the man. She was aware of a stand of dwarf birch trees to her left, along what was clearly a frozen river, but paid no particular attention to the scenery. They were climbing a gentle slope now, moving up the mountain, away from the snow-covered river, its snaking course defining itself as they rose. They drove slowly, the engines just ticking over. For once, Nina thought, they could just make out the sounds of nature as they rode. She paused to remove her helmet and continued, still wearing her *chapka*.

A deafening shot obliterated the noise of the engine. Nina felt an electric jolt of shock. A shadow darted ahead, to her right. She realised what it was when she saw a bulky silhouette on skis, gesticulating in front of her colleague's snowmobile. The man had burst out from the higher ground above them and came to a halt across Klemet's path, in a cloud of powdery snow, forcing him to make a sudden stop. Nina watched as Klemet calmly lifted his visor, while the other man yelled at him in anger. Nina couldn't believe what she was seeing. The other man had just fired on them – or fired a warning shot in their direction – but Klemet remained perfectly calm and unresponsive, taking the furious reprimand on the chin.

Instinctively, Nina knew this must be Aslak. She lifted the earflaps of her chapka to hear what was being said.

'. . . hell out here right now. But dear God, how many times must you be told? You can't come this way. My reindeer are just down there. If they take fright because of you, they'll make off over to the other side where there's nothing to eat. It's hell, I tell you. God almighty! You have to go around the other way, not through here, is that clear?'

The tone was authoritarian, even threatening, though there was no call for that. Everything about the man suggested he was a force of nature, radiating power and charisma. Aslak was living up to his reputation, Nina thought. He looked as if he might throw himself on Klemet at any moment and devour him whole. And bizarrely, it seemed to her that Klemet would do nothing whatever to defend himself. Strange.

Aslak was wearing a reindeer-skin poncho like Johann Henrik's, but longer, as well as reindeer-skin leggings, boots and gloves. No helmet, just a thick chapka, like those worn by the Reindeer Police.

Nina dared not move. In the growing daylight, she watched her partner's motionless silhouette, and saw Aslak's dark eyes, his fury expressed in every keenly etched line. His face was deeply furrowed and shadowed by several days' growth of beard. His jaw was squarer than most Sami men, but he had his people's high, proud cheekbones, a sharply defined nose and a broad, sensual mouth. Most of all, Nina was struck by his penetrating gaze. He emanated raw energy. Aslak moved slowly, but each gesture involved the whole of his body. Beneath his thick clothing, he was astonishingly fit and alive. He held his gun in one hand and a long stick in the other. In a flash, Nina realised she and Klemet weren't armed – the Norwegian police seldom were. Their guns were stowed in a safe back at headquarters. Helpful.

At length, Aslak turned to look in her direction. His piercing eyes seemed to take in every detail. Nina stared right back. He no longer seemed threatening, she thought. Now, she sensed an overwhelming

fatigue in the Sami's expression. Their interview would be complicated, to say the least.

Then another sound left her frozen to the spot. An unearthly
shriek, echoing around the landscape. A long, harsh, guttural cry,
expressive of terrible pain. The cry came from a long way off. But
where? The horror was nowhere to be seen, but the cry ricocheted
across the valley. Just as suddenly, it stopped, leaving nothing but
the moaning wind that had carried it to them. Nina was seized with
a sudden nameless dread. They would have to do something. She
turned to the two men. Aslak said nothing, showing no sign of
surprise. His eyes remained fixed on her, but Nina was shocked
to see the change in his expression. Pinched tight, his lips had lost
their sensual fullness now. She broke the silence.

'What was that?'

10 a.m., Kautokeino

André Racagnal walked into Kautokeino's rod and gun store.
Almost immediately, he noticed the police car turning and parking
outside. A cop got out – the same man who had interviewed him
the previous day. Shit. For a moment, he considered making an
about-turn, but decided it would be better to stay where he was,
rather than attract the sales assistant's attention. Racagnal managed
to move to the back of the store, where the knives were kept.

Rolf Brattsen walked in and headed for the fishing tackle along
the left-hand wall, apparently absorbed in the coloured flies.
Racagnal turned away, concentrating on a detailed comparison of
the broad blades. His back prickled. Someone was standing right
behind him.

'That one's for the real big game.'

Racagnal looked round. Greeted Brattsen with a forced smile.

'You never know, I may get lucky out in the *vidda*. Would this
be a good blade?'

'Don't know anything about knives,' said Brattsen, fixing him
with a hard stare. 'So you're a hunting man?'

'I'm off prospecting, like I told you. Once I get the permit from the council, which shouldn't take long. Just getting the last of my equipment together.'

Racagnal replaced the knife – he didn't need it, and since the policeman showed no sign of leaving, he went on:

'Any news on your case?'

'We're searching for clues. Still searching.'

Brattsen was standing very close. He looked less like a cop now. Seemed almost affable, though the smile was a little forced. He was clearly trying to adopt a friendlier, less stubborn expression. The worst of it was, he couldn't even manage that, thought Racagnal. The Frenchman was eager to get away, but he knew that after yesterday's interview he had to watch his step. He couldn't afford to set the cop on the scent of what had happened in Alta. Racagnal thought back to his visit to the pub, but quickly banished the image from his mind.

'No trouble since last night?' asked the policeman.

Jesus. Racagnal thought for a second before replying. Could the cop suspect something? No. Impossible.

'No. So much for my little tête à tête in the smoking area! Too bad. But I'll be in town for a while. Don't want to upset anyone.'

'No, indeed.'

The two men stood silent for a moment. Then Brattsen spoke.

'Fancied her, though, didn't you? The girl behind the bar. Eh? I could see that.'

Racagnal looked closely at Brattsen, trying to figure out where he was going with this. The policeman maintained his air of forced affability. Or perhaps he really was just being friendly.

'She was . . . interesting.'

'Bit young, though?'

'Over eighteen, I believe,' Racagnal ventured.

'No doubt, no doubt.' Brattsen stared him in the eye. He had reverted, unawares, to his natural expression – stubborn and hard. He forced another smile.

'So when are you heading out into the *vidda*?'

'Once I've collected the last of my equipment. And above all, I need a guide. Someone local.'

'Ah, yes, of course, a guide! Who will you take?'

'Don't know yet. I need someone tough who can stay the course. Someone who knows the terrain.'

'Oh, you'll find plenty around here. They may not be office material, but they're strong, dependable, and they're in their element out there. If you don't get landed with a drunk, that is.'

'I've been recommended a breeder by the name of Renson. Swedish, originally. Very sharp, apparently.'

Brattsen interrupted, with a suspicious look, 'Renson? I'd take someone else if I were you.'

'Why?'

'Find someone else, that's all. A word of friendly advice. If you don't want to get held up with your mission.'

Racagnal could see there was little point in insisting. But this wasn't helping. Renson's qualities had been roundly praised at the Villmarkssenter. An atypical breeder, liked to do things his own way, but he knew what he was about, with a great many contacts, and above all he was available – he belonged to a powerful clan who could take over his herding duties while he was away.

'Too bad. Well, I'll find someone.'

'Sure you will,' declared Brattsen. 'And don't you worry, you'll find yourself a little girlfriend hereabouts, soon enough.'

With that, he turned on his heel and left the store, looking at nothing, making no purchases. As if he hadn't stopped in by chance at all.

14

Friday 14 January

10.30 a.m., Central Sápmi

Nina didn't hear Aslak's reply. In fact, she couldn't be sure he had answered her question at all. His lips were still pinched tight, as if in acute pain. With that look in his eyes, a mixture of fire and ice. Nina felt exasperated. For once, her expression betrayed nothing, but she felt frustrated and annoyed. She didn't understand these people, with their long silences, let alone her partner, who seemed to find their behaviour perfectly normal. As a police officer, she had the right to expect an answer, to demand one, even. But Klemet stood as silent as Aslak. Not a word. As if Aslak's presence robbed him of his authority, his defences. That was it, she thought. He's in awe of Aslak, too.

As a new recruit, she had been taken to meet the Reindeer Police chief in Kiruna, on the Swedish side. He had warned her about the special nature of the squad. The Reindeer Police was no ordinary unit. They didn't usually take such young recruits, he had told her. But for the moment, the officers were all men, and they needed women. The *vidda* wasn't a woman's world, though. The chief had hesitated before going on:

'Probably no place for us non-Sami, either, come to think of it.'

The shriek seemed to die back to the far end of the valley, but Nina still felt the goosebumps on her neck and arms. She looked around her. All that whiteness, the bare mountains with their sparse stands of dwarf birch, the scattered rocky outcrops and the blue gleam of the sky where the sun struggled to rise. From their position on the mountainside, the view extended far and wide, with no sign of human life. Aslak's camp would be on the far side of the peak.

'Aslak, we need to ask you a few questions,' said Klemet. 'Nina will follow you back to camp. You can talk to her.'

Nina had been expecting anything but this. A complete change of plan! She was about to object, but Klemet carried on, avoiding her gaze. He was actually avoiding her eye! He wasn't looking at Aslak, either. What was the matter with him?

'I need to get back to the hut, I'll explain later. Let me know when you've finished. I'll come and find you here. Or somewhere. We'll see.'

He glanced at her quickly, then lowered his eyes again. Nina had never seen him like this. She saw Aslak staring intently at them both, but he made no reply. Deftly, quickly, he picked up his gun and slung it across his back before setting off, pushing silently through the snow on his skis, towards the summit. Nina followed.

They soon reached Aslak's camp on the far side. Nina sat for a moment on her scooter, with the engine off. She was fascinated by what she saw. The camp consisted of three tents covered with branches, earth and moss. Smoke rose from the biggest of the three, through an opening at the top. Nina saw an enclosure next to the furthest tent, with ten or so reindeer. The animals began to turn and jostle at their approach, indicating their alarm. They weren't used to engines. Nina couldn't see a snowmobile anywhere. It was like looking at a postcard from the pre-war days, a photograph from the book she had leafed through in Kiruna, about traditional Sami lifestyles. Camps like this didn't exist any more. She hadn't visited many herders on patrol, but those she had met so far afforded themselves a few modern comforts, at least. Not Aslak. He was a different character altogether. Beside the entrance to the biggest tent a scaffold of slender birch logs was hung with quarters of meat drying in the wind. They would be frozen rock-hard, she thought.

She sensed that she was about to enter an unknown world, far stranger than anything she had seen up to now. She was crossing a new frontier. The wind pushed at her back, urging her towards the entrance of the main tent, with Aslak's shouts, the gunshot and the terrifying shriek ringing in her ears. She knew, now, that she was about to discover its source.

Aslak went ahead, bending to step under the tent flap. He disappeared into the semi-darkness, then paused, lifting a thick tarpaulin that served as an inner door, inviting Nina to step inside. Nina prepared to stoop down. Aslak was staring at her, his dark eyes gleaming intently, framed by deep creases. His chiselled features were partly obscured by his coarse growth of beard. Nina was unsure how to interpret the look. She bent forward, took another two steps and found herself in front of a fire, in the middle of the tent. She coughed. The air was full of smoke, stinging her throat and eyes. She spotted a free space to her left and went to sit down. At ground level, the air was breathable. She removed her chapka and was about to shake her blonde hair free when Aslak entered the tent. Sensing his gaze on her again, she felt somehow indecent, exhibiting her hair. Hurriedly, she tied it back, then wished she hadn't. Aslak said nothing, waiting for her to settle.

Nina found herself unable to speak. She felt so far from anything she knew. Her eyes were getting used to the semi-darkness, and only now did she see a shape moving on the other side of the fire. She shifted slightly and saw a woman swaddled in a heavy, reindeer-skin garment, wearing a chapka, its straps knotted under her chin. The woman moved very slowly. She had a fine, slightly receding chin and high, prominent cheekbones, though less pronounced than Aslak. Her almond eyes were magnificent, but for their blank, soulless expression, Nina thought. No light there at all. She shivered. Without knowing why, she was certain that this woman had uttered the terrifying shriek. The woman didn't seem to have noticed their presence. She turned slowly, took a birch log and placed it delicately on the fire. Nina watched her. She felt acutely on edge. But the woman didn't seem to be suffering physically. Just far away, absent, not of this world ... Suddenly, she gave a deep, long sigh. Nina held her breath, dreading another shriek. But nothing came. The woman stared into the flames, her features a frozen mask.

'This is my wife,' sad Aslak. 'She doesn't speak. She is elsewhere.'

His voice seemed to draw the woman out of her torpor and she began to chant quietly. Nina recognised a guttural melody like the one she had heard Mattis sing. Another *joïk*. She found it impossible to tell how old the woman was. She might have been anywhere between thirty and sixty.

'Is she the one who screamed?' Nina asked at length, breaking the heavy silence.

'She is.'

'Why?'

'It's her way of speaking.'

He fell silent again.

'Like an infant,' he said, in a dull voice.

Nina looked at him. He seemed to be weighing each word. They were separated by much more than the hearth. She thought of Klemet's odd behaviour in Aslak's presence. Nina could almost feel the tension between the two of them, like a tightly stretched net. She couldn't understand why she found it so difficult to start the questioning. Something indefinable mingled with the floating tendrils of smoke. She tried to pull herself together, think rationally and concentrate on the inquiry. She focused on Aslak. Was he more than just Mattis's neighbour? Did he have a sufficient motive for murder?

'You have questions to ask me.'

Nina knew she was not welcome.

'We're investigating Mattis's murder. You are aware that he's been killed, that his scooter was set alight and his trailer searched. We're calling on all his neighbours. I have some questions I'd like to ask you, all of which are purely routine, and part of our inquiry.'

Nina was justifying herself more than was necessary, she knew that. But she felt impotent faced with Aslak's stare, his intense silence. And annoyed at herself.

'Where were you on Monday and Tuesday?'

'Where do you think I was?'

Nina stared at him. Aslak's lips formed a sneer of disdain. But their raw sensuality was apparent, even now. The glowing fire reflected in his eyes. He looked dangerous, she thought. This man was capable of killing.

'Where were you?' Nina asked again.

'With my reindeer.'

'With your reindeer. I see.'

Nina knew Aslak would do nothing to make her task any easier. He was obviously unaware that he risked arrest. She found herself in the same situation as Klemet, the day before, with Johann Henrik. She glanced at Aslak's wife. The woman was gazing up into the smoke rising through the hole at the top of the tent. She would find no help there, either.

'When did you last see Mattis?'

Aslak bent forward to the cooking pot, hanging from a birch tripod over the fire. He dipped a birchwood mug into it and drank a gulp of scalding-hot reindeer broth. Only after he had helped himself did he invite the policewoman to do the same. She plunged her own mug into the pot.

'I saw him on Sunday,' Aslak revealed at length. 'Sunday. He was in a bad way. Always bad. He could no longer cope. He ate here. Our paths crossed to the west, three-quarters of an hour from here. I told him to take better care of his reindeer. Some of them were over on my side. And Johann Henrik's side. He couldn't handle them alone.'

He took a long drink of broth, slurping loudly from the bottom of the mug, then helped himself to more, staring intently in Nina's direction.

'You killed him. All of you. Your rules, your lines on the map. We cannot live by reindeer breeding, as we did before.'

'No one was forcing him to drink,' said Nina.

'What would you know about that? No one was helping him, either. He hadn't opened a letter in six months. He didn't dare. He was scared.'

'What was he afraid of?' asked Nina.

'He was afraid he had lost his way. Failed.'

'You mean as a reindeer breeder?'

'As a breeder, and as a man. A breeder who doesn't know how to take proper care of his reindeer is not a true man.'

'From what I understand, from what I've seen of your lifestyle, a breeder working alone doesn't really stand a chance,' Nina objected. 'It's nothing to do with whether he's a real man or not. I thought people always helped one another out in the *vidda*....'

'Hah! Yes, of course. Did Klemet tell you that? Being Sami doesn't mean he understands what goes on out here.'

'Mattis got himself into his own mess,' said Nina. 'It wasn't the system's fault. Where were you *exactly* on Monday and Tuesday?'

Asking the question, Nina realised that whatever answer Aslak gave would be almost impossible to check. Aslak kept his contact with the town to a minimum. He didn't need to stock up on fuel, and he had no mobile phone that could be tracked. A dead end. She sensed that there would be no point coming down hard on him, as Klemet had done with Johann Henrik. Aslak was a different character altogether.

She would have to try another approach. As the inquiry progressed, it seemed to her that they were groping further and further into the dark. Klemet was too careful in his handling of the breeders, she thought, not to mention his inexplicable behaviour with Aslak earlier. Was he too close to their world? Yet the Sami seemed suspicious of him. She thought again about what the Sheriff had said before they left: if Aslak has no alibi, arrest him.

'Aslak, you do realise that if you can't tell me exactly where you were at the time of Mattis's death, you are making yourself a suspect?'

The herder looked at her with cold disdain, or indifference. Nina held his gaze.

'What was your relationship with Mattis like? I get the impression you were close. But that you had had your differences, too.'

Aslak clenched his jaw, still staring Nina in the eye. She forced herself not to look away and was astonished at the powerful emotion expressed in his face. Powerful, and tragic. She understood why people were in awe of him. But she didn't feel afraid.

'Mattis had lost his way. A long time ago. But especially since his father's death. I knew his father. He was a true Sami. He knew our people's past. People tell many stories about him. Good, and bad. But people knew nothing about him, really. He had power. He had knowledge. He had the memory. Mattis had none of those things. But he thought of himself as a shaman.'

'What do you mean?'

'You met him before his death?'

'Yes, why?'

'He didn't try to read your fortune?'

Nina pictured the scene in the trailer, Mattis half drunk, leering at her breasts.

'Yes, he offered to tell my fortune.'

'Mattis was like a child. His father was too great for him. And your society, your system drove him down even further. Led him even further astray.'

Nina had no interest in that particular line of discussion. She remembered what Johann Henrik had told them about Aslak's exceptional strength and powers of endurance.

'Aslak, is it true that you killed a wolf by thrusting your fist down its throat?'

He hesitated, bending over the fire, stirring the embers. Nina looked at his hand. It bore several scars, reaching up higher than his wrist. Marks left by the wolf's teeth, she thought. Her heart beat hard.

'It is true.'

'They say you followed it for hours, on your skis?'

'It may have been hours.'

'How many kilometres can you cover in a day?'

But Aslak had closed himself off once more. His lips pursed tight in a thin line. His wife began to shake her head gently, from side to side. A guttural murmur rose in her throat. Her lips parted. The murmur grew louder.

'Get out!' said Aslak, urgently.

His sudden fury took Nina by surprise. She had touched a raw nerve, she decided.

'Get out, now!' he roared.

Nina watched as he got to his feet. His looming silhouette was terrifying, but he made no move against her. His mere presence was enough.

Aslak's command was final. His wife's murmuring grew louder. Nina was acutely aware of her own situation, now – far out in the tundra, facing a man with a mysterious reputation, surrounded by nothing but ice, snow and desolation, a long way from her partner. She felt suddenly cold, but her shivers expressed something she dared not admit, even to herself. The smoke stung her eyes. She buckled her bag. She had to get away from the hypnotic chant.

She got her feet and bent down, making for the entrance to the tent. Aslak followed her, then stood guard outside. Nina was about to start her snowmobile; the murmur became a wail. She turned to Aslak. He lifted the tent flap, preparing to go back inside. The wailing grew louder still. Nina forgot all about her questions, her terror. She forgot all about the inquiry, but gazed at him, speechless, her eyes full of empathy. Aslak was breathing hard, his chin thrust forward in defiance, fists clenched. Through the tent flap, Nina could just see his wife, her arms lifted skywards, her face a mask of intense suffering.

And then she heard it. The sound filled her head, on and on, for hours on the journey back to base. The shriek.

15

Friday 14 January

11 a.m., Kautokeino

Berit Kutsi arrived for work later than usual that morning. She was afraid Karl Olsen would appear, but the irascible old farmer was nowhere to be seen. Fortunately, she had no need of his instructions before setting about her tasks. Berit knew perfectly well what she had to do. If the truth be told, she had always known what was expected of her. She had known that since childhood. She knew her place. People like her always knew their place. Berit had left school when she was barely eleven years of age. School was not a happy memory. She had learned the basics of Norwegian – there had been no choice in the matter. Learning Norwegian was the reason she had been sent to school in the first place. And once she knew enough to get by, she had left. As simple as that. She understood enough to know where she belonged in Norwegian society.

She entered the barn to see to the cows. The cattle spent the better part of the year indoors. There were few dairy herds in the interior of the Finnmark. The wild country barely supported any livestock, apart from the reindeer. But a handful of countrymen like Olsen had managed to make a living dairying here, though they were in the minority and barely tolerated by the Sami. Olsen was an unjust man, and mean. Berit was wary of him. Afraid, too. But she belonged to an ill-reputed local clan, and finding work when you came from a family with no reindeer of their own was next to impossible.

Thanks be to God, her faith was her rod and her staff for the challenges she faced. The Lord was a hard master, but merciful. Berit trusted in Him, though she didn't always understand His ways. She cursed Olsen sometimes, when he humiliated her. But she always forgave. The pastor insisted on that. Only those who forgave their fellow men and placed themselves in the hands of God were fit to enter the kingdom of heaven. It was as simple as that, the pastor assured her categorically. 'No salvation without forgiveness.'

Berit was a devout, trusting, God-fearing Laestadian. She had shunned any notion of personal fulfilment, dedicating her life at an early age to her younger brother and the trials he faced in the sight of God. She moved along the rows of dairy cows, the gentle creatures she knew and loved like the children she had never had. After so many years with them, she understood them better than she did other people. Sometimes, she thought to herself, her fellow men did not repay the effort, not if they were like Olsen, at any rate. The more she saw of them, the better she liked her cattle. She had worked on the farm since she was twelve years old. And now she was fifty-nine.

But she must do what she could to help people, too. Or God would not approve. Berit smiled. Really, her wayward thoughts shocked even her sometimes. The idea that the Almighty might stoop to think about her and her cows. God was love, but He was to be feared, too.

The pastor wouldn't approve if Berit dedicated herself solely to her animals, either. He had great need of Berit. But the cows were her responsibility. The pastor took a close interest in the day-to-day business of his parishioners. He was a friend of Olsen's, and God smiled when Karl Olsen's business prospered, Pastor Jonsson had told her that. Because cattle were God's creatures, unlike reindeer.

Berit couldn't really see the difference. As a rule she felt the pastor took altogether too close an interest in local politics, even though she understood little of such things herself. In her heart of hearts, Berit thought the pastor did not care for each member of his flock quite equally. She took better care of her herd than the pastor did of his flock. She had even told him so one day, and his temper had flared. The pastor reminded her about it, quite often.

The business with the drum had angered him. He had heard Olaf Renson, the member of the Sami parliament, talking on the radio about how the theft of the drum was a threat to the Samis' identity. And on that same day, Olaf Renson had called the pastor a 'drum burner' at the crossroads. The churchman had confided his frustration and anger to Berit. 'God did not speak Sami, Berit! Never forget that!' Berit could well believe it; she had learned to read using a Norwegian Bible.

No, Berit did more than just look after Karl Olsen's cows. She had a duty to watch over the weak in spirit, the poor souls who risked being led into temptation, out in the *vidda*. She watched over the pure of heart, too. And when she thought of one and the other, two images came into her mind, as clear as day. Mattis and Aslak. The two men stood like figureheads for the herders, for the down-trodden people of the *vidda*, their misery and greatness, their sufferings and their fierce pride. Berit followed the rhythm of their lives. Her spirit went with them into the mountains, warmed them during their endless vigils in the cold of winter.

Berit prayed for them, too. The Norwegian gospels were full of good words for the souls of the *vidda*, and the great lineage of Laestadian pastors had never failed to communicate the word of God. But when she thought of the things she knew, Berit shivered. She paused in her milking, then went to wash her hands, wiped her face and slipped away to a small corner at the back of the barn, where she always went to collect her thoughts. She made the sign of the Cross, and she prayed for the salvation of the weak in spirit, and the pure of heart, out in the *vidda*.

*

When Nina rejoined him from the camp, Klemet made no attempt to explain his strange behaviour with Aslak. Patrol P9 rested for a few hours. Reindeer Police rules stipulated an overnight stay in one of the huts for any journey of more than two hundred and fifty kilometres, but Nina had insisted they move on and try to make headway with the investigation. The inquiry was stagnating, she said, and Klemet allowed her to twist his arm. He just hoped their GPS wouldn't be checked back at headquarters.

She's eager to prove herself, he thought. And he remembered the quotas again. The idea had preoccupied him ever since it had first crossed his mind. He couldn't help acknowledging that although he was the boss right now, through experience and seniority, she was the one with a career ahead of her. She'll be my superior one day, he told himself.

For the moment, he had to find a way forward with the inquiry. And avoid getting himself into any more awkward situations, like the one with Aslak. Luckily, Nina hadn't persisted with the matter. Had she understood? Had Aslak told her anything? He didn't think so. That wasn't Aslak's way.

The Sheriff was waiting for them in his office, helping himself to too many *salmiakki* from the bowl on his desk. Deputy Superintendent Rolf Brattsen was seated opposite him. Klemet knew what was going through the Sheriff's mind: Tor Jensen pictured Brattsen taking his place one day. Brattsen was ambitious. It annoyed the Sheriff, Klemet knew that. Brattsen's hard-line views didn't sit easily with the delicate balance to be maintained across the region. Kautokeino was a Norwegian town, much like any other, but it was also one of the few genuinely Sami towns, with a special status of its own: the Sami inhabitants were allowed to use their own language in their dealings with the authorities. Most of the population was Sami. It had always been that way. Not only that but the Reindeer Police, with its cross-border jurisdiction, had to tread very carefully, too. They covered Norwegian Sápmi, and the Sami territories in

Sweden and Finland; their headquarters were in Swedish Kiruna. The national government, and the regional administration, saw the Reindeer Police as a model of Nordic cooperation. But it was a fragile balance, as Klemet knew only too well. His own post counted for the 'Swedish quota'. He had trained at Sweden's police college. But that didn't matter to him. His parents were local people, originally. And national borders meant nothing to the Sami. They counted for him, as a man of the law, but still . . .

'So, Rolf, getting anywhere?' The Sheriff turned to Brattsen first. 'You know Oslo are talking about sending some crack teams up here. That'll go down well. Our confidence rating in Oslo and Stockholm isn't exactly high after that business with the paedophile ring. So do me a favour and show me some results, as they say down there. Where are we at, right now?'

Klemet watched Brattsen closely. The deputy took his time, looking around the room before speaking. Apart from the Sheriff, Nina and Klemet, the only other person present was a Swedish officer sent from Kiruna to provide back-up for the scene-of-crime team.

'Well, I think Fredrik here should update us on the forensic team's findings. Fredrik . . . ' Brattsen invited the other man to take the floor.

The Swede from Kiruna was a tall blond with a beer gut and a toothbrush haircut. He stared around, looked hard at Nina – a new face – opened a file, glanced at it quickly and addressed Jensen, who fidgeted impatiently, crunching his *salmiakki*.

'OK. First the murder. We should be getting the report from forensics soon. But I'd be surprised if we get the highest priority. The murder of a Sami herder is never going to be top of their list. I'd need to see the report before coming to any conclusions about one or two things, anyway: the type of knife used, the length of the blade. These will be important leads. And any traces of blows, the cuts around the ears. They look pretty clean, as you know. We found a lot of prints in the trailer. We haven't made much head-way there – there are fingerprints traceable to all the breeders

120

roundabout, and to Patrol P9's visits the day before, and after the body was discovered.'

The forensic officer looked across at Nina and Klemet, saying nothing. But Brattsen wasn't about to miss his chance.

'Yeah, well we can't expect the Mounties to be well up on scene-of-crime procedure, can we, Chubby?'

'Enough, Brattsen,' the Sheriff interrupted. 'What else, Fredrik?' he asked.

'We went back to the trailer after it had stopped snowing. Guess you won't be needing a Powerpoint presentation from me to explain the slim chance of isolating snowmobile tracks under fresh snow. But this was the first snowfall for a while, and the layer underneath was quite compact, hardened in places by the wind. It might seem overzealous, but I think if we removed the top layer of powdery snow around the trailer, we might find something.'

'Idiotic waste of time!' Brattsen made no attempt to conceal his scorn. 'What tracks? A snowmobile? Someone on skis? What we need is a motive, then we'll know where to look. And the motive is staring us in the face. It's a case of breeders settling old scores.'

'Rolf,' Klemet cut in, 'you know perfectly well that you can have every motive under the sun, but if you can't connect a murder to evidence found at the scene, you haven't got a case. One thing I learned from my time on the Palme investigation.'

Brattsen ignored Klemet and addressed Fredrik.

'You can put your snow-blower away for a start. Look for traces on the breeders' knives if you want proof. But don't go wasting your time poking around in the snow. We haven't got limitless resources. Remember the powers that be want results,' he added, glaring at the Sheriff. 'They won't want to hear we've been out hoovering the tundra.'

The room fell silent. The Sheriff turned to Klemet.

'What about the breeders?'

'We've questioned Johann Henrik and Aslak,' said Klemet. 'Nothing conclusive. Johann Henrik seems to have an alibi, though it's quite light for part of the period of time we're interested in. I should say, too, that Johann Henrik doesn't think this is a case of breeders settling their scores.'

'Oh really, doesn't he? Well, that's that, then,' exclaimed Brattsen. 'He's a fine one to talk. Let's see, when did he get shot at? Ten, twelve years ago, wasn't it?' Brattsen grinned. 'Bunch of innocent choirboys, the lot of them.'

'He was shot at, yes, but you know perfectly well the other man was dead drunk. People don't settle scores that way here. Just because someone has a hot temper doesn't make him a criminal.'

'Yeah, of course,' said Brattsen. 'Bullet holes in the trailers. All part of the décor. Nothing at all to do with intimidation.'

'Can we get back to Johann Henrik's questioning?' the Sheriff interrupted.

'Well, if we follow Brattsen's logic,' said Klemet, 'I can't see what his motive would be. The theft of a few reindeer wouldn't be sufficient provocation, even Brattsen would admit that.'

'Unless it's the last straw, unless Henrik was drunk that night. Things can get out of hand. Any excuse.'

'Maybe,' said Klemet, quietly. 'But we need more than just a motive.'

'Dear God.' Brattsen was visibly annoyed, 'Old Chubby-chub's giving us a lesson in police procedure now. Served you well in the Palme investigation, didn't it? Remind me – how many years is it since the Swedes saw their prime minister assassinated, and the murderer is still at large? Unless I'm very much mistaken?'

'Thank you, Brattsen, this is getting tiresome,' warned the Sheriff. 'What about Aslak?'

Klemet was about to speak when Nina cut in quickly, 'Another suspect alibi.'

She had been lost in thought for a moment, reliving the extraordinary encounter with Aslak. She realised now that when he spoke – despite his awe-inspiring, powerful, almost brutal aura – he had a strange way of making you feel you were the centre of the known universe. Something in those eyes, perhaps.

'There's no one to confirm it,' she went on.

'What?' the Sheriff interrupted brusquely, thumping his fist on the table. 'And where is Aslak now? You've brought him in, I hope?'

Nina glanced uncomfortably at Klemet, who gave a jerk of the chin, inviting her to continue.

'Well, something strange occurred at his place. Or rather, it began before we arrived. We heard a terrible scream. At first, we didn't know what it was. And then when we left, we heard the cry again. It was his wife. She has some sort of condition. She utters these awful shrieks.'

'No way?' scoffed Brattsen. 'And what's that got to do with the case? The woman's got a screw loose, what about it? Mattis wasn't the brightest spark either. Normal, really. They're all inbred. You know perfectly well, Mattis's father was his uncle – his mother's brother!'

Klemet was about to respond when the Sheriff burst out, 'Brattsen! For Christ's sake, you're overstepping the mark. You're a police officer, and never forget it. Not some damned gossiping fish-wife. Can we please get back to the serious business in hand?'

Klemet and Brattsen glared at one another. Nina went on:

'I think we are making progress with Mattis's murder investigation, in spite of everything – at least from our perspective on the Reindeer Police. We've eliminated a number of potential suspects. We've been focusing on the breeders for the moment, because that's our field. But I think it would be useful to start looking at other areas, too. And I'm sure Deputy Superintendent Brattsen is working on that.'

She spoke with assurance, encouraged by her male colleagues' bitter silence.

'Regarding the drum, if Deputy Superintendent Brattsen has no objection, I'm prepared to travel to France to meet with the donor. I feel sure he has information that will help us.'

'Yeah, the drum ...' Brattsen muttered, clearing his throat. 'Travelling to France is probably a good idea, especially if there are documents to be seen, as your report suggests.'

'I think it's such a good idea, I'd like Klemet and Nina to be more closely involved in the drum investigation,' said the Sheriff. 'To be perfectly honest, I think it needs more careful handling than you've been demonstrating, Rolf.'

Brattsen flushed with suppressed anger.

'What careful handling? Why would the breeders need careful handling? Because they're Lapps? Is that it?'

Tor Jensen looked calmly at his deputy. He made no reply. His silence, and the slight smile at the corners of his lips, said it all.

'Fine,' the Sheriff went on. 'Nina, when you will be leaving for France?'

Nina turned to Klemet.

'In the next couple of days.'

'Good. The sooner the better. Perhaps we'll get somewhere now.'

Nina spoke quickly, before Tor Jensen could go on:

'And I think it's important to stress the coincidence of the two cases – two major inquiries, two days apart: the theft of a Sami drum, and the death of a breeder who was fascinated by drums. I don't see how they can't be connected, even if the link isn't clear at the moment.'

'That's pure speculation, Nina,' said Klemet. 'We can only go on tangible proof, which we don't have. In the Palme affair, we spent years following up attractive hunches that proved futile in the end.'

'Klemet, in the absence of any other leads for the moment, I want you to carry on questioning the breeders,' instructed the Sheriff, firmly. 'For now, that's still our most plausible lead in both cases, it seems to me. But I'm astonished you let Aslak off the hook, when he has no verifiable alibi. You'll have to answer for that sooner or later.'

16

Friday 14 January

5.30 p.m., Kautokeino

The group filing out of Tor Jensen's office looked thoroughly out of sorts. Fredrik left first, eager to get back to Kiruna and the analysis of his findings and samples.

Klemet caught up with Nina. Before heading back out into the *vidda*, he wanted to talk to Helmut Juhl, the German museum director, in preparation for Nina's trip to Paris.

Patrol P9 found Juhl in the museum's reserve collection, overseeing the opening of a set of packing crates from Afghanistan. He escorted Klemet and Nina to his office, overlooking Kautokeino in the valley below. It was late afternoon, and twilight had long since engulfed the town. No one had contacted him, Helmut said. He had heard nothing more about the drum. No rumours or speculation, nothing. He seemed genuinely affected by what had happened.

'Was the drum insured?' asked Klemet.

'Yes, but not at its true value, nowhere near that,' the director admitted. 'If its true value can indeed be estimated, that is. I was due to get an expert opinion on it in the next couple of days.'

'You mean you weren't convinced it was genuine?' asked Nina.

'Oh, it's genuine, of course, but we accepted it on the basis of what Henri Mons told us – the French collector who presented it to the museum. I've no reason to doubt him, or the drum's authenticity, but from a strictly financial point of view I wasn't able to give a reliable valuation. And no one in France had the required expertise.'

'I understand the drum was here for a week before it was stolen,' said Nina, 'but its case remained unopened. You weren't in any hurry to take a look at it. That seems odd, to me. A specialist in Sami culture like youself . . .'

Juhl looked uncomfortable, guilty even.

'I can understand your surprise. But we are right in the middle of preparations for the UN conference in a few days. The delegates are coming to visit Kautokeino, and of course they will come here to the museum. The drum was going to be one of the highlights of their visit. We had a thousand other practical details to attend to first. I was very busy with all of that. But my mind was very much on the drum, I can assure you.'

'I see,' said Klemet. 'So you have no idea what the drum looked like?'

The director pulled another guilty face.

'I know Henri Mons by reputation. He was one of the collectors closest to Paul-Émile Victor. I can assure you he is a thorough-going professional, and a very great gentleman. If someone of his calibre gets in touch, with something exceptional to give to the museum, you take him at his word. And especially as no money was changing hands. He wanted nothing, only that we should cover the transport and insurance costs.'

'And no photograph was taken for insurance purposes?'

The director threw his hands up in a gesture of impotence.

'Were you surprised by the Frenchman's approach?'

'How could I not be surprised? If someone calls to say they have a genuine Sami drum for you, you have every reason to be surprised, believe me. Especially when you know about the drums, as I do. There are apparently only seventy-one historic Sami drums left in the world. Seventy-one. Can you believe it? Hundreds, maybe thousands, were burned by the Lutheran pastors. And this is the first one to be returned to Sami territory.'

'Seventy-one, you say,' said Nina. 'And was this one of those known drums or not?'

'A priori, I would say no.'

'A priori?'

'Well, some drums have been identified and authenticated, but then they disappeared from circulation. Most are in European museums, but some have vanished. We have precise descriptions of seventy-one drums – copies of the designs on the skins.'

'Vanished? You mean stolen?'

'In some cases, yes indeed. Stolen to order for private collectors, you know. There are always cases of that.'

'So there could be an illegal trade in the drums?' asked Nina.

The director said nothing for a moment, apparently deep in thought.

'I would tend to say not. Sami culture is not so well known or widespread as to encourage such behaviour.'

'I don't want to insist on this point,' said Nina, 'but I do wonder why you weren't desperate to open the case and see what it looked like.'

'Well, listen. A drum like that – if it is authentic – has to be handled with extreme care. That's another reason why I hadn't looked at it. I was waiting for a conservation expert, I didn't want to take any risks. And he was supposed to come the day before yesterday. So there it is. But I assure you, I feel desperately bad and frustrated about this whole business. I feel I have betrayed the Sami.'

Helmut seemed genuinely, profoundly affected.

'When did Henri Mons first contact you?' asked Klemet.

'Not very long ago, in fact. I can find the exact date, if you're interested, because he wrote me a letter. But I would say it was about a month ago, roughly. Yes, a month almost to the day. It must have been *Lusinatt*, or the day before that, because I remember joking with my wife that we could celebrate with a St Lucy

127

dressed up as a shaman, chanting to the beat of a genuine Sami drum.'

Klemet thought this was an extremely odd idea, to say the least, but made no comment.

'Who else knew about the drum?'

Helmut spread his arms wide.

'Everyone hereabouts, I would think. The press had been talking about it. We had no reason to keep it a secret. Although now I think perhaps we should have done.'

'Do you know Henri Mons?'

'By reputation only. I have some of Paul-Émile Victor's books. Perhaps you do, too?'

'Er, no. Who is he, actually?' Klemet asked.

'I see,' said Helmut. 'He was a very well-known French explorer, a specialist on Polynesia and the Polar regions. He made a journey across Lapland – Sápmi – just before the Second World War.'

'And Mons worked with him?'

'Yes. He was a geologist by training, and an ethnologist, too. He was one of that great generation of polymath adventurers, before it all became ultra-specialised. Expeditions frequently took along multi-talented people like him. It was cheaper that way, I imagine. But Mons was highly qualified in both his fields.'

'How did he come into possession of the drum?'

'Well, I don't know the details, to tell you the truth. But I believe one of the Sami guides gave it to him. Was it a personal gift? I don't know. We were going to ask Mons, and then this business turned everything upside down. The drum's exact provenance is less of a priority now. We simply must get it back.'

'If the drums are as rare as you say, then it was quite an extraordinary gift, wasn't it?' asked Nina.

'Indeed it was! But did the Sami guide know its true value? We cannot be sure. Most of the drums still in existence were no longer in the hands of private families. People had no use for them any more. The Sami had been largely Christianised by that time. But it's an object of great significance for the culture of the Far North. And

Europe, after all. The Sami are our last aboriginal population. How we treat them, and their culture and history, says a great deal about our ability to apprehend our own past.'

'No doubt,' said Klemet. The director's comment had touched a raw nerve. 'But we're getting off the point . . .'

'You alone can be the judge of that, Inspector.'

'What about Mattis Labba, the breeder who was murdered?' Nina decided the question was worth a try. 'You wouldn't happen to know anything about him?'

'Mattis? Of course,' said Helmut, to both officers' surprise. 'I knew him quite well, as a matter of fact.'

Klemet and Nina stared at one another in astonishment. Helmut gave a small sad laugh.

'Mattis was a remarkable character.'

'We've mostly heard him described as someone down on his luck, alcoholic, unable to cope,' said Nina, looking hard at Klemet.

'Well, yes, he could be seen in that light, too. I would say he was more complicated than that. He had vision and ambition, beyond what he felt he was capable of achieving. And so he became depressed. I can understand that. He took it very seriously.'

'What do you mean by his ambition?'

'Well, you know who his father was? A very mysterious man, a true shaman, so people say. No one believes in all that nowadays, but there is a strong sentimental attachment to the idea. There's a certain nostalgia for it. Not to mention its historical and cultural importance.'

'What about Mattis's ambition?'

'I think he lived very much in his father's shadow. I wouldn't say he saw himself as a shaman, but he certainly had quite a gift for making drums.'

'Making drums? What sort of drums?'

'The same as those used by the shamans of old. That's why I was in regular contact with him, in fact. I sold his drums in the shop here at the Centre. I may even have one still in stock, I think. The customer hasn't come to collect it yet. They demand a great deal of work, you know. So Mattis made them to order. The big ones, at any rate, the ones for private collectors. Then there are the tourist versions – they take less time, and they are less expensive, of course.'

Nina thought of the equipment and raw materials neatly arranged on Mattis's shelves. So that was how he had spent his time when he wasn't out watching his reindeer: drum-making and drinking. She pictured him alone in the trailer, cut off from the world in a snowstorm, bending over a piece of wood, working it laboriously, his eyesight blurred by alcohol. She forgot her disgust at the leering herder.

Naturally, her thoughts turned to Aslak. His tormented gaze, his implacable, troubling expression.

'When did you last see Mattis?' asked Klemet.

The museum director stroked his beard.

'I saw him . . . a good two weeks ago, I believe.'

'What did he want?'

'Oh, the same as usual, you know. We saw one another about every two months or so. Mostly when he needed money. So I would order a few drums. I liked Mattis very much. He was one of a dying breed. There's no room for the little people like him, nowadays. Not with the fixed outgoings the breeders have to put up with today, and the pressure from the Reindeer Administration. But I'm talking out of turn. None of that is my business.'

'How did he seem to you?'

'Mattis could go from one extreme to the other. It depended on his state of mind . . .'

'Whether or not he'd been drinking.' Nina finished the phrase.

'Yes,' said Helmut, with an uncomfortable look. He glanced at the two officers and continued: 'I don't wish to sully his memory.'

'We're not asking you to do that,' said Klemet. 'Carry on.'

'I saw Mattis as a very sensitive man. He was not made for this world.'

'We're none of us made for this world,' said Klemet, very softly under his breath.

'What? Say again?' said Nina.

Klemet ignored her, turning his attention to the museum director.

'Did he seem any different from the last time you had seen him? How long had you known him?'

'I met Mattis almost as soon as I came to Scandinavia, over thirty years ago. He was young then, a teenager. He worked for the other breeders.'

The German director smiled with pleasure at the memory.

'I arrived just as the reindeer breeders were becoming mechanised,' he said. 'The Sami were discovering snowmobiles. Mattis was a wild rider on his – really reckless.'

Helmut smiled again and fell silent. Then he looked up at Klemet and Nina in turn.

'He had changed. He was always changing. He was on a slippery slope. Alcohol played its part, but he was sinking fast even without that. I think something was bothering him. No, it was more than that. Something haunted him, possessed him. That sounds far-fetched. But I think he carried something within him that he couldn't share with another living soul. And it dragged him under. Yes, there was something dragging him down. You asked about the last time he came to the Centre: he hung around the workshop, watching the other artisans at work, and he took a look at the exhibits. There was no one else here, much. It was nice and quiet, and I think he appreciated moments like that, before returning to the *vidda*, the cold, the danger, the endless work with the reindeer. I like to think he found a few moments of peace here.'

The police officers said nothing. They had no more questions. Each was lost in thought. For their own, quite different reasons. They left the Centre, and when Klemet asked Nina if she wanted to come over to his place that evening, she accepted with relief.

17

Friday 14 January

7 p.m., Kautokeino

Nina knocked on Klemet's front door at seven sharp. She wore a close-fitting parka jacket and a colourful knitted hat with a red pompom bouncing to one side. It felt strange to be calling on Klemet at home – this was the first time – and even stranger for him to see her in plain clothes. There was no logical reason for it, she knew that. But she felt more exposed, all the same. There was no reply. She knocked again. No reply. She turned around, looking along the brightly lit street. Klemet's car was parked. She looked down the side of the house, towards the garden, but the path was too dark to see anything. She knocked again, harder this time, then called Klemet's name. At last, she got a response.

'Here!'

'Where's "here"?'

'In the garden!'

Nina walked around the side of the house, picking her way carefully over the compacted snow and ice, until she saw a light glowing at the bottom of the garden. A light inside what could only be a Sami tent. The canvas flap lifted and Klemet's silhouette appeared.

Nina crossed the garden, then bent down to step inside. Klemet stood back, holding the flap. Nina straightened up and gazed around in amazement.

Klemet had installed a *lavu* – an authentic Sami tent – right there in his garden. In the middle, a blazing fire radiated heat on an open hearth, filling the top half of the tent with smoke. The ground was covered with reindeer skins, apart from the space in front of the entrance, which was carpeted with birch twigs.

'Sit wherever you like,' Klemet invited her.

'Where are you going to sit?'

'On the other side of the fire from you, don't worry,' he said. He wasn't smiling.

'I'm not worried.'

Nina sat to the left of the fire and looked around once again. All around the circumference of the tent, between the reindeer skins and the canvas, stood a series of long, narrow wooden chests about thirty centimetres wide. Some were covered with richly coloured, silky cushions, adding a definite touch of refinement. Opposite the entrance, behind the hearth, stood a polished antique trunk, solid but not bulky, at the foot of a beautiful, elaborately carved cupboard, its corners reinforced with decorative copper fittings. Klemet had used string and strips of wood to hang reproductions of paintings and photographs celebrating the magnificence of the *vidda*: enchanting, magically lit landscapes, and abstracts in the colours of the earth, forest and sky. Nina looked at the pictures, fascinated. Half obscured by the smoke, they seemed to hang in space, adding to their mystery.

Looking higher, she followed the trails of smoke rising to the very top of the tent, which was open to the sky. The upper part of the roof space was hung with dozens of pairs of reindeer antlers, carefully interlocking and suspended thanks to an invisible but obviously ingenious system. Nina was impressed by the harmonious effect of the tightly knit barrage of antlers, glimpsed through the smoke. Like a mysterious filter, catching at thoughts and dreams, keeping them inside. Everything had been chosen with taste, to create a warm, welcoming atmosphere. Nothing she had seen of Klemet so far suggested this secret refuge. Nina was impressed and intimidated. The intimacy was almost too sudden. She felt the need to talk about something more banal, more practical.

'I've booked my flight to France. I leave on Monday, late morning.'

'Perfect,' said Klemet, simply. He added nothing, conscious of the atmosphere he had created inside the *lavu*. Conscious, too, that Nina needed time to get her bearings.

'What'll you have to drink?' he asked, at length. 'There's some food, too, but no reindeer shanks, I promise.' He looked at her with a half-smile.

'Klemet, this is . . . extraordinary. This space. I'm really impressed. It's like being transported to another world. It's so . . . harmonious, cosy, magical. Unexpected, too. What an idea, to set up a *lavu* in your garden.'

'With or without alcohol?'

Nina was still looking around. She had visited twenty or so trailers, huts and breeders' tents since her first days with the force, but she had seen nothing like this.

'I'll have a beer.'

Klemet opened the antique chest and extracted two bottles of beer, from the Mack brewery in Tromsø. He opened the cupboard door and took out two glasses, handing one to Nina, with the opened beer bottle.

'We need to find out everything about the drum, the pre-war expedition, the Sami guide and the other collectors, if possible,' he said. 'Whatever Helmut says, we shouldn't exclude the possibility that it has been stolen for some sort of illicit trade. We need to know for sure whether it's one of the known drums or not. If the culprit's local — Olaf, or anyone else — there must be a solid motive.'

'Did you hear the radio news on NRK? They're saying it could have been the Far Right, even the Laestadians. They say the Far Right want to prevent the Sami from reinforcing their identity with the drum, and the Laestadians want to protect the Sami from the temptations of the old religion.'

'I heard. Those are motives, not proofs.'

'Who are the Laestadians? I've never heard of them down south.'

Klemet looked perfectly relaxed now. He raised his glass.

'Skål.'

'Skål,' said Nina.

'They're a Lutheran sect,' said Klemet. 'My family were Laestadians.'

Her eyes opened wide in unconcealed astonishment.

'The name comes from a Swedish pastor who was part Sami, who went to great lengths to set the Sami back on the path of right-eousness, because he thought they were too much under the influence of alcohol. That was a hundred and fifty years ago. There are still some congregations that follow his teaching. The real, hard-core traditionalists. Not my cup of tea at all. No TV, no alcohol, no curtains at the windows, all that. A lot of my family were practis-ing Laestadians. That's why we fell out. I never could stand their bigotry.'

'What did they do? Were they breeders?'

Klemet took a slow sip of his beer.

'No, like I said, my grandfather had been a breeder, but he had to give it up. He couldn't carry on. People would find themselves ruined in the space of just a few years, which is what happened to him. He could have gone under when he lost the herd. But his Laestadian moral fibre kept him going. He went to work as a labourer for a local farmer. He lived on a farm beside a lake, on the other side of the mountain, two days' walk from Kautokeino. When my father was a boy, he worked with other people's reindeer, and sometimes in the fields, too. But my grandfather never drank. Nor my father. They were both very proud.'

'You said you were Swedish.'

'On my mother's side,' he reminded her. 'My father met her while he was doing seasonal work in Sweden. He lived part of the year with us in Sweden, and the rest of the time in Norway,

135

depending on where he could find work. I grew up partly in Kiruna, in Sweden, where the iron-ore mine is. I was born there. I was fifteen when we came to live in Kautokeino.'

Nina felt drowsy and comfortable, sipping her beer, stretched out on the reindeer skins, warm and slightly light-headed. She could tell Klemet was in a talkative mood, unusually.

'Klemet, why did you set up this tent?'

He gave an embarrassed laugh.

'I like the atmosphere. It's cosy, intimate.'

'Would you have liked to be a reindeer breeder?'

Preoccupied, he didn't answer straightaway. 'No. Not that I don't think it's interesting work. But I think you have to be born to it. I wanted to run a garage. I worked in one when I was a teenager here in Kautokeino. It was fun. There were all sorts of cars. We serviced them all. The ice-cream van, the police cars, the ambulance. My favourite was the funeral hearse. Very classy. I drove them back after we'd finished. I loved doing that.'

'Was that what you had always wanted to do?'

'No.'

He looked uncomfortable again.

'This will sound idiotic. But what I always wanted to do was something no one did around here. No Sami has ever done it. But I wanted to be a whaler.'

'A whaler . . .'

'Yes. Daft, really, when you're born so far inland, in Sápmi.'

'My father was a whaler,' said Nina.

Now it was Klemet's turn to stare in surprise. He waited for Nina to go on, but she said nothing.

'Well, well!'

Klemet thought for a moment. He was about to ask Nina a question when he caught the dark look on her face.

136

18

Monday 17 January

Sunrise: 10.07 a.m.; sunset: 12.52 p.m.
2 hours 45 minutes of sunlight

8.30 a.m., Kautokeino

Karl Olsen walked into the municipal council offices in a thoroughly bad mood. He was naturally ill-tempered, but this was worse. The mining affairs committee meeting was scheduled for late morning, and he hadn't had time to read and prepare his files as he would have liked.

As the Progress Party councillor, he represented something of a minority in Kautokeino. But the party's twenty-per-cent support rating at the national level earned him a degree of respect nonetheless. Some of the party's opponents tried to brand it as a Far Right organisation, but Olsen knew it was nothing like that at all. It was just that here, in Kautokeino, the Sami thought they could get their own way in everything, and it couldn't be allowed to continue. He, Karl Olsen, would do everything in his power to make sure of that. Not for nothing had his family been farmers in the region from generation to generation. Yes, the Olsens were pioneers, among the first to conquer the Far North in the name of the Norwegian Crown.

They'd been the first to clear the frozen waste, when all the Lapps did was run along behind their reindeer. The problem was that here, in the interior of Lapland, the Lapps were few enough in number, but they were still the majority. Down on the coast, it was different. Here, you had to accommodate them.

And Olsen certainly knew how to accommodate people. He had mollified the other parties and secured himself a seat on two committees – agricultural affairs and mining affairs. He spent one day a week at the council offices, as a rule, which was a lot, but he saw it as a duty – the best way to keep an eye on whatever schemes were being hatched. Olsen twisted from the waist to greet the receptionist – his neck was still stiff. He didn't like her; he knew she voted Labour, but hers was a pivotal role. When the Mayor's secretary was away, she was often the one who kept day-to-day business running at the council offices.

'How are you today, Ingrid, my dear?' Olsen affected a jovial, honeyed tone.

'Fine. I've printed the agenda for the mining affairs committee. It's in your pigeonhole, along with the guest list for the UN conference on indigenous peoples – the people coming to the Mayor's reception here.'

'Wonderful! Many thanks, Ingrid, dear. In haste . . .'

Olsen collected the agenda and guest list, together with a clutch of other envelopes and newspapers. Ramrod-straight, he directed his short, quick steps to the Progress Party office. As expected, there was no one in. His fellow PP councillor was an incompetent buffoon for whom Olsen felt nothing but scorn – a pretty face who preferred parading about on his snowmobile on market days. Pathetic. The guy ran a small IT shop, and had joined the Progress Party only when he realised they had plans for a massive drop in taxation, and a spending spree funded by the nation's oil riches. He understood nothing about what really went on here, but Olsen needed him, so he put up with him.

Karl Olsen thought over the recent events. There was a lot happening. Too much, in fact, but it got the police off their backsides, at any rate. He took the list of UN conference guests, balled it up without a glance and tossed it into the waste-paper basket. His mind was on another gathering, of far greater importance for him – the regional committee that would meet soon to issue mining licences in Lapland.

Meanwhile, Kautokeino's mining affairs committee was meeting later that morning. Olsen pondered the agenda, leafing absently through the pages of the *Finnmark Dagblad*. There was a report about his party's protest in Alta. This drum business was stirring up controversy. Down on the coast, people had had enough of Lapps dictating the law. Very good, thought Olsen. Very good. He turned the pages. A car crash on the Hammerfest road, a fishing boat in difficulty off the North Cape, a schoolgirl raped in Alta, a cigarette trafficker arrested in Kirkenes, approval at last for renovation work on the school in Tana Bru. He binned the newspaper.

The handful of mining companies working in the region had brought plenty of development to Kautokeino, true enough – there was even a small aerodrome now. But that was nothing compared to what would happen after the latest round of drilling licences had been handed out. Dear God, no. That would be big, as Olsen knew only too well. He had got himself appointed to a seat on Kautokeino's mining affairs committee precisely so that he could keep a close eye on things. His pretty-boy colleague could have the popular stuff, like the budget committee. Yes, the opportunities were huge, especially if you knew the system and where to look.

'Dear God, dear God, if only . . .' Olsen swore, bitterly.

The damned UN conference was just around the corner, the next round of drilling licence attributions was due at the beginning of February, and he still didn't know exactly where to strike, even where the hell he should apply to explore. He was staring at the agenda for the Kautokeino meeting when the phone rang.

'Karl, there's a gentleman in reception. He wants to see someone from the mining affairs committee.'

'Well, tell him I'm busy,' muttered Olsen. 'Tell him to come back this afternoon.'

Olsen listened to a muffled exchange. The receptionist spoke into the receiver again.

'He's insisting, Karl. He's French. A geologist. He says he's submitted an application to prospect. He wants to know if it's been accepted.'

God almighty, thought Olsen. The character Brattsen had told him about. Quickly, he thought back over everything the Deputy Superintendent had mentioned at their latest rendez-vous, two days previously, in a secluded spot behind the farm. A bit conspiratorial, all that, but it was his way of testing Rolf Brattsen's will. If he could get the policeman to come to secret assignations in out-of-the-way places, he could get him to do a great deal more, too, he told himself. He had to keep the lad under his thumb. Brattsen had told him about the geologist. He might even be a suspect, who knew? After all, he had arrived in town just before the recent dramatic events. What was he after? It wouldn't be too difficult to get him put away for a bit while things calmed down, until the wretched UN conference had passed and the tension had eased.

Two days back, Olsen had listened carefully to Brattsen's news, narrowing his eyes, thinking hard, before turning sharply in his seat to face the policeman.

'Can't you see, lad? The man's a blessing from heaven! Better than anything we could have hoped for. You can see that, can't you?'

Brattsen hadn't seen at all.

But he, Karl Olsen, had the grain of an idea. An idea that sprang from an obsession. Perhaps, at last, the time had come, he told himself, massaging the nape of his neck. But he couldn't act alone. He had never trusted the local geologists. Too hand-in-glove with the authorities for his liking. The whole economic and industrial apparatus of the Far North had been infiltrated by the Labour Party, and that included the geologists, he was sure of that. Bureaucrats in the pockets of the powers-that-be, the whole lot of them. They wouldn't know how to keep a secret. Their loyalty was never to the likes of him. And now here was a foreign geologist, heaven-sent.

The receptionist was still waiting for an answer.

'Ingrid, ask him to wait a moment.'

Olsen hung up, then dialled Brattsen's number. The policeman answered and Olsen got straight to the point.

'Rolf, what else do you know about that Frenchman?'

Olsen listened and his face broke into a broad smile. He grunted an acknowledgment from time to time. He was still listening carefully when his gaze alighted on the *Finnmark Dagblad* in the waste-paper basket. He fished it out and smoothed it on the desk with his free hand, opening it at the relevant page – the local news in brief. Then he thanked Brattsen and ended the call. Olsen rubbed his hands, cut an item from the newspaper and picked up the phone once again.

'Ingrid, can you tell the gentleman I'm not free to see him before the committee meeting. We don't want him trying to influence any outcomes, do we?'

'I hadn't thought of that, Karl, but you're quite right, of course. That's good thinking. If only we could say the same for some of our other councillors.'

'Indeed, my dear, indeed. Well, must get on. No more calls until the meeting, understood?'

Olsen hurried to his office window. The Frenchman was climbing back into his four-by-four. He looked angry and seemed in a hurry. He drove a large Volvo, an XC90. Olsen noted the direction he took as he drove off, waited a few minutes, then left the council offices by the back door.

He soon caught up with the Frenchman. He waited until they were on an isolated stretch of road, then flashed his headlights twice. Up ahead, the geologist slowed and flashed his indicator.

Olsen pulled alongside.

'You wanted to see someone from the mining affairs committee?' he asked, lowering his window. 'Follow me.'

They drove further out of town, to the spot near the reindeer enclosure where the farmer had held his first rendezvous with Brattsen, just after the disappearance of the drum. Olsen leaned across and opened the passenger door, wincing in pain from his stiff neck. He unscrewed the thermos he had brought from home that morning.

'Coffee?'

Racagnal sat in silence. He didn't seem particularly surprised to have been brought to this deserted spot by a complete stranger. The man was clearly no innocent, Olsen thought, used to underhand business, dirty tricks. He would have to tread very carefully.

Olsen shifted round in his seat and held out his hand with what he hoped was a benevolent smile. Racagnal stared at the cold rictus, unmoved.

'Karl Olsen,' the councillor introduced himself. 'Mining affairs committee. Spot of bother back at the office, there, couldn't see you right away, but it's all taken care of. So, tell me . . .'

Now it was Racagnal's turn to take a closer look at the farmer. He turned to face him.

'I don't drink coffee, thanks,' he said, in French-accented Swedish. The Frenchman seemed to be assessing the situation, absently stroking the identity bracelet on his left wrist.

'My company – the Société Française des Minerais – has lodged an application to prospect. I was promised a positive response today. I've jumped through all the hoops at the ministry, the Mining Administration, the regional council. I just need your council's stamp. And I was told that wouldn't be a problem.'

'Really? Not a problem?' Olsen chuckled. 'So our little committee counts for nothing at all, is that it?'

'That's not what I said. I've complied with all the criteria for prospecting in winter, avoiding the reindeer pastures and—'

'Reindeer, reindeer.' Olsen waved his hand dismissively, indicating that reindeer were not a problem. He lowered his voice. 'Now, listen.'

Olsen paused, as if weighing his words one last time, reviewing the many options he had in mind.

'The Kautokeino committee's in a restrictive mood right now. There's been a lot of debate on the town council, and some people think things are moving too fast.'

This was not entirely true, but Olsen turned a little further in his seat, to judge Racagnal's reaction. Nothing. The Frenchman was not making this easy. He went on.

'We've already turned down an application to prospect from the air, as you are probably aware.'

That was true, as it happened. Another glance at Racagnal. Still nothing. God almighty.

'So it's not looking good for you. But I can help. You seem like a serious player. You know the region, so I've been told?'

This time, the message seemed to hit home.

'My very good friend Deputy Superintendent Brattsen – fine policeman, a dead cert for the local top job – told me about you.'

'And?'

'You've already done some work in the region?'

'Yep. For a few years. I've worked a lot in Africa, too, and Australia, Canada. All over.'

'Always with the same company?'

'No, for the Chileans too, but I've been with the SFM for ten years now. The biggest French outfit. Very competent people.'

'Excellent, excellent. I've taken a look at your application. Very well put together, it has to be said. Shame the local committee is such a tough nut to crack. But there's something else I'd like to discuss.'

The Frenchman stared at him, harder than before.

'You see, I'm interested in mineral ores, too. Very much so. Have been for a long time. But I need a geologist. A good one. Not someone in the pockets of the Labour Party, or anyone else from around here. Someone who can go about their business quietly and discreetly, if you see what I mean. Answering to no one.'

'I see what you mean,' said Racagnal. 'Go on.'

'I can offer you a partnership. In a mine. A big one. Something that will make us both rich.'

Olsen's eyes narrowed further. He spoke slowly and carefully. He could picture the mine, right there before his eyes.

'I just don't know where it is.'

'Ah . . .'

'But I have a map,' he added quickly.

'A map. But you don't know where the mine is. I don't follow.'

'It's a geological map, see? No place names. An old map and, well ...'

Olsen left off in mid-sentence again, gauging Racagnal's reaction. At the mention of the geological map, the Frenchman looked very interested indeed.

'A map dating from when?' Racagnal cut in.

'Well, the date isn't marked anywhere, but from what my old father told me before he died, it must be from just before the war.'

'And what makes you think your huge seam exists? What would we be mining?'

Karl Olsen massaged his neck, his features lined in pain. He leaned in closer to the Frenchman.

'Gold,' he said quietly. 'Quantities of gold.'

Olsen sat back in his seat, unable to hold the painful pose for long.

'And what do you want from me?' asked Racagnal.

'You're an expert prospector. With a permit from your company. But you'll be looking for my gold seam too. As a priority. I'll give you an exclusive share. You'll be a rich man.'

'How can you be sure?'

'Because my old dad said people had talked for years about a fabulous seam here in the region, but one had ever found the damned thing. Except no one else had the map.'

Racagnal said nothing. Olsen watched him closely. At least the Frenchman was giving it some thought. At least he hadn't laughed out loud.

'We're holding our next committee meeting at noon, as you know,' he said. 'But it won't be difficult for me to get it postponed a few days. Which will give you time to submit an additional application to prospect. My name won't appear, of course. So by our next meeting, you'll need a clear picture of where the seam might be located, to be sure to strike in the right spot. Because the licences they're handing out at the end of this month cover the whole of Lapland,

144

and they're the biggest ever granted up here in the North. There won't be another round of licences on that scale within the decade, you mark my words. It's now or never!'

The Frenchman looked straight at Olsen, who had begun massaging his neck again.

'Sounds interesting, potentially. Give me some time to think. I'll need to make a few arrangements.'

Olsen shot him a dark look, winced in pain, then slowly reached for his wallet, with the newspaper cutting slipped inside. But he thought better of it.

'The committee meeting's at noon today. I need an answer before then. An exclusive share, remember. Here's my number. Now go.'

10 a.m., Kautokeino

Karl Olsen returned to his parking spot behind the council offices and entered unnoticed by the back door. It was easily done. You could walk in and out of the place, and no one was any the wiser. Anyone could come in from outside and go straight through to the offices without ever being noticed. People didn't worry about things like that here. Kautokeino was an innocent backwater. Just as well, Olsen grinned to himself.

He opened the door to the Progress Party office. No one was there. Excellent. He walked through to reception. Ingrid was talking to a small group of councillors, including his Progress Party colleague, still wearing his snowmobile suit.

'Any messages for me, Ingrid?'

'No, Karl. And I told the personal callers you were busy working.'

Ingrid opened the morning mail, chatting amiably with the other councillors. There were two hours to go until the meeting.

'Is the room ready, Ingrid?' one of the councillors asked. 'The overhead projector wasn't working the other day.'

'I'll go and check.'

Ingrid walked across the reception area to the corridor opposite and headed for the committee room. After a few moments, a piercing scream sent the group scurrying as one to where she stood. Ingrid had her hand over her mouth, eyes wide in terror.

'There,' she said, pointing to a shape on the floor.

Everyone looked. The thing lay next to an open plastic bag. It had curled in on itself and turned black in places. But its outline was unmistakable. It was a human ear.

146

19

Monday 17 January

10.30 a.m., Kautokeino

Brattsen was questioning Ingrid when Klemet arrived at the council offices, alone. Nina was making final preparations before leaving for the airport in Alta. The two had parted in melancholy mood on Friday night.

Brattsen paid no attention to Klemet. A police officer was taking pictures of the ear while another looked for fingerprints. Ingrid explained that she had found the plastic bag fixed to the door with a drawing-pin. She had no idea how long it had been there. The meeting rooms hadn't been used that morning – the mining affairs committee was the first of the day, so she couldn't be sure anyone else had been in that part of the building earlier. Brattsen continued his questioning, but clearly wasn't getting anywhere, Klemet thought: the council offices were wide open. Anyone could walk right in.

He bent over the ear. It lay untouched on the floor. There were clear marks cut into the lobe. His blood ran cold.

Matttis's ear – Klemet was certain of that – had been marked like one of his herd. Like a reindeer calf, its ear incised by the breeder as a mark of ownership. Klemet kneeled down to take a closer look. There were cuts in two places. The first, at the bottom of the ear, was circular in shape, but incomplete, like a three-quarters full moon. The second, at the top of the ear, was more elaborate, like a curved claw, and, just below that, a curling movement described a shape like a fish-hook. Yes, some kind of sharp hook. Klemet got to his feet.

Brattsen finished questioning Ingrid and the receptionist left, still in shock, supported by one of her colleagues.

'Chubby! Quick on the scene as ever . . .'

With that, Brattsen hurried away, leaving Klemet to speak to the photographer.

'I'll need copies of the shots.'

Klemet wondered what the marks referred to. Could they be traced to an individual breeder? Why make them? The discovery of the ear, in this state, put the inquiry in a completely new light. What sick individual was capable of this?

He hurried back to the station, shut himself in his office and reached for the Reindeer Administration handbook, listing the marks of every reindeer breeder in Sápmi, across the three Nordic countries. There were thousands of them, some no longer in use but still existing in law. Klemet rubbed his forehead. Some of the marks looked vaguely familiar. But vague familiarity was nothing to go on. There was nothing for it but to check each one, systematically. He picked up the phone to let Nina know what had happened, then collected a pen and notebook, and set to work.

11 a.m., Kautokeino

Brattsen made a wide-ranging tour around town, looking for suspect vehicles. He was returning to headquarters when he saw the Frenchman's four-by-four parked outside the pub, where the fight had broken out the other evening. He should have been getting back to the station. Instead, on an impulse, he parked next to the Volvo. From the evidence of the parking lot, there was no one else around. People wouldn't be turning out for lunch for another quarter of an hour or so, at the earliest.

He pushed the door soundlessly and saw Racagnal at the bar, nursing a beer and apparently deep in thought. Brattsen was about to approach him when he saw the waitress coming out of the kitchen. Not Lena, but her little sister, two years her junior. Brattsen watched as Racagnal reached across the bar and caressed the girl's cheek, stroking her lip with his thumb. She smiled shyly and pushed his hand away before turning and heading back into the kitchen. Racagnal inclined his head slightly to the left, eyeing the curve of her tight jeans. He looked round further and caught sight of the policeman silhouetted in the shadow of the doorway. The two men stared at one another, then Brattsen moved towards the bar.

'A light beer please, Ulrika.'

The girl poured a beer and placed it on the counter, catching Racagnal's eye as she did so. Then she returned to the kitchen. Brattsen raised his glass to his fellow drinker.

'Still not left town?'

'Nearly all done. Just waiting for the green light from the council.'

'Of course, the council.'

Brattsen said nothing about the discovery of the ear. He sipped his beer then spoke, lowering his voice.

'Definitely not eighteen, that one, I can tell you that for a fact.'

Racagnal said nothing.

'One sweet ass on her, though.'

Racagnal was taken by surprise, but let nothing show. He couldn't make the police officer out. Brattsen's allusion to the girl's shapely figure put him on his guard, but it set his mind racing, too.

'The young ones, like her, they're the easiest.'

Racagnal held his breath, gazing straight ahead, wondering what the policeman was after.

'Used to it, too. Even their own fathers screw them around here.'

Ulrika emerged from the kitchen at that moment. The two men stared at her. She looked away, intimidated now, and turned around, disappearing back through the door. 'There for the asking,' said

Brattsen. 'And her old man wouldn't kick up a fuss, believe me. Ulrika,' he called out.

The girl appeared from the kitchen.

'Come over here.'

Ulrika made her way around the bar and stood between the two men. Racagnal's breathing quickened, but still he said nothing. Brattsen reached up to stroke the girl's cheek. She seemed startled.

'How are things, Ulrika?' Brattsen continued to caress her cheek with his thumb, with a gentleness unusual for him. 'School all right, is it? Things at home OK?'

He was stroking her lip with his thumb now, the gesture at odds with the everyday niceties of the conversation. Ulrika clearly had no idea how to handle the situation. She looked somewhat at a loss, but she was letting him get away with it. Brattsen leaned back slightly on his stool, noting Racagnal's reaction. The Frenchman watched in fascination as Brattsen's thumb brushed the young girl's lip. The gesture was fatherly, but highly sensual, too. Brattsen dropped his hand suddenly.

'Ulrika, you look after my friend here, won't you? Be a good girl ...' He got up to leave.

Ulrika looked at Brattsen with a submissive air, then returned to the kitchen without a backward glance. Racagnal's eyes blazed. He stared at the kitchen door.

20

Monday 17 January

11.10 a.m., Highway 93

Nina was driving along the highway between Kautokeino and Alta, heading for the airport. She drove slowly, with plenty of time before her plane. Thick, dark clouds covered the region, softening the temperature to a mild twenty degrees below zero. A strong wind was blowing too, swirling flurries of snow. The sun had risen above the horizon but it was still dark as night, the surrounding landscape invisible in the snowstorm. Sections of the road were covered with packed ice, and Nina drove even more slowly here. The road turned slightly, the wind rose and she found herself blinded by the blizzard at times, her headlights bouncing off an impenetrable curtain of snow. She was heading downhill now. Soon she would be level with a lake much favoured by snowmobile riders in winter. Visibility was bad and she could barely make out the sides of the road.

A shadow sprang out from the right. She tugged the wheel left and skidded, avoiding the dark shape. A reindeer, she told herself, heart thumping. She straightened up and accelerated, pushing forward over the ice; but new shapes appeared, coming closer fast, too fast. She hit one of them straight on. The muffled shock made her swerve again. A big truck was bearing down on her in the opposite lane, flashing its headlights furiously, sounding its horn. Nina swung the steering wheel round hard, accelerating again, skidded and drove straight into a mound of snow on the bend ahead. She was thrown around violently in her seat and heard a dull crump as the car's right front wing buried itself in the deep drift. Then nothing.

She kept her hands on the wheel, feeling the adrenalin flooding her system, unable to move. She pressed her right hand against her heart, feeling its wild beat, then turned around. There was nothing to see behind her. The truck hadn't even stopped. Nina reversed and parked in a small lay-by. She left the engine running and the hazard lights on, pulled out her flashlight and put on her chapka and gloves. The blizzard clawed at her face. She had lost all sense of distance. The wind almost blinded her, biting at her skin, pouring through the gaps in her hurriedly fastened snowsuit. Nina felt the sudden grip of the cold. She tried to retrace her tyre-tracks but the blizzard had swept everything away, and her powerful flashlight shone barely three metres into the near-horizontal, driving snow.

At last, she made out a shape to her left. The reindeer was half leaning against a deep drift, its hind quarters still sticking out into the road, its pelvis apparently shattered by the impact. The ground before her was a mess of blood and ice. It was still alive, its tongue lolling to one side, its large eyes expressing sheer terror. Or pain. Or both. Nina was in shock, deafened by the storm, shaking with cold and adrenalin, completely at a loss in the face of the animal's plight. She turned away, tears in her eyes, and gave a terrified shriek at the silhouette of a man, standing just behind her. The wind had drowned his approach. Aslak. He was a fearful sight, his beard half frozen, his muscular jaw clenched, his bloodshot eyes sunk deeper than ever, expressing profound rage. Nina was seized with dread. He was wearing his reindeer-skin cloak. In fact, he was clad from head to foot in reindeer skins. She could hardly believe her eyes. He had appeared as if from nowhere, at the height of the storm.

152

'What are you doing? What are you doing here?' She found herself shouting, not to make herself heard, but to release her pent-up tension. She was furious with Aslak for frightening her so badly.

He showed no response, but stepped around her, moving towards the mound of snow, and bent over the reindeer, feeling the animal's body. Its eyes were still wide and staring, but it seemed soothed by Aslak's presence. Nina watched the surreal scene in the shaft of her flashlight. She stood stock-still, shaking, gripped by the cold. Aslak was kneeling in the snow, stroking the reindeer now, with a gentleness Nina would have found it hard to imagine earlier. She felt overcome with emotion: the sight brought other images crowding into her mind, bright and sharp, powerful and absurd. The image of her father, that wounded soul, stroking her hair on the evening she had been too scared to sleep, after seeing him suffer one of his attacks. Nina struggled to contain her feelings. She did not notice immediately that Aslak had taken out a dagger. Only once he had plunged it into the reindeer's heart, straight and sure, killing it where it lay, did she realise what he was doing. He closed the animal's eyes and stroked it for a while longer.

'Are you going to Alta?'

Nina looked up, astonished to hear him speak.

'Yes.' Her voice shook.

'Then I'll carry the animal to your car and you will take it to the police. They'll do the paperwork.'

He bent down, gathered the reindeer in his arms and followed behind Nina. He stowed the carcass in the boot and took a seat next to Nina in the front of the car. She was about to start the engine when Aslak stayed her hand.

'I'm staying here, I have other reindeer to bring in.'

'In this storm? Without a snowmobile?'

'I'm on skis.'

'You're crazy!'

'Crazy? Yes, that's what people here say,' he said, quietly. The rage was gone from his eyes.

'Was that one of your reindeer?' asked Nina, miserably.

153

'Two of my reindeer.'

'Two . . .'

'A mother – one of my favourites – she was intelligent. She was in calf. It would have been born this spring. Don't forget to tell them that in Alta.'

Nina felt as if she might break down in tears. But she clenched her jaw, got a grip, stared straight ahead.

'Aslak, I'm so sorry. You'll be compensated for the two of them, is that right?'

He was silent for a moment.

'If you weren't a Reindeer Police officer, I wouldn't report the accident.'

'But why not, if you can be compensated? The Reindeer Administration will ensure you get a fair deal, like everyone else.'

'I don't believe in your justice. I don't believe in it.'

'But you're wrong. You're entitled to fair treatment, the same as anyone.'

'Am I? Really?'

Nina felt a rush of sympathy. Aslak looked so embittered that it hurt her to see him. Almost without thinking, she placed her hand on his, then took it away again just as quickly. She was badly shaken, had no idea what to do next, only wanted him to go. She looked for some hint of a response in his eyes, but all she saw was the reindeer's terror-struck gaze, clouding her vision. She buried her face in her arms, crossed on the top of the steering wheel, then straightened up again in her seat, feeling a little calmer. Aslak was holding something out to her in his hand. A small leather pouch.

'It contains a pewter pendant. I made it myself. Carry it with you, and carry the souls of the reindeer with you. You must not feel guilty.'

And without waiting for a reply, he opened the passenger door and disappeared into the darkness.

21

Monday 17 January

11.30 a.m., Kautokeino

News of the discovery of the ear had travelled all over town and far beyond. Journalists were calling from across Norway. The roadblock at the crossroads had been lifted. Pastor Lars Jonsson had been talking with Berit Kutsi when the information reached him.

'What a dreadful fate for Mattis Labba,' said the pastor, quietly. 'He was a sinner, but he was a poor, lost man. He lived his life far beyond the reach of the Gospels.'

'His fate was perhaps not entirely his fault,' ventured Berit.

'We must place our lives in Jesus's hands, Berit, there can be no salvation without that. Mattis lived by the old superstitions. And no good can come of that, for anyone, believe me,' he added with a cold, unsettling stare. Hurriedly, Berit took her leave.

She climbed into her old Renault 4 – a familiar sight and something of a local attraction – for the short drive to Olsen's farm, on the edge of Kautokeino. As a rule, she worked there every day, but Mattis's savage murder had left her deeply affected, more than anyone could have imagined. She parked behind one of the barns, but stayed in her seat, reciting a prayer, eyes closed, before walking to the cowshed to feed the herd.

Olsen had just finished a call to Rolf Brattsen when he saw Berit arrive.

'God almighty. Dragging her feet, as always.'

He was on the point of stepping outside to urge Berit to hurry up when the telephone rang.

'We need to talk terms,' said a French-accented voice, in Swedish.

'Come to the farm straightaway. I have to get back to the council offices before noon.'

Olsen forgot all about upbraiding Berit. Silently, he climbed the stairs to his bedroom, crossed to the back wall and opened a low door leading to a built-in storage space. No one was in the house at this time of day, but he turned to check behind him, with a suspicious look, nonetheless. He bent down and stepped through into a small, dimly lit room cluttered with storage chests, rolled-up maps and documents, and old newspapers. He reached out to a small safe and carefully input the combination. Opening it, he took out a large envelope, smoothed it against his chest, closed the safe and the door behind him and went back downstairs. He was just entering the kitchen when the Frenchman's Volvo pulled up outside the farmhouse.

Olsen greeted his guest on the kitchen doorstep and invited him to come in and sit down. He placed the envelope prominently on the table, to his right, and noted with satisfaction that Racagnal seemed unable to take his eyes off it as they spoke.

'This is going to be difficult with regard to my company,' said Racagnal, straightaway.

'You'll find a way to reassure them – it'll be worth the effort, believe me.'

'You have the map?'

Olsen pushed the envelope slowly across the table. Racagnal took out the yellowed sheet of paper inside and unfolded it carefully. No doubt about it, this was a geological map all right. A real work of art, produced with all the care and skill of a bygone age, though Racagnal saw immediately that it was the work of an amateur geologist. He looked at the curving lines, the symbols and colours: the result of a painstaking land survey, carried out sixty or seventy years before. It brought back memories for an old-school geologist like himself – someone who still knew how to work with a notebook and crayons, not like the rookies today, reaching for their computers at the first sight of a chunk of rock.

'Interesting,' he said. 'Granite layers . . .'

He fell silent and pored over the sheet, lost in concentration. A geological map represented hundreds, sometimes thousands, of hours of work on the ground. You had to know how to read the landscape, look beyond appearances, see what was invisible to the naked eye beneath the layers of soil, the vegetation, the moraines. Maps like this were irreplaceable; they contained a mass of fine detail, of the kind that had been eliminated little by little as map-making became increasingly modernised. Nowadays, people focused on the principal rock masses, nothing else. Judging by its appearance, this map was the result of direct observations and readings on the ground. It was dotted with numerous pinpoints, small nicks in the paper, cross-references. An original map based on data noted down in the field by one or more geologists, with an abundance of priceless information.

A true geologist always looked for the original map, the very first one, the oldest, the one that smelled of sweat and times past, because a field geologist was always ready to note down the tiniest anomaly. And those anomalies were the sign of a true expert. Racagnal's hunter instinct was aroused. With it came a rush of adrenalin and a sudden, vivid image of Ulrika, the young serving girl from the bar.

He knew the complexity of the local terrain – typical of a region crushed under the weight of glaciers for thousands of years. He looked closely at the map's captions and annotations, but nothing suggested a precise location for the survey. The corners and edges of the map were worn and stained, as if it had been handled a great deal. Someone had taken it out, over and over again. Trying to solve the mystery.

'Where does the map come from?' he asked after a long pause.

Olsen shot the Frenchman a look of undisguised suspicion. He didn't have much time left before the mining affairs committee meeting, though it was very likely to be adjourned following the discovery of the ear. Still, he would have to lodge this blasted new application to prospect.

'I inherited it from my father. He drew it.'

Racagnal looked at him, saying nothing.

'Who else have you shown it to?'

'No one! What kind of a person do you take me for? My father told me on his deathbed that there was a huge gold seam indicated here. But the old fool never gave me the name of a place. Or he did it on purpose, the sly son of a bitch. That wouldn't surprise me. Never wanted us to think food would drop into our plates from heaven.'

Racagnal pointed to the map.

'There are several places in the region with this type of configuration. And given that there are no place names, the only thing to do is go and look. Out in the field. See for yourself, test it out, get a feel for it, scratch the surface. There's no other solution. You say aerial reconnaissance is out of the question in winter?'

'Yes, thanks to the damned reindeer. Also because uranium prospecting is taboo around here: they don't want people prospecting for radioactive areas from the air, or on the ground.'

'And what do you think about that?'

'I couldn't give a damn about their uranium. I want my gold. So are you in or not?'

Racagnal traced the broad curves with his finger, crossing the map, feeling the tiny pinpoints, the little nicks in the paper.

'You see all the spots of yellow metal marked by my father, indicating gold. You see those?'

'I see them,' said the geologist.

But his tone suggested he could see much more than that. Olsen pictured a seam even more vast than he had imagined so far.

'So you'll say yes?'

'Yes.' Racagnal's decision was firm.

'Well, I'll get along to the council offices then,' said Olsen, brisk and business-like now. 'You'll need to sign this, here, and fill in this form. I'll do the rest. Everything has to be passed along to the Mining Administration. How long will you need to prospect and identify the right place, based on the map?'

Racagnal looked at the farmer, scornfully.

'Think we can do this with a click of the fingers?'

'But you're ready to go ahead, aren't you?'

'Now I need to check every geological map of the region, to see which ones correspond more or less to your father's survey.' Racagnal was exasperated by Olsen's tone. 'And don't try to tell me how to do my job.'

The older man pressed his face close to the Frenchman's, ignoring the pain in the nape of his neck.

'You think we're just a rag-bag bunch of peasants up here, good for nothing. Is that it?' he said, very quietly. 'If you try and double-cross me, or fail to get the job done as quickly as possible, I can ask the right people to take a closer look into just what you were up to in Alta the other day.'

He pushed his chair back and unfolded the press report on the rape of the Alta schoolgirl.

'A good friend tells me you've a liking for little girls. You were in Alta that day, weren't you?'

'Think you can blackmail me?' Racagnal jumped to his feet. 'I went to Alta to buy equipment. That's all.'

'Just sit down and shut up!' Olsen's voice was raised now. 'If you don't locate that seam in time, we have a nice fresh statement from a little girl name of Ulrika, on our local deputy superintendent's desk, right now.'

'What the hell are you saying?'

'Think we're a bunch of hicks, do you? Well, see here, we can be quick off the mark too. Now you get on and do your job. And if you play your cards right, you'll get an exclusive share. Sole partners. And all the little girls you want. You've got a week. Like I said before, I can get today's meeting postponed, but probably only for a week at the most. And you're going to sign this piece of paper here, too. But that's strictly between ourselves. A private contract that says I'm the owner of the land. And this is going to stay right here at home, in my safe, with little Ulrika's statement and the little newspaper article all about Alta. So if anything happens to me, they can follow the trail all the way back to you.'

'Don't even think I can get this done in a week without a guide.' It was worth a try.

Olsen softened.

'The best guide around here – but he's a difficult customer – is Aslak Gaupsara. He lives on the mountain. A wild man, but he's a wolf-hunter and a skilled tracker. Knows the region like the back of his hand. When you've collected your equipment, come back and find me here.'

12 noon, Kautokeino

To convince Brattsen about the gold seam once and for all, Olsen had promised him a role as head of security at the mine, with a salary he could barely dream of, even if he was promoted to the top job at the station in Kautokeino. A small price to pay, the farmer told himself. At the same time, having a security chief all lined up for his gold mine, when the seam hadn't even been located yet, made it seem almost real. Olsen felt the project was within his grasp, after decades of dashed hopes. But there was still the blasted missing link.

He pushed the thought to the back of his mind. Lapland was vast. He had come so close, and then . . .

He braked hard in front of the council offices. The police had left already. Idle layabouts.

Olsen thought of his father. He had told Racagnal that his father had drawn the map. The Frenchman didn't need to know the truth. He didn't need to know that Olsen's father had stolen it; that the fool had never managed to decipher the precise location. Throughout his youth, Olsen had seen his father set out on endless hikes,

160

armed with a metal detector and that damned map. He had found bits and pieces, but never anything resembling the fabulous gold seam promised by the myriad yellow dots on the sheet.

The four committee members were already seated around the table when Olsen took his place. As expected, the president – a member of the Sami People's Party – opened the session and declared straightaway that he was asking for an adjournment in light of recent events.

Around him, the others nodded their heads in silence. The committee president was a well-respected man locally, an elderly sage, and his opinion counted, Olsen knew that.

'We still have some important decisions to take. The Mining Administration's next licence round will have lasting implications for our town, for the next ten or twenty years. Many companies are interested in the region's mineral deposits. We're the richest in Europe on that score, and most of Sápmi remains unexplored, let alone exploited. We have to face facts: the pressures are huge. People know, or suspect, that vast deposits lie undiscovered out there.'

Olsen found it hard to sit still. Discreetly, he turned from the waist, checking the reactions of the rest of the committee. He was the only non-Lapp. Which way would they go? Would the promise of riches prove too much for them? He hoped so.

22

Monday 17 January

1 p.m., Kautokeino

Klemet had spent hours searching through the handbook of reindeer breeders' marks, checking certain pages several times over. He was forced to admit the evidence of his own eyes: the marks cut into Mattis's ear were virtually identical to one of the marks registered to Olaf Renson. It was unthinkable, but the evidence was there on the page.

To be absolutely certain, he needed the second ear. Only the two combined would confirm the owner's mark beyond doubt. But why would the murderer insist on marking both ears, as with a reindeer? The act was a clear reference to the breeders and their world. The second ear was bound to turn up sooner or later.

He headed downstairs to the Sheriff's office, entered without knocking and sat down opposite Tor Jensen, slapping the handbook onto the desk, open at the relevant page. Next to it, he placed one of the pictures requested from the police photographer, showing the severed ear.

Tor Jensen slurped his liquorice sweet, staring at the photograph and the diagrams of breeders' marks. No need to spell it out. Klemet knew Jensen would understand perfectly what he was getting at.

Jensen took another sweet, leafed through the pages of the hand-book, paused, then continued dipping into his bowl of *salmiakki*.

'So you think this is it? You think the cuts on the ear are a clue leading us to an individual breeder?'

'What else?'

Silence again.

'Well, it seems logical enough, you might say. Except . . . Except where it falls down: you think the murderer wanted to implicate somebody else? I don't get it.'

Klemet said nothing for a moment. Then a thought occurred to him.

'Unless Mattis – if it really is his ear – worked for the breeder whose mark this is.'

The Sheriff whistled and threw himself back in his chair. He crossed his hands behind the nape of his neck and looked attentively at Klemet.

'So the murder might be some sort of warning to a big-time breeder? Is that what you're thinking?'

'I have no idea,' said Klemet.

'But who, in that case? That would represent one hell of an esca-lation in the tensions between breeders.'

Klemet said nothing.

Jensen continued, 'So in addition to his victim, the murderer would be targeting a wealthy breeder – Olaf Renson – and we would need to find out who has a bone to pick with him. Still, you'd have to be more than stupid to sign a murder like that. And there can't be that many breeders seriously at odds with Olaf. Did Mattis work with him sometimes? And if so, when? Know anything about that, Klemet?'

Klemet was on his feet. He left the room without saying a word.

2 p.m., Kautokeino

Klemet had no desire to call Olaf. The Sami militant was no fan of his, dismissing the Reindeer Police officer as a collaborator. Searching online, Klemet was forced to admit that Renson's name cropped up very little. He hadn't been involved in even minor reindeer rustling for more than a decade. Nothing of note at all. The only thing that came close was a case involving two animals that had been hit by a small truck, as declared by Olaf. Their ears hadn't been been brought into the Reindeer Administration offices, as required by law, but Renson had claimed compensation nonetheless. The claim had been refused. Case closed.

Klemet read through each report. A boundary dispute caught his attention – a fence torn down by a hot-tempered neighbour of Olaf's. He read through to the end, but that was harmless enough, too, he decided.

The last two entries featuring Olaf's name included some more interesting material. Olaf had been investigated back when Johann Henrik had been shot at. Klemet shivered as he read that the weapon used had come from Olaf's place. Johann Henrik had narrowly escaped being killed. Was he dealing with a vendetta?

8.15 p.m., Paris

Nina Nansen had made it to the French capital and checked into her hotel, a small place on Place du Général Beuret, that evening. Henri Mons lived in the 15th arrondissement, near the *mairie*. She went to her room, called Paul and arranged to see his father early the following morning. The old man was feeling much better and looked forward to meeting Nina. Actually, Paul said, his father seemed quite reinvigorated at the prospect of her visit. He had spent the last few days in his study and attic, rummaging through his archives.

The call ended and Nina realised, once again, that speaking to Paul had awoken painful memories of her youthful Paris experience. Had she been too naive? She had often mulled over the episode, but couldn't see how the fault could have been hers. She had liked the young man. She remembered the sound of his voice. Paul Mons's voice had stirred the same feelings. It was deeper, but the timbre and cadence were the same.

Not wanting to face the evening alone, she called Klemet, who told her about his discussion with Tor Jensen. Jensen's conclusions showed common sense, she felt. But she could tell Klemet was annoyed to find her siding with the Sheriff.

'Are you going to question Johann Henrik again, tomorrow?'

'Nina, you're as bad as Jensen! One ear doesn't prove anything.'

'But you'll question him all the same?'

'Of course! I'll have to take a stronger line with him this time. Check back over every dispute he's been involved in. We'll see. I'll need to look back further than two years if we really are dealing with a full-scale vendetta. I may find something that connects him to Olaf. I haven't talked to the Sheriff about that yet.'

'Will you go alone?'

'Want me to take Brattsen along for company?'

'Why do you two dislike each other so much?'

'The man's an out-and-out racist. He has no business being a policeman. That's all there is to say about him.'

Nina could see the discussion was closed. Afterwards, she still didn't feel like sleeping so she took out the file on the drum. There were photographs of the Juhl Centre and photocopies of the designs on known Sami drums. She studied them with interest. They were mostly oval in shape, covered with strange symbols. Some she could identify, though they were highly stylised. She recognised the reindeer, of course, and birds. Other symbols were trees perhaps, and boats. She saw tents like the ones she had visited, Klemet's included, and figures of people, simplified in the extreme, almost like a child's drawing. But there were a great many other symbols she couldn't place at all. Deities, even abstract concepts? But which ones? Again, she felt like an explorer in an unknown world.

Norwegian schoolchildren were taught very little about the Sami, perhaps because the country's nomad population was so small. From the police course in Kiruna, she knew that they numbered in the tens of thousands, but not even a hundred thousand, as far as she could remember, and those were scattered across Norway, Sweden, Finland and Russia. They had their own parliaments in each country.

At this, she remembered Olaf, his seductive smile, his mocking nickname. And what was the Spaniard's role in all this? It was a world very far from her own.

Nina lay down on the bed, closed her eyes and thought about her home region. Her father. Vivid memories came flooding back. Papa. Softly, she began to cry.

10.45 p.m., Kautokeino

André Racagnal had said nothing to the old farmer, but if there was a map, there would be a field book, too. That was how it was, never anything different. Every geologist worked that way. A map always led back to a field book, where the geologist had recorded his observations out on reconnaissance, before drawing the map. And if an old, hand-drawn map like Olsen's was worth its weight in gold, compared with those issued by professional institutes today, an original field book was the Holy Grail itself. So where was it? It would speed up his search for the location of the gold seam. If there really was a gold seam. Olsen had held on to the map for now, but Racagnal had made a mental note of the main characteristics. Olsen wasn't a professional, luckily. He associated maps with buried treasure, like some antiquated adventure novel. That was about the level of his limited imagination. Just as well. It gave Racagnal the advantage.

Still, he was furiously angry with Olsen. That hard-faced cop had pretended he was on Racagnal's side, but he was in the old man's pocket, too. How could Olsen have known about the little bar-girl otherwise? That little minx. She'd done as she was told all right. But he could forget all about fooling around now.

The Frenchman mulled over Olsen's proposition. An exclusive share in the exploitation of a seam – a rich seam, as Olsen claimed – was tempting indeed. He could stuff the lot of them then – the Paris bureaucrats and the stay-at-home geologists with their slick Power-Point presentations and no clue how to survive in the field without their GPS and computers. Those arrogant white-collar salarymen, giving him the cold shoulder on his return from Kivu, coming over all shocked and horrified when they heard how he had handled the mission in the Congo. Or, rather, when they read in the papers what had been done out there in the company's name. Because if the papers hadn't got hold of the story, you could bet your bottom dollar headquarters would have left him in peace; probably paid him a hefty bonus, too. They had been happy enough all those years ago when he had secured the coltan seam in what was probably the most corrupt and dangerous region in the world.

Four years. He had spent four years down there, with the crazed militiamen, drink-sodden killers the lot of them. Travelling the length and breadth of the region, locating the seam, then setting up and securing the mine, so the Paris pretty-boys could get their precious coltan for their precious mobile phones. And then they had the nerve to take the moral high ground with him, André Racagnal, because he'd had the guts to get down and dirty with the monsters running the show out there. He didn't give a toss about any of them. Oh yes, they were all so terribly shocked and upset. Still clung on to their mobile phones, though. Fuck every last one of them.

Four fucking years. Even so, Racagnal had had his fill of little Kivu girls. One of the militia men, one of the craziest types he'd ever come across, fancied himself as the local Chuck Norris. Little clipped beard and sleeveless gilet, just like the action hero himself. Except that compared to him, the real Chuck was a liberal intellectual. Commander Chuck, as he liked to be known, was mad, bad and in charge of security at the mine. Racagnal had supplied him with dope and cognac, and Commander Chuck had kept him supplied with little girls. Fair exchange. But the guy was genuinely dangerous. One day, completely off his head, he had killed an engineer from the Société Française des Minerais in cold blood, right before Racagnal's eyes. Over nothing. Racagnal had told him he couldn't touch the ex-pats, but Chuck didn't give a flying fuck about that. That was when the trouble had started.

He pushed Kivu to the back of his mind.

The field book. Did it still exist? And if so, was it at the farm? He would have to try to find out. What if it existed, but wasn't at the farm? Where might it be? At the council offices, the local museum? The Geological Institute in Malå, perhaps. That high temple of geology, home to the complete geological archives of the Far North.

Racagnal had been there several times, back when he had last worked in Lapland. The institute was an unrivalled source of documents for anyone with the knowledge to decipher them, keeping records of every survey carried out in the region for over a century. Even the Americans couldn't match that. It had maps, field books, samples, aerial surveys, everything. All archived and accessible. A treasure house.

But why would the map and field book have become separated? It made no sense.

23

Tuesday 18 January

Sunrise: 10 a.m.; sunset: 12.59 p.m.
2 hours 59 minutes of sunlight

9.30 a.m., Central Sápmi

Klemet set off early, taking two other police officers with him. He didn't think Johann Henrik would show much resistance, in spite of his hard-bitten character, but you could never be sure. The faintest blue light softened the darkness, but the three snowmobiles moved swiftly nonetheless, racing along the final stretch of frozen river. Five kilometres from Henrik's trailer, they left the river and climbed a slope covered in thick snow. After four kilometres of difficult terrain, threading through buried rocks and dwarf birches, Klemet came to a halt on the summit of Searradas, the highest hill in the area, rising to a height of some six hundred metres. He took out his field glasses and scanned the surrounding countryside, one knee propped on the seat of his scooter, searching for the slightest movement. The engines had been switched off and the silence was near-total. There was no wind, but still the cold stole through the slightest chink in his snow gear.

Johann Henrik kept his trailer on nearby Vuordnas, on a shoulder of land from which two slightly higher peaks rose to the north. It was still there, sheltered by the higher ground. Vuordnas rose only a hundred metres or so above the surrounding terrain, but it gave Henrik a perfect vantage point. Klemet hadn't called ahead on this occasion.

The previous night, after Nina's call, he had studied the herder's file one more time. Henrik was the youngest of five brothers. In accordance with Sami tradition, he had inherited his father's herd, together with his house, furniture and land rights. A helping hand for the youngest in the family, and a reward for taking care of his ageing parents. The herd had prospered under Johann's expert husbandry, but he had gone into the tourism business, too, filling the slack periods when there was less to do with the reindeer. He organised fishing trips and showed visitors around a corral with a few reindeer, where he sold Sami handicrafts. Perhaps even a few drums made by Mattis, Klemet thought. He would have to ask about that. Henrik kept a fleet of agricultural vehicles, too, renting them to the council as required, especially for snow-clearing. His wife kept a small café on the Alta road, selling home-cooked reindeer dishes, sandwiches, drinks and cakes. In the high season, Henrik commanded a team of fifteen men. With all that, Henrik must be earning a tidy living, Klemet thought. Not at all like Mattis. Henrik was a local entrepreneur and a member of the Sami Nomad Party – the biggest political contingent in Kautokeino.

Klemet lowered his field glasses, having spotted a few groups of reindeer. They seemed quiet enough. Smoke was rising from the trailer's stove-pipe. A snowmobile – only one – was parked out front. Had Johann Henrik heard he was now a murder suspect? If he had, it wasn't from the newspapers.

'That's probably Henrik's scooter down there,' he called over to his colleagues. 'Looks like he's alone. Let me take charge and ask the questions. Nothing aggressive. This isn't Oslo. No need to play cowboys and Indians.'

He liked giving orders to Norwegian police officers.

The trio made their way down from Searradas, crossed a frozen lake and began the climb to the top of Vuordnas. Klemet reached the plateau and looked across at the trailer, about three kilometres away on the northern side. He was halfway across when he saw a dark silhouette emerging from the shelter. Klemet accelerated hard. The figure spotted them at last. Klemet saw him move forward, then jump aboard the snowmobile. The machine tore around the trailer, along the north side of the plateau and away into the distance. Klemet swore and accelerated again. He spoke into the helmet's fitted radio, giving the two other officers instructions to go on ahead of him while he turned off, taking a lower route. He stared into the distance, looking for the scooter, but could see nothing. He would have to act fast. The other two officers weren't used to this, and Henrik would have no difficulty shaking them off.

Klemet accelerated down towards a lake just visible to his right. He followed the contour of the hill, avoiding hidden obstacles, anomalies in the snow-covered relief that might suggest a buried birch trunk, a boulder, or a crevice. He looked up repeatedly from the path ahead of him, checking the direction of the lake. He had to reach it before Henrik, whose only way down was through a narrow ravine, opening onto the expanse of frozen water. Losing concentration for a moment, Klemet hit a rock. The heavy snowmobile went into a skid. He felt the machine swerve to the left, sinking into the snow. He threw his weight to the right, turning the accelerator handle away from him as far as it would go. The machine leaped forward. He managed to get back on course. In less than half a minute he had reached the lake.

He followed the shoreline to his right and stopped at the mouth of the ravine. There were no tracks as yet. Then Henrik's scooter burst into view, bearing down on him fast. Klemet stood up on his footplates, waving his arms. He saw one of the police snowmobiles following behind. The man riding the front scooter – it was clearly Henrik – realised his way was blocked. He slowed down and stopped just short of Klemet's machine.

'What the hell do you think you're playing at?' he shouted. 'Let me through, I have to catch up with my reindeer!'

'Your son can take care of them.' Klemet's voice was raised over the noise of the engines. 'You're coming with us back to the trailer right now, for a little chat. And after that we'll see if I decide to let you go see to your reindeer.'

Henrik muttered under his breath, gunned his engine and set off in the direction of the trailer, escorted by Klemet and the other police officer. A little higher up, they found their colleague, fresh from heaving the front end of his machine out of a hole, to judge from the tracks. He was apparently unhurt.

Johann Henrik led the way into the trailer, followed by Klemet and the first police officer. The interior was like that of any other shelter in the *vidda*: two bunk beds down one wall, a fitted bench seat opposite and a table in the middle. Klemet invited Henrik to take his seat first, hemmed in by the others. The herder shifted reluctantly along the narrow space between the bench and the table, and sat down.

'We'll start by searching the trailer,' said Klemet, raising a hand for silence before Henrik had time to object. 'You may have heard we found a severed human ear at the council offices yesterday. It had been marked – incised along the edge with a knife.'

Johann Henrik stared at him incredulously. His mouth twisted, but he said nothing. He took out a pouch of tobacco and began rolling a cigarette.

'What's that got to do with me?' he asked, with an unpleasant glare. 'That why you've come out here to stop me going about my work?'

'The marks look strangely like one of Olaf's. Very similar, in fact.'

Henrik looked unfazed. He lit his cigarette.

'Brilliant. One more ear notched up for the Spaniard.'

'You didn't tell me about that business between you and him.'

'What the hell are you on about? What business?'

'That time you were shot. Seems you were in a dispute over pasture, you and Olaf. More of a long-standing grudge, actually, from what he told me. Mattis was working for him at the time. Seems he was caught up in it, too.' No harm in giving Henrik the impression he'd been talking to Olaf.

'Ah.' Henrik sighed. 'And so you reckon I killed Mattis, cut off his ears, marked them with Olaf's notches and left one of them in the council offices? You're a crack squad in the Reindeer Police and no mistake.'

He broke into a dark grin this time, cackling with laughter.

'I don't think anything, Johann Henrik,' said Klemet. 'There's nothing to link the mark to you, but I have to explore the possibility.'

Henrik stared at Klemet through clouds of exhaled smoke, while the two officers searched the trailer. After a few minutes, the men placed their finds on the table: three daggers and a bottle of cognac, three-quarters full.

'We'll take the knives with us, if you've no objection.'

Henrik blew smoke.

'Not arresting me, then?'

'We know where to find you. We'll be back,' said Klemet, closing the door behind him.

24

Tuesday 18 January

9.30 a.m., Paris

It was raining when Nina left her hotel to go to the Mons apartment. She pressed the button twice next to the name 'Mons' on the intercom. The building dated from the early twentieth century and was clearly well maintained, with a recently cleaned stone façade. Paul answered immediately and buzzed her into a smart, well-appointed hallway. She took the stairs to the second floor. Henri Mons himself was waiting for her outside his door. The old man welcomed her with a broad smile.

'Ah, Mademoiselle! I have been waiting impatiently for you!'

Nina was surprised to find him so bright and alert. His gestures were quick, almost nervous.

'Your visit has restored him to a state of robust health!' said Paul, shaking her hand in turn. 'But be careful not to wear him out,' he added, smiling.

Nina looked at the two men facing her. Henri Mons sported quite a full head of hair for a man of his age, snowy white and brushed straight back. His face was thin and gaunt, with a slender nose and disproportionately large ears. His narrow shoulders stooped slightly, but this in no way detracted from his fine, distinguished air. He returned Nina's gaze with kindly, bright blue eyes.

At his side, Paul wore his own, chestnut-brown hair in exactly the same style. He was roughly his father's height, with a slim, fit build, his healthy complexion shadowed by a well-cut three-day beard.

Nina glanced around the spacious apartment, lined with paintings, panelling, expensive curtains and expedition souvenirs. The impression was cosy, comfortable, bourgeois. She was unfamiliar with the smell of polished wood, but thought it added to the refined atmosphere. It was all a far cry from Norway's timber-framed houses with their pale, untreated birch and pine.

They moved to a set of deep leather armchairs in the sitting room. Paul served tea while Henri Mons, clearly the lord and master, addressed Nina with a smile.

'I am delighted to receive a visit from such a charming representative of the Norwegian police, Mademoiselle.'

Nina smiled politely. The usual gallant compliments. She knew enough about French men to expect no less. She acquiesced with a look of suitable, modest delight, trying not to simper, all the same.

'Do you have news of the drum?'

'Still none, *Monsieur*. We have several teams of investigators on the case. We're following up various leads, but until we know a little more about the piece, and its history, we're groping in the dark.'

'I understand, of course. And how may I be of help?'

'First, could you tell me what you were doing in Lapland before the war?'

'I took part in an expedition organised by Paul-Émile Victor. I was conducting an ethnological study. We travelled with the Latarjet brothers – both doctors. We crossed the whole of Lapland, apart from the Soviet section, of course.'

'So all four of you were—'

'The four of us made up the French contingent. Paul-Émile and the Latarjet brothers were old friends. I went along as a sort of alibi. The Musée de l'Homme funded our expedition, and as the token ethnologist I provided proof that it was more than an exotic jaunt among friends. It was that, too, of course, but that's another story. Two Swedes came along with us, and a German. The Swedes were anthropologists from Uppsala: they seemed quite charming at first. And the German was from somewhere to the east, I think, or the south-east. The Sudetenland. Or Bohemia. I can't really remember. But no matter, he was German at any rate, and a geologist. And then there were the guides and porters, of course. Laplanders – Sami as we must now call them – who travelled with us the whole way.'

'You said the Swedes seemed charming "at first" . . . ' ventured Nina.

'Well, Paul-Émile was a man with a passion, you know. He adored people. He was absolutely committed to learning about other cultures, discovering other perspectives on the world – be it in Polynesia, where he went later in life, or the Far North, at the time of our expedition. The stranger and more exotic a place and its people, the better he liked them. His journey across Lapland was conducted absolutely in this spirit of authentic discovery. So it was for me, too, and for the Latarjet brothers. But we discovered quite early on that our Swedish colleagues felt otherwise. In fact I find it quite hard, with hindsight, to refer to them as "colleagues" at all. What Paul-Émile and I both failed to realise, when we were planning the trip, was that the two anthropologists from the University of Uppsala were also connected to their country's State Institute for Racial Biology, the SIFR.'

Henri Mons paused, apparently assessing the impact of this revelation on Nina. She stared back with wide-open eyes, confirming her complete ignorance on the subject.

'Paul, would you be so kind as to fetch the book I left on the armchair in the office?'

Mons took the book, leafed through its pages, then held it out to Nina.

'This is the sort of study our Swedish gentlemen were carrying out at their institute, at the time.'

The book was in Swedish. Nina took her time looking through the yellowed pages, watched intently by Mons. The old man had kept it all these years, and it was obviously of some importance to him. It deserved close attention – and the contents were fascinating indeed. A series of photographic plates was included at the back. It didn't take Nina long to realise that they were clearly intended to illustrate the racial superiority of the Scandinavians, and the inferiority of not only the Sami, but also the Tartars, Jews, Finns, Balts and Russians. The caricature even extended to the types selected to illustrate the Scandinavian peoples: students, pastors, business leaders and doctors, while the other photographs looked like criminal mugshots. Indeed, many of the people chosen to represent the 'sub-races' were actual criminals. Nina was shocked. She looked up.

'The two Swedish researchers were highly cultivated men, perfectly charming,' said Mons. 'Their conversation was fascinating and often very funny – one was a Social Democrat, the other a staunch Conservative. They sometimes disagreed on matters of race. The Social Democrat spoke in terms of the coming welfare state – the march of progress, which antisocial elements could not be allowed to hinder. The other man applied a more overtly racist logic. I should point out that very many academics were pro-German in Scandinavia during the war. We French were horrified by their views. At night, in camp, we had some very lively discussions. But we were worlds apart, in truth. Privately, Paul-Émile was furious. He saw how the Swedes manipulated scientific facts to their own ends. But we needed them nonetheless. And they had done a great deal of work on the Sami. To them, the Lapps – as they called them – were an inferior race, doomed to extinction. Their arguments often sounded rather like those advanced today with regard to the inevitable demise of the polar bear – can you imagine? It was revolting. Quite revolting.'

'And the drum?'

Mons continued, apparently disregarding Nina's question. 'The guides were aware of our disagreements. One of them was particularly sensitive to it, because he had been a subject of the Uppsala gentlemen's scientific studies. They had measured his skull, as they had those of hundreds of people.'

Henri Mons got to his feet and invited Nina to follow him. They walked the length of a panelled corridor decorated with small gilt-framed paintings of Arctic hunting scenes, each topped with a brass lamp. At the far end, Mons's study was a spacious room with book-shelves on two walls and a small two-seater divan in the corner. A large cupboard partly filled another wall. A mahogany desk was placed diag-onally, almost facing the door, with a large window to the left. Henry Mons took his place behind the desk and invited Nina to sit opposite. The old man had clearly planned their meeting very carefully. Neat piles of papers had been placed within reach, to his left. First, how-ever, he showed Nina a photograph to his right. He leaned across, holding it out for her to examine. Nina bent forward in her seat.

'This was the beginning of the expedition. Paul-Émile is in the middle, of course, with the Latarjet brothers to his right, and the Swedish and German researchers to his left. The Swedes are the two stood right next to him.'

'And this is you,' said Nina, pointing to a man with a frank, open smile, standing to the right of the French doctors.

'Exactly. In my prime! Ah, I would have tried to work my charm on you back then, Mademoiselle, believe me,' he said, with what was clearly intended as a gallant smile. 'And here are our three guides, our interpreter, and our cook.' Mons ran his finger over the photograph.

The printed caption noted that the picture had been taken in the foyer of a Finnish hotel. The group posed stiffly, as in so many pre-war portraits, like solemn heralds of the dreadful events to come. Everyone was dressed in thick overalls, clearly about to set off. The Sami guides were wearing their traditional costume: moccasins with pointed, upturned toes tied into place with straps criss-crossed around their calves; light-coloured reindeer-skin trousers and woven wool tunics decorated with braid. The photograph was in black-and-white, but Nina recognised the royal blue cloth and multicoloured strips still worn by the older Sami at the market in Kautokeino. The Samis' differently shaped hats indicated their region of origin. She noted that one of the guides wore a four-pointed hat, like Aslak.

Henri Mons pointed again to the German geologist.

'Poor Ernst. He had been to Lapland before, but he wanted to go there again with us, to revisit a particular place. He died on our trip. He had gone off for several days to make a survey of a location that interested him, taking one of the Sami guides along. But on the way back, he suffered a fatal fall. He was buried in the cemetery in Kautokeino. Ernst was not like his fellow Germans – he never spoke about politics, never said anything for or against Hitler. And he showed no interest in the racial issues that obsessed the two Swedes. Mostly, he kept himself to himself. I surprised him one evening, working by the light of his lamp. I could see he was making notes on a geological map, but he covered it up when he saw me coming. I didn't ask what he was doing, of course. We geologists always respect one another's little secrets.'

'Who is this man, with the four-pointed hat?' asked Nina.

'Ah, you mean the devil's hat.' Mons smiled. 'That's what the devout Christians called it, in the Far North. The devil's hat. That was Niils. I don't remember his family name. He was the guide who set off with Ernst and who broke the news of his death to us. He was very badly shaken. He felt responsible, I think. Ernst died when he, Niils, had gone off to kill a reindeer for food. Apparently, Ernst had fallen into some sort of crevice, invisible under the lichen. His head was smashed on the bare rock. Yes, Niils felt guilty. I had become quite friendly with him. I understood his humiliation at the Swedish researchers' views. But he would never speak out. I think he thought that all White men – his phrase – shared the same opinion of the Laplanders. His shame was apparent in his expression: a mixture of pride, distance, incomprehension at times, even terror. I was deeply moved by what I saw. I didn't dare speak to him about it at first, because we had to go through the interpreter, but I showed him, with my own expression, that I knew how he felt. Towards the end of our trip, when I knew I could trust our interpreter, we talked about it one evening. I was dreadfully affected by what I discovered, because it revealed the most extraordinary injustice.'

Mons paused for a moment. Nina saw the beginnings of tears in his eyes.

'I think you should get some rest now, Father,' said Paul, entering the study. Mons looked tired indeed. He made a show of protestation but finally agreed to take a nap. Nina would have to wait.

25

Tuesday 18 January

10.30 a.m., Kautokeino

André Racagnal parked in front of his room at the Villmarkssenter. Each had its own front door, motel-style, and guests did not need to pass through reception on their way in or out. He was free to come and go undisturbed from his wing of the building. He had taken a suite: one bedroom and one large sitting room, where he stored all his equipment before loading it into a set of sturdy trunks for transportation. His preparations for the expedition were unaffected by recent events.

Racagnal took out his rock hammer. He had left it soaking overnight in a bucket of water, to swell the wood of the handle and prevent it from splitting. It was a Swedish model, with a long shaft, also useful as a hiking staff in difficult terrain. Efficient, too, because its long handle gave extra momentum when it came to breaking rocks. He did a final check on his instruments, each in its proper place: his camera, the GPS – though he hardly needed it, nor knew how to use it – his magnifying glass. He had a compass, a stock of soft-leaded pencils for drawing and some coloured crayons, too. Next, he opened a box full of maps, taking time to select the ones he would need, drawn to differing scales, making sure to take several copies of each. Sixty altogether. He began by loading a metal trunk into the back of his Volvo, followed by the rest of the equipment. He took enough clothing for two weeks, and food for two people, for the same length of time.

He thought of stopping in at the pub, but quickly decided it was a bad idea. Shame. For now, at least.

Instead, he focused on recalling the map he had glimpsed briefly at the old farmer's place. It was highly detailed. He would have to compare it with each of the maps he was taking with him. He knew from experience that geological maps never represent the landscape exactly as it appears in reality. Old and modern maps of the same section of terrain could look completely different. It would be painstaking work, but not impossible. He had an eye for it. He was good at his job and he knew it. Once he had pinpointed a location, he could begin his analysis of the terrain. And then he would be in his element.

He hadn't said anything to Olsen, but the map seemed to indicate scattered samples, fragments of some unidentified mineral, rather than a concentrated seam. Indicators like that were priceless – if they were properly marked and accurate. But mineral traces in the surface rock were no guarantee of a seam below, except in the imaginations of treasure-map geologists. And Racagnal was no treasure-map geologist. On the contrary, he was well known in the profession for his formidable intuition, based on a flawless ability to read the geologies of the regions he worked in and an encyclopaedic knowledge of geological structures, acquired on his many travels. He could read a landscape better than almost anyone else in the business.

He stopped at the service station to fill his jerrycans with petrol. Then he headed out to Olsen's place. He had work to do.

26

Tuesday 18 January

1.30 p.m., Paris

Nina took a walk outside to collect her thoughts. She was disturbed by what she had heard so far – horrified by some of it. She had grown up firmly believing that the Nordic countries had created one of the best, most just societies in the world. Perhaps Mons's account of skull measurements, the racial biology institute, was exaggerated. She had never heard about it before. It couldn't have been that important.

Paul buzzed her back into the hallway seconds after she had pressed the bell. 'Come in. My father has finished his nap. He's very eager to continue your discussion. I think he still has a great deal to tell you.'

Nina went straight into the study and sat down opposite Henri Mons. The old man looked up from a document he had been reading.

'Niils was a man of many talents, Mademoiselle,' he began immediately. 'Like most Laplanders, he had no formal education. Not as we would understand it, at least. But he was highly sensitive, intelligent. He seems to have had something of a gift as a shaman. As for me, this was my first visit to Lapland and I knew very little about these practices. Paul-Émile was fascinated by them and knew a great deal more. He had already had occasion to observe shamanic rituals in Greenland and was passionately interested. But it was to me that Niils confided his feelings, as I have already mentioned. As I was to learn later, a true shaman never tells anyone that he is a shaman. But I did know that Niils was deeply anxious.

'The anthropologists' views infuriated us French, but the Sami did not feel anger like us. No – they felt fear, and with good reason. They lived in Scandinavia and would remain there after we had gone home. I have no idea what their perception was of the impending crisis in Europe, the rise of Hitler. Even we hadn't fully understood what was afoot, after all. But Niils had a sense of foreboding. One evening, he drew the interpreter and me aside, then took a drum out from under his cloak. From what I could tell – we were looking at it by the light of an oil lamp – it was a magnificent piece. And in very good condition. It was oval in shape and scattered with small symbols that I found it difficult to make out.

'I asked Niils what it was, and he told me the drum belonged to him. It was a very solemn moment, and I sensed that this was not the time to conduct a scholarly interview about it, though I was longing to do so. I was very excited, too, because I knew that to find such a drum was one of Paul-Émile's long-cherished dreams. I would have to be patient. Niils told me that it was in danger. I said I didn't understand, and he explained that in light of the racial theories gaining credence at the time, anything pertaining to his people and their lifestyle was under threat. I tried to reassure him, but I could see that he was genuinely alarmed. And I have to admit that even though I tried to put a brave face on things, I knew he was right.

'That was when he asked me to take care of the drum, to take it back with me to France and keep it safe, but to return it eventually to Lapland at a time of my choosing. He trusted my judgement. I must confess, Mademoiselle, that I was deeply touched by his show of trust, more than I can say. I was the repository of one of the treasures of Sami civilisation.'

183

Henri Mons paused for a moment. He had spoken eloquently, moved by his vivid memories. Nina touched his forearm. The old man returned her smile – a tacit expression of gratitude for this moment to catch his breath. Nina was similarly affected, but for different reasons. This stranger had made her aware of an uncomfortable truth about her home country, a truth she had known nothing about until now and which she found hard to assimilate. She would need time to adjust to this new perspective. She was grateful for the inquiry – a rock to cling to.

It was early afternoon. Henri Mons asked his son for more tea. While they waited, he sorted through a handful of photographs taken during the expedition, attractive pictures of the everyday lives of people encountered along their route. There were Sami families inside their tents and some family groups posed out of doors. Some of the photographs showed mothers holding their swaddled babies in cradleboards. Some breeders had had themselves photographed standing next to a reindeer – doubtless the head animal of their herd, their favourite. Looking at the pictures, Nina saw an entire people on their guard. One thing struck her: almost no one smiled. And when anyone did, the effect was so forced, so out of place, that it was almost embarrassing. She glanced quickly through the remaining photographs. A few showed members of the expedition posing with groups of Sami.

'Did you know that Lapland is a fascinating area, geologically?' said Mons. 'Rich in mineral deposits. There were many mines active at the time, not least the iron-ore mine in Kiruna. The Germans showed a great deal of interest in that. The Nazis' armoury was made from Kiruna iron ore. But I remember rumours circulating about a vast gold seam. Some people spoke of it almost as a kind of legend. We were surprised, because it had seemed to us that the Sami were not especially concerned with material wealth, in that way. At the time, they were still living an essentially nomadic life. But rumours about the fabulous seam were rife. When Niils entrusted me with the drum, he gave me to understand that it was linked to the gold in some way. But he became very – how can

I put this? – very solemn when he spoke about it. He told me the seam was cursed, that it had brought great sorrow to his people. And this was another reason why the drum had to be kept in a place of safety, far away from Lapland, so that the truth about the seam would not fall into the wrong hands, at the wrong time.'

'What was the curse he referred to?' Nina wanted to know.

'You will accuse me of a dreadful lack of curiosity, Mademoiselle, but I did not ask about it at the time. I was caught up in the solemnity of the moment, the feeling that we were watching the dawn of a political cataclysm, the magical but sinister atmosphere – the lamplight, the dark, hostile wilderness all around, the deafening wind, so far from my own civilisation, with this man, his extraordinary face, his four-cornered hat. It was quite overwhelming, I assure you.'

'And what do you think about it now?'

'I believe the drum is connected to the story of the gold seam, but as to the curse, I really have no idea. How could the seam affect the fate of his people? I do not know. Had they been deprived of pastures that were rightfully theirs? Or land routes vital to their seasonal migrations? Had the mine resulted in the loss of livestock, had the reindeer been starved and died? Or did the curse touch the Sami themselves? I have asked myself these and many other questions.'

'I was given to understand that we have no pictures of the drum?' said Nina.

'Almost certainly not, if Juhl hadn't photographed it before the theft. I certainly don't have any.'

'But you must be able to tell me what the drum looks like.'

'You overestimate my powers of recall, Mademoiselle. But I will try to describe it for you. Now, let me see . . .'

Mons closed his eyes and kept them closed for some time.

'A horizontal line, drawn across the upper part of the drum, divided the surface into two. I remember that in this upper section there were stylised reindeer and one or two quite simply drawn human figures, also very stylised. I would guess they were hunters, but I couldn't be sure. I think there were trees and maybe some mountains, though the peaks may have indicated tents.'

Nina scribbled in her notebook, glancing up at Mons, who sat with his eyes still closed.

'The bottom section was more complicated. There was a cross in the middle, with different symbols on each branch of the cross and at the centre, too, contained within a small lozenge shape. What else? There were other symbols around the edges. Stylised, simple figures. And others, more elaborately drawn. Deities, perhaps. And there were fish and a boat. One motif that struck me – I remember it quite clearly – was that of a snake. I think there were more trees and mountains, and other symbols that were more difficult to interpret. I always meant to do some research on these, but you know how it is – I had a thousand other matters to attend to. I respected Niils's wish – I showed the drum to no one. And I did not photograph it, or have a copy made, for the same reason. Paul-Émile resented that, of course, but I know he respected my integrity.'

'Who else knew of the drum's existence?'

'Very few people altogether,' said Mons, after a moment's thought. 'Until I told Juhl about it, at any rate.'

'Did anyone contact you about it?'

'Oh yes! A piece like that inevitably attracts jealous collectors. It didn't have the monetary value of a work of pre-Columbian art, naturally, or an Egyptian antiquity, but I can safely say that it was a very fine object – an absolutely unique work, it would seem. And a testament to a dramatic period in Scandinavian history. All the drums are, as you must know.'

Nina remembered Olaf's accusations, calling Pastor Jonsson a drum-burner.

'Who contacted you?'

'Well, most recently there was a German museum in Hamburg. I think they worked with Juhl in Kautokeino. They wanted to see the drum, provide an estimate of its value.'

'But you showed it to no one . . .' Nina nurtured a faint hope that Mons might have chosen to reveal it to the museum experts. They might even have photographed it.

'They never came, in fact. And I sent it directly to Juhl in the meantime. As I recall, two other people got in touch over the years. One was from a museum in Stockholm, and another was a gentlemen who did not make his identity known – a dealer, I think, acting on someone else's behalf; a collector, no doubt. I assumed they were people Paul-Émile knew and had spoken to about it. But I had no intention of selling it, so their approaches came to nothing.'

'Have you kept the names of the museum and the intermediary?'

Mons looked through one of the piles of papers, eventually found what he was after and noted the details on a sheet of paper, in a fine hand, using a fountain pen. Nina glanced at the sheet. The Nordiska Museet in Stockholm. The intermediary's name looked Norwegian. There was an Oslo telephone number.

He gave Nina permission to take the photographs away with her, together with a handful of documents relating to the expedition.

She was about to leave, but paused for a second on the landing outside the door.

'Why did you decide to return the drum to Kautokeino now?'

'Because of my great age, first and foremost, Mademoiselle,' replied Mons, with a tired smile. 'I do not want the drum to be lost to the Sami after my death. I asked myself whether returning the drum now would have gone against Niils's wishes. And it seemed to me that it did not. There can be no doubt that the ideas circulating before the war have no credence whatever in modern-day Scandinavia. I hope that I am not proved wrong.'

27

Tuesday 18 January

3.30 p.m., Kautokeino, Highway 93

André Racagnal pulled up in front of the Olsen farmhouse. The old farmer had seen him arrive and stood waiting on the doorstep. He couldn't make the Frenchman out; he gave nothing away, so it was hard to tell what made him tick. He wasn't as easily manipulated as someone like Brattsen. But there was his taste for young girls, of course. Rolf had been quick to pick up on that. Any right-minded person would have taken exception to the police officer's insinuations. Not him. God almighty. He'd been outraged all right, but only at the prospect of being blackmailed. Nothing else.

The old geological map was on the kitchen table. Racagnal walked across and picked it up immediately.

'Remember,' Olsen told him, 'time is running out. We need to file an application to prospect with the regional Mining Administration, so that it can be approved by the mining affairs committee here in Kautokeino after that. Things move fast with the Administration, they have people working more or less round the clock, but the local committee takes decisions only at the scheduled meetings. We can't miss the next meeting – the one that's just been postponed, or we'll be too late for the licence round at the beginning of February. It's now or never.'

Racagnal's silence was disconcerting. Olsen pointed to a spot on a second, modern map of the region.

'Aslak is here. He's a strange character, but definitely the best guide. I'm sure you'll find a way to talk him round,' he said, turning his body to look at Racagnal.

Still the Frenchman said nothing. He pored over the two maps, then folded them, glanced at Olsen and turned to leave.

The geologist headed north, then turned east on the Karasjok road. Aslak was over this way. The farmer's words of warning left him unfazed: 'A strange character.' The old fool had no idea. No idea at all. The strangest Aslak in the world couldn't possibly be worse than Commander Chuck. Olsen was a pitiful hick who had never left his own godforsaken hole. That much was obvious.

Racagnal made for a small roadside café. Renlycka, the Lucky Reindeer. He'd spotted it before, the only place between Kautokeino and Alta, at the intersection with Highway 92, as it turned east. He parked outside. Once the expedition was under way, he'd be forced to sleep in whatever shelters or trailers he could find, or in his tent. That didn't bother him. But for the work he had to do right now, he would be far more comfortable inside.

There were no other customers. A woman aged about sixty emerged from a small room at the back and installed herself behind the cash register, saying nothing. She was a Sami, wearing an apron in the same bright colours as the traditional Sami tunics. Racagnal sat at a long table in the corner, near the windows. Ten or so tables in pale wood, with chairs to match, were laid with small, embroidered mats representing scenes of Sami life: reindeer marking, traditional reindeer caravans, sorting the animals into corrals. Small tealights had been placed on each table in glass pots. The woman came to light the one on Racagnal's table. A glass vitrine displayed handicrafts, Sami dolls, small tambourine-style drums covered in naive figures, stickers. From here, he could see the road skirting the foot of a low hill and, to one side, the vast expanse of wilderness he would soon be venturing into. The scene looked peaceful enough, slumbering under a blanket of snow. But he knew that wasn't going to last.

He took out the maps, then walked over to the till. The Sami woman sat waiting and stared at him dully. He ordered a sandwich and coffee, and paid. The woman thanked him.

'Do you know Aslak?' he asked.

She stared at him for a long time before answering.

'Yes.'

She waited again.

'Is he easy to track down?'

'No.'

'Can you tell me how to find him?'

Silence.

'No.'

Racagnal didn't like being caught unawares. He stared hard at the woman, forcing a smile. She lowered her eyes. He turned and walked back to his table.

Finally, he unfolded Olsen's geological map as well as a handful of the other maps he had brought along. He needed to act fast. Kautokeino's mining affairs committee had postponed its meeting until the following day. He had to locate the area where he would prospect for the seam and call the details through to Olsen before then. The old farmer had promised to complete the paperwork in time and secure approval for both applications to prospect – his own, and the SFR's. Now Racagnal would make this damned map talk.

6 p.m., Kautokeino

Nina arrived back in Alta late that evening. Klemet came to fetch her. She appreciated the gesture.

'We're expecting the full forensic report tomorrow,' he said. 'Not before time. So how was Paris?'

On the hour-long drive back to Kautokeino, Nina delivered a full and faithful account of everything she had learned from Henry

Mons. When they passed the spot where she had hit a reindeer the day before, she gave a brief report of her accident and Aslak's strange response, the gift of the small piece of jewellery. Klemet showed no reaction and she returned to her meeting with Henri Mons.

'That business about the racial biology institute is absolutely extraordinary. Incredible,' she said.

'Yeah, I guess.'

'Don't you find it revolting?'

Klemet drove, concentrating on the road ahead. He turned to look at her, said nothing, then looked straight ahead once more. They had reached the edge of Kautokeino. The town was dark and quiet.

'We'll get a coffee at my place.'

It was not a question. She was happy enough to make a return visit to Klemet's tent. The car came to a halt and he pointed to her bag.

'Bring that with you.'

Nina stared at him quizzically, her head tipped slightly to one side, pondering her colleague's proposition.

'I mean, bring the documents from Paris in with you.'

'Oh, of course.'

He could have sworn she was blushing and decided he would play along.

'Do you want to take a shower?'

Nina stopped in her tracks. She had no idea whether her colleague was teasing her or not, but declined the offer politely. Klemet trudged through the snow and lifted the tent flap to allow her to step inside first. He put some logs on the hearth. The fire, almost extinct, soon sprang into life. Nina relaxed and looked around in delight.

'Klemet, would you mind taking a photo of me in front of the fire?'

He forced a smile. Nina held out her camera. He knew what to do and focused on the flames. Nina thanked him, checked the picture and gave a small, irritated sigh.

'Klemet, I'm all in shadow. You know perfectly well if you're taking a picture with a light source from behind, you need to—'

'Give me the camera.' He was losing patience.

Another picture, very slightly askew. Nina seemed satisfied with the result, put the camera away and took out the file. She handed him the first photograph Mons had shown her and described the different members of the group.

'Who took the picture?' asked Klemet.

Nina stared at him, caught red-handed. She hadn't thought to ask.

'What will you have to drink?'

'An alcohol-free beer.'

He took out two bottles and poured himself a glass of three-star cognac. An old habit – the sole remnant of his Laestadian upbringing. In his family's hard-core branch of Laestadianism, alcohol was strictly forbidden, with one exception: three-star cognac for medicinal purposes only. He had always been amused by this. Three-star cognac remained his brandy of choice – one way of not completely denying his origins. He drank half the glass, followed by a long sip of beer.

Nina sat next to her partner this time, her legs stretched out on the reindeer skins. She looked at the photographs hanging overhead in the tent, her mind buzzing with the events of the past two days. Klemet's question bothered her. She took out the other photographs entrusted to her by Henri Mons. There were fifty in all, mostly depicting scenes of Sami life. Fifteen showed members of the expedition team at different stages on the trip. Klemet separated them into two lots. Members of the research team appeared in every picture, though not everyone was present in every photograph. Apart from the formal group picture in the lobby of the Finnish hotel, at the start of the expedition, all the photographs had been taken out of doors, either in the tundra, or at their camp. The later pictures were less posed, suggesting the busy life of the expedition, in tough conditions.

'There. That man isn't on the first photograph.' Nina pointed to a figure, shorter than the Swedish and Norwegian scientists, though he was not Sami, it seemed. They found the same man on a second photograph. He seemed strangely out place, as if slightly apart from the rest of the group. He had a fine, narrow nose and a moustache covering the corners of his mouth. 'I'll ask Mons about him.'

She leafed through the other photographs and found the man again. She spread out all the pictures between them, in several rows. The fire gave just enough light to see by. She sipped her beer. Klemet did the same, poring over the images. He took one, turned it over and discovered what he was looking for: the date.

'Sort them into chronological order.'

They rearranged the sequence and pored over the pictures once again.

'What are we looking for, exactly?' asked Nina after a while.

'I'm not sure,' he admitted. 'But we know something happened on the expedition, something involving the drum, these men.'

He had drained his cognac, and served himself another small shot.

'Well, if we're tracking the drum, the logical thing would be to track Niils, the Sami guide. He's in the first pictures and the last.'

'But not in the middle,' said Nina. 'He isn't there, because he went off with the German geologist.'

Nina turned over the last photograph showing Ernst and Niils with the rest of the group, then the next picture in the sequence, without them.

'This one's dated twenty-fifth July, and that one twenty-seventh July. So Ernst and Niils left in the last week of July 1939.'

'And here,' Klemet pointed to one of the photos, 'Niils is back. Alone, of course, because Ernst has been killed.'

He turned the picture over.

'Seventh August. And the preceding picture, without him, is dated ... fourth August. So Niils came back sometime between those two dates.'

He let the photograph fall and sank back against a long, low chest covered with cushions.

'Niils comes back highly disturbed from his mission with the German geologist, and shortly afterwards he confides in Mons and entrusts him with the drum.'

Klemet put down his glass and picked up the file of documents relating to the expedition. There was a certain amount of official correspondence, together with lists of equipment, letters of introduction, sheets of expenses, tickets, a whole pile of uninteresting, yellowing paperwork. Klemet searched for any mention of the drum. Finally, he found one, on a customs docket.

Under the heading 'Description' a handwritten note in Swedish read: 'Cheap handicrafts'. Under 'Value', the same hand had noted 'Nil'.

6 p.m., Highway 93

André Racagnal's mind leaped from valley to valley, following the curves of the geological contours dancing before his eyes. Five maps were spread on the table in front of him. He homed in on Olsen's once more. He could easily imagine the hours its maker must have spent in the field, identifying the geological formations, looking for fossils, tracing the outcrop patterns, where the different bedrocks became visible on the surface. Racagnal was taking his time, though he had precious little at his disposal. The old map seemed to suggest a granitoid pluton in the Finnish province of Karelia, making the rock around 1.8 billion years old. The European Far North was one of the oldest terrains he had studied.

When he wasn't out trekking in the field, studying these maps was the only way to chase his demons. Even then, the curves and contours could be dangerously evocative. Racagnal traced the lines on the map, muttering to himself. The plutonic rock had formed in the surrounding host rock, part of a shale belt. Racagnal read the maps with ease. The belt was composed of quartz, diorites and granites. It all made sense. Gold could be found in terrain of this type, no doubt about that. The real question, as so often, was whether the mineral was available in sufficient quantities, not too deep, and

194

whether the market justified embarking on the exploitation of a mine in the Far North, in difficult conditions, in terms of climate and human resources.

There was a lot to think about and Olsen's deadline gave him no time to come up with all the answers. Even a really competent geologist – especially a really competent geologist (and Racagnal considered himself one of the best) – needed time to get a feel for the terrain, to walk it, to follow his intuition, even if it drove the new recruits and bureaucrats crazy. Everything had to fit one of their models. They could never be expected to understand the workings of a mind like mine, Racagnal thought – nor his taste for very young girls either. The picture of purity. His only response – the only rational response, in his view – was to dirty that picture. Their innocence unsettled him. Terrified him. Challenged the way he felt about himself. He felt comfortable in the company of characters like Olsen – manipulative and crafty. Or that hard-faced cop. These people reassured him, confirmed his view of the world as a grey, shifting, unjust place.

The granite deposits had been eroded by the glaciers that had covered Scandinavia for millennia. The last great glaciers had retreated just ten thousand years ago, leaving smooth, bald summits in a landscape dotted with lakes. Olsen's map showed eruptive terrains forming a host of small veins. Its author had described quartz-pebble conglomerates, too. As he pored over the map one more time, the evidence looked pretty consistent, in Racagnal's view..

Geologically speaking, Lapland was a stable region, part of the Scandinavian belt, though faultlines existed in places. For geologists like himself, the faultlines were especially interesting. And there was one on the map.

He turned to the modern maps from his own collection. Most of the details indicated on the old map were absent, not to mention their scale, which was quite different. You had to know how to read between the lines. He stroked the curves with his finger. Other curves soon sprang to mind. Ulrika. That little minx had to go and get mixed up in all this. But that didn't matter now. If he found what he thought he could find here, she'd come crawling to him all over again, with her little angel face. Olsen would have some crawling to do, too.

7.20 p.m., Kautokeino

Before accompanying Nina home, Klemet had kept her at the tent for a few minutes more. He had something to say.

'Watch out for Aslak.'

She was about to object, but he placed a finger on her lip.

'Hear me out.'

She almost misinterpreted his gesture, but realised she was mistaken.

'Just now, in the car, you asked me why I wasn't horrified when you talked about the Swedish researchers. We only ever spoke Sami at home, on my parents' farm. When I was seven years old, I was sent to a boarding school where almost all the pupils were Sami. We were forbidden to speak our own language. The schoolmaster was Swedish. He spoke only Swedish. On purpose. They were turning us into little Swedish children. Things had moved on a bit since the war, certainly. People like Mons had been observing the death of the Sami as a people, recording what they could in the name of science. In my day, it was all about assimilation. Complete assimilation into Scandinavian society. Grinding us down. We were beaten if we spoke Sami, even in the playground. See this scar?'

Klemet pointed to his temple.

'I was seven years old, Nina. I was seven years old and I was forbidden to speak the only language I knew. I couldn't speak. So don't talk to me about seeming horrified, I . . .'

Nina watched in astonishment as her partner's eyes brimmed with tears. She had never seen him like this. He broke off and left the tent, holding the flap for her as she stepped outside. Then he let it fall back. The time for shared secrets was over.

*

The old Sami woman was still sitting behind her cash register, motionless and silent. She should have closed up by now, but she sat waiting. One other customer had come in during the past hour. A truck driver who had left his engine running outside.

'Evening, darlin'. Bored, are we? Fancy a bit of fun in the back of the rig? How about it, eh?'

The Sami woman stared at him in silence, showing no reaction.

The driver was Swedish, Racagnal noted, eyeing him briefly, taking in the tattoos plastering his forearms. The Swede roared with laughter and turned to Racagnal, certain his wit would be appreciated. Racagnal stared at him for a moment, then went back to his maps.

'Pardon me, I'm sure. *Hej*, old hag, any sign of my sandwiches? Sorry if I've interrupted the start of something beautiful between you two, eh?'

He roared with laughter all by himself, ignoring the geologist now, tapping his fingers on top of the cash register, waiting for the sandwiches, beating out the rhythm of a silent song. Probably a regular at the café, thought Racagnal. He hadn't needed to say what he wanted in the sandwiches.

The woman returned with two sandwiches wrapped in clingfilm. She placed a bottle of Pepsi next to the cash register, took out an exercise book and made a note of everything. On the slate.

'*Hej*, old hag. Look at the tits on that. Got me in your little black book of favourite customers, eh? Know just what I like, don't you? We should have some fun, you and me, I've told you before. Yeah, baby! Hands off old Sexy Sami, mate,' he called over to Racagnal. 'She's all mine! *Hasta la vista*, baby!' He left, slamming the door, still humming and tapping the fingers of his free hand against his thigh.

The Sami woman closed her notebook, shook her head quietly for a couple of seconds, then resumed her impassive pose behind the cash register.

Racagnal had made progress, meanwhile. Much remained to be

done, but by cross-referencing the information on the modern maps and identifying the geological structures, he thought he was getting somewhere.

The old map-maker seemed to have concentrated on the central section, which was much more thoroughly annotated. Racagnal thought he could see why. It was scattered with the yellow marks indicating metal, pointed out to him by Olsen. Racagnal, on the other hand, was much more interested in a geological deposit in the top right-hand section – a tertiary formation combining a fair amount of rubble and large rocks, mostly shale. This was also where two basement layers of differing ages rubbed up against one another. Here was the faultline he had spotted, marked by the unknown geologist with signs indicating marble deposits. The presence of marble in this area, even in small quantities, bothered Racagnal. He tapped his pencil on the map, thinking hard, then decided to leave that till later and focus again on the yellow markers, clearly suggesting an abundance of gold.

After another hour of calculations and comparisons, Racagnal was satisfied he had found three possible matches for the area described on Olsen's hand-drawn sheet. He spread the old map out flat and folded it over several times, hoping it would correspond to an area on the modern map. The two showed a number of variations and anomalies, of course, but these could be explained by the differences in the approach, the means and, of course, the professionalism of their respective makers. Setting all these aside, he saw clearly where he should search. In an ideal world, he would collect samples and analyse them back at base. But he had no time for that. He'd have to draw on every last scrap of his intuition and expertise. And he would need Aslak, given the few short days available. There wasn't a minute to lose.

He would radio the three areas through to Olsen, for the exploration permit. Play it by the book. His tracker's instinct was aroused. Racagnal felt the familiar adrenalin rush. Shame the old Sami woman wasn't a fresh little minx. As if reading his thoughts, she turned to look straight at the Frenchman for the first time, staring after him as he stepped out into the cold and dark.

28

Wednesday 19 January

Sunrise: 9.54 a.m.; sunset: 1.07 p.m.
3 hours 13 minutes of sunlight

8 a.m., Kautokeino

The radio announcement of the discovery of the second ear came as no surprise to anyone, though it was a terrible shock for the cleaner who found it, behind a door in the main hallway of the annexe to the Reindeer Administration offices in Kautokeino. It was barely 7 a.m. and no one was at work yet. As a rule, the door was kept open, and the woman had only closed it to run the vacuum cleaner behind. The ear must have been there for several days. No one had noticed, because the hoovering was done only once a week. Like the first ear, the second had been marked with incisions.

News of the find spread fast around town, especially because the cleaner had been unable to contact the police. Shocked and frightened, she had called her neighbour Tomas Mikkelsen, the reporter. He was sure to know what to do. Mikkelsen had arrived fifteen minutes later, microphone at the ready, and interviewed her on the spot. He was careful not to touch anything, but took photographs from all angles. A scoop of the first order. The police had tried to conceal the fact that Mattis's cadaver had been found minus its ears, but Mikkelsen had already heard the rumour. The second ear, shrivelled and curled, was incontrovertible proof, in his view, that this was an important case and more than a simple, if murderous, feud.

There was very little time before the eight o'clock bulletin. After that, he would post the photograph of the ear on the newspaper's website. It would be a busy day.

Tor Jensen's office was crowded and the Sheriff looked particularly out of sorts. He hadn't picked at his bowl of *salmiakki* yet. It was barely 8 a.m. Everyone present had just heard the radio news. Coffee was doing the rounds. Pastries were swiftly disappearing from two loaded trays. Brattsen appeared to be sulking, sitting in a corner at the back. Nina was in discussion with Fredrik, from forensics, who had arrived from Kiruna the previous evening with the forensic pathologist, Anders Sunneborn. The latter sat poring over his files. Fredrik seemed very interested in Nina, whispering quietly to her. Two other officers were present, from Brattsen's team.

The room was waiting for Klemet, who had gone to place the second ear in the Reindeer Police freezer. Located in the station's map store, the freezer held a curious assortment of exhibits including several reindeer ears, a couple of Siberian geese and other quarry from illegal hunting expeditions. Now the collection included two human ears.

Klemet returned holding a sheaf of documents. The Sheriff raised a hand, calling the meeting to order.

'The first ear has been identified as belonging to Mattis Labba, beyond any doubt,' said Fredrik.

'Same goes for the second ear, almost certainly,' added Klemet. 'Same size, same cutaway sections, same type of incisions too, though the marks are different.'

'So this definitely points to one of the breeders?' the Sheriff cut in. Klemet took his time pouring a cup of coffee.

'Well, I'm not so sure about that now,' he admitted. 'The cuts on the two ears still seem to indicate Olaf's clan, and Olaf himself, but it's a fairly loose interpretation, admittedly.'

Brattsen jumped to his feet.

'I've always said Olaf was involved one way or another. There's something not right about him. He's got a guilty conscience, you mark my words.'

'Let Nango finish, Brattsen.'

Brattsen sat down, clenching his jaw. 'Come on then, Chubs. Amaze us.'

Klemet ignored Brattsen, as usual.

'What I mean is, that's just one possibility, based on a fairly loose reading of the incisions, which may have been made in a hurry. And remember we're looking at them several days later, when the ears have atrophied. There did seem to be a likeness to Olaf's clan mark, but now that we have both ears, I'm less convinced. If we're looking for a strict comparison, then . . . Well, the marks don't correspond to anything in the handbook.'

A heavy silence greeted his words. The Sheriff signalled for Anders Sunneborn, the forensic pathologist, to take the floor.

'Doc, please. I hope you've got plenty to tell us – you've been rather quiet these past few days.'

Sunneborn flashed a broad smile at Tor Jensen.

'Procedure, Superintendent, procedure. And for us, as a transnational unit, procedure is even more important, so as to avoid any possibility of misunderstanding between our two exceedingly punctilious administrations. Procedure states that nothing is to be divulged, either by telephone or by—'

'I'm familiar with procedure, Doc. I would just like us to be given a somewhat higher priority than usual, for once. But that won't have crossed your minds, over in Kiruna.'

'Klemet has summarised the situation regarding the ears, but I'll come back to that in a moment. Just one clarification about the incisions. I haven't examined the second ear yet, but I imagine the same observation will apply. The incisions – meaning the marks made on the lobe and in the upper part of the ear – are clean-cut.

I mean that whoever was handling the knife did not think twice. The flesh is cut with some precision, not torn. There is no sign of multiple cuts, which might indicate that the person with the knife had changed their mind, going back over their work.'

He opened a file.

'Now, the cause of death. The examination found that Labba received a violent thrust from a sharp, pointed instrument, with a blade measuring between 3.5 and 3.8 centimetres at its widest point, apparently a knife identical or similar to the Knivsmed Strømeng models used by the breeders, found in the rod and gun stores here, and also popular with tourists as souvenirs. The wound is not that deep, but the force of the thrust is apparent from the fact that the knife passed through several layers of clothing. The murderer is strong – just one thrust was enough. Labba was wearing his snow-suit, two sweaters, one of which was quite thick, a shirt and two T-shirts. These layers of clothing also explain why very little blood was found at the scene – it was all absorbed by the fabrics. The wound was nonetheless deep enough to cause renal scarring. Judging by the apparent width of the blade, the corresponding length would be seventeen centimetres, which also corresponds to the depth required to pass through the layers of clothing and reach the kidney.'

He paused. Everyone was listening attentively.

'You see, a renal wound is not fatal, unlike a wound to the heart, for example. Which brings me to my point: Labba was not killed by the knife wound. Under normal circumstances – by which I mean, at normal temperatures, if the body had been indoors, for example – he could have survived for about six hours. But outside it was minus twenty, give or take a couple of degrees. He was well covered, well protected from the cold, but still, hypothermia would have set in very quickly. His suffering was all the shorter for that. And I would estimate the time of death at around one hour after the infliction of the knife wound.'

Sunneborn waited for this information to sink in.

'But that's not all. This brings me back to the ears.' He was working the room, for maximum impact.

202

'At the risk of disappointing some,' he paused, 'I can confirm that the severing of the ears was not an act of torture.' All eyes were on him now, some expressing astonishment and impatience.

'I can say this quite simply because Mattis Labba had been dead for two hours already, when the ears were severed.'

Glances were exchanged around the room. A low murmur circulated. Even Brattsen looked incredulous.

'Almost no blood flowed from the ears, barely a few drops, so we are already in the presence of quite advanced vaso-constriction. Bleeding does not occur after death because there's no circulation of the blood. If Mattis had been alive when the ears were severed, we would have seen far more bleeding. But in fact we see nothing of the kind. Added to which we have the effect of the extreme cold. The body had already begun to freeze when the ears were severed. Which explains the clean appearance of the flesh cuts.'

'Which means,' said the Sheriff, 'if your observations are correct, that the murderer would have spent three hours at the scene after stabbing Labba, perhaps looking for something, before cutting off his ears and leaving?'

The group sat deep in thought.

'Unless,' said Klemet, 'we're dealing with two different people.'

10.30 a.m., Central Sápmi

André Racagnal had found Alsak Gaupsara's camp without too much difficulty. Olsen had indicated the precise spot on the map. He hadn't needed the unhelpful old bag at the café after all. En route, he stopped in a small lay-by to take another look at the map. He could get closer by car and after that he would have to continue by snowmobile. He had made sure the track wasn't off limits – no need to attract unwelcome attention. He was less sure of how to approach this notorious breeder. Olsen's warning left him unfazed: he wasn't one to go to pieces over some nutcase with a scary reputation. On the contrary. He had plenty of form when it came to dealing with characters like Aslak.

He continued on his way, taking a short cut across country in the direction of a lake, frozen solid, like everything else. He drove slowly for a few kilometres and reached the shore, where a few huts stood waiting for their summer users – anglers from Alta or neighbouring villages. They were deserted at this time of year. Racagnal parked his Volvo, unloaded his snowmobile, hooked up his trailer and piled it with equipment. He made a final checklist. No room for mistakes on an expedition like this. He was naturally cautious, even extremely so. He hated leaving things to chance – something his colleagues misunderstood. Because Racagnal trusted to instinct when prospecting, they dismissed him as reckless, even negligent. The opposite was true. He trusted to instinct only once he had recorded every last detail, eliminated every possible uncertainty from what he knew. Only then would he set off, every sense honed and alert, the ultimate tracker.

He cast a glance at his surroundings. It would take him at least two hours to reach Aslak's camp. He would bivouac on the way in a shelter he had spotted on the map, then arrive early in the morning. Surprising people when they were half asleep gave you an undeniable advantage.

Aslak Gaupsara kept his breathing deep and regular. He moved forward, repeating the same movements over and over again. His skis glided almost without noise. He had one last, small valley to check, making sure that the small group of reindeer that had strayed yesterday had enough to eat. Aslak liked to feel his body responding without complaint to his most extreme demands. He was in no hurry. His day was almost over. He wasn't too worried about the reindeer. His herd was in his own image. Tough, capable of surviving in the most extreme conditions, impervious to the cold, resistant like no other creature on earth. They could sniff out lichen buried under two metres of snow, walk for days without eating to find pasture. And yet there was no more disciplined herd in the *vidda*, none more responsive to its breeder.

Aslak's three dogs were in their master's image, too. They knew how to find a lost faun, coax rebel reindeer back to the fold, block dangerous trackways, sniff out danger in the *vidda* before anyone else. All lived in perfect harmony with the surrounding landscape.

Aslak had had no formal education. He was not like the youngsters you came across sometimes in Kautokeino market, idealising his lifestyle and the old ways. There was nothing to idealise. This was his life. He understoood that he was different. And he understood, too, that living as he did, as his ancestors always had before him, was likely to provoke extreme reactions.

He was often asked why he refused the advantages of progress. Aslak didn't really understand what that meant. He saw the other breeders doing the same work as him, but with scooters and quad bikes, even helicopters, using electronic neck tags fitted with GPS transmitters. And to pay for all that, they needed even bigger herds, which meant greater expanses of pasture. And all that led to conflicts between the herders, under the beady eye of the authorities, who had found the perfect excuse to keep up the pressure on the Sami, make them do as they were told – keeping the peace out in the *vidda*, they said. Was that what they called progress? To be a slave to official census forms, and tax declarations, accounting for your lifestyle to people who understood nothing about it whatsoever? Small-time herders like Mattis, who just wanted a quiet, simple life, had been left with no choice. Aslak paused for a moment, leaning on his stick. He closed his eyes and clenched his fists, invisible inside his reindeer-skin gloves. Anyone watching would have thought he had stopped to collect his thoughts, perhaps even to pray. He seemed to be looking in upon himself, with a silent intensity. Mattis, he thought to himself, straightening up. That poor soul. He set off once more.

Some years, Aslak's reindeer were thin but they never starved. They retained a certain prestige, setting them apart from the other animals, the ones that were left to their own devices for too long by herders who got up too late, or were in too much of a hurry to get back to the warmth of their trailers. Aslak stopped on the crest of the hill. He could barely see in the dim light, but he knew what he was looking for. His dog never failed to lead him where he needed to go. After a quarter of an hour, he spotted the old reindeer. One of his toughest head animals, one of the wisest, too. A beast who always led his group to the right place, at any cost. Aslak trusted him. If he was there, you could be sure there was enough lichen to feed the others. He moved forward, quietly. His dog knew what to do. When his master moved closer to the great reindeer, he had to keep well back.

At Aslak's approach, the great reindeer lifted his head, surmounted by thick, elegant antlers. Slowly, he moved away just a few steps, then stared back at Aslak. Aslak glanced around, seeing other reindeer digging at the thin covering of snow. They seemed to have no trouble finding the lichen so they could stay where they were for a few more days. His great reindeer had found the right place.

Satisfied, Aslak turned to go, followed by his dog, and made his way back to the track leading to his camp. Back to his wife. He hurried on, redoubling his efforts, leaning on his stick, impervious to the freezing air rushing at his throat.

29

Wednesday 19 January

10.30 a.m., Kautokeino

The forensic pathologist's findings, and Klemet's theory of two suspects instead of one, sparked an animated discussion among the assembled officers. With a second suspect responsible for severing and marking the ears, the case was taking a new turn. Two suspects meant twice the likelihood of finding further evidence, new clues. There had to be something else, something they had missed.

The Sheriff called for quiet. To give everyone a chance to collect their thoughts, he asked Nina to summarise her visit to Henri Mons in France. Klemet listened as his colleague delivered a precise account of the main points, including the pre-war political background and the dark shadow cast by the Swedish ethno-biologists.

'The Swedes got something right for once.' Brattsen grinned. 'Joking! Of course!' This in response to a furious glare from the Sheriff.

'What about the various contacts who approached Mons about the drum?' he asked Nina.

'The Nordiske Museet tried to secure it for their collection, but pulled out when Mons made contact wth Juhl, here in Kautokeino. Which leaves the private dealer who contacted Mons, apparently acting as an intermediary. There's an Oslo telephone number, apparently. I can soon follow that up.'

Tor Jensen picked at his bowl of *salmiakki*. He looked uneasy. On edge.

'Any more from the crime scene?' he asked Fredrik.

The forensics officer from headquarters in Kiruna hadn't bothered to open the folder in front of him on the conference table. He straightened up in his seat and directed a smile at Nina.

'Well, hoovering the tundra wasn't a complete waste of time,' he said, with a sidelong glance at Brattsen. 'We managed to get some fairly clear prints of the scooter tracks. They don't match Labba's machine, and they run over the top of his tracks, so whoever made them arrived after him. But there's something else. The tracks are deep-set. To my mind, that means there were two riders on the second scooter. It's most apparent when you focus on the places where the scooter had to slow down. It sinks even further into the snow. Two riders on board, then. Make what you like of that.'

'Can you tell whether they left together, as well?' asked Klemet.

'I would say yes, they did.'

'Any way of identifying the machine?' asked the Sheriff.

'No. Obviously, if it's going to carry two men across the *vidda*, it would have to be pretty powerful. But there are plenty of powerful machines around here. I did find traces of grease on Labba's poncho. I was told he inherited it from his father. Took great care of it, unlike the rest of his stuff, it has to be said. So I was interested in the stain – it was clearly fresh. It certainly isn't animal fat. I don't exclude the possibility that it came from the murderer's snowsuit. The stain could have transferred in the struggle, when he stabbed Labba. Like the doc said, it was a powerful thrust. He may have pressed all his weight against Labba to push the blade home.'

'Fine, fine,' muttered the Sheriff. 'Anyone got anything else? If not, class dismissed.'

Klemet raised a hand.

'The GPS,' he said. 'Mattis's GPS. Have we been able to get

anything off that? I know his machine was set alight, but we might be able to find out something about his last movements.'

The Sheriff looked inquiringly at Fredrik.

'We're on to that, of course.' The forensic officer gave a thin-lipped smile. 'Going to need a few more days. Patience!'

Clearly, the GPS hadn't crossed his mind until now.

The meeting was over. Fredrik pushed passed Klemet, looking preoccupied, even shamefaced. Klemet couldn't resist whispering in his ear, to the effect that Nina already had a boyfriend. The Kiruna officer clearly fancied himself as something of a Casanova. Klemet didn't like that.

Leaving the Sheriff's office, Klemet tugged at the forensic pathol-ogist's sleeve while the other officers were dispersing along the corridors, then showed Sunneborn into his own office and invited him to take a seat.

'I have a question. It may not be important, but—'

'You mean you didn't want to ask it in front of Brattsen.' He was right, of course.

Klemet looked at him, saying nothing. His expression said it all.

'Klemet, everyone at headquarters knows the situation you're in, with Brattsen. But that makes it all the more important that you should be here in Kautokeino. Brattsen has allies further up the ranks. The Norwegians seem perfectly happy to have someone like him in a place like this, but, I can assure you, everyone on the Swedish side thinks you're doing a great job in the circumstances.'

'Which means no one's going to lift a finger to get him to shut up.'

'You know we can't do that, Klemet. Now, what was your ques-tion?'

'When you examined Labba's body, did you notice anything about the eyes?'

'The eyes?'

The question seemed to take the forensic pathologist by surprise. He gave it some thought.

'Anything in particular?' he asked.

'I couldn't be sure, but it seemed to me that the skin around them was very dark. Bluish in colour. Or purple. I remember Nina commented that he seemed to have very dark rings under his eyes. I wonder what to make of that.'

'I'll take a look when I get back to Kiruna,' said Sunneborn. 'I'll make it a priority this time. Promise.'

Nina was leaving the station, on her way to the stores, when she met Berit Kutsi. The older Sami woman gave her a kindly smile.

'So! How are you, Nina? I hope you aren't getting any bother from Klemet? He's quite incorrigible!'

Berit's mischievous expression was enhanced by the crow's feet at the corners of her eyes. Nina returned her smile.

'He's a great partner to work with. Don't worry. But I'm keeping your advice in mind,' she added, with mock seriousness.

'It's strange to think,' Berit went on, 'I've known Klemet since we were both young. He wasn't in the police force then. He was mad about cars and anything mechanical. And rather awkward when it came to girls. One of the superintendents here suggested he stand in when the station was short-staffed one summer. Klemet was a sensible boy. He didn't drink. Those were all the qualifications you needed here, then. He just drove the patrol van, to start with, but by the end of the summer he was in uniform and driving the inspector's car. That was when they sent him to the police academy in Sweden. Not before. And when he came back, all fit and muscly in his smart uniform, I think he decided to get his own back on a few people. One or two harsh fines here and there, but he soon got over that. And then he was posted to all the small towns in the region. Little towns like here. Being a policeman was much simpler back then.'

Her face darkened and she shook her head.

'I can't help but think of poor Mattis. So awful . . .'

'Did you know him well?' asked Nina, leading Berit gently into the shop doorway, out of the cold.

'Those boys, I've known them all since they were small. Mattis was a wild one, and—'

'Berit,' Nina lowered her voice. 'I need to ask you something. Between ourselves, please don't tell anyone else.'

Berit looked intently into Nina's face.

'There are rumours about Mattis. I've heard people say he was, well, "simple". Some say it was because his parents were ... closely related. Blood family.'

Nina detested herself for relaying Brattsen's malicious gossip. Giving it credence, in a way.

Berit looked at her, sadly. Gently, she clasped Nina's left hand.

'Nina, my dear girl. Mattis was a good, decent boy. A kind boy. I wish I could say as much for everyone here. So I can tell you this: what you have heard is wrong. I knew Mattis's father. I knew his mother, too. I helped her when she gave birth to Mattis. So you will understand my close connection to him. You don't want to say the word, my dear, and I don't blame you. So I will say it for you. Mattis was not a child of incest – which is the substance of that abominable rumour. It has even come to the ears of our pastor. And I have heard Karl Olsen spreading it around, too. I know him, I work for him at his farm. And I will tell you something else, Nina, because I see in your eyes that you have no prejudice against us, no wicked thoughts. Even today, people are still trying to bring the Sami down. I don't know why that should be so. Why it should be so hard to live together when there is room enough for everyone in the *vidda*. But that's how it is. I pray to Our Lord every day, but every day I see bitterness, jealousy, pettiness and suspicion.'

Nina placed her right hand on Berit's. The two women were a strange sight, standing in the entrance to the general stores to one side of the door, near the bottle bank. They looked out of place amid the toing and froing of shoppers and trolleys, hurried customers laden with grocery bags, children shouting and pushing.

'God's peace,' said Berit.

Nina gave her a parting smile, then disappeared into the shop. Berit stood for a long while, looking after the young Norwegian woman from the South.

*

Anders Sunneborn, the forensic pathologist, left for Kiruna with Fredrik, the Casanova from forensics. Klemet headed for home: his house, not the Sami tent in the garden. His house was home, after all, not the *lavu*, which even he considered a kind of exotic retreat.

Klemet's family were no longer breeders, though they had had their own reindeer mark once. Sami society followed a complex hierarchy, with the reindeer breeders at the top. Klemet's tent had been a show of bravado to begin with, a gesture to some of the local breeders, who looked down on him because he came from a family that had been forced to give up their herd. Luckily, most of the herders didn't think that way. They knew the rigours of the work too well to point the finger at people who, for whatever reason – weather, bad luck, sickness, predators – had quit. They knew the same thing could happen to them.

There were the hard cases, too, like Renson. Klemet was a collaborator in his eyes. But Renson's scorn was purely political, Klemet knew that, nothing to do with being exiled from the breeders' caste. Then there were characters like Johann Henrik, a herder of the old school. A real hard nut. Sly, too. But he owed nothing to anyone. Henrik knew his livelihood and lifestyle were hanging by a thread. Klemet didn't like Henrik, but he respected him. The same could not be said of Finnman, secure in his powerful clan, always ready to show Klemet exactly what he thought of him.

And so Klemet had decided to put up the tent one day, in his garden, just to infuriate arrogant types like Finnman. The neighbours had found it a little strange at first, but after a while they came to like the idea. Klemet, for his part, had discovered other advantages to the *lavu*. The mysterious tent, with its stylish, cosy interior, had acquired quite a reputation throughout the area, and it clearly appealed to the opposite sex. Only later did the tent awaken vague, folk memories of a distant past Klemet had never known, except in stories retold by his mother, and his uncle Nils Ante.

Klemet seldom went to the tent alone, spending his evenings indoors, at home. His house was far more conventional. Some visitors felt more comfortable there. Setting yourself apart from other people, with a tent in your garden, could give the impression that you felt different from everyone else. And feeling different meant feeling superior. Which was a sin, even a mortal sin, around here.

In the kitchen, Klemet helped himself to a glass of milk, and spread margarine and cheese on a slice of bread. He turned on the small TV next to the microwave, in time for the local news. Most of the bulletin was devoted to Mattis's murder, of course, but there were no new details. Speculation and supposition were rife. One breeder, interviewed anonymously, stated that what had happened was the result of deteriorating trust between the breeders and the authorities. Mutual suspicion that had been brewing for years. It was becoming harder and harder to survive in the business, he said, and people were driven to extremes. The breeder told of several cases of warning shots being fired at trailers in the *vidda*. Things would only get worse as climate change took hold, said an expert. Normally, there was far less snow in the interior, and the reindeer had little difficulty digging down to the lichen. But warmer temperatures brought alternating bouts of rain and snow. The rain froze and impenetrable ice layers meant the reindeer risked dying of hunger. With that came competition for access to decent pasture and heightened tension.

Next came an interview with Helmut Juhl. The German curator spoke about the missing drum and showed other drums on display at the Juhl Centre. He made a point of displaying one very fine example.

'This one was made by Mattis Labba. The buyer who commissioned it never came to fetch it. We're keeping it here, in memory of Mattis,' he said.

Klemet heard the reporter ask if the old Sami beliefs were still current in Lapland.

'Not that I'm aware of,' came the cautious reply. 'But everyone respects what they represent. Mattis may have believed in the power of the drums, to an extent. But it didn't save his life.'

The news presenter moved on to a new subject. Klemet felt a rush of sadness at Helmut's words. He emptied his glass and got to his feet. He hesitated for a moment, then reached for his bottle of three-star cognac in one of the kitchen cupboards. He pulled the cork, then froze, pushed it back into place and made himself a coffee first.

The TV news continued with a report on preparations for the UN conference. Tonight's angle was the economic benefits of the jamboree for the region as a whole. Some two hundred delegates would be visiting for several days. The report ended just as Klemet finished making the coffee. He uncorked the cognac again and poured himself a generous glass, then set cup and glass on the kitchen table and turned off the TV. He sat thinking for a moment about the TV report, and Nina's reproach when he had refused to consider her intuition of a link between Mattis and the theft of the drum.

Klemet freely admitted his almost obsessive need to tie every hunch down to palpable evidence. He sipped his coffee and drank some cognac. Nina wasn't bound by such constraints. The advantage of a proper education, he told himself. You're not afraid to think big, explore avenues, make mistakes, start again. He wasn't like that. Not at all, he thought to himself. Absolutely not. It was the price he paid for his Sami origins. He didn't want – couldn't afford – to put a foot wrong. He had to prove himself every step of the way. The fact was, he was afraid people would poke fun if he came up with anything too far-fetched. The garage mechanic getting above himself! He'd surprised himself in the Sheriff's office earlier, when he had floated the possibility of two suspects. He'd never admit it to a living soul, but he was proud that no one had mocked the idea. Not even Brattsen!

He drained the glass of cognac. He wasn't that far off retirement, and here he was moaning about his lot like an old woman. What with that and his adolescent insecurities, like a persistent bad smell.

And at his age. Klemet, he told himself, you're pathetic. He looked at his glass, drank more coffee and got up to pour more cognac. Did him the power of good. He felt a warm, spreading glow. He wasn't in the habit of drinking and now he felt that hint of intoxication. His usual signal to stop, telling him he'd had enough.

What had he been thinking about again? Mattis and the drum. Poor Mattis. He raised his glass and drank a silent toast. What did I know about Mattis, really? His father? Never knew him. A shaman? Not my world.

He, Klemet, had been raised a Laestadian. The real hard core. The ones who only drank cognac when they were half dead already. He filled his glass. Another toast.

'To the Laestadians!'

He drained it in a single gulp. He was feeling great now. Just that nice sensation of being slightly drunk. He was glad he knew his limits. Saw so many drunks on his patrols. Hated seeing other men get themselves into that state. The women even more. And the men, too. Undignified. He never understood why people had such a hard time knowing when to stop.

But what had he been thinking about? Laestadians, Laestadians. The Lutherans' crack squad. He'd had his fill of Laestadians. Must have been the only one in his family who didn't go to the big annual gathering in Lumijoki. The only one not to follow the precepts. His family took it all very seriously, of course. His great-grandfather had even been baptised by Lars Levi Laestadius himself. In person. That was enough to mark an entire family for generations! No alcohol. No dancing, no sex before marriage, no sport at school, no TV. No wonder they'd called him Chubby-chops. Watching the others dance. Snatching a quick snog under the Midsummer pole. Here's to the Laestadians!

Klemet heard a knock at the door. He checked his watch but it wasn't on his wrist. He got to his feet, found himself holding onto the table. Uh-oh. He chuckled. Good thing I know when I've had enough. He headed slowly towards the door, calling out that he was coming. No idea what time it was. Never mind. Couldn't be too late. Didn't feel tired. Yeah, those Laestadians. And their drum. Funny business. He opened the door. A pretty young blonde stood right there on the doorstep. Not only that, but she was smiling at him.

'I'm sorry to bother you, Klemet. I went to the tent, but you weren't there. I've been looking at Henri Mons's photographs and I think I may have found something ... Klemet? Are you OK?'

'Yeah, hi ... Nina!'

Klemet clung to the doorframe with one hand, bent forward and kissed Nina full on the mouth. A second later, he felt a sharp, stinging slap in exchange. The second after that, he found himself focusing – with some effort – on her retreating back.

30

Thursday 20 January

Sunrise: 9.47 a.m.; sunset: 1.14 p.m.

3 hours 27 minutes of sunlight

8.15 a.m., Central Sápmi

Aslak put more logs on the fire, rekindling the flames and lighting up the interior of the tent. His wife was still sleeping. It was good when she slept. She seemed not to suffer. Sleep was good for her. But she slept very little. She woke often. Often, she woke shriek-ing.

Aslak warmed his usual breakfast of reindeer-blood broth. Some years back, Mattis – when he was still in his right mind, not terri-fied of his own shadow – had invited him over to drink coffee and eat bread. Aslak hadn't liked either. Fortunately, the reindeer pro-vided for all his needs. As they always had. He had been born during a migration, a long time ago, it felt. He had suckled at his mother's breast in forty degrees of frost, but his mother had died after the birth and he had been raised on melted reindeer fat. The reindeer was a good animal if you knew how to take care of it. It fed people and clothed them. Skilled craftsmen knew how to turn its antlers into caskets, or knife handles, or jewellery. Aslak knew.

And he knew how to work silver, the Sami nomads' precious metal, the metal handed down from generation to generation, from migration to migration. He knew all these things. And he knew that, after him, it would all be lost.

He looked at his wife. They had met when she was a young woman. She had not suffered then. Not as she did now. Not as she had for so long. But she was in the grip of evil. And with evil, came misery.

Aslak ate slowly. Soon he would have to go back out to see to the reindeer. He was ruled by the law of the pasture. The reindeer followed the pasture, and the herder followed the reindeer. That was how it was. Sometimes, he would be gone for days. He was not worried about his wife. She would not starve. There was always enough for her. She could not live like others, but she knew how to survive.

She was still asleep when Aslak heard a snowmobile approaching. The radio had not announced any visitors. Aslak finished collecting his things. He was ready for his reindeer. The tent flap lifted and a man stepped inside. He kneeled down, facing Aslak, and smiled.

Aslak did not return his smile. He looked at the man for a long while, his jaw clenched. And he saw that evil had come again.

8.30 a.m., Suohpatjavri, Kautokeino

Klemet Nango woke in a pitiful state, having fallen asleep on his sitting-room sofa. He emerged from the shower, watched the TV news, drank a stronger coffee than usual and collected the *Finnmark Dagblad* from his mailbox. He didn't have a headache, the advantage of good-quality cognac. But he felt idiotic. Despicable. He couldn't believe he had tried to kiss his colleague. The very last thing he should have done, of course, though it had crossed his mind a few days before, in the Reindeer Police chalet.

Now he would have to carry on working with Nina, try to look her in the eye. Would she report the incident? If it reached the Sheriff or, worse still, Brattsen, his life wouldn't be worth living. He wouldn't be thrown off the force, but he might find himself transferred to a small station in some godforsaken hole. Back to the hellish, solitary patrols of all the bars in all the villages along the coast. He tried to remember everything that had happened the previous evening. A thought struck him, and he forgot all about feeling guilty.

Mattis and the drum. Nils Ante. He had to speak to his uncle. Nils was an old man now, but he was the only person Klemet could think of who might be able to answer his questions. What about Nina? He should take her with him, of course. But he couldn't face her just yet. She'd get over it, he knew that. Scandinavians were used to office parties. Colleagues getting intimate for an evening over too many drinks. Everyone suffering collective amnesia the following morning. The great unwritten rule. Nordic people were pragmatists, he thought. It had its advantages, he had to admit. Still, he decided to leave it a few hours before contacting Nina. He would go to Juhl's with her. But it was quite normal to visit family on his own. Yes, that's what he would do. He didn't want to let her know straightaway. He didn't want to have to apologise.

He called the station and told the secretary to leave a message on Nina's desk: he had to check something and would be back in the afternoon.

Twenty minutes later he came in sight of his uncle's house. By Nordic standards, Nils Ante was something of an eccentric. 'Not a joiner,' one might say. A marginal outsider. Someone different, in short. Unclassifiable. And unsettling, therefore, in a society that was the world champion of classification. For Klemet, Uncle Nils Ante had always represented the spirit of freedom denied by his own Laestadian upbringing. He had opened the doors to an extraordinary world. Klemet had lacked the wild spark needed to break away from his roots, but Uncle Nils Ante had planted a seed. A seed that flowered from time to time. Unconsciously, the idea for the *lavu* had come from him. Klemet's decision to join the police force could be seen as a victory for his upbringing. An assertion of strict values – though the Laestadians thought the law of the land was far too permissive and lax. But Uncle Nils Ante had breathed something of his spirit over Klemet's cradle.

His uncle lived in a simple house, about ten kilometres from Kautokeino on the south road. It had been painted yellow, a long time ago. The hamlet (population: nine) was called Suohpatjavri. Apart from the house, Nils Ante owned a barn painted Falun red, a tool shed and a fourth structure – a traditional conical tent supported on birch logs covered in moss and earth, with a heavy door, padlocked shut. No smoke rose from it.

Nils Ante lived alone, and this, too, singled him out from his Laestadian relatives and their large families. Klemet wondered why his parents had allowed him to spend so much time with this rebellious character. They must have regretted it, he thought, seeing as he had never managed to follow the Scriptures, and start a family.

The snow was pure white, undisturbed, reaching the windowsills in places. Small electric candles burned in each window. An old Chevrolet station wagon stood in the yard in front of the main house – another whim of his uncle's that had set him apart from the rest of the family. Klemet smiled at the sight of the car he had repaired so many times over the past twenty years. He hadn't been able to do anything about the rust – bodywork wasn't his thing. But the engine kept on going. Like his uncle.

Klemet sounded his horn twice. Nils Ante was getting old. He didn't like to be taken by surprise and the telephone wasn't his style. No one came to open the door. He sounded the horn again, in vain. Nils Ante's advancing age had left him hard of hearing, too.

Klemet forged a path through the thick, uncleared snow. He stamped his feet, opened the door and went inside. He removed his boots and explored the house, going from room to room. There was no one on the ground floor, but two coffee cups stood on the kitchen table. Yet Klemet hadn't seen another vehicle outside. He called his uncle's name and decided to look upstairs. At last he heard voices, speaking a language he didn't understand. Strange. Cautiously, he moved towards the room the voices were coming from and pushed open the door. Nils Ante was sitting with his back to it, rocking back and forth in front of a computer, beating time, wearing a set of outsize headphones. He was listening to music. Someone was sitting to his right. A woman. She was talking and wearing headphones, too. The computer screen was filled with the image of another woman, gesturing animatedly.

Klemet had expected anything but this at the house of his uncle, whom he had thought at death's door. Neither of the two had heard him enter. Klemet cleared his throat, not wanting to give the old man a heart attack. The woman turned around first. She was young, and not in the least alarmed. She tapped Nils Ante on the shoulder. Nils looked towards her. Finally he turned around. At the sight of Klemet, his face lit up with a broad smile. He took off the headphones and hurried to clasp his nephew in a warm bear-hug.

'Miss Chang, would you mind telling your grandmother you will call her back later? I'd like to introduce you to my favourite nephew.'

Nils Ante positioned himself in front of the camera and waved to the grandmother, signing off with words Klemet did not understand. The woman answered, smiling. The Skype connection was cut, and Nils Ante made the introductions.

'Klemet, this is Miss Chang. Miss Chang is the extraordinary individual who has saved my life by preventing me from becoming a doddery old fool. You know me, Klemet. You know how far I had slid down the slippery slope.'

'Don't exaggerate, Uncle, you were still—'

'Oh, enough of your false politeness, Klemet. It's true. But this delightful young lady is a rare pearl. She has energy enough for two, fortunately. Miss Chang is Chinese, as you can see. She came here last year with a group of farmworkers from the Three Gorges, berry-picking. They indebted themselves to get to Norway, and of course she was hoodwinked. You know how the berry-pickers are exploited. There was a solidarity concert for them. I saw her and, well, here she is. We had a fine time securing a residence permit, but we got there in the end.'

Nils Ante kissed the young woman, who must have been about fifty years his junior. She stroked his hair, tenderly.

'Miss Chang has no family apart from her elderly grandmother in China. She has a very up-to-date neighbour, fortunately, who has been able to install a small, inexpensive, uncomplicated computer, with Skype.'

Miss Chang held out a hand to Klemet.

'It was my grandmother who see you come in behind us, on the camera,' she said laughing, in near-faultless Norwegian.

'What were you doing with the headphones?' Klemet asked his uncle.

'I was on Spotify. Little Miss Chang-Chang showed me. Checking out the competition.' He winked. 'Some of the young *joïkers* today aren't bad. And you know I've an ear for it.' He pointed to the shelves lining the room, loaded with hundreds of cassettes. Recordings of traditional *joïks*.

Nils Ante adopted a stern expression.

'But what brings you here, Klemet? Spotted the vultures circling, did you? Worthless nephew!'

'You don't seem to be in any need of me to take care of you,' said Klemet, looking at the young Chinese woman nestled close to his uncle, stroking his chest. 'Can I ask you something?'

'Let's go and get some coffee. Miss Chang, send your grandmother a kiss when you call her back, and tell her I have almost finished her *joïk*.'

He took Klemet back downstairs.

'Extraordinary girl,' he said, making coffee. 'Well, Klemet, you've got plenty to occupy you at the moment!'

'That's really why I came to see you. I'm worried about the business with the drum. We're trying to see if there's a link between Mattis's death and the theft. But we don't know much about the artefact itself. I thought maybe—'

'Well, let's get one thing crystal clear, right now. Drums really aren't my thing. I'm a singer, a poet, whatever, but I want nothing to do with religion – even our own ancient religion.'

'I know, I know.' said Klemet. 'And that's why you're the only person in the family I can stand to be with.'

He took fifteen minutes or so to summarise the situation. Nils Ante knew almost everyone concerned. Klemet gave him all the information Nina had collected in France, too, trying to leave nothing out. When he had finished, he took a long drink of coffee and waited.

'Listen, Klemet. About Mattis's murder. I hope you find the culprit. I didn't know Mattis well, though I knew his father. An extraordinary man. But too absorbed in his mission to be a good poet. He had a screw loose.'

'What mission?'

'He saw himself as a kind of minister. He must have caught it from the pastors he fought against all his life. Because the Sami aren't given to preaching, as you know. Not when it comes to shamanism, anyway.'

'Yeah, I've heard all that already. The great, respected shaman, his unworthy son who couldn't match his father's legacy, and all the rest of it. But I—'

'Let me finish, Klemet. I'm intrigued by something else you said. The curse that you say Niils the guide talked about.'

'The curse associated with the gold seam?'

'Yes, of course, the gold seam. Klemet, stop repeating what I say, like an old woman. There are stories told in the *vidda*. Ancient stories.'

'Sure. I haven't come to hear all the old legends again, Uncle. I'm not seven years old any more.'

'Enough of your insolence! You enjoyed my stories back then.'

'And I'll listen to them again with great pleasure another day. But right now, I'm working a police inquiry. I need clues. And leads. Proof. Not some legend that's been doing the rounds of the *vidda* for centuries.'

'Fair enough. But you must accept, like it or not, that Sami culture has been written down only for the past half-century or so. Before that, everything was passed on by storytelling and *joïks*.'

Klemet fell silent. If his uncle got onto the subject of *joïks* they would be there all morning, and a long morning at that. Suddenly, Nils Ante began a chant. Klemet forgot his impatience. The song filled his consciousness. He felt all his old childhood emotions flooding back. His uncle had a remarkable talent. His chanting could transport you beyond the mountains, to the very heart of the wild dance of the Northern Lights. What was most fascinating, thought Klemet, was that even non-Sami who had no under-standing of the language were enchanted by the music of his *joïks*.

Nils Ante's song told of a cursed house, a malevolent stranger who cast a dark spell on its inhabitants, all of whom were struck dumb. Klemet was seized by a strange idea. He looked at his uncle, rapt and absorbed in his song, and wondered whether Nils Ante could read his nephew's mind. The *joïk* awoke memories of school, where his own language had been forbidden. The inquiry into the murder and the theft of the drum seemed a long way away. But the vision that sprang to mind from his distant youth left him troubled. He listened to his uncle's guttural singing, and the shadowy sil-houette of Aslak rose before his eyes.

31

Thursday 20 January

8.20 a.m., Central Sápmi

Racagnal shifted the weight from his knees, sitting himself down opposite Aslak without waiting to be asked. He maintained his smile, frozen now in a sinister rictus. Aslak observed the change at work in the stranger's face, saw the attempt to appear friendly. But the stranger couldn't fool him. Aslak knew the face of evil. He looked at his wife sleeping, savouring the few moments of peace afforded to her each day. The stranger's arrival had not woken her. Aslak breathed deeply, calmly. He waited, jaw clenched, his eyes fixed on the new arrival.

'My name is André. I'm a geologist. The people I work with here tell me you are the best guide in the region. I need your help. For just a few days. You will be well paid.'

The stranger spoke in odd-sounding Swedish. He affected his amiable expression again, but Aslak saw the true face behind the façade. Aslak knew how to read such things. The stranger opened a large bag. He took out some smoked salmon and black bread, pushing them towards Aslak, inviting him to help himself. Aslak ignored the bread but cut a piece of salmon, which he ate in silence. The stranger helped himself in turn, and cut a thick slice of black bread. He remained silent, too, and seemed to be in no hurry. His expression took on a new intensity when he noticed a movement behind Aslak. His wife had just turned over, presenting her sleeping face to the glow of the fire. Aslak looked at the stranger, and the stranger looked from his wife, back to Aslak.

Aslak had worked as a guide before. The request was nothing new. But he was busy with his reindeer now, keeping constant watch over his territory to make sure the other herds didn't mix with his own. He worked alone. He sensed that this man represented danger. Aslak knew nothing of fear. If anyone asked whether he was afraid, he would stare at them, uncomprehending. Mattis had asked that very question, once. He hadn't known what Mattis meant. Fear? Aslak disliked questions that had no meaning. People might ask whether he was hungry, or tired, or cold. But not whether he was afraid. Aslak knew the things he needed to know. Fear was of no use to him and so he knew nothing about it. But he knew how to recognise danger. That was an instinct. A matter of survival, whether the source of danger was a wolf, or a storm. Or a man.

'It's not possible now,' he said.

Clearly, the stranger had not been expecting a refusal. Aslak watched as his eyes narrowed. Like a fox stalking its prey. The man chewed slowly on his black bread. He took his eyes off Aslak for a moment and looked around the tent, as if taking a detailed inventory.

'I must insist,' he said, calmly. 'It's very important. And you'll be well paid.'

Aslak shook his head but made no effort to reply. And to show that he had finished with the stranger, he left the rest of his salmon and helped himself to a beaker of reindeer broth, sipping it slowly, staring hard at the geologist all the while. The stranger stared back, nodding slowly. All at once, he seemed to reach a decision. He gathered his things and got to his feet, half disappearing into the smoke.

'I would advise you to think again. You're alone here. It would be a dreadful thing if any harm should come to your head reindeer. Or your dogs ... Or anyone else you care about.'

The stranger wasn't trying to look friendly now. He fixed his gaze on the sleeping woman.

'I have things to do. I'll be back in two hours.'

He stepped outside.

Immediately, Aslak's wife opened her eyes. She was wide awake. Aslak saw that she, too, had sensed the presence of evil.

9.15 a.m., Suohpatjavri

'You know, dear nephew, the legends told out in the *vidda* aren't all hunting, fishing, migrations, love and poetry.'

'I've never heard anything else from you,' said Klemet.

'True enough. I have a fondness for the finer things in life.'

'You were saying that the business about the mine and the curse reminded you of something.'

'More than "reminded". There are many strange tales told in the *vidda*. Did you know, for example, that when the Karelians came, invading our lands, bringing the curse with them, we—'

'Karelians? You mean Russians?' Another thought occurred to Klemet. 'You think organised crime might be behind this?'

'Ignorant boy. I'm talking about the time before the Scandinavians. Over a thousand years ago. Two thousand, perhaps, for all I know, that's not important. When they invaded, we Sami lacked strength, but we had plenty of cunning. The Karelians were cruel, but very stupid. We lured them to the edges of precipices. Some places in the *vidda* are still known as the Russian Cliffs today, because the rocks and lichen are stained red. With the blood of the Karelian monsters.'

Klemet decided to say nothing. He took a deep breath. Patience. His knew his uncle wouldn't listen until he'd done his party-piece. Told a few old stories.

'I hope you haven't been telling Miss Chang about what the Sami did to their foreign visitors. You'll frighten her to death.'

227

'You think so? Oh, she has heard far worse tales than that, believe me. Stop interrupting an old man, Klemet. My days are numbered, indulge me for once. Yes, there is a legend about a fabulous seam. A hidden realm, deep underground. Unbelievably rich, but terrifying, dangerous, even fatal. The legend is a little like the story of the Karelian cliffs in reverse. Sami villages were decimated by a terrible evil brought by the White man.'

'The White man?'

'Try to keep up, Klemet! Has your uniform corrupted you to that extent? White men, the Swedes, the Scandinavians, the colonists, the invaders, call them what you will, but know that they brought with them a strange evil for us Sami.'

'What period are you talking about?'

Nils Ante frowned, thinking hard.

'It's a legend, of course. But it dates from the time when Sápmi was first colonised for its mineral riches. So the seventeenth century.'

'How could a gold seam decimate entire Sami villages?' said Klemet. 'And what would that have to do with the drum, the theft, or Mattis's murder today?'

'Well, you're the cop in the family.'

All at once, Klemet felt the lingering effect of his hangover. Which reminded him, he would have to confront Nina soon. He drank some coffee.

'The very existence of the legend is proof of a kind,' Nils Ante went on. 'Don't forget that, at the time, the Sami were press-ganged into working in the first iron-ore mines established here. Until then, they had had very little contact with the outside world.'

'I don't see the connection.'

'Think what happened to America's First Nations. They were decimated by diseases previously unknown to them.'

Klemet sighed. He rubbed his temples. Nils Ante's legends were taking them too far from the object of the inquiry. Still, he was intrigued by what his uncle had to say.

'How would you establish a link between this legend and the stolen drum?'

'There's your Sami guide, back in 1939, the man who entrusted the drum to the Frenchman on the expedition. There's the legendary gold seam. The curse. What was it the old gentleman in Paris said, to your young colleague?'

'He was making suppositions. He thought the gold seam was real, too, but that the curse might be linked to the destruction of pasture or migration routes, leading to the death of entire herds.'

'And back then,' said Niles Ante, 'the death of a herd meant the death of the Sami whose lives depended on it.'

'Fair enough,' said Klemet. 'But why would this drum in particular still be of interest to anyone today?'

'Well, we would need to see it in order to find out.'

'And there we are, right back where we started. Fuck!'

Klemet couldn't help swearing out loud. His uncle stared at him in astonishment, then amusement. Miss Chang popped her head around the door, making sure everything was all right, and disappeared again just as quickly. Klemet took another deep breath.

'Dear God, why didn't I think? We don't have any pictures of the drum. But I have a photograph of the shaman who gave it to Henry Mons.'

Klemet went outside and came back a few minutes later with an envelope. He spread a number of photographs on the table in front of his uncle, and pointed to the Sami guide.

'His name was Niils. We don't know his family name.'

'Look no further. That's Niils Labba.'

'Mattis's father?'

'His grandfather, Niils Labba. Mattis's father was called Anta. Funny, when you think of it, their two names come together to make mine. Niils was the grandfather Mattis never knew, I would think.' Klemet's uncle reckoned up the dates in his head. 'How old was Mattis? About fifty?'

Klemet took out his notebook. 'Late forties. He was born in 1963.'

'That's right. I think his grandfather died before or just after the war. As for Anta, Mattis's father, he died ... about five or ten years ago.'

Klemet rang his finger over the rest of the group in the photograph.

'These are the French, and those two are the Swedish researchers from Uppsala. This man was German. He died on the expedition, and the others are Sami. I imagine most of them would have come from Finland – the expedition started out from there.'

'Very probably. Though people around here aren't afraid to travel long distances. Do you know, I even went to Ikea last weekend? I found a small chair, perfect for sitting in front of the computer.'

Klemet smiled. The locals had been like a bunch of excited kids since Ikea had opened in Haparanda on the Swedish-Finnish border. The store was over four hundred kilometres from Kautokeino, but, as his uncle said, distance counted for nothing in the Far North. People would drive a hundred kilometres to buy cigarettes. Like a trip to the corner shop.

'This person looks like someone from around here. But I can't quite place him.'

Nils Ante was pointing to a man with a narrow nose and a drooping moustache covering the corners of his mouth. Klemet remembered that he and Nina had wondered who the man was, noting that he seemed slightly apart from the rest of the group, and didn't appear on some of the photographs. Klemet said he was neither Sami, nor French, nor one of the scientists.

Nils Ante bent over, peering closely at the photograph. He straightened up.

'Chang-Chang!'

The young Chinese woman appeared almost immediately.

'My sweetest amber pearl – would you be so kind as to fetch my magnifying glass, on my desk?'

Miss Chang brought the magnifying glass and left it on the kitchen table, planting a delicate kiss on Nils Ante's forehead at the same time. He watched her leave the room with an expression of rapt enchantment.

'An angel has come into my life, Klemet. And what about you, my favourite nephew? Still unattached?'

'You wanted to check a detail in the photograph,' said Klemet, holding the magnifying glass out to his uncle.

Nils Ante shook his head and took it from him.

'No, I can't put a name to him. I couldn't swear he's from around here, but he does look familiar.'

Klemet took the magnifying glass and peered slowly at each figure in turn, coming back to the stranger with the elegant moustache. Then he noticed the man was carrying something at his side, slung on a strap across one shoulder. He could only see part of the device, but it looked like a metal detector.

Clearly, he thought, the 1939 expedition had been interested in more than Sami customs and costumes.

10.05 a.m., Central Sápmi

It was extraordinarily quiet. Profound, almost deafening silence. André Racagnal could hardly remember the last time he had experienced such silence. Not for months. Maybe even years. The tiniest sound carried far across the landscape.

He watched from a distance as Aslak put on his skis. He could just hear them gliding and crunching on the frozen snow. He hadn't expected Aslak to be an easy customer. Hadn't expected him to say yes straightaway. On principle. Racagnal was a pragmatist. He always got his way in the end, because he was always ready to do what had to be done. He knew when to step back. He wasn't burdened with pride. Not like so many others, people who gave up and had no clue what to do at the first sign of serious resistance. The geologist adjusted his field glasses. Men living like Aslak were easy to handle, really: every decision was a matter of life or death for them. There was nothing superfluous or trivial in the breeder's existence. He wasn't a victim of consumer society. Trapping people who were in debt wasn't difficult either, for example. The same rules applied – the tricks were just that little bit more subtle and technically advanced. With Aslak, he was working in the raw. Anything the Sami lost would have a direct impact on his survival out here. The survival of his herd, too. And his wife. Simple as that.

It hadn't taken him long to come up with a plan. That was the advantage of a character like Aslak. His entire life was there in plain sight. No hidden bank accounts, no second home. His reindeer were grazing in the distance. Here were the camp, his wife and his dogs. Racagnal was almost sure he had singled out the right one. It would come as a shock, but it would kick-start negotiations. The Frenchman didn't want to miss this.

He trained his field glasses on Aslak. There was enough light now. It had been difficult earlier, in the dark, but he had found one of the dogs keeping watch. He had been discreet. He couldn't afford to spread panic among the animals, or noise.

'Now,' said Racagnal to himself. Aslak had his back turned just at that moment, dammit. But the Sami stood frozen to the spot. He had just discovered his dog's body. Or, rather, its head.

Racagnal decided to give it another thirty seconds. Time for the herder to absorb the shock and realise the immense loss represented by the dog's killing. Time, too, to make the connection between the killing and Racagnal's visit. Thirty seconds, but no longer. He musn't give Aslak time to recover and think about how to respond.

Now.

The geologist unhooked his radio and called Aslak. From where he hid, he could almost catch the crackling inside the tent. After a moment's hesitation, the Sami went back inside. A few seconds later, he answered the call.

'Treat the dog as a warning,' said Racagnal straightaway. 'I'm serious. We need your help. If you refuse once more, we'll kill your head reindeer. Refuse again, we'll kill your wife. Come with me, and your dog will be replaced. You'll get three new ones. The best. I'm coming over now. And we'll be taking a trip, just the two of us. Not for long. Any trouble, and my men will deal with your reindeer. If you've understood, come out of the tent and take off your chapka.'

Racagnal ended the call. He reckoned Aslak would appear in about fifteen seconds. He raised his field glasses. Nothing moved. The silence was absolute. Racagnal could feel his fingers turning numb.

At last, the tent flap moved. He had underestimated. Twenty seconds. Aslak stepped outside and stood motionless for a long time, scanning the surrounding landscape. After what seemed to Racagnal like an eternity – another fifteen seconds – he raised his hands to his head and removed his chapka.

32

Thursday 20 January

11.30 a.m., Police Headquarters, Kautokeino

Klemet glanced at his watch and realised he had to get back to the station. He had stayed at his uncle's house for as long as he could, but now it was time to confront Nina. Running away was not an option. He promised his uncle he would be back before the vultures, took his leave of Miss Chang, who waved cheerily, and set out along the road back to town, driving at an abnormally cautious speed.

He took a deep breath before knocking on Nina's office door, then entered, his opening phrase at the ready. He stood staring open-mouthed at what he saw. She was there, hands stuffed into the pockets of her navy-blue police fatigues. But her office was transformed. Copies of the expedition photographs were arranged on the wall opposite her desk. A dozen reproductions of Sami drums were Sellotaped to the windows. Photographs of all the protagonists encountered so far were pinned to a large board resting on an easel. She had even found some Sami music online and was playing it on her computer, to add to the mood. The office had become an operations centre.

'You're forgiven,' said Nina brightly, leaving Klemet no time to mumble his excuses. 'Next time you'll get my fist in your face. Now, look at this.'

Taking one hand out of her pocket, she led him over to Henri Mons's photographs. Klemet was dumbfounded – as much by her work as by her reaction to him. She had decided to keep control of the situation by taking the initiative. Once again he was left speechless, out of his depth.

'Nina, I just wanted to—'

'Don't make things any more complicated, please, Klemet. Now, look at these photos.'

He went along with it, feeling relieved, in fact. He concentrated on the pictures, especially the fifteen shots of members of the expedition.

'So, what do you see?'

Nina seemed excited. She must have found something. Which would explain why she was in such a hurry to forget last night's incident.

'No idea, yet,' he said, looking closely at each picture. 'I'm thinking. But I can tell you something. Niils, the man with the four-pointed hat – his family name was Labba. Ring any bells?'

'Mattis's father?'

'His grandfather.'

Nina's eyes opened wide in astonishment. She seemed to be thinking fast.

'So Mattis's grandfather was in possession of a drum that was stolen seventy years later, and which may have caused the death of his grandson.'

'Don't take short cuts, Nina.'

'Sure. But it's bizarre all the same. The drum goes off to France for seventy years. And a few days after it's returned to its place of origin, the original owner's grandson is murdered. Klemet, do you really believe we're still dealing with a vendetta between reindeer rustlers?'

He was silent for a moment, mulling over the problem, looking at the pictures.

'Well?' she asked.

Klemet remembered the detail that had struck him on the photographs he had taken to his uncle's house.

'There's a metal detector in one of the pictures. They were searching for ore. I think the drum, or the expedition, may be linked to the existence of a gold seam.'

'It's quite possible. Was Mattis involved in mineral prospecting, in any way?'

'Not as far as we know.'

'Look again.'

Nina's eyes sparkled, to Klemet's great discomfort. He focused on the pictures again, thinking aloud.

'We found out that the German geologist had gone off . . . on the twenty-fifth. No, between the twenty-fifth and twenty-seventh July 1939, accompanied by Niils Labba.'

He checked his notes.

'And that Niils came back alone between the fourth and seventh August.'

'Yes. And?'

'And . . . the others are all there, and they carry on with their expedition, because they're all on the later photographs.'

'Really? Are they?'

'Yes. The French contingent. The two Swedish researchers. The interpreter. The cook. The . . . '

Klemet thought again about his uncle. If he hadn't singled out the man with the slender nose and the drooping moustache, he would have forgotten all about him. He was easy enough to overlook on the photographs.

'There's someone missing on the later pictures. The one with the moustache.'

'Bingo.'

'I saw my uncle this morning. He said that man reminded him vaguely of someone local, but he couldn't remember who. Why isn't he on the later photographs?'

'I don't know. But we have a drum and a death in 1939. And

another death, and the same drum now. And a connection to both deaths: the Labba family.'

'We don't know for sure that Mattis's death is linked to the drum,' he interrupted, quickly.

'Oh, Klemet, for heaven's sake!' Nina looked suddenly exasperated. 'I know we don't have concrete proof yet, but still, it's staring us in the face.'

'And the cut ears? What about them?'

Nina did not want her colleague's excessive caution to affect her own thinking. When Patrol P9 entered the Sheriff's office fifteen minutes later, she decided to push her advantage. The case was outside the Reindeer Police's usual remit. You had to think outside the box, but it was plain to Nina that Klemet's obsession with evidence and proof prevented him from thinking imaginatively.

Paradoxically, Klemet's experience was against him – not so much his time in the Reindeer Police as his years on the Palme assassination inquiry in Sweden. In Kiruna, before he had been posted to Kautokeino, his Swedish colleagues had shown him great respect as a former Palme investigator, in the biggest inquiry ever undertaken by the Swedish police. To his Norwegian and Finnish colleagues, the case had been a laughing stock. But in the career of a Swedish cop, it was tantamount to a service medal, despite the inquiry's undeniable failure: the only suspect to come to trial and be sentenced had finally been acquitted on appeal.

Tor Jensen greeted them. His bowl of *salmiakki* was nowhere in sight. He indicated the Bodum coffee pot, inviting them to help themselves,, but said nothing for the moment. A bad sign. Nina wondered vaguely whether the reason was bad news, or the absence of his bowl of sweets.

'So?'

The Sheriff seemed on edge. Nina knew his post was politically sensitive. And doubly so in light of recent events. Tensions between the Sami and the Norwegians were nothing new, especially now that the success of the populist Progress Party had loosened many people's tongues. But they were new to Nina. Her innate sense of right and wrong, good and bad, told her that the Sami had not initiated the confrontation. Henri Mons's testimony had shaken her. She was unprepared for this new perspective on her fellow Norwegians, and the Swedes, as the bad guys.

Something else bothered her, too. The legend of the curse, and the Swedish ethno-biologists, all added to the disturbing nature of the case. This was no random settlement of old scores.

The Sheriff was growing impatient. Klemet hesitated to speak first. Exasperated by her patrol boss's cautious nature, his religious devotion to proof, Nina spoke out.

'The theft of the drum and Mattis's murder must be linked. It's only logical,' she said. 'What's the likelihood of two such exceptional events taking place within the space of twenty-four hours, in a place like this?'

'Go on,' said the Sheriff.

'We know that two people visited Mattis at his trailer, riding the same snowmobile. Did they come to talk, or were they looking for something? Was it the drum? That seems to be the logical conclusion. Is Brattsen still talking about breeders settling their scores? Nothing in the inquiry corroborates that, though it's the easiest and most tempting solution. I would add that some people have a vested interest in encouraging everyone to believe the breeders are given to murdering one another or engaging in open conflict. All the more reason to keep a tight grip on their apparently incest-ridden, gangster-ish world. That's what we're talking about here, isn't it?'

Klemet said nothing. Nina might have been reading his thoughts. He was astonished that she felt bold enough to venture into the minefield like this.

'I know we still need proof,' she went on. 'But I think something is going on under our very noses. I firmly believe these crimes are linked to the events of 1939. The expedition. A gold seam. Deaths, a theft.'

'And the marks on the ears?' interrupted the Sheriff.

Nina glanced at Klemet. Her partner had responded with the

exact same objection. Now he said nothing. He wasn't hostile, just silent. The ball was in Nina's court. Tor Jensen waited.

'The ears are the biggest missing link. Not the only one, but the one that will give us the final, conclusive answer to the mystery. Or part of the mystery.'

Klemet was thinking.

'What Nina has said holds together. And what she hasn't said, too. The missing pieces. I think we should investigate the story of the gold seam, the gold mine. My uncle Nils Ante told me about a similar story. I detest rumour and speculation, but there does seem to be a cluster of evidence here.'

'Well, get over to Malå and clear up this business of the gold seam, then,' said the Sheriff.

'What's at Malå?' asked Nina.

'It's near Västerbotten,' said Jensen, 'a little town in northern Sweden. The Nordic Geological Institute. Its archives, at any rate. Not sure they aren't even the oldest geological archive in the world. Bring me something back.'

11 a.m., Central Sápmi

André Racagnal pulled up on his snowmobile, five metres from where Aslak stood. He sat watching the herder for a few moments. He cut an imposing figure for a Laplander. His square-jawed face registered no emotion. The geologist knew he was dealing with a highly determined man. Before moving closer, he made his way around to his snowmobile trailer and retrieved his radio. He spoke into the handset, addressing a nameless contact at the other end, making sure Aslak could hear.

'I'm in the field, with the guide. He's ready to help. You'll get a message every two hours. If not, you know what to do.'

He cut the call without waiting for a reply. Finally, he approached Aslak.

'Know how to read a map?'

'Yes.'

'Let's go inside.'

Racagnal and Aslak spent the next two hours studying the maps. The Frenchman was on his guard, but the herder showed no sign of rebellion. Racagnal was anything but naive – he knew a hard nut like Aslak would not give in quite so easily. But he knew, too, that primitive, isolated individuals like him did not react in the same way as men accustomed to the petty intrigues of everyday society. Aslak had to be convinced that he had no choice. Perhaps the promise of replacements for his dog had been enough to persuade him. When you lived under such extreme conditions, you accepted the twists of fate. No point trying to fight the will of the evil spirits. You just knuckled down and put up with them, hoping they'd soon move on, trying to forget them once they'd gone, yet living in fear of their next appearance.

Racagnal could see why Olsen had insisted he take Aslak as his guide. The Sami didn't know how to read geological symbols, but he recognised the curves and contours, he could feel his way, knew how to describe a location with a wealth of precious detail. Still, the Frenchman had to allow for a double margin of error: Aslak could make a mistake, and he himself had no idea whether or not he could trust the old geological map. Its maker had deliberately omitted the place name. And he might well have laid other traps, too, to put inquisitive souls off the scent. It was a possibility Racagnal could not exclude.

Aslak rolled up his bundle and wrapped it in reindeer skins, tying it tight. He moved closer to his wife. She would have to manage alone for up to five days. Aslak could not be gone for too long, he knew that. Her sufferings were too great.

Aslak had suffered too – the absence of a mother, and his father's death when he was still very young. He had succumbed to the cold after setting out to recover a group of reindeer that had crossed into Finland. The regulations were harsh and pitiless back then. Aslak's father risked a heavy fine if the Finnish patrols found him. He had no way to pay. He had set out in haste. Too much haste. He had been too ill equipped and caught unawares by a snowstorm the like of which had seldom been seen. They had found his body two months later.

And then the tragedy of Aslak's wife had struck, when they were first betrothed.

Aslak looked at her, placed his hand on her head. They had not spoken for so long. The eyes were enough, in the rare moments when she seemed to share his existence. She knelt up. He did not take his hand away. She stared at him intently. A look like that usually preceded one of her attacks. But no cry rose from her throat. On the other side of the hearth, Racagnal was getting impatient. Aslak's wife stared at him, then turned her gaze on Aslak, as he cradled her face. She placed her left hand over her husband's. But with the other hand – out of the Frenchman's sight – she drew a sign in the dust of the hearth. A sign that turned Aslak's blood to ice.

33

Thursday 20 January

3 p.m., Kautokeino

To reach Malå, Patrol P9 would have to drive almost seven hundred kilometres due south. A good ten hours or so on the road.

Klemet and Nina decided to leave at the end of the afternoon, taking turns at the wheel to arrive the following morning, sleeping for a few hours in one of the Reindeer Police cabins.

An afternoon nap was essential, preceded by lunch at the Villmarkssenter, just across the main street. Nina paused for a moment as they left the station, watching the pale, orange afterglow on the horizon, and the encroaching, relentless dark of the Polar night. The light was one of the great discoveries of her new posting to Sápmi, even more raw and magnificent than that of her native fjord. She felt its impact still more powerfully in the biting cold. That was something new, too. Where she came from, the Gulf Stream ensured tolerable temperatures all year round.

A gust of wind struck their faces. They bent their heads and hunched forward, Nina shielding her mouth and eyes with her arm. It became suddenly, aggressively cold. As they hurried over to the restaurant, she lost her footing on the black ice covering the slope leading to the entrance, practically skating the last few metres, and almost laughed out loud when Klemet rushed to help her and slipped himself. The last gleam of sunlight had disappeared, obliterated by the clouds covering a section of the sky.

It was already past lunchtime, but Mads laid two places for them and brought out the dish of the day – salmon with dill, boiled potatoes and a white sauce. The dining room was empty, and the proprietor sat with Klemet and Nina as they ate. The low cloud dispersed and the wind swept the sky clean. The Villmarkssenter stood on high ground overlooking the road, with a view over the whole of Kautokeino. At this time of day, the town's lights were all that was visible, snaking in a gentle curve along the Alta river.

'So, have you found the bastard who killed Mattis?' Mads asked Klemet.

'Not yet.'

'What are you playing at? People are starting to ask questions, you know. Everyone's very tense.'

Klemet nodded. 'Anyone staying here now?'

'No. The retired Danes have left, and the truckers come and go as usual. The French prospector left yesterday.'

Klemet and Nina stared at one another.

'What prospector?'

'You know, that Frenchman! He'd been here a while. But he left with all his stuff. Loaded with equipment, he was. He's off to look for some kind of ore, a big seam. Don't know what. Always top-secret, all that. Oh, he had all the paperwork – all in order, so he said. He was annoyed about the mining affairs committee taking its time. But it was all sorted in the end.'

'Did he leave on his own?'

'Far as I know.'

'And you say he'd been here for some time?'

'Let's see, he arrived ... before all this business, I'd say. Well, yes, the first day back to school, the third of January. A Monday. I remember because he was very keen on helping Sofia with her French homework. She's in eighth grade now, started French last autumn.'

'And where was he off to?'

'Oh, you'd have to ask at the council offices about that.'

Klemet glanced at his watch. Still time to drop by. They drank their coffee quickly.

'What was he like, this Frenchman?'

'Oh, a decent enough type. Seemed a bit bored waiting around for his permit. Told me some tall stories about his time in Africa. He speaks Swedish. He's worked around here before – he was prospecting then, too. But you should ask Brattsen if you're interested. He interviewed him about a week ago, after a punch-up in the pub. The Frenchman looked a bit shaken up about it, in fact.'

Klemet stared at Nina, who stared back, eyes wide, indicating this was news to her, too. Why had Brattsen said nothing about questioning the prospector? This suggested a whole new line of inquiry.

Just then Sofia entered the restaurant, back from school, her bag slung over one shoulder. She waved to the table and grinned broadly, then came over to hug Klemet and shake Nina's hand.

Klemet and Nina got up to leave.

'Put both the meals on my slate, Mads,' Klemet told him. 'I'm hoping I'll be forgiven for something . . .'

Nina smiled.

'You already are.'

Sofia spread out her exercise books on a nearby table.

'So, how are you getting on with your French, Sofia?' asked Nina. The girl's face darkened.

'Why do you want to know?' she retorted sharply, to everyone's surprise.

'No reason,' said Nina. 'Seems you had a private tutor for a few days.'

'That creep, with his vile wandering hands? Five minutes it took him. Five minutes.'

Mads stared at her in astonishment.

'What do you mean, "wandering hands"? You didn't say anything at the time.'

'Well, I'm saying it now, so there. Now leave me alone!'

The girl gathered up her things and stormed out of the restaurant.

Mads was speechless.

Nina was the first to react. She ran after Sofia and came back five minutes later, looking furious, but she addressed Mads calmly and methodically.

'Nothing serious happened,' she reassured him straightaway. 'She knew how to say no ... and how to make herself thoroughly understood.'

Nina paused, swallowed nervously. For a fraction of a second, Klemet saw how upset she was.

'But I would advise her to file a complaint of sexual harassment all the same,' Nina went on. 'I think it's important for her to do that. This sort of thing needs to be taken very seriously, right at the outset, at the slightest gesture. And we must show her that we're backing her up.'

'Of course, of course.'

Mads looked as if he was in shock, gradually realising that he had accommodated the Frenchman for two whole weeks alongside his family, who lived in a private wing of the hotel.

'Everything will be fine,' said Nina. 'She's under age, everything will be very discreet and, if need be, she can talk to someone who can help.'

'Do you really think it's that serious?' asked Klemet. Nina shot him a furious glance.

'Of course it's serious! And it's about time men understood as much,' she said, marching out of the hotel. He hurried after her.

3.45 p.m., Council Offices, Kautokeino

While Klemet called at the council offices alone, anxious not to attract too much attention, Nina returned to the station and began drafting a report on the incident involving Sofia.

In reception, Ingrid greeted the Reindeer Policeman with a delighted smile.

'Well, hello, Klemet! Goodness me,' she lowered her voice to a whisper, 'I thought you'd disappeared. You haven't invited me over for a drink in your tent for a while.'

Klemet leaned over the counter and whispered back, 'Just let me get through all this business and I promise, we'll have an evening all to ourselves.'

Ingrid giggled, but quickly pulled a straight face as one of the Progress Party councillors walked in wearing a brand-new snow-mobile suit, hair slicked back, face freshly tanned from the solarium. Olsen's fellow councillor – the young man he referred to as 'Prince Charming' – barely bothered to acknowledge the council's Labour-voting receptionist, nor the Lapp policeman, whom he suspected of harbouring similar political sympathies.

'Arsehole,' muttered Ingrid. 'Makes that old hypocrite Olsen seem almost bearable. So, you haven't come to invite me over to your place, if I've understood correctly.'

'It seems a Frenchman came by to see the folks on the mining affairs committee,' said Klemet. 'I'm interested in him, but keep that to yourself. No sense in worrying everyone, if you see what I mean.'

'I see. Big Bad Wolf's on the scent . . .' Ingrid's pet name for him. 'Yes, I remember him. Good-looking guy! That hint of danger, just my type. He was angry the last time he came in. He wanted to see someone from the committee. Old Olsen was the only one here, but he wasn't free to see him. Don't know what happened after that.'

'Olsen here now?'

'No. He must be back at the farm. He usually comes late in the afternoon, unless there's a meeting.'

'When was the last meeting?'

'It was scheduled for Monday. He was here that day. But – oh God, Klemet! Monday was when I found that hideous ear. I haven't seen the Frenchman since.'

'Was Olsen here long, before you found the ear?'

'No, just a couple of hours, perhaps.'

'Anyone enter or leave the building between Olsen's arrival and the moment you found the ear?'

'Not on that side of the building, no. There was no need for anyone to be there. But I've already told Brattsen all this, as you doubtless know.'

'Brattsen! Again . . .'

'Meaning?'

'Nothing, just thinking aloud. Any other committee members in today?'

Ingrid glanced at her list. 'No. Why, are you interested?'

Klemet leaned over the counter once again. 'I want to know where the Frenchman was planning to go digging. And I'd like to know soon, because I'm leaving for Malå this evening to make some inquiries with Nina.'

'Ah yes, young Nina. She hasn't been here long, but people are already talking about her, quite a lot. Very bright girl, apparently. And cute, too, wouldn't you say, Klemet? Invited her back to the tent, have you?'

'Ingrid, please. I really need to know where the Frenchman was headed. I'm carrying out a criminal invesigation here, remember?'

'So you have, haven't you?' Ingrid pursed her lips.

She stared at Klemet in silence for a few seconds, apparently sizing him up.

'And what's more,' she went on, 'Brattsen says he's in charge of the murder investigation. Still not exactly your biggest fan, of course. He's a really nasty piece of work. You should watch out.'

'Thanks for the tip, Ingrid,' said Klemet drily. 'So can you give me anything on the Frenchman?'

'I must be the dumbest blonde in town. But I suppose the documents aren't confidential. They're just the applications to prospect, received from the Mining Administration for our approval. Nothing top-secret – residents in the area concerned have to be able to consult them here. They're not as detailed as the applications for drilling and mining licences. They're often quite vague, actually. Wait here, I'll go and take a look in the back.'

247

Ingrid got to her feet and disappeared down a nearby corridor. Klemet felt a pang of emotion. He remembered her at twenty. Fantastic-looking, with a devastating smile, irresistibly fresh and natural. Not much of that left now. She had turned him down at the time, like all the others. He didn't hold it against her. Much. She hadn't been unkind. She had just said no, laughing, like the rest. A quick kiss on the mouth, meaningless as far as she was concerned. She had haunted him, like the others. Klemet had suffered, but the worst of it was, he had taken it for granted that a quick stolen kiss was all he deserved. Nothing more. He had settled for the crumbs at the feast. When he was posted back home after his years on the Stockholm force, he had relished his new status in the eyes of the local women, Ingrid included. Obsessed by the rejections of his younger days, he had seen them all as if they were still twenty years old. Now, he saw them for what they were: women worn down by the trials of life, struggling to hold on to their looks and claim their share of happiness. They had become like him, happy with a furtive kiss. It had taken thirty years for them to call it quits.

Ingrid reappeared. Klemet smiled at her. She held a thin file in one hand.

'You'll be disappointed if you're after precise details, but take a look at this.'

She motioned for him to move behind the reception desk, keeping the file out of sight. He made his way around to the other side.

Quickly, he glanced down the topmost form. André Racagnal, date of birth, contact details. Société Française des Minerais. Project at the research stage. And, finally, the geographical details.

'Can I get a photocopy of this?'

'I'd rather not, Klemet, if you don't mind. I'd be worried that was a step too far.'

He didn't insist but took out his notebook. The prospecting area mentioned on the form was huge. The envelope contained two applications, in fact.

'Why two applications?' he asked.

Ingrid took a look.

'He's applied to search in two different areas, that's all. The first request covers a vast area north-west of Kautokeino. That was lodged last autumn and seems to have been stamped by the committee yesterday, Wednesday. The second request looks like more of a rushed job. It mentions three zones within a large area extending east and south-east of here. Seems to have been sent over from the Mining Administration sometime yesterday morning. And it was stamped late yesterday afternoon. Well, that was quick.'

'What makes you think it's a rushed job?' asked Klemet.

'Not sure really. These are only applications to prospect in the field, I suppose. We've had quite a few through from the Mining Administration in recent months. They usually take a while to compile and process, but the second one looks as if it was done in a hurry. The final decision on the licences for exploratory drilling will be taken on the first of February.'

Klemet was taking notes, saying nothing but trying to fit together the pieces of the puzzle. When he had got all the information he needed, he moved closer to Ingrid and cupped his hand tenderly around her face, gazed at her for a second, then kissed her on the forehead.

Ingrid smiled and raised her hand in a discreet wave as he walked away.

'Call me,' he said, and left the building.

4 p.m., Central Sápmi

André Racagnal had very little time to pull off an extraordinary feat. The wretched hick farmer was insisting he find the gold seam double-quick, because he had no idea of the work involved.

After studying the maps on his own at the café, he had isolated three zones within the vast area suggested by Olsen's geological map, and confirmed them again the next morning with Aslak. Even that had been a near-impossible task in such a short space of time. The obstinate old git had been right on one thing, at least. His Sami guide seemed to know the region inside out.

Aslak lay stretched out on the trailer behind Racagnal's snow-mobile, packed in between the bags and storage boxes. The Frenchman paid little attention to him, but he needed his local knowledge. He was forced to drive slowly and avoid shaking him up too much. At this speed, it would take three hours to reach the first location he wanted to look at. He had set off just after the passage of a low bank of cloud that had barred the horizon for some time. Now the sky was clear again. A sky for the Northern Lights, he thought. He had no idea why, but the spectacle of the aurora borealis was the only thing that moved him. Really moved him, not just excited him, like the young schoolgirls. He had realised this on his first visit to Lapland years before. The wild dance of the Northern Lights seemed to embody the desperation of his own life. He saw its fleeting beauties, its irresistible energies, its chaos.

According to the map, he could follow the course of a frozen river for the whole of this first stage of the journey, which made driving easier. There were few bumps, nothing to crash into. The wind had swept the sky clean, and a bright moon lit up the way ahead. The ride was smooth, and Racagnal's thoughts turned again to the mine. His initial observations were insufficient for a clear, precise picture. He would have to compare various coordinates and details, to see if they concurred with the old map. He didn't believe in luck. He had been spared such naivety. His creed was simple: life was the sum of a set of choices. Leave nothing to chance. Anticipate everything. And accept the outcome of your choices. Live with every decision. His personal creed had kept him alive this far, and made him one of the best geologists in the business: what envious colleagues saw as his exceptional instinct was in fact the result of diligent hard work. His approach to life also meant he could pursue his urges in relative peace. Still, he knew he had made a series of blunders over the past few days. The hick farmer and the cop had trapped him. He would have to find a way to redress that anomaly in his career. He turned his attention to the frozen river, rounding its curves. The moonlight dimmed. He couldn't allow his concentration to lapse. He slowed down for a moment, turned to check on the Sami, then focused on his driving again. The surrounding terrain was relatively flat, punctuated by clumps of young trees struggling skywards. Racagnal could see for some distance, in spite of the dark. He was riding over the high plateau now, a rolling landscape of low hills and gentle dips, having travelled for over an hour with no sign of a light. He stopped at the mouth of a small valley, taking advantage of the view, and cut the snowmobile's engine. They were engulfed in total silence. When he moved away from the warmth of the scooter, the cold bit suddenly, and hard. Racagnal lifted his eyes for a moment. No sign of the Lights yet. He took out his radio and sent a message. Then he turned to look at the Sami. Couldn't make out the expression on his face – it was too dark. But he could see the man watching every move he made.

5.30 p.m., Kautokeino

Nina and Klemet would be away for at least two days. They met at the agreed time, at the station in Kautokeino. The Sheriff had asked to see them before they left. Tor Jensen liked to keep his troops on a tight rein.

The bowl of *salmiakki* was back. Klemet raised a hand in greeting. The Sheriff held out the bowl. Klemet declined the offer, as did Nina. Tor Jensen frowned, pushing the sweets to the very edge of his desk, as far as possible out of reach, then slid a folder over to Klemet.

'A photograph of your Monsieur Racagnal. And a few bits of information picked up here and there. Nothing much. Why the interest?'

'He's suspected of sexual harassment. But it turns out he works in the mining industry. Which makes him doubly interesting.'

Jensen frowned. 'Not much to go on, is it?'

'Well, the sexual harassment is important, of course,' said Nina, pointedly. The Sheriff caught her tone, but said nothing.

'So, Malå. What was all that about again?'

'After looking at the photos from the 1939 expedition, we're convinced the link between the drum and the Sami legend about the cursed mine is worth exploring,' said Klemet. 'The Geological Institute archives may have something.'

The Sheriff frowned, apparently less convinced than at their meeting earlier that day. He leaned forward and pulled the bowl back towards him, picking out three liquorice sweets at once.

'You know the UN conference is almost upon us,' he said, with his mouth full.

Klemet and Nina nodded.

'It's been made abundantly clear to me that all this has to be resolved by then. So don't go saddling us with even more investigations, please! On your way back, stop in at Kiruna. They've promised me the latest forensic results from the murder scene.'

Jensen looked at the two officers. 'So? Still here?'

Klemet hesitated.

'There are a lot of us on this case. But I get the feeling some people are keeping their cards close to their chest. For example, we only just found out that Brattsen questioned the Frenchman a week ago. A week! And we knew nothing about it.'

'Well, let's ask him, shall we? I'm assuming you've been sharing with the rest of the class as required, Klemet?'

'Of course. Everything we can be sure of, at any rate.'

The Sheriff pressed a button on his phone panel.

'Rolf, can you come in here, please?'

Silence reigned. Tor Jensen picked at the bowl of sweets.

Brattsen entered the room two minutes later. He didn't bother to acknowledge Klemet or Nina, but shot a questioning look at Tor Jensen.

'You're aware of a certain ... Racagnal around town?' asked Jensen, reading the unfamiliar name from the case file.

'Racagnal? French? Yeah, I questioned him a few days ago.'

'And why did you not tell the Reindeer Police about this?'

'Why would I? It was just a pub brawl. Nothing to do with this case. Wouldn't want the Mounties to get too overloaded, would we?' he added, underscoring the heavy irony with a look to match.

The Sheriff seemed to be weighing up the situation.

'What happened, exactly?'

'A pub brawl, like I said. Between the French guy and Ailo Finnman. John and Mikkel were involved, too. Nothing serious. The Frenchman didn't even want to file a complaint. I had to insist on taking a statement.'

'So the Frenchman was the plaintiff?' asked Klemet, disappointed.

'Yes, why the surprise? The breeders jumped him. Ailo, followed by the other two, as per usual.'

'Why?' asked the Sheriff.

'The herders were the worse for a few beers. All it takes with that lot, believe me.'

'And where's the Frenchman now?' asked Klemet.

'How should I know?' Brattsen's response was sharp, irritable. 'He was here to prospect. He'll be out doing that somewhere.'

'Alone?'

'No idea. He knows the area. I expect he's capable of setting out unaccompanied.'

'And he shows up at the council offices a few hours before Ingrid finds the ear,' Klemet insisted.

'So?'

Brattsen glanced suspiciously at Klemet. 'What is this? Taking me in for questioning, are you?'

'Seems he was there to try and see Olsen,' Klemet continued. 'Do you happen to know whether they saw one another, finally?'

'No, he didn't see him!' Brattsen barked his reply.

'How do you know that?' Klemet's tone was even, unruffled.

'I don't think he saw him,' Brattsen corrected himself. 'I don't know. What does it matter anyway whether he saw him or not?'

Jensen sighed heavily and pushed the half-empty bowl to the end of his desk. Brattsen reverted to his usual hard glare. Klemet glanced at the Sheriff. With a jerk of his chin, Jensen indicated the door.

Klemet had been at the wheel of the Reindeer Police's Toyota pick-up for a good hour already. He had loaded what seemed to Nina to

253

be a great deal of superfluous equipment for the trip – sleeping bags, camping stove, provisions for two days.

'Old habits,' he explained, when she commented.

'We don't go by the clock in the Reindeer Police,' he told her as they drove. 'That's meaningless here. Three-quarters of what we do is connected with disputes over reindeer breeding, across vast areas. Sometimes you get a call and you'll be gone for four days.'

Nina peered through the car window. Black night. The head-lights showed nothing but snow-covered slopes and sparse dwarf birches. The tarmac was covered with packed ice, but with a top layer of grit, and his snow tyres, Klemet maintained a steady ninety kilometres an hour. The road ran straight, over long distances. In the darkness, the lights of oncoming vehicles were visible from a long way off. Since leaving Kautokeino they had passed one car and two big trucks, throwing up swirls of powdery snow in their wake.

They crossed the Finnish section and drove on into Sweden. The thermometer showed the outside temperature: minus 25°C. Klemet slowed and parked in a lay-by at the top of a hill. He left the engine running, suggested coffee.

Nina got out to stretch her legs. She was wearing a heavy snow-suit over her uniform, with her chapka and thick gloves. She stood still, her face turned to the sky.

'If it's this cold, should we see the Lights tonight?'

'Nothing to do with the cold,' Klemet told her. 'It's just that you need clear weather for the Lights. And in winter, clear weather means cold weather.'

'What produces the aurora?'

'Not really sure. Something to do with the sun. The Sami say the Lights are the eyes of the dead. And because of that, you should never point your finger at them.'

He handed Nina a plastic cup full of coffee.

'The eyes of the dead,' she repeated his words. 'Well it looks as if the dead are blind, tonight.'

34

Friday 21 January

Sunrise: 9.41 a.m.; sunset: 1.20 p.m.
3 hours 39 minutes of sunlight

7.30 a.m., Central Sápmi

André Racagnal and Aslak Gaupsara had slept just a few hours in a herder's shelter before hurriedly setting off again. It was dark, with banks of low cloud blocking the faint hint of light that should have been felt at this time of day. They had not spoken once. Racagnal had slept lightly, fitfully, attentive to the Sami's every move, ready to knock him out flat if necessary, tie him up if it came to that. Or worse, if Aslak caused him too much trouble. Racagnal had formed a clear picture of what was at stake; he wouldn't hesitate to take the necessary measures. If the Sami had to die, then die he would. Racagnal's task would be all the more difficult, for sure, and probably impossible in the timeframe imposed by the old farmer, but he knew he could find what he was after, alone. Perhaps the SFM would cover him then, if he discovered a really superb seam.

He knew his methods looked wildly unorthodox in the eyes of any professional in his field. His expedition was doomed to failure in the eyes of any rookie geologist. He could hear the youngsters now, laying down the law, telling him all about aerial geophysical surveys, moraine samples, bore holes, laboratory tests, studies of old and recent maps, field-book research, studies of field reports. Fastidious, scrupulous research. A mix of fieldwork, lab work, archive work: the mysterious alchemy that was the pride of his profession. And here he was, flouting it all. If his bosses knew what he was up to, they would probably earmark him for early retirement. But that was a risk he would take. Double or quits. If he drew a blank, he had a great deal to lose. But if he came good . . .

He glanced back. Aslak was still on the trailer. Racagnal couldn't see the man's eyes, but he felt his constant gaze. The landscape rose and fell more than yesterday, but the vegetation was unchanged. No pines, just a few skimpy birch trees, their trunks twisted in torment. He couldn't be far now from the first observation point he had identified: the snow cover was thinning. In the light of his powerful headlamps, Racagnal could even see patches of earth, blown clear by the wind. This section of the Finnmark deserved its reputation as an Arctic desert, there was so little precipitation.

Racagnal rode on for another half an hour, then looked for a place to set up camp, finally choosing a spot above a bend in a river. Rivers were cherished friends for people like him. Lapland consisted of vast expanses of granite. You had to find the faultlines – these were where the water ran off, carrying the minerals with it. A river meant a faultline, a weak point in a fractured expanse of rock, used by the river to carve out its bed.

He explained to Aslak what he planned to do. The Sami raised a makeshift shelter and spread the reindeer skins on the ground, then cut some wood. Soon, smoke was rising from inside the tent. Everything had to be in place before the first rays of the sun broke the horizon. They could not afford to lose a moment of daylight. Racagnal looked up. The clouds were thinning. The sky brightened. With luck, it would be clear within an hour, for the start of his exploration. He looked again at the modern geological map of the area and compared it with the old, hand-drawn sheet. The author had been at pains to conceal the exact spot. Subtle and clumsy all at once. The map looked quickly drawn, he thought. Too quickly, perhaps. Yet its fine detail suggested hours of painstaking analysis of the rock fragments collected, in order to record them on paper.

He sipped his coffee. The geologist who had made the old map was becoming something of an obsession with him. He wanted to discover his secret, find out who he was. His taste in women. Or men. His sexual likes and dislikes. Was he the average type, or an adventurer in the field? Racagnal liked to think of himself as an adventurer, a man unafraid to experiment, pushing the boundaries of convention.

He firmly believed that a man's sexuality spoke volumes about his willingness to venture into new, unexploited terrain. He turned to the Sami, stretched out in a corner of the shelter, his gaze lost in the flames. Racagnal thought about the woman he had seen in Aslak's tent. He'd seen plenty like her on his first trip here. Had some fun with one or two. They had been less willing than the Scandinavians. He wondered if the Sami had a taste for young girls, too. What red-blooded man wouldn't, he thought.

The sky was clear now. He collected his things and held a second pack out to the Sami, who took it without a word. They stepped outside into the cold and began making their way slowly upstream, along the frozen river.

10 a.m. Malå, Sweden

After a night in a Reindeer Police refuge on the Swedish side, Patrol P9 continued south. The landscape now was a vast, almost unbroken expanse of thick forest, mostly pines and birch trees, nothing like the dwarf birches of the *vidda*. Yet they were still in the Sápmi interior and very far north. Roads plunged straight through the forests, occasionally touching the shorelines of small lakes, or following the banks of broad rivers.

Nina was discovering this part of northern Sweden for the first time. It seemed scarcely more populated than the Norwegian section of Sápmi, but was clearly more exploited. In places, tracks disappeared into the forest, which was evidently replanted and carefully managed. Signs pointed to mineworks at regular intervals. Tall pylons supporting thick electric cables soared above the birches and pines, crossing the road and marching into the distance down deep cuts through the trees, carrying electricity to the rest of the country. They passed through hamlets of houses painted Falun red, each settlement arranged around a central petrol-station-cum-general store. Finally, after more pine trees and birches, stretching monotonously for kilometres, they arrived in Malå.

The Nordic Geological Institute stood on the edge of the small town. Some of the archives were still held in their respective countries, but for practical purposes the Nordic countries had grouped everything relating to Sápmi – and its unique geology – here. Malå was served by just one road connecting it to the Gulf of Bothnia several hundred kilometres to the south-east, but it was visited regularly by mining company representatives from all over the world, preparing to explore in the region. The Nordic archives had joined the Swedish institute, established here for over a century with its own, unique archive collection, especially on the results of drilling carried out since 1907.

Klemet and Nina reported to reception in the main administrative building. The director's office was one of several leading off the reception area. The director greeted them in person, and escorted them to a corner fitted out with tables and a coffee machine.

Eva Nilsdotter had a bad-tempered look about her. Her thick grey hair was piled on top of her head in a bun she clearly couldn't be bothered to keep under control. Her fine, sharply lined features were lit by magnificent eyes of an intense, pale blue. She had worked at the NGI for twenty-seven years, she said, including the last five as director. If everything went according to plan, she would hold the post until she retired in two years' time. She hoped the Reindeer Police weren't planning to rock the boat, as it were.

'So what do you want, exactly?' The tone was direct, even abrupt. Her jaw worked busily, chewing gum. 'Our Director of

Information is away in Uppsala. He hasn't the faintest idea of the amount of work we get through out here. He'd do better to get his arse off his office chair, in my humble opinion. He told me to see you, so I'm seeing you. But I'm warning you now, I don't like probing questions. We get a lot of visitors here who mind very much about discretion. The bedrock of our reputation, you might say. Geologists know they can work here in complete confidence. Many of our clients are listed on the stock exchanges in Asia and North America, if you get my drift. They come here to prospect and, ultimately, possibly, to invest a great deal of money. They don't like people making waves. So we ask uniformed officers of the police – even a couple of good-lookers like you two – to be discreet. And the more so since our dearly beloved ministry has ordered us to pay our way, making money on the backs of our users, instead of providing the service for free at the expense of the taxpayer. But you're in luck. It's quiet today.'

She paused to light a cigarette, flouting the no-smoking rule strictly enforced in all Scandinavian public buildings.

Klemet and Nina hadn't expected a welcome like this. Nina wondered how such a woman – clearly not a natural diplomat – had managed to get where she was and hold on to the job. Eva Nilsdotter seemed to read her thoughts.

'Didn't even shag for it, dear. But you know what, I'll tell you a secret: I was the best. For a long time, no one wanted to give me any responsibility – I was too good. They needed me as a geologist out in the field. One day, I'd had enough of seeing complete incompetents promoted to the top jobs because they had to be parked somewhere. So I got angry. Decided I'd be the boss. And you know what, I was the best at that, too.' She stubbed out the remains of her cigarette.

Nina stared at the director in disbelief; Klemet in delighted amusement. He recognised the tough, dyed-in-the-wool character of women from the North, unconcerned with social niceties and politesse.

'So what brings you to my neck of the woods? The Reindeer

259

Police. What the hell is that? Never heard of you.'

'Well, I think with a little imagination you can probably work it out,' said Klemet. 'All you need to know is we're investigating a murder. And we have reason to believe that it may have something to do with a story relating to a mine.'

'And in particular, a story related to an expedition to Lapland in 1939,' Nina added. 'Something about a cursed gold seam, that has brought great misfortune on the Sami people, and—'

'I see.' Eva lit another cigarette. 'Go on. I adore anything about old treasure maps. That's what got me into this business in the first place.'

Klemet spent the next fifteen minutes delivering a summary of what they knew so far. The theft of the drum, Mattis's death, the suspicion of foul play between breeders, the 1939 expedition, the legend of the gold mine, the rumours of a curse. Everything. Eva Nilsdotter listened with rapt attention, interjecting with enthusiasm, indignation, sympathy and compassion as the story unfolded. Klemet made a good job of it. Even Nina was surprised to find herself hanging on his every word.

The director sat in silence for some minutes. Then she jumped to her feet, disappeared into her office and returned with a perfectly chilled bottle of Chablis and three glasses.

'To our collaboration! Because you haven't said as much, but I'm guessing you're after the location of the mysterious mine. Am I right?' she asked, popping the cork, before downing her first glass in one, while Nina looked on in astonishment.

Half an hour later, the first bottle had been finished – there were more in the fridge, Eva promised, having drunk three-quarters of it herself – and the director of the NGI and Patrol P9 were walking slowly through a hangar on the other side of the road. It was one of several large buildings housing tens of thousands of flat wooden chests, each containing ten geological core samples measuring a metre in length and several centimetres in diameter. Eva seated herself on a stack of chests.

'You see, each core sample is numbered. These chests contain a series labelled "U".' She pointed to the coded labels. 'For uranium. Great for warming your backside!' She gave a husky smoker's laugh, lit another cigarette and blew out a cloud of smoke, mingling with Klemet's and Nina's breath in the icy air.

'If I was at all sensible, I wouldn't smoke in here on the uranium chests. Venerable old samples, these. They give off a rather nasty gas. Odourless, colourless, tasteless. Radon. It occurs in the landscape, too, but it's radioactive, and it accumulates in places like this or, worse still, in mineshafts. Causes lung cancer. We do ventilate this place, a little. But the worst thing is if you inhale it and smoke at the same time. Double whammy . . . Well, where were we? The stolen drum may have something to do with your gold seam. You think the German geologist was on to it. And you wonder if your French geologist might be on to it, too, because his arrival on the scene coincides with all the recent revents. What do we have to go on, to try to locate the buried treasure?'

Eva's question met with a heavy silence.

'I see. You do know that Lapland covers an area of some four hundred thousand square miles. Bigger than the whole of Finland, or Japan?'

'All we've got is some information on the areas the French geologist was planning to explore,' said Nina.

Eva moved over to a desk installed in a corner of the hangar, switched on a computer and entered the coordinates from Racagnal's second application into the database. She studied the maps on the screen and fetched the corresponding paper maps – on a readable scale – from a plan chest near by, then spread them out on a huge reading-table.

'Here are the places your Frenchman is planning to go walkies,' she said. 'Is he alone?'

Eva bent over the maps, running her finger over the symbols, following the curves of terrain, grunting and muttering to herself.

'You see, when a geologist draws a map, he notes down a multitude of details and readings taken out in the field. The maps we have here are simplified, based on the originals. When someone plans to go prospecting, they start by visiting our website, to check the geological maps, like these. Then there's a list of reports on the targeted areas. Those are the archives we hold here, together with the core samples all around us in this building. We get out the reports people ask for. Some of them date from before the Second World War.'

'The expedition photos,' Nina suggested.

She took out her portable computer and began showing Eva the scanned pictures.

'The expedition took place in the summer of 1939. The French organised it and took with them a Swedish research team, a German geologist and—'

'What was the German's name?' Eva interrupted.

'He was called Ernst, but we don't know his family name. We know he was from the Sudetenland,' said Klemet.

Eva frowned and noted the name on a piece of paper. The police officers said nothing for the next few minutes, trying to decipher the changing expressions on the director's face. She lit another cigarette, taking her time, poring over each picture. She spent a long time looking at the pictures featuring the German geologist.

Nina broke the silence.

'We think they took metal-detecting equipment with them, too.'

Eva took a long drag on her cigarette.

'Metal detection. Yes . . . But that's not all. What you see there is a Geiger counter, the very first portable model – though the buggers weighed twenty or twenty-five kilos.'

'A Geiger counter?'

'Well, I know what you're thinking, but don't jump to conclusions. No one was looking for uranium as such around here, in those days.'

'But the first atomic bomb was made during the war, so people must have known about uranium in order to carry out the research and develop it?' said Nina.

'Yes, but they obtained it from a mine in the Congo. I don't think this expedition has anything to do with uranium.'

'So why the Geiger counter?'

'Before the war, uranium was just something people were inter-ested in for its luminous properties. Radium was a useful component in phosphorescent paint, for watch dials and other instruments, for medical applications, too. Of course, today we howl at this, but at the time we knew nothing about the effects of radioactivity. Marie Curie, mother of us all, worked on ores from the Joachimsthal in Germany, or from Czechoslovakia. Can't remember which.'

'So the German geologist might have been looking for radium?' asked Nina.

'The Germans were interested in it at the time, for instruments or whatever. And with this equipment, your geologist would have been able to identify areas containing it. Which doesn't mean he was looking specifically for radium, either. Like most geologists, he was probably after various different ores at once. Letting Lady Luck be his guide. And, don't forget, radioactivity exists everywhere in nature, all around us. Take the tiniest chunk of granite and pass it in front of a Geiger counter, you'll soon see!'

Eva Nilsdotter went back to examining the photographs, leaving Klemet and Nina to their thoughts.

'Your German may have been looking for your fabulous gold mine. But I can tell you where he disappeared, at any rate,' she said suddenly.

Klemet and Nina stared at her in complete incomprehension. Eva burst out laughing.

'Oh, look at the pair of you, poor dears! Now, see here and listen closely. The last photos with our man Ernst were taken on the Norwegian coast. You see, in the distance, that mountain peak, the sort of hooked nose, and, just behind, the lake shaped like a little dinghy sail. No doubt about it.'

Eva fetched a map of the region.

'The lake is here, and the crooked mountain top is there. Given the angle, and the distance, I'd say the picture was taken . . . here.' She pointed to a spot on the map, took a soft red crayon and marked it with an X. 'So that's the last picture with Ernst. You told me earlier they had come from Inari, which is here. So they must have passed this way. And now, let's see the picture where your Sami guide makes his reappearance.'

Eva pored over the picture showing Niils after his return.

'Given the direction they took, you've got the Sami camp here. It's abandoned today. I camped there myself in my younger days. But it was on a reindeer migration route, with this river, and the rather unusual delta — not at all common in the region. So,' she brandished the red crayon again, 'the second photo was taken ... here!'

Ernst had died somewhere between the two points, searching for the mine. Or perhaps he had found it.

'And now,' Eva continued, 'let's see if we can define a radius within which Niils and Ernst travelled. Because they set off on foot, you say? We don't know how many days' walk it took them to reach the spot Ernst wanted to explore, nor how long they remained there.'

'But we know that Niils walked there and back,' said Nina.

Eva was studying the map again. She moved around the long table, poring over the three maps corresponding to the areas Racagnal planned to explore. She went back to the little desk and seated herself in front of the computer. Tapped something in, peered at the screen, picked up a telephone and began talking in English to someone at the other end. She waited a long time, saying nothing. Then her interlocutor came back on the line. Eva noted an email address on a piece of paper and ended the call.

'Log your machine on to the institute's wifi,' she instructed Nina. 'And send the photos of your German to this address. Just tell them in the message who it is you're trying to identify.'

Eva's tone was firm, brooking no questions or objections.

'The difficulty is, we don't know whether your German back in 1939 and our French geologist today are after the same mine. Nor whether you are after the same seam or another one altogether. So, one mine, or two, or three?'

'I think we're after the same mine as Ernst,' said Klemet. 'It's a hunch, but I'm trusting my intuition for once. The cursed seam . . . Niils knew about it. The drum spoke of it, one way or another.'

'And the French geologist?' Nina broke in. 'All we see here is that he set off to explore three different places, with the required permits. Eva, can you see any common characteristics in the three areas, anything hinting at what he might be looking for?'

Eva bent over the maps, saying nothing for a long while. She smoked two cigarettes before she spoke again.

'Look,' she said finally. 'First factor in common: the course described by the main river crossing the map in each case. On all of them it flows, broadly speaking, from the north-west towards the south, then curves back up to the east, then bends round and down again to the south-east.'

Klemet frowned slightly, but Nina nodded in agreement.

'Then there's the relief,' Eva went on. 'The altitudes are different, the surfaces are different, but in all three cases you clearly have the higher ground – the high plateau – with a lake to the south-east, and the presence of faultlines and fractures in the north-east.'

Nina nodded vigorously. Klemet maintained his frown.

'I'm not giving you a precise, clinical description here,' said Eva. 'More of an Impressionist landscape than your Flemish Masters. Big blocks of colour, blurred detail. I see strong similarities. And I haven't said anything about the third factor yet – the geological composition.'

'OK, suppose you're right,' Klemet cut her short. 'I get that the Frenchman doesn't know exactly where he's headed. But he's looking for somewhere that corresponds to the criteria someone else has provided. From those, he has deduced a fairly precise geography for the area he's after, and he's looking for places that correspond to that.'

'Spot on!' declared Eva. 'He must be one hell of a professional to have isolated these three areas. I'm ready to bet there isn't another spot anywhere in the region combining all these characteristics. But these maps cover vast expanses. If you're planning to search them in detail, you'll need weeks, perhaps months. Now, I think you'd better check your email,' she suggested to Nina.

Nina read a message in English from a man named Walter Müller.

'Ernst Flüger,' she said. 'The German geologist is called Ernst Flüger. Trained in the mid-1930s at the Mining Institute in Vienna.'

'An excellent school,' Eva commented. 'Shame they were all hired by the Nazis afterwards. But that wasn't the case with your Flüger. He died beforehand.'

'He may have worked for them,' said Klemet. 'The Nazis came to power in 1933, well before the expedition.'

'I doubt that,' Nina cut in, still reading her email. 'Flüger didn't complete his training. He was expelled at the end of his first year. He was Jewish.'

The news left a cold silence. No one was sure how to react.

'Perhaps his fatal fall in Lapland was a lucky escape,' said Klemet, after a moment.

It occurred to Nina that she might put in a call to France. She did so and came back after a few minutes.

'Henri Mons thought he remembered Flüger's name,' she said. 'Flüger and his guide headed north when they set out together. And according to Niils on his return, they walked for about two or three days before setting up camp, where they stayed for two days, until Flüger suffered the fall.'

Eva went back to the main map.

'Two possibilities, then. Here ... and here. If we take it that the gold seam is somewhere here, that still leaves a huge area to explore. If only we knew whether the geologist had drawn a map.'

'He did,' said Nina. 'Henri Mons saw it. But it has disappeared.'

'Well, that changes everything,' said Eva. 'Our man Flüger must have kept a field book. Every field geologist keeps field books. They use them to draw their maps afterwards.'

She marched back to her computer screen with a decisive air, seated herself, tapped something in and waited, drawing nervously on her cigarette.

35

12.30 p.m., Central Sápmi

Racagnal had trudged more than a kilometre upstream along the frozen river, followed by the Sami herder. As he had hoped, the snow was thinner on the ground in this part of the *vidda*. He could see numerous rocky outcrops. His initial observations confirmed the information recorded on his most recent map. Determining whether or not this coincided with the old geological map would be a more difficult task. Even if he had the unlikely good fortune to hit on the right place first time, it would take a lot of imagination to single out the area he was in now from the drawings on Olsen's sheet.

A pale blue light lay over the river and the bare hills all around. With his hammer Racagnal struck an interestingly shaped rock rising through the ice. He picked up the clean-cut fragment but resisted the urge to lick its icy surface. In these temperatures, he risked losing a piece of his tongue. He examined the rock in the bright light of his headlamp, then discarded it.

He continued up to the bend in the river. A rocky bluff rose from the river to a height of about two metres, giving him a chance to read the local geography. Old rocks. No surprise there. A layer of granite, unaltered garnets, some gneiss – mesocratic or thereabouts – a layer of clay about five centimetres thick, sloping up and away at an angle of fifteen degrees. Further down, he could see a matrix of sand and clay. Hurriedly, he noted his observations in his field book, but time was running out. The jottings lacked his usual precision.

He called Aslak and asked him to fetch a small device he had wrapped in a wool blanket, then aimed the pistol-shaped attachment towards the rock. The device emitted a faint whine. He directed the pistol at various points on the bluff. The changes in tone were scarcely noticeable, barely a hundred shocks per minute. He closed the device and held it out to Aslak, who wrapped it inside the blanket.

They continued up the thick ice sheet covering the river. Racagnal spotted a rock on one bank that had a fine, rounded form with multicoloured spots of lichen, from dark green to yellow. He raised his hammer again and took a fragment, observing its texture and striations, then cast it aside and moved on.

A small shoal of pebbles had accumulated in a bend of the riverbank. He kneeled down, turning them over one by one, examining them through a magnifying glass, taking his time studying every detail. The light was good now, clear and strong with the glare from the snow. It wouldn't last, although the hours of sunlight were lengthening day by day. A brighter gleam caught his attention. He passed his magnifying glass over the glint in the stone. It was a fleck of gold. An amateur would have jumped for joy, but he knew it meant nothing, only that gold was indeed present here, which came as no surprise. Everyone knew that. Dozens of companies were looking for gold in the region. The Canadians were a particularly strong presence, because the local geology resembled their own, back home.

Racagnal stood up, climbed the riverbank and looked slowly all around. The bare hilltops extended as far as the eye could see. He glanced at his map and walked on. There was still a lot to do. A lot to see. And very little chance of success.

*

Eva Nilsdotter led Klemet and Nina to a large, dimly lit side room. Two of its walls were fitted with floor-to-ceiling shelves loaded with files and archive boxes.

'Right, let's start here,' she announced, pointing to a small series of folders high up on the longer wall.

She pulled down a file with a yellow cover.

'If I've understood correctly,' she continued, summing up, 'your man Flüger's map disappeared with him. But I imagine it hasn't been lost to all mankind. As a student I often heard stories about curses, as well as in my own research, meeting elderly Sami. People talked about a fabulous seam that had brought bad luck. No one was ever able to identify it. Your dear uncle, Klemet, knows nothing more about it either, it seems. And yet, in his way, he does. Unsettling, isn't it?'

'What do you mean?' asked Nina.

'I spent part of my career abroad, like all geologists, in fact. Did quite a lot of time in Asia. Mining stories tend to have similar endings, you know. The local population carries no weight faced with the might of the State, determined to exploit its resources.'

Eva pulled out an archive box from a high shelf and climbed back down the library steps.

'Here, catch this,' she ordered the two police officers.

The box was full of brown envelopes. Eva pulled one out, read the references and put it back. She reviewed the contents of the entire box and found what she was looking for.

'Sit down,' she said, opening the envelope and removing a field book, which she placed carefully in front of her but didn't open straightaway.

'This is Ernst Flüger's notebook. There's only one, which is quite unusual. Geologists generally keep whole series of field books. Veritable works of art, in many cases. That's how I see them, at any rate. How did this field book come to be here? I have no idea. You should ask your elderly French friend about that, my dear. But I'm sure it's no exaggeration to say that it hasn't been opened since Flüger's death. His body must have been brought back with his personal effects. Someone at the time must have decided to bring the field book here. And it was forgotten. The same is true of many of the archives we hold. Most bits of land and rock have been explored at one time or another, but, for reasons best known at the time, the analyses may not have been considered interesting or valuable. They can become so, of course, a century later, when needs and technologies have evolved. And so we dig down into our old treasure trove.'

Klemet and Nina were having a hard time concealing their impatience. Eva shot them a small smile and lifted the battered leather cover. The notebook's pages were covered in a small, dense hand recording precise data on every observation carried out in the field, great or small. The officers peered in fascination at the diagrams and geological cross-sections, the detailed drawings of relief, all to scale, filled with differently textured motifs indicating the types of rock. The notebook was in German. Eva translated a few passages, selected at random.

'Flüger was a conscientious, meticulous man. He may have had just one year of training, but he had an excellent grasp of the techniques needed to draw up his reports.'

Eva skimmed through the book to the end. The last page was dated 1 August 1939. She sat for a long time, saying nothing.

'I have to say, this field book is highly unusual. For someone with an eye for these things, at any rate. In some ways, it describes the presence of mineral ores just as you'd expect, geological cross-sections, the age of the rocks, the way they overlap, the probable geological history of the area of land observed, suggestions for subsequent searches.'

'But . . . ?' Klemet made no effort to hide his impatience now.

'But Flüger annotates some of the diagrams and readings in just a few, scattered places, in an utterly fascinating and really rather . . . mysterious way. He had already made one visit to the region before this. Most of the field book relates to that first trip. What's very strange, for a document of this type, is the complete absence of precise coordinates. Surprising. Given Flüger's painstaking approach to every other aspect of geological cartography, I can only think that it was an oversight, or a mistake. Perhaps he noted all that down on the geological map he drew up, based on the information in the field book. Very likely. But let us continue.'

'What about the mysterious annotations, Eva? What are they? Can you give us an example?' Nina was losing patience, too.

'As a rule, a geologist's field book is a very dry thing. Highly technical. Only another geologist would appreciate the poetry in it. Some aesthetes will add decorative touches, little sketches, some of which are genuine works of art. But the text tends to be very succinct. Technical, as I said, using abbreviations and incomprehensible jargon – to the uninitiated, at least. But here, Flüger provides short commentaries that have apparently nothing to do with geology. You have to look carefully, but they're there, slipped in among the multitude of observations. I didn't notice them at first. They're quite incongruous. So Flüger had indeed made a first visit here, and knew he would have to come back in order to complete his research. Which explains his presence on the French expedition in the summer of 1939. He had a precise objective. The seam. There can be no doubt about it, as far as I'm concerned.'

Eva went back to reading the book in silence, then took a piece of paper and covered it with notes of her own.

'When you know what a geology field book ought to contain, the things it shouldn't normally contain jump out at you,' she explained. 'Rather as if you came across quotes in Russian in a Swedish text. There, you see, Flüger spent just a few days on this section. His observations fill a few pages, no more. Five at the very most. And what he wants to say is contained in two phrases, here, two pages apart: "The gateway is on the drum." And "Niils has the key."'

'Niils's drum!' Klemet spoke under his breath.

'The location of the mine must be indicated on Niils's drum,' exclaimed Nina. 'That's why he was so insistent it should be taken to a place of safety. And whoever stole it knew what it meant. They knew! It's obvious! Klemet, we've been on the wrong track since the beginning. The drum is no ordinary drum – it points to the location of the gold mine!'

Nina was gripped with excitement. Klemet saw the plain fact of the matter, too. The drum was the key.

'Wait,' said Eva suddenly. 'I didn't say anything about any gold mine.'

'What then? I don't understand.' There was just a hint of annoyance in Nina's voice.

'Flüger makes no direct mention of gold, anywhere. He does everything to give that impression – little touches here and there. Perhaps it is gold. But he never mentions the word "gold". He talks about yellow ore and altered black blocks. He says he thinks he's close to something huge, something unimaginable. But I'm not sure he knew himself what he was on the point of discovering. And, don't forget, he never completed his training. He's a technically excellent cartographer – I imagine that was the beginning of his course in Vienna – but he was not qualified to identify rocks. Logically, that would have come at the next, more specialist stage in his training. Theory often comes before practice, you won't change that. Solid experience is gained only after years and years of reconnaissance work in the field, in a variety of terrains, and poor Herr Flüger here was only half trained in the mid-1930s. He had had no time to develop those skills. He may have been mistaken, or unsure of himself, when he identified the ores.'

Klemet turned to Nina.

'Remember, Niils didn't want the seam to be discovered. What if he accompanied Flüger just to keep an eye on him, to make sure he didn't find it?'

'Then you're suggesting that Niils may have killed Flüger and made up his story afterwards?' said Nina. 'Flüger knew about the drum. He talked about it. He must have heard about it from Niils himself. So why would Niils have killed him?'

272

'Eva, can you give us a moment? I need to talk things over with my colleague.'

'Take your time, constables. I'll go and pop a bottle of white in the fridge and you can join me in my office when you're ready. Don't sit on the uranium samples for too long, they'll give you piles,' she added, leaving the hangar.

Klemet and Nina stared after her, unsure whether she was joking or not.

'What an extraordinary woman,' said Nina after Eva had gone. 'She must have ruffled a few feathers in her time. I think she's great.'

Klemet made no comment on the character of the director of the NGI. 'The problem is,' he said, 'we still don't know what the damned drum looks like. My feeling is it must look like a traditional drum, or it would have attracted attention. We still haven't followed up that Oslo number, the intermediary you were going to try to find. The one who wanted to acquire the drum for an unknown collector.'

In the small office area in the corner of the hangar, Nina put in some calls to Oslo. Klemet left its warmth to pace the beaten-earth floor between the rows of piled-up chests. The tallest stacks were six or seven metres high. He stopped in front of one, pulled open a drawer and lifted a core sample.

'Don't touch!' a voice rang out.

Eva was back with a bottle of white and three glasses in a basket, this time wearing a thick chapka, slightly askew, giving her a rather impish look.

'The samples absolutely must stay where they are, in the chests. The slightest mix-up is like changing your ancestors' birth dates on your family tree – the whole thing becomes meaningless and useless. Here, I didn't want to wait back there by myself. Have something to drink.'

'Well, just a finger. We have to drive back to Kiruna.'

'Skål!' Eva stood the bottle on a nearby chest and toasted Patrol P9 with a glass filled to the brim. 'Gold in these here boxes.' She smiled, patting one set of chests.

Klemet took a drink of wine, slooshing it around his mouth to warm it before swallowing it down. The alcohol, even in such small doses, delivered a feeling of mild well-being in the icy hanger.

'Hard to know what you're looking at, really,' he said, peering at the core samples.

'Most rocks keep their secrets close. Like a woman of a certain age.' Eva smiled. 'Can you possibly imagine the unbelievable quantity of ore, and labour, and smelting, and transforming, and energy it takes to extract one kilo of gold?'

'But this gold mine, so unbelievably rich that it's become a legend in the *vidda*. It seems strange that no one has ever found it, surely?' said Klemet.

'Strange? No, not really. For one thing, people look for different ores at different periods in history. Our archives are full of unsuspected, hence undiscovered, treasure. Renewed interest in a particular ore, and technical progress, changes in the extraction costs, are all factors that will bring someone back to our archives today, to read them afresh, with new insight. And some ores are better at concealing themselves than others.'

'You were talking about radium earlier.'

'For example. A sneaky customer, that one. Highly radioactive. Lurking in uranium ores, talk about underhand. In big demand a while back for its luminescence. Watch hands and instrument dials, as I said. Right up to the 1950s. Very important for fighter pilots in the war. Radium is white, but if you expose it to the air, it camouflages itself, turns black. Clever, no? Like its cousin uranium. And just as cunning. In the form of uraninite, uranium is black. But when it's altered, it changes colour. Ever heard of yellowcake? I'm simplifying here, of course. But it's quite the chameleon.'

'You've been a fantastic help already, Eva, thank you,' said Klemet. 'But we really must find the mine quickly. We have every reason to believe the French geologist is headed there. And we believe that if we find the mine, we'll find the answers to the theft, and the murder. I shouldn't be saying this to you, really, but it's a case of intuition over hard facts.'

'Have no fear, my dear boy. Officer. I'm no stranger to intuition. It's eighty per cent intuition and luck in my business. Anyone who tells you otherwise is a liar. But intuition is fed by things seen and lived, you might say. The product of hard work and experience. You still need a nose for it, though.' Eva savoured the bouquet of the Chablis before swallowing another mouthful.

Klemet smiled. 'If your intuition ever brings you over to Kautokeino, you must come and visit me in my *lavu*, Eva. I'll keep a bottle of white chilled just for you.'

'A Sami tent with a supply of chilled white wine? Now there's an offer I can't refuse,' she replied, raising her glass in his direction. 'Well, to get back to the matter in hand. The only way to find the place, in my view, is to find the geological map that accompanied Flüger's field book. We clearly don't have it here. Does it still exist? I have no idea. The presence of this one field book here is a mystery to me.'

'Find the geological map . . . But surely that's Mission Impossible if it isn't here already?' said Klemet.

'You said it, not me. Your only possible lead, as far as I can see, is to contact all the surviving members of the 1939 expedition.'

'You're right, up to a point,' Klemet admitted after a moment's thought. 'It's the only logical lead. Most of the explorers are dead. We might be able to trace their families, ask to see their archives. But, well, frankly—'

'Frankly, I can see your intuition is telling you the same thing as mine, dear boy. Officer. Things are slow to come together, but patience is a virtue, in your line of work and mine.'

'I know. But now I just don't have the time.'

'Well, all I can do is wish you good luck.'

Eva was toasting Klemet one more time when Nina emerged from the little office, her eyes shining. She asked him to step inside, making her excuses to Eva.

'I began by calling a colleague in Oslo. The antiques dealer has a shop between City Hall and the Stortinget, so quite a chic address. He specialises in antiquarian books, Polar and scientific literature,

275

Arctic fauna and flora, that sort of thing. He sells through the shop and online, but he also does searches to order for private clients.'

'Why would he be interested in a Sami drum?'

'It wasn't for him. He was acting as an intermediary. His specialisation makes him a useful contact. The Sami are an Arctic people ... According to my friend, he's had a hand in a couple of shady affairs too.'

'Someone you'd get in touch with for a rather special job.'

'So I called him,' Nina went on. 'He made no secret of the fact that he had contacted Henri Mons. The rest is complicated. He didn't want to break his professional confidentiality by giving me the name of his client, especially since it came to nothing anyway, because Henri Mons didn't want to sell.'

'How did he know Mons had the drum?'

'From what he said, his client had spoken to him about the pre-war expedition. The dealer did some research – not too difficult for him. One of Paul-Émile Victor's colleagues had published an account of the trip. He didn't go into detail because he knew nothing about it, but apparently the book mentioned that the drum had been given to Mons. Nothing more. The lead to Mons was easy enough for the dealer to follow.'

'So who commissioned him to approach Mons about the drum?'

'Someone who knew about it long before it hit the newspapers.'

'Someone close to the expedition at the time ...'

'Or a descendant of one of the participants,' Nina finished her colleague's sentence.

'Mattis? I can't see Mattis getting in touch with an antique dealer in Oslo. Nor any of the other Sami on the trip, most of whom were Finns, in any case. We can discount the French contingent. Flüger's dead.'

'There are the two Swedish scientists,' Nina added.

'And the moustachioed character with the thin nose who disappears just after Flüger and isn't seen again.'

'And whom your uncle thought he recognised.'

'What did Mons say about those three?'

'Nothing. He had lost touch with them, what with the war breaking out just after the end of the expedition. One of the Swedes spent two years in Germany at the beginning of the war, at the Kaiser Wilhelm Institute of Anthropology, Human Heredity and Eugenics in Berlin. He was called back to Uppsala in 1943.'

'Yeah, when things started to turn bad for the Germans in Stalingrad. Neutrality is a flexible concept. Typical of Sweden. I always felt ashamed about that.'

'He spent a few years in the Directorate of Health and Social Affairs,' Nina went on. 'And he died in the mid-1950s, in a car crash. The second one had a successful career as a doctor. He ended up as professor of geriatrics at the Karolinska Institute, and sat on the Nobel committee. He died, too, in the late 1980s.'

'So that leaves our friend with the moustache.'

'He was from around here. From the Finnmark,' said Nina. 'A Norwegian. A local. He provided logistical support.'

'If he was from the region, he's either left the area or died some time ago, or I'm sure Nils Ante would have identified him.'

'It might be worth paying your uncle another visit, just to be sure. That's our only firm lead now, at any rate.'

36

Friday 21 January

4.55 p.m., Central Sápmi

Aslak had followed the stranger for hours, in silence. In the thick darkness, a sliver of moon was enough to make the *vidda* sparkle. Ensnared in the bushes, clumps of snow glittered in its eerie light. He obeyed orders without protest. He was watching. Ever since this man had set foot inside his tent, he had been pondering the best way to kill him. He could have done it there and then. He knew how to handle a dagger better than anyone. His father had given him his first knife when he was five years old and impatient to have one of his own. He had whittled toys out of birchwood, like one of his uncles who carved figurines – reindeer, or toy sledges. His father had indulged his efforts, giving him a man's knife, even then. That was important, for a Sami. He still had that knife today. The birchwood handle was well greased. The finely carved reindeer-bone sheath was broken in places, but the blade was still almost perfect.

Aslak had other knives, but he kept this one for his most important tasks. His way of honouring his father. He had never known a mother's love. He regretted that, but he had never missed his own mother. How could he? Mattis had asked him about that one day.

278

But how could you miss someone you had never known? Aslak had not understood what Mattis meant. Mattis could be strange at times. Mattis had lost his way and harboured odd notions. The only comfort, the one soft touch Aslak had known as a child was the thick reindeer skins lining the floor of his tent, and the sledges. A good feeling. Like the clothes he wore now. Reindeer skins kept you warm when you needed it most. They could save your life. One day, when Mattis had been drinking, he had ventured to talk to Aslak about gentleness, and the lack of tenderness in his life. Another strange idea, a sign of how far Mattis had strayed. Reindeer skins showed no tenderness. Tenderness couldn't save lives. Reindeer skins saved lives. Aslak's father had shown him how to treat the reindeer skins, how to bring out their softness. It was the most important skill his father had handed down to him. He never spoke, other than to tell his son to respect the reindeer and to name the lead animals in the herd. His father was often away. Aslak had gone with him, sometimes. But he had been absent a great deal, too. And one day, he hadn't come back. His father had been a God-fearing man, but men had killed him. Aslak knew that. Men brought nothing good, no tenderness. He thought of his wife. She had enough to eat for a few days, enough wood and reindeer skins. Perhaps she could hold out. If her attacks were not too violent.

She had held out for so long already.

Sometimes her shrieks were unbroken for hours at a time. She would tear at her throat. In her worst fits, she would raise her arms to the sky, shriek and wail. Aslak knew there was nothing he could do. He had to let her scream, show her that he was there. She would calm down once he managed to catch her eye, after her gaze had wandered for hours over the sky. As if she had found her way once again. Often, though, his wife stared straight through him. That was a strange feeling, like being invisible, and then she would cry out, with her arms lifted to the sky. He knew why she screamed. He understood why she screamed. It was necessary for her to scream.

One day, a representative from the Reindeer Administration had come by on his rounds, to try to talk about it to Aslak. He was a decent man, a Sami who had known Aslak's father. He had asked Aslak if he thought his wife should see a doctor. Out of respect for the old friendship between this man and his father, Aslak had said he would think about it. The man came back several times but, finally, he had understood that there was no point in talking about it further. Aslak's wife's unearthly shrieks had become a legend in the *vidda*, like the mysterious seam that made everyone so tense.

He looked around. They were on the surface of a frozen river. Low on the horizon, a thin band of cloud merged with the mountains to their left, earth and sky forming a single, grey mass. Only by the bare, snow-free rock could one tell them apart. The wind had cleared the snow in places, revealing strips of bare earth parallel to the crest of the ridge. On the gentler, flatter slopes at the foot of the mountain, a few thin tree trunks held the thicker snow cover in place. A handful of reindeer, mostly indifferent to their presence, were digging into the layer of white, looking for lichen. They lifted their heads to watch as the men passed, then plunged into the snow once more, their bodies almost completely covered.

The mountain dipped gently down to the river. Massive boulders lay scattered over its flank. The geologist made his way up to inspect them – some were huge, others smaller. He looked at them carefully, taking a special interest in the larger ones, rapped them with his hammer and scanned them with his strange device. He took notes, consulted a map. The stranger reminded Aslak of a fox on the scent, every sense sharp and alert. Ready to bite and run. As he had done with Aslak: bitten hard, then kept his distance. Protected by the invisible threat at the other end of the radio. Aslak thought again of the sign his wife had traced in the dust.

The stranger was a fox. But Aslak was a wolf. He had spent his life in the wild, tracking animals. He was close to them. Knew their behaviour. He did not see them as strangers. A wolf could bite, too. And never let go. He was waiting for the right moment. He would wait a long time if he had to. The wolf was more patient than the fox. The fox gave up if he was not quickly satisfied. Not the wolf.

'Get a move on, dammit!' the stranger yelled. 'I need the bag. Quick, while there's still some moonlight!'

Aslak hurried over, but still his movements were supple, minimal, his chest thrust forward, arms at his sides, his disturbing presence undiminished. The stranger was kneeling beside a round boulder the size of a sleeping reindeer. He took the equipment he needed out of the bag, scratched the stone and poured some sort of liquid onto it. From time to time he glanced suspiciously at the Sami, but Aslak gave nothing away, responding with a vacant stare that seemed to irritate the other man intensely. His face was set in an ugly grimace, one corner of his mouth raised, creasing his cheek.

The stranger peered at the shard of rock under a magnifying glass, apparently disappointed. He swore in an unknown language and put away his equipment. Then he sent a short radio message, similar to the others. Showing Aslak that he was still under threat.

'We'll get back to the bivouac. Carry on along the river tomorrow. Move! I can hardly see my hand in front of my face. Get a fucking move on, we need wood, and supper. Move it, damn you!'

Aslak loaded the bag onto his shoulders and turned away. He barely felt the twenty-five kilos. He could carry a reindeer weighing fifty or sixty kilos on his back, if he had to, over long distances. The other herders had seen him do it. Even the ones who thought of themselves as real hard men had been impressed. Walking ahead of the stranger, finding his way with ease in the fading light, Aslak heard the man swearing in his wake. He couldn't understand what he was saying, but he felt that the longer it went on, the better it was for his purposes.

5.50 p.m., Kautokeino

Berit Kutsi crossed herself. She had just finished her day's work at Olsen's farm. The old man was nervous and jumpy, even more unpleasant than usual. Berit had spent a long while seeing to the cows. They were far less shy than the reindeer and allowed themselves to be stroked quite happily. You could talk to them. Berit told them things she dared not confess to the pastor. The cows were good company, for sure.

At this season, there was little work to be done out of doors. Olsen checked and repaired his machines. When his back wasn't playing him up, he would clear the roads with his snowplough. But he grumbled and cursed all day long. Occasionally, he would ask Berit to dust indoors. But he kept the house obsessively clean: there was seldom anything more for her to do. Berit sometimes thought he called her in just for the pleasure of taunting her. She was ashamed to think such things, but God knew she was a good woman at heart.

She always crossed herself on leaving the stable, so that the Almighty would spare a few thoughts for her companions. Cows did not have souls, but they were God's creatures, Berit knew that. Their good nature deserved some small reward. One day, she had confided her little ritual to Pastor Lars, and he had become angry.

For the first time in her life, she had decided to lie to him. When he asked her next if she was still praying for her cows, she had assured him she was not. She felt bad about that, of course, and now she dreaded talking to the pastor for any length of time. She was terrified he would give her one of his penetrating stares and force her to confess. He was quite capable of that.

Berit had feared her father the same way. He had been a strict Laestadian. She never remembered seeing him laugh. Not once. He wore the thick neck-beard of the older faithful, and a white shirt buttoned up the neck. He was hard but fair.

Berit's mother had converted in adulthood. She was a believer, of course, raised as a Protestant. But she had found the true Laestadian faith late in life. She had confessed to Berit that, before her conversion, she had always wondered whether her faith would hold fast in the face of death. A friend had told her mother that she knew a man who had just such faith. That man had become Berit's father. Since her conversion and marriage, Berit's mother had never doubted. Berit's six brothers and sisters were all Laestadians, too. Her mother's faith was unshaken by the death of two of them. It had grown stronger, if anything, in the face of adversity. Berit had grown up hugely impressed by her mother's radiant light. Her smile – because she did smile – was never excessive, always measured, and she knew how to contain her laughter. An admirable woman, who had passed too soon.

She once told Berit that she had been attracted to the Laestadian faith because it did more than take the forgiveness of sin for granted. You could actually confess your sins. Like the Catholics, Pastor Lars had assured her. Of course, the Catholics were no example in a great many other matters, everyone was agreed on that. But confession, and the forgiveness of sin, were wonderful gifts from God that enabled weak and fearful people like Berit to live with themselves and keep the fires of hell at bay.

Pastor Lars had always told her that for a person to come to the faith, they must first feel the nature of sin.

'He who did not kill the Lord Jesus his Creator has no need of salvation,' Pastor Lars had told her one day, shaking a trembling finger in her face. 'And he who comes not begging the Lord for salvation from sin will never make a true Protestant.'

There had been a time when Berit's father had nurtured the idea that Pastor Lars would make a good husband for his daughter. But fate had decided otherwise. The pastor had returned from his travels one day with a taciturn Finnish woman. During his wife's first pregnancy, the pastor had insisted to Berit, several times, that it was necessary to feel the nature of sin, in order to come to the true faith. He seemed to be insinuating that Berit was not of the true faith. She had expressed her anxiety over this to her mother. And her mother, not smiling at all then, had stayed behind at church after the Sunday service to have a brief exchange with the pastor. Berit had no idea what was said, but the pastor never again alluded to Berit's need to feel the true nature of sin. After the Finnish woman came into the pastor's life, there had been no suitors for Berit. She had devoted much of her time to her younger, mentally handicapped brother. And she had allowed the few opportunities that had come her way to pass her by, fearful of the word of God and submissive to the will of her parents. And yet Berit burned with ardent fire, though she never dared talk about it. Even after her parents had both died, she led the spartan Laestadian life, far removed from the worlds of fashion, and television, and consumerism. These things were easy to renounce. The people she liked and spent time with – reindeer herders for the most part, though not necessarily practising Laestadians – were hard workers, often living simple lives of poverty. Like Aslak.

Berit closed her eyes. She crossed herself again and left the cowshed just as a car pulled up outside. She recognised the policeman at the wheel, the one who detested the Sami, and saw him rush inside Olsen's house. Brattsen had been coming to see Olsen often in recent days. The old man seemed more and more restless, and nervous. Berit wondered if he was in trouble with the police. She couldn't imagine why. But then a lot of things escaped her.

6.05 p.m., Kautokeino

'They've reached the spot. I got a radio message from the Frenchman. He must have found a way to persuade Aslak to go with him.'

Olsen thought for a moment, then rubbed his hands together.

'Ha! We may have picked a winner with this one at last,' he said.

'Perhaps, perhaps. Don't go counting your chickens, though. I had to tell the station that the Frenchman had left alone. And Nango knows he wanted to see you. I had to tell him you never saw one another.'

'Well, you did right, lad. Didn't meet him officially, did I, eh? And don't you worry, your Frenchman and Aslak might not get along. Sparks may fly. Wouldn't be at all surprised if they came to blows.'

'What do you mean?' Brattsen had no idea what Olsen was getting at.

'You told me the first time you saw the Frenchman was in a fight at the pub?'

'Yeah, so?'

Olsen was losing patience. He would have to spell it out.

'You told me yourself, your first thought was that you suspected him of murdering Mattis.'

'That's true.'

'So? See my point?'

'But since then, I've been thinking it really was a vendetta between reindeer breeders.'

'Bravo!' exclaimed Olsen emphatically. 'And you're the cop, you know better than anyone about all that. I'm just an old farmer. Intuition? Not me! All I know is the colour and smell of the soil. I'm just saying, your Frenchman aroused your suspicion; and you followed your instinct, and that led you to the business with the little girls. See? You were right, there.'

'True. I was,' said Brattsen.

'That's what good cops do, isn't it, follow their instinct?'

'Yeah, sure,' Brattsen replied cautiously. He still wasn't catching Olsen's drift.

Karl Olsen frowned and turned to face the policeman.

'And now your instinct is telling you that this business is all about the Lapp breeders settling their scores.'

'Yes. But the Reindeer Police think the Frenchman might be implicated in some way. Because of the business with the mine and the drum. And the Sheriff seems determined to follow their lead.'

Olsen exploded. 'Stuff and nonsense!' Hastily he softened his tone. 'You know what, lad? Your father – back when we were hunting Commies, they tried to lead him a dance every now and then, laying false trails. But he wasn't fooled, not him. He had the measure of them. He always caught them out in the end. And I remember he used to say he had a sixth sense. He'd always flush them out, the bastards. Ha! You're his boy and no mistake. A proper bloodhound! Am I right? There's no telling you stories, is there, eh, lad? You can see it's the breeder's business. See what I mean, boy?'

Rolf Brattsen fixed Olsen with his usual hard stare. Perhaps he understood, but Olsen wanted to be sure.

'See, lad, what I'm getting at is, it would be a shame if the police wasted time and resources chasing after the Frenchman out in the *vidda*. And it won't do our bit of business any good to have them on his tail. See what I mean, lad?'

Brattsen seemed to be turning it over in his mind. Now Olsen was sure the policeman had taken his meaning. The old farmer watched the officer's tortured expression, thinking that Brattsen looked every bit as stupid as his father. He had hardly known the man in truth, but it was there in his face.

'Yeah, I see what you mean,' said Brattsen finally. 'But there's not much I can do to put Nango off the scent. The Sheriff doesn't trust me.'

'So the Sheriff's the problem?'

'In a way, yes. The Reindeer Police just do as they're told. And the Sheriff's under pressure to deliver results, with the UN conference coming up.'

Olsen was deep in thought.

'And what if your Sheriff, Superintendent Jensen, was relieved of his duties. What would happen then?' he asked, suddenly.

'Relieved of his functions?'

'You heard.'

Brattsen thought hard. Suddenly, his face brightened into an expression of boyish delight. He was Deputy Superintendent, after all. Dear God, he looks almost simple, Olsen thought. But the old farmer smiled indulgently.

'If Jensen was out of the way, I could call off the Reindeer Police,' said Brattsen.

'Good lad. See, your old dad would have been proud. I've had a little idea. We'll have to act fast, but it might just work.'

7 p.m., Highway 93

Nina was sleeping in the passenger seat, curled deep in her snow-suit, her head resting on a cushion, her blonde hair tucked into her chapka. The heater was on full. Outside, the temperature was still glacial. The wind had risen again, blowing in from Siberia. Nina was tough, but she had sunk into the car after leaving the Geology Institute, grateful for a chance to rest.

Klemet headed straight for Kiruna, to the north. Patrol P9 was expected at Reindeer Police headquarters the following morning. Isolated in the midst of the tundra, the mining town was home to the regional police headquarters for central Sápmi. Kiruna was Klemet's home town. He had been born there, and he'd lived there for a few years, too. He liked the plump, regular silhouette of the mountain, excavated into a series of steps.

The mine had moved underground in the 1960s: an invisible labyrinth of subterranean roads, four hundred kilometres in total, made possible by ever more sophisticated technology. For the local Sami, the mine traffic had disrupted their way of life, cutting across migration routes, bringing noise pollution, destroying pasture. Klemet's father had worked in the mine at times when the farms in Norwegian Sápmi had less need of hired labour. Plenty of miners were seasonal, like him. People in Sápmi often had several different jobs throughout the year. No one was afraid of travelling long distances. Migration was in the blood, up here in the North. Klemet had tried to break away from all that. He had cherished a mad dream of becoming a whale-hunter once, as he had told Nina, but he had never taken the idea any further. He dared not admit to his colleague that the nearest he had come to a seafaring life was two summers spent working in a fish factory in the Lofoten Islands. The work had been well paid, but held no appeal otherwise. And it had been made quite clear to him that the factory was no place for a Sami. But was he a true Sami, really? A true Sami was a reindeer herder. His father had never insisted on their Sami identity.

Sami society was close knit and highly structured. The breeders were a caste apart, very much at the top of the pile. The aristocracy. They were the big families, the ones who owned vast herds, the ones who called the shots, who could tell the Reindeer Administration how many reindeer they intended to keep, not the other way around, without fear of reprimand, or almost. After that came the young people who had chosen to study. There were fewer of them, and the phenomenon was quite recent, but there were one or two Sami lawyers now, and doctors. And then came the anonymous ranks, the ones who didn't really know whether they were Sami or Norwegian, Finnish or Swedish. And at the bottom of the pile came the people the world of reindeer breeding had spat out. The ones who had failed. The pariahs. Like his grandfather.

Klemet wondered who had found that the hardest. His grandfather, who had thought it over and made a choice, because he could no longer feed his family, and who had thrown himself into farming and fishing on the shores of the little lake where Klemet had spent his early years? Or his father, who had known the free nomadic life as a child, with its reindeer and its pride, and who suddenly, without understanding why, had found all that taken away and been subjected to the taunts of adolescents his own age? Demoted. When Klemet was old enough, his father had insisted he go to school to learn Norwegian, wanting to make a proper Norwegian of him, never to feel the shame. He'd wanted him to live his life far from the world of the breeders who scorned the family. But it hadn't been that simple. At boarding school, he had found himself studying with the sons of nomadic breeders. With Aslak.

Klemet was overcome with tiredness. They were nearing Kiruna. Already he could see the familiar floodlights and the silhouette of the mine. He liked the lights. They reminded him of coming home as a child from the family farm in Kautokeino, on the other side of the mountain, after hours on foot, or by boat, depending on the season. After anxious, exhausting hours journeying through the dark, the magic of the lights awaited him still.

They arrived just as the nightly explosions began to shake the entrails of the mine. Nina was still sleeping. Klemet headed for the Reindeer Police hut on this side of town. Gently, he nudged her awake.

They had been in their bunks just a few minutes when the hut shuddered slightly. Business was still booming.

37

Saturday 22 January

Sunrise: 9.35 a.m.; sunset: 1.27 p.m.
3 hours 52 minutes of sunlight

9 a.m., Kiruna, Sweden

Officers in the Reindeer Police were used to keeping odd hours. And just occasionally, they managed to convince their colleagues to adapt to their needs. The Reindeer Police headquarters were housed in a converted fire station – an unusual building with an attractive turret, all in white-painted timber, not far from the huge red church, the pride of Kiruna.

The other members of the Reindeer Police were nowhere to be seen – out on patrol in the four corners of Sápmi, or on leave. Klemet made coffee and placed the thermos in the meeting room. Its windows overlooked the church, which was due to be dismantled and moved in a few years – part of a plan to displace Kiruna's town centre, so as not to slow the march of the iron-ore mine beneath their feet. Nina took some photographs out of the window – 'On a long exposure,' as she explained to Klemet. They were several hundred kilometres south of Kautokeino, but it was still not fully light in Kiruna at this hour.

Anders Sunneborn, the forensic pathologist, arrived at 9 a.m. precisely. He looked half frozen, wrapped in a huge fur-lined parka. He had slipped on a sheet of black ice just outside and entered the room limping and cursing.

'Time you started wearing those shoe cleats your mother-in-law bought you,' advised Klemet.

'Spare me the topical tips. Try to understand there are some depths a Stockholmer will never sink to.' He winced in pain as he spoke.

Klemet liked Anders. They had worked together in Stockholm on the Palme investigation. He had seldom met anyone so open-minded and unprejudiced. They had drunk a few beers together at Pelikan or Kvarnen, when the doc had tried to make a Hammarby supporter of him. But Klemet was completely uninterested in foot-ball, as Anders had soon realised. Still, Klemet never felt the need to be on the defensive in his presence. And that was worth a cer-tain amount of self-sacrifice: evenings spent following the match on a giant screen, surrounded by bellowing fans in green and white scarves, Anders included.

Fredrik, from forensics, was not on time, which came as no sur-prise to Klemet. He had agreed to attend the meeting against his will and it was just like him to make a show of discontent by turn-ing up late.

'Here's Fredrik,' said Nina, waving through the window.

Klemet looked at his watch. Only five minutes late. The man clearly wasn't trying. Fredrik entered the room, removing his cash-mere scarf and camel-hair hat with a theatrical gesture. He was freshly shaven, smelling of quality aftershave. He directed a charm-ing smile at Nina.

'Let's get started then.' Klemet did not attempt to conceal his irri-tation and made a show of looking at his watch, too. 'We've got a long drive back to Kautokeino.'

'Oh, you're not staying tonight? What a shame.' Fredrik gave Nina a meaningful look. 'There are some groups in town for the UN conference. They're giving a concert this evening.'

Nina smiled politely and turned to Klemet. Anders spoke first.

'Well then,' he said, opening his file. 'So our man Mattis died about an hour after being stabbed with a knife of this type.' He slid a photograph across the table. 'And the ears were cut off roughly two hours after the time of death. Nothing new there. The second ear is Mattis's, predictably enough. I've done some blow-ups of the marks on the ears,' he said, pushing more photographs across the table to the officers. 'Have you got any further with the identification of the marks?'

Klemet frowned.

'I was getting further with just the one ear. The cuts on the second ear took me away from my initial lead.'

'Could that mean two different breeders?' asked the examiner.

'Normally, you need the marks from both ears to identify one owner,' Klemet told him.

'But since the breeders aren't in the habit of incising their own ears, perhaps we shouldn't be reading these signs in the traditional way,' observed Fredrik drily, happy to put Klemet in his place.

'Quite,' said Klemet, without looking at Fredrik. 'Except the marks on the second ear really don't suggest any breeder in particular, in the way the first ear did. And that makes me think they may not point to the reindeer breeders at all.'

'On the subject of breeders and their marks, I've done tests on the knives taken away from Johann Henrik's place,' said the doc. 'Traces of blood on all of them. Reindeer blood, except on one knife where I found human blood. But not Mattis's. A harmless accident, perhaps.'

He slid a few sheets of paper over to Klemet.

'And the GPS?' asked Klemet, somewhat impatiently.

Fredrik got to his feet. 'It's all there. I managed to recover some of the data. Think I did a pretty good job.'

'What did you recover?' Nina pressed him.

'Data on his positions, basically, so we have a record of his movements over the past six months. I've printed out the week prior to his death. Let me know if you need more, Nina.'

'Print out the week before that, then,' said Klemet, irritated that Fredrik was ignoring him and talking to Nina. 'And do it now, so we can get going as soon as possible.'

Klemet watched with satisfaction as Fredrik's ears reddened. Double satisfaction when he complied straight away and left the room. Immediately, Klemet and Nina began examining the documents. The GPS data was fairly scant. The device was damaged, and it hadn't been possible to retrieve any maps. But the raw data were there, at least, from which it would be possible to identify co-ordinates and times. A lengthy, painstaking task. And there was no indication as to whether the data were complete. This would become clear only once the coordinates were plotted on a map.

Fredrik returned after five minutes with a handful of stapled sheets, dropping them onto the table.

'Oh, I almost forgot, Mattis's poncho. I picked it over very thoroughly. All kinds of stuff there. The list is in the file, too. You were interested in the grease stains. It's motor oil, but not the kind he used in his scooter. That's about it. If you've got no more questions for the moment, I'll be getting along.'

Fredrik was clearly annoyed. Swedish good manners demanded a gesture of reconciliation on Klemet's part, but he really didn't feel inclined. Arrogant, self-assured types like Fredrik exasperated him. He let him go without a word, leaving it to Nina to thank him.

Anders smiled broadly when Fredrik had gone.

'What an idiot,' he commented to Klemet. 'You won't change him.'

'The guy doesn't even realise he's doing it. Behaviour like that just comes naturally to him. All airs and graces. A proper Stockholmer,' he added, with a wink for Anders.

'Well, hark at you,' the doc joked. 'Pay no attention to him, Nina – I can see you think he's overreacting. Your partner has old scores to settles with a certain section of humanity.' Meaning Casanovas like Fredrik.

'Absolutely not!' Klemet burst out, amiably. 'I'm not out to settle scores with anyone!'

'No . . .' The doc's reply was heavy with irony. 'Anyway, Nina, you should know you're working with one hell of a cop, a real obsessive for the fine detail that can make an investigation. A dedicated seeker after proof. Klemet, you remember the dark circles under Mattis's eyes? You asked me to take a look.'

'That's true,' Nina interrupted, 'they struck me, too, when I saw the corpse. Dark rings, maybe bruises. He must have suffered terribly.'

'Well, they were smears, not bruises.' The doc was staring straight at Klemet. 'Smears of blood.'

9.30 a.m., Central Sápmi

Aslak and Racagnal had set out early, in the same direction as the day before. Racagnal continued sending radio messages at regular intervals. This morning, he had taken the gun lent him by the proprietor of the Villmarkssenter, too. One of the reindeer they had spotted yesterday would make a nice change for supper. Before setting off, he had spent a long time poring over the map, asking Aslak about this or that faultline, the cliffs, a river. The Sami had an encyclopaedic knowledge of the region. And he could describe the shapes and colours of particular boulders in just a few, terse words. No substitute for a geologist's observations in the field, of course, but enough for Racagnal to narrow the area of his search.

Aslak had said nothing since leaving the camp, but the geologist was unconcerned. Racagnal walked slowly, astronaut-like in his thick, fur-lined snowsuit and field boots, his face almost completely hidden by a scarf. As always when out in the field, he began talking to himself, out loud. And Aslak made a great audience. He listened to everything, acquiesced to everything, in silence.

'A nice little reindeer tonight, what do you say, Sami? We'll cook up a feast, you'll see. I can be out prospecting for two, three, even four weeks. And you can't carry food for four weeks. But a true geologist will get by. Give me a fishing rod and I'll feed a village. But a little reindeer will do just nicely. Got a problem with that? No comment? Just as well. Ah, look at that boulder. Magnificent. You won't mind if I give it a scratch. I'll just take my hammer – this one's Swedish, did you know that? – and smash it good and hard in the face, there, job done. See that, Sami? The boulder didn't put up much a fight, eh? But you don't know what "boulder" means. Well, I'll tell you, it's a nice piece of rock stuffed full of mineral ores, see? No, you don't see. Yes, you see. Well, just listen, you seem happy enough doing that. This one's a fine little piece of magma. See how it glitters there? That's a pretty bit of quartz. Couldn't give a damn, could you? You're right. It's shit. Pretty, but shit. But see here, the old farmer's gold, you can find it in quartz like that. So get a move on. I want to get on round the bend in the river. Scratch around a bit down there. Won't take too much out of the day.'

Racagnal felt good now. He was in his element. King of all he surveyed; on the scent, every sense honed, dredging his memory for rock classifications, comparisons with a faultline observed in another place twenty years ago, something that might help him interpret what he was seeing, something that no other geologist alive would think of. All because he, Racagnal, had an unerring sensory memory.

He could remember every single one of his sexual conquests. Kept a precise inventory, allowing him to re-create every last detail – the texture of the skin, the feel of the hair, the plump curve of a hip, a budding breast. And the look. The eyes. Racagnal had seen so many. A whole gallery. He saw them one by one in his mind's eye now, intimidated, submissive, blank, conquered. Rebellious, begging, terrified. Conquered. Every one of them conquered.

They had reached the bend in the river.

'Here,' he held out his hammer to Aslak. 'Break some ice there. We'll take a look.'

Racagnal installed a makeshift shelter against the cold and spread out the reindeer skins Aslak had been carrying. He took out his field stove and boiled some water, diffusing a hint of warmth in the shelter. It would be a tough day. The cold devoured your energy, fast. He slipped fresh handwarmers inside his gloves, stepped outside the shelter and looked around. The river wasn't very wide at this point. To the east, an open stretch of ground extended for several hundred metres, covered in a fine layer of snow. Even the smallest swellings and mounds broke through the white surface, revealing clumps of heather crystallised by the cold. He could practically count the shrubs in sight, they were so few, so thin. Further off, a low mountain barred the horizon, with what looked like a lake at its foot, judging from the flat, uniform sheet of white. This was a sleepy, gently rolling landscape, glittering now in the rays of the rising sun. Not enough to warm the bones, but it meant the day's prospecting was about to start in earnest.

Racagnal had very little time. The more he thought about it, the more he realised how important it was for him to make a success of this hare-brained mission. He couldn't afford to become the object of a police investigation. Couldn't let his victims' eyes become the eyes of his accusers.

38

Saturday 22 January

9.55 a.m., Swedish Lapland

Klemet and Nina hadn't stayed long in Kiruna. Preparations were in full swing to welcome some of the delegations attending the UN conference. Huge Sami tents had been put up, housing exhibitions or seminars. Workmen were unloading sound equipment in the foyer of the Ferrum hotel. Klemet and Nina walked the length of the red-brick City Hall, with its clocktower of metal girders. Nina was wide-eyed, seeing the capital of Swedish Lapland in daylight for the first time. She had come here when she joined the Reindeer Police just a few weeks ago, but it looked quite different now in the early sunshine. She managed to persuade Klemet to take a photograph of her in front of City Hall. Her partner was half asleep this morning – she had to ask him to take the picture three times, to be sure to get everything in: Nina, the City Hall and the mine in the background.

They drove out of town. Immediately, the tundra asserted its presence. Yesterday's clouds had cleared, the sun shone and the intense glare ricocheted off the hills. Sápmi lay sparkling and glittering all around. The immensity of the landscape, its vast horizons, were plain to see. So different from what Nina had known in the furthest part of her deep, narrow fjord, with its sheer cliffs plunging straight into the sea, its scraps of moorland and its fields perched high above the water. You had to go to the mouth of the fjord and gaze out west to the horizon, to experience anything on the scale of Lapland. The tundra would have its secrets, Nina thought, like the sea. She had learned all about that. She had suspected nothing, as a young girl, until her mother spoke to her about her father's problems. He had gone down to the bottom of the sea, and he had never been the same. The sea that seemed so predictable, so knowable, concealed forces that had almost killed him.

Nina opened her rucksack and pulled out the folder containing the report on Mattis's poncho.

'Motor oil, but not from Mattis's scooter,' she said, thinking aloud.

'Yes, it could have come from the scooter that left the deep tracks,' said Klemet. 'We'll have to look into that when we get back. We need to look again at the list of all the scooter models and fuels and oils used by each of the herders. We'll check out all the service stations locally. Might speed things up.'

'Klemet, what do you think about the blood under the eyes?'

Nina's partner seemed transfixed by the icy, sparkling road.

'Blood smeared under the eyes, severed ears, it's looking more and more like some kind of ritual. But . . . .'

Klemet fell silent. Nina knew he was stuck, like her.

'Ritual? Could that really be some sort of Sami rite? It's so savage, so far from anything Scandinavian people would do. Yet the Sami are always portrayed as such a peaceful people.'

'They are, as a rule. Don't say no one's told you this yet – the Sami language has no word for "war".'

Hours passed in which Klemet and Nina took turns at the wheel. They turned on the radio after stopping for a short break. They were in Finland now, but the radio was picking up a Norwegian station. The NRK regional news for the Finnmark would be on soon. Nina poured coffee while Klemet drove. The presenter began with the weather forecast, followed by news of a catastrophic road accident in Alta. Two dead, including a young man from Kautokeino. Nina stared at Klemet, who shook his head as the victim's name was read out.

'A young breeder. Decent guy. A tragedy for his family.'

The NRK bulletin continued. There was important news from Hammerfest, the region's gas port. A major investment had just been finalised, bringing one hundred new jobs. Then news of preparations for the UN conference, and a host of cultural events taking place at the same time all over the region. Local associations were also organising to get their voices heard.

'Difficult to imagine so much activity when all you can see is the empty tundra,' said Nina.

Gradually, the sky turned an astonishing, intense royal blue, matching the new intensity of the presenter's voice, for the next item:

'And some news just in: Kautokeino police superintendent Tor Jensen has been suspended and summoned to an emergency meeting at regional police headquarters in Hammerfest.'

Klemet slammed on the brakes. Nina spilled her coffee but ignored the hot liquid dribbling down her snowsuit. She sat riveted, like Klemet, to the radio news.

'Speaking from Kautokeino, NRK reporter Tomas Mikkelsen says the emergency summons is highly unusual. Regional police headquarters intervened following the theft of a unique Sami drum from the museum in Kautokeino. With the UN conference in Kiruna just days away, the drum has still not been found. The artefact was due to go on public display for the first time, as a strong signal of UN member states' reconciliation with their indigenous populations.

'Still in Kautokeino, the identity of the murderer of reindeer breeder Mattis Labba remains a mystery. The savage crime has shaken the local population. Signs indicate that Labba suffered torture, with both ears torn off. Anxiety and surprise at the slow police response have been growing in the region, with Superintendent Tor Jensen taking the brunt of criticism. Sources close to police headquarters suggest the summons to Hammerfest may lead to his permanent dismissal.'

*

10 a.m., Kautokeino

Berit Kutsi concealed her surprise when Karl Olsen called her over to the house earlier than usual, while she was still in the cowshed. She worked for just a couple of hours on Saturdays, making sure milking proceeded without a hitch, and the cows were well supplied with feed and water. She had barely finished when Olsen yelled for her. Berit hurried out of the cowshed straightaway. The cold bit hard, and the cowshed was heated to the minimum, to keep down costs. Berit wore an old, dark blue wool tunic over her snowsuit. An unorthodox look, but practical for seeing to the cows in such extreme temperatures. Emerging from the barn, she saw John and his inseparable friend Mikkel, clad in mechanics' overalls. The two young herders earned extra cash by doing maintenance work on the local farmers' machines. They climbed into a small van and drove off the farm.

'God almighty, Berit! Get a move on, woman!' shouted Olsen.

Poor Berit scurried over to the farmhouse, a sizeable, rectangular block in yellow-painted wood, its door- and window-frames painted white, its entrance protected by a carved wooden portico. She almost slipped on the ice in her reindeer-skin boots, saved herself as best she could, then hurried up the steps under the portico and in through the door, eager to get into the warmth. She removed her boots and went through to the kitchen. Olsen was waiting, in his usual chair.

'You took your time. Can't spend my life waiting around for you. There's cleaning to do here. I'm expecting people. And you can do a bit upstairs, too. You haven't been up there for years. Make sure you're finished by lunchtime. Well, get to it, woman!'

Berit turned and walked through to the back room leading off the kitchen. She collected the broom, the dustpan and brush, and the cleaning products. Olsen's old wooden house wasn't that big, but it was well maintained. The wooden floors, and the few pieces of furniture in the kitchen and sitting room, were all of pale wood. Long narrow rugs, woven by the local women and sold in the market, added a touch of colour. The ground floor had an impersonal look. No mementos, no sign of family life. The few items lying here and there were all related to Olsen's business: equipment, tools, trade magazines, parts in need of repair. Old Olsen didn't entertain often, and his sitting room was more of a workshop than a reception room. When he did have guests, he would invite them into the big kitchen, where he himself spent most of his time.

Downstairs, the cleaning was soon finished. Berit tidied up the sitting room, but dared not touch the tools and dismembered parts, knowing the farmer would fly into a rage if she moved anything. She tidied the magazines and a handful of Progress Party tracts into a neat pile next to the television.

Berit was more curious to clean upstairs. She had been up there only once in ten years, at Olsen's express wish, shortly after the old man's wife had died. Olsen had asked her to fetch his wife's clothes and do with them as she saw fit.

'Burn them if you want, Berit, but get them out of here,' the old farmer had grumbled.

It was no secret in town that the Olsens' marriage had been cold, to say the least, for a good thirty years. Husband and wife had slept in separate rooms after their only son left home. He had gone to study engineering in Tromsø and never came back to Kautokeino after that. Olsen's wife had been even more ill-tempered than her husband – a tigress by all accounts, a thoroughly uncompromising woman, harder and more moralising than a platoon of Laestadian preachers bent on redemption.

Cleaning upstairs in the past, Berit had seen one or two family photographs, pictures of relatives she had never come across in person. These had soon disappeared after his wife's death. Olsen had been quick to stow the severe faces out of sight, in a trunk, which he had taken to the attic.

'The old scold wouldn't even have portraits of my family on the walls.' Olsen had spat the words out. 'Reckoned they were lost to the true faith. Degenerates, she said! Well, her lot can choke in there!' And he had slammed the attic door shut.

Berit remembered that day well. She had seen no portraits since. So her curiosity was aroused when she noticed that the top landing and bedrooms had been hung with pictures again, but nothing like the ones she remembered. These were landscapes of the *vidda*. Berit was in a hurry to finish, but lingered in front of each one, nonetheless. She identified one or two views of Olsen's land: regular, well-maintained fields, their owner's pride and joy. At the top of the stairs, Berit recognised a picture of his first ever combine harvester. She went into his wife's bedroom. There was just room to stand under the low ceiling. It was bare, apart from a mattress thrown onto the floor and some boxes piled in a corner. The room was unused since her death, yet it seemed clean and dusted. Berit crossed herself and closed the door behind her.

'Haven't you finished yet?' hollered Olsen from below.

'Soon, soon. Just your room to do.'

Berit slipped along the corridor and pushed open the door. The old farmer lived simply, and his bedroom was no exception. His bed stood immediately inside the door, fitted into an alcove in the old-fashioned way, the wooden panels painted with folk motifs. There were drawers underneath, and it was closed off with a curtain. Laestadians forbade curtains at the windows, but Olsen had found a way to get around his wife's prohibitions by installing some for his bed, to shut out the endless summer light. Berit was not surprised that he still had none at the windows, even long after his wife's death. That was like him. Anything to save money.

Berit wiped a damp sponge and duster over the antique piece, opened the curtains and shook the coarse sheets. She dusted the large, pale wooden wardrobe occupying the wall opposite the bed. She listened out for sounds elsewhere in the house, then opened it. The shelves were half empty. A few thick sweaters and shirts, pairs of jeans. Everything carefully folded. Berit dusted the shelves quickly.

She looked around her and saw framed photographs on the other two walls. She went over and examined them all in turn. They formed a gallery of individual and group portraits. Olsen's family, she thought, remembering the old farmer's rage when he had thrown his wife's pictures into the attic. One photograph of Olsen's son showed the boy at his high-school graduation, but there were no more recent pictures of him. Other, older pictures depicted what must be Olsen's parents. Berit had never known them. A strict-looking couple, too. Olsen's father wore a curious cowboy-style hat, unusually for a local farmer. He had been something of an eccentric, people said. Other photographs were of his grandparents. Berit dusted the frames.

'Berit, for God's sake, woman, haven't you finished yet?'

She dusted faster. When she had finished the frames, and a shelf supporting a scant row of books, she paused and looked around. At the far end of the room she saw a low door, possibly leading to a built-in cupboard that she had never noticed before. She listened, then moved towards the door. It opened outwards, making no noise. It was dark on the other side. She felt for a light switch, revealing a small, dimly lit room. A cubbyhole, really. A tiny table with a rickety chair tucked under it were the only bits of furniture. The small space was cluttered with trunks, rolled-up documents and maps. Moving these to one side, she found a small safe. Old Olsen probably didn't trust the banks, she thought to herself. She wiped its top with a sponge, then carried on cleaning, intrigued but not daring to unroll the papers or open the trunks, in case Olsen crept up on her. I'm doing nothing wrong, thought Berit. Why should I be afraid? She shrugged nervously and dusted some more before stepping back into the bedroom and closing the little door behind her.

A silhouette loomed in the doorway beyond the bed. Berit started and stifled a cry: Olsen had climbed the stairs silently in his stockinged feet. He looked at her, saying nothing, his legs planted firmly apart, arms hanging loosely at his sides.

39

Saturday 22 January

2 p.m., Kautokeino

Patrol P9's pick-up drove down the main street in Kautokeino. The sun had set, but a steely afterglow clung to the tops of the low mountains surrounding the little town. The buildings followed the curve of the river Alta, slumbering under the ice. On the west side of town, the ground rose steeply from the river to a summit barring the horizon, below which the sun had disappeared, silhouetting it now in a gleam of deep, clear blue. The western slope was home to Juhl's museum, the Villmarkssenter hotel, the new Sami University College and the gas station. The opposite bank offered a broader expanse of gently sloping ground rising to the eastern mountains, much further away and already shrouded in darkness. The advancing shadows had stolen over the church and the comfortable villas scattered along the western shore. Olsen's farm stood near the river, on the edge of town. People joked that Olsen guarded the south, while the church guarded the north. The Sami had always lived mostly to the west, though many people had spilled over to the east side in recent years.

On a normal Saturday afternoon, the police station would be standing empty. Police budgets didn't allow for 24/7 manning, and the station's public opening hours were those of any public administrative building – nine to five, Monday to Friday. In summer, you were lucky to find anyone there on a Friday afternoon, either. And in the moose and partridge season, absenteeism rocketed.

Klemet pushed the door and found the station open. News of Tor Jensen's summons to Hammerfest had sent shockwaves through his small team. Klemet knew Tomas, the local NRK reporter, quite well. Well enough to know that the Sheriff's official reprimand was more than hearsay. Tomas Mikkelsen was a news hound; he knew everyone, and his friends in the Labour Party, the controlling force in the region, made sure he got the gossip on every local intrigue. Klemet had thought about giving him a call, but held back.

He spotted the station receptionist. She looked utterly defeated. Her eyes filled with tears at the sight of Klemet, and she burst out sobbing when he comforted her with a hug, patting her on the shoulder.

'What's going on?'

'Oh!' Her words stuck in her throat.

Klemet patted her on the shoulder again, then walked on down the corridor. Nina hugged the receptionist briefly and followed him in the direction of the Sheriff's office. Klemet pushed the door. The room was as empty as Jensen's bowl of *salmiakki*. There were voices coming from the kitchen where a group of officers were discussing the matter. They fell silent when they saw Klemet. He was about to ask them all what was going on when the kitchen door opened again and Rolf Brattsen entered. He glanced around, spotted the steaming coffee pot and filled a mug, taking his time. Klemet's hackles rose. Brattsen looked a little too sure of himself. The other officers said nothing. Cups and biscuit tins littered the big table. A plate displayed the crumbs of a round of pastries. One of the officers picked at them.

Nina broke the heavy silence.

'What's happened with Tor?'

Brattsen stood cradling his mug in both hands, blowing lightly across the surface of the coffee, eyes flicking around the room. One of the officers glared at Brattsen, then looked up at Nina.

'Tor left early this morning for Hammerfest. It all happened very quickly. The chief ordered him in straightaway. Sounded pretty angry, from what the Sheriff said. The guys at the station in Hammerfest reckon it's all politically motivated. Something came up during a sitting of the regional council yesterday evening, it seems. Completely unannounced. Not even on the agenda. The Conservatives, the Progress Party and the Christian Democrats all demanded an explanation from the Sheriff about the "unbelievably slow police response to the exceptional events sullying the region's reputation in the run-up to the UN conference". Their exact words. People are saying it all started here.' He caught Brattsen's eye. 'In Kautokeino, I mean, not the station.'

'Why would the regional assembly get mixed up in this?' Nina wanted to know.

'They get mixed up in matters that concern them,' Brattsen cut in suddenly, banging his mug down on the yellow plastic table-cloth. 'We're treading water here. And you can't blame the politicians for getting edgy, with the UN conference around the corner. It's what I've been saying from the start. We've been taking this too softly-softly. Making too many allowances for the Sami. We're cops, for Christ's sake, not fucking ethnologists, zoo keepers, mediators or whatever else they'd have us be. Things need to get moving!'

'What do you mean by that?' Nina continued. 'It seems to me we're making progress, even if no one's been arrested.'

'Oh yeah, making progress, are you? News to me. Truth is, we're a laughing stock.'

'And what's your suggestion?' Klemet hadn't taken his eyes off Brattsen since he entered the room. 'Because you've obviously got an idea up your sleeve. Go on, let's hear it.'

12.30 p.m., Kautokeino

Olsen's silence was even more disturbing than his usual violent outbursts of rage. The old man seemed to be sizing her up. Berit felt utterly transparent, as if he was trying to see into her soul, read her intentions. She lowered her eyes to the floor.

'I just finished,' she said quietly. She walked quickly past Olsen, who watched her go, rooted to the spot, turning his head until the pain of his stiff neck cut in.

'Dear God. Get on home! Wretched woman! And don't think you'll be cleaning up here again. You're not needed!'

Berit wasn't arguing. She hurried downstairs and busied herself dusting the hallway one last time. Olsen followed, grumbling under his breath. He pushed past her, watched as Berit finished what she was doing and climbed into her car, then went back into the kitchen.

He was waiting for Rolf Brattsen to drop by with the latest news. The old farmer had called up all his contacts on the previous evening. He'd spoken to Prince Charming at the council offices, too. Even managed to convince him this was a great opportunity for the Progress Party to stir things up a bit. He hinted strongly that his fellow councillor should contact his good friend, the Conservative member for Kautokeino and Alta, and use the current session at the regional assembly to make some noise about the whole business of the drum, and the murder. No harm dramatising things a bit. Olsen had been suitably flattering, hinting that, with the municipal elections coming up, he was thinking of stepping down as head of the Progress Party list in Kautokeino.

Prince Charming had been quick to take his meaning. Started sounding off as if he was already the town's Mayor. Olsen had forced himself to listen, responding with great enthusiasm to his colleague's vacuous ideas. He had advised caution, too, before the kid seized the telephone, calling contacts, pulling strings. Ideally, Olsen had suggested, with heavy emphasis, the intervention at the assembly should come from the Conservatives. Prince Charming had failed to see why the Progress Party should hide behind their centre-right colleagues. Olsen had been expecting that.

'Like this, you can gauge reaction, lad,' he said. 'If the assembly goes our way, you can get out your big guns, and then you'll be in the front line when they're handing out the plaudits – you'll be the man with the solution.'

Olsen's benign mask had almost slipped when Prince Charming fixed him with his usual, incomprehending stare. The solution? What solution? He was eager to know.

'I'll explain later, lad.' Olsen was evasive. 'But if the question falls flat, public opinion will come down hard on the Conservatives, see? Your backside's covered!'

Now his colleague understood. Especially the bit about saving his own backside. Olsen had to admit, Prince Charming had acted with lightning efficiency after that. He had got the message out and the Conservatives had fired the question straight as an arrow during other business at the end of the session. It had struck home even better than Karl Olsen could have hoped.

The old man had rubbed his hands in satisfied glee for a good half an hour, all alone in his kitchen, when his colleague had called to report back. He grinned to himself and massaged the nape of his neck. The Conservative Party man had got all fired up, it seemed, the more so because he had been sent packing thirty minutes earlier by a Labour councillor, over some business about funding for a community association. Everything had fallen into place perfectly after that. Now for the second phase of his plan. Olsen massaged his neck hard, looked at his watch and cursed that ass Brattsen for his late appearance.

6.30 p.m., Kautokeino

Klemet was hungry for more. He wanted to find out what Brattsen was planning, what he really had in mind to sort this business out, as he had put it. Brattsen had come over all indignant and walked out, after which everyone had headed home. They would have to wait until Monday morning for more news. Klemet and Nina had already used up quite enough of their weekend. The investigation would resume on Monday, when the Sheriff's fate became clearer.

Klemet wanted to invite Nina over, to mark the end of an intense week, but he didn't feel he could ask her back to the tent again. Not after his recent blunder.

'Nina, do you fancy getting something to eat at the Villmarkssenter?'

'I'm exhausted, Klemet. Not tonight. I'm off to get some sleep. I'll take some of the GPS data, you take the rest. See you on Monday!'

He found himself alone at the station. He had got used to that, ever since his younger days. Over the years, he had grown accustomed to his own company. He was hardened to it. It had even become a strength. He had understood: there was no one to rely on but himself. He had steered his own course. Other people thought of him as a solitary type, a little shy, perhaps. He didn't see himself that way. Thought he was pretty friendly, really. He always spoke. It didn't matter what people thought of him.

He wondered whom he could call tonight for a drink in the tent. He thought of Eva Nilsdotter. Too far away to invite, though they could talk on the phone. A terrific woman, a real character. Who else?

He switched off the light in his office, stood for a moment in the corridor. He pushed the door opposite, leading to the map room and the chest freezer packed with exhibits from the Reindeer Police patrols. He lifted the lid. Mattis's frozen ears were in separate plastic bags, labelled individually and tied together with string. Small chance of confusing them with the dozens of reindeer ears piled alongside, he thought. He took the bags out and examined them from all sides. The incisions hadn't kept their shape. Thoughtful, he put them back in the freezer and left the room. He went back to his office and reached for the handbook of breeders' marks on the shelf. Some Sunday reading. Tonight, too, perhaps. He was tired. He wouldn't call anyone.

The blue afterglow had disappeared by the time Klemet crossed the road on foot. Greenish lights flickered fitfully in the sky on the church side of town, quite low overhead, seeming to spring from out of the mountain. A lively night in store up there, he thought.

A few minutes later, he pushed open the door to the Villmarks-senter. He had hesitated to go alone. But he wanted to talk to Mads, ask after his daughter. The restaurant was busy, as always on a Saturday evening. In the corner furthest from the cash register, the biggest table was occupied by a group of twenty men. Klemet recognised some workers from the quarry taking shape along the Finnish border. The Saturday evening menu was always the same: reindeer hash with chanterelle mushrooms and potatoes. Sami families occupied the other two tables in the bay windows overlooking Kautokeino, each generation wearing traditional dress. A handful of other clients were scattered at tables around the room. A band was busy preparing the small podium.

Mads emerged from the kitchen and raised a hand in greeting when he saw Klemet, who took the table nearest the cash register. Apart from the quarry workers, he knew everyone in the room. The two families came from the same *siida* to the west of town, three generations sitting down together. The meal was a special occasion – the men were home just for this afternoon, before returning to the *vidda*. They came back to take a shower, fill their snowmobile tanks and jerrycans with petrol, and shop for supplies for the week ahead at the trailer. A chance to see the wife, kiss the children. Klemet looked at the youngsters. Two of them were about seven years old. The age he had been when he started boarding school in Kautokeino. Seven years old. Plunged into a strange world where people he didn't know spoke to him in a language he couldn't understand.

He stared out of the bay windows. The lights of Kautokeino shone at his feet. The town stretched along the valley with the church to his right, picked out in floodlights. He couldn't see the boarding school from here. It was lower down, beyond the centre of town, near the banks of the Alta. But Klemet didn't need to see it to remember every nook and cranny.

Mads interrupted his thoughts. The hotelier slipped a plate of reindeer hash in front of him, brought a couple of beers over to the table and sat down opposite. The two men clinked their glasses and drank in silence. Klemet put down his glass and began to eat, savouring the melting flavour of the chanterelles on his tongue. He nodded appreciatively. Mads raised his glass again in Klemet's direction, acknowledging the compliment.

'Is Sofia around?'

'In her room.'

'How is she?'

Mads thought for a moment, shaking his head slowly, as if weighing up his reply. He sported a thick brown moustache, a rare enough attribute in the locality. His face was full and round, and he had lost most of his hair. Local rumour held that one of his grandfathers might have been Italian.

'I think she's feeling a bit better. When was it you came by? We're Saturday. It was—'

'Thursday.'

'Yes. She shut herself up all day after that, didn't eat anything. Dear God, Klemet, I didn't see it coming.'

'I know.'

'Same thing yesterday morning. I wondered whether to send her to school or not. But I thought it would be better for her to go, rather than brooding here.'

Klemet nodded, chewing his food.

'You did the right thing,' he said, his mouth half full.

'Yes, I think so. She was better when she came back in the afternoon. And she spent the evening with a girlfriend in her class. And the same girlfriend spent the day with her today. They did a lot of talking apparently. All highly top-secret, but they talked.'

'Good, that's better.'

'And . . . that character, the Frenchman. Did you get him?'

'Not yet. He's out in the *vidda* somewhere, prospecting, but we don't know exactly where. We're looking. We'll get him soon enough. I should warn you, Nina's really on her high horse about this, and she's right, of course. But if the guy denies everything, there's not a lot we can do.'

Mads nodded, taking another sip of beer. The group's opening chords filled the room. Klemet pushed his empty plate away.

'I wouldn't mind a quick word with her, if that's all right?'

Mads got to his feet, took Klemet's plate and the glasses, and led him into the kitchen where his wife was emptying one of the dishwashers. Klemet saw Berit peeling potatoes, raised a hand in greeting and reflected that he would have to question her on Monday. No need to let her know in advance. No point in worrying her. They went through to the private wing of the building. Mads tapped on a door. Heard no reply. Knocked harder. The door opened. Sofia peered around it, with an annoyed expression that turned quizzical when she saw Klemet.

'Hi, Sofia.'

'Hi.'

'Just wanted to say hello.'

She stood inside the doorway, poking her head into the corridor, and smiled.

'So, hello then. That it? Can I get back to my friend now?'

'Could I just have a quick word?'

Sofia sighed. 'OK, OK.' She turned back into the room. 'Just a minute.'

The girl failed to get her friend's attention – she was obviously listening to music, earplugs in place. Sofia yelled, 'Ul-rik-a! I'll be back in a minute!'

Then she stepped out into the corridor, keeping hold of the handle, leaving the door slightly ajar.

'Is that Lena's younger sister, the one who works at the pub?'

'Yeah, why?'

'I just wondered how you were?'

'I'll leave you to talk, if you prefer,' said Mads. 'I'll get back to the dining room.' Sofia watched her father disappear along the corridor.

'So did you get that creep?'

'Not yet, Sofia. But we're on his trail. He's out in the *vidda*, not easy to find, as you can imagine. But we'll find him and bring him in for questioning.'

'Questioning?'

'Yes, to hear his version of events.'

311

'Why, mine's not good enough?'

'Well, no, we have to hear everyone and then we decide. Well, the judge decides. Well, if it gets that far, of course. How can I explain – cases like this can be . . . complicated.'

'What's so complicated?' Sofia cut him short. 'The guy's a creep and a bastard. Nothing complicated about it. Honestly.'

'That's just how the justice system works, Sofia. I thought I should warn you. We take cases like this very seriously, I can assure you. Nina is just as angry as you.'

'And you're not?' Sofia retorted, drily.

'Sofia, listen. I have to tell you that in the judge's eyes, "wandering hands" won't be enough to convince him the Frenchman is a bastard who needs to be put behind bars.'

Sofia's expression changed abruptly. She glanced quickly behind her into the bedroom, then quietly shut the door. She was standing right under Klemet's nose now, her chin lifted almost horizontally, staring up at him, straight in the eye.

'The guy's a bastard. A real bastard! You've got to catch him and put him in jail.'

Then she turned on her heel and disappeared back into her bedroom, slamming the door. Klemet stood in the corridor, stunned and perplexed. Had he handled things that badly? He was never at ease with cases like this, he had to admit. He should have told Sofia that he, too, took the case very seriously. He reached for the door handle, then hesitated. Should he apologise or not? He didn't like making apologies. But she was just a kid. He should make an effort. There were no adults around to see.

He took a deep breath, gripped the door handle, hesitated again. Had Sofia told him everything? Had the Frenchman gone any further? Had Ulrika been giving her ideas? He released the pressure on the handle. Stared at it. He would talk about it to Nina.

He returned to the restaurant. A folk song was playing. In the kitchen, Berit was still peeling potatoes. She worked from morning till night, he thought. She wasn't much older than Klemet, but she belonged to that sacrificed generation that had had virtually no

312

access to education. Berit turned around as if she had felt his gaze on her back. She saw Klemet, watched him closely for a moment, then nodded and went back to her potatoes.

Klemet crossed the dining room. Mads was clearing the quarry workers' table. The men were watching the musicians, talking and laughing. The children clapped their hands to the music. He collected his parka in the hallway and prepared to leave the building.

A group of young people hurried inside at the same moment, jostling him as they passed. He pressed himself to the wall to let them through. There were at least twelve of them, with a handful of girls, laughing and cursing the cold. He saw they were wearing miniskirts, in this cold, under their parkas. They took off their fur-lined boots and donned reindeer-skin ankle boots. The men were mostly young reindeer breeders. Ailo Finnman, apparently the group leader, led one of the girls onto the small dance floor in front of the band. They began to dance, to general applause. Klemet spotted Mikkel, too. And John. The inseparable trio. He remembered he wanted to tell Mikkel something, but couldn't remember what it was exactly. Two other young men Klemet didn't recognise were with them, one busy removing his leather jacket, the other shuffling out of a set of filthy mechanics' overalls. He saw a tattoo on one of the men's arms. In a flash, he remembered. The truck driver who had insulted an elderly Sami woman at the crossroads. He went over to Mikkel, who had just finished taking off his snowsuit, took him by the elbow and led him aside.

The herder started in surprise, then glared at Klemet's hand on his arm.

'Mikkel, that guy with the tattoo ... Friend of yours?'

'Er, not really. I know him a bit. That's all.'

'If he's a mate, make sure you tell him to mind his language next time he talks to his elders and betters.'

Mikkel exhaled deeply.

'Oh yeah, why's that?'

'You were in his truck the other day, weren't you? He's a Swedish

313

trucker, isn't he? The day of the protest – remember what he said to the old lady?'

The young man reddened like a guilty child.

'I'd appreciate it if you made sure he didn't talk that way again. Let him speak to your granny like that, would you?'

'I'll tell him, Klemet. You can count on me, honest. He won't do it again.'

He seemed relieved that was all Klemet wanted and was ready to promise anything.

'Good kid. You promise. And no taking the piss. I'm serious about this, OK?'

Klemet put on his chapka and stepped outside. In a way, Mikkel reminded him of Mattis. Small-time herders, on the margins of Sami society, unable to make a go of it, liable to sink at any moment. Hard times for people like them.

Before climbing back into his car, he looked up to see how the Lights were doing. The aurora had expanded, rippling across almost half the sky, drawing strange motifs. Messages from space, he thought. As indecipherable as the cuts on Mattis's ears. He drove away.

40

Monday 24 January

Sunrise: 9.24 a.m.; sunset: 1.39 p.m.
4 hours 15 minutes of sunlight

8.15 a.m., Kautokeino

Tor Jensen, alias the Sheriff, was a popular chief, close to his team. His departure in such murky circumstances left his troops anxious and confused.

No one had any news, and the Sheriff's mobile was switched off. He was still in Hammerfest, it seemed. The whole squad was called in earlier than usual to receive urgent announcements 'in the interest of the service'. Klemet had spent part of Sunday reviewing the local breeders' earmarks one by one, heightening his sense of frustration. He had tried every possible combination, even the most unlikely, and ended up throwing the handbook across the sitting room.

At the station, Nina had begun tracing Mattis's GPS positions on the map, a painstaking task that would take hours to complete. Klemet had just finished telling her about his visit to Sofia on Saturday when Rolf Brattsen entered the room, preceded by a tray loaded with biscuits.

'All present and correct,' he observed in satisfied tones, looking around. 'Good.'

Rolf seemed to be revelling in the turn of events. He helped himself to a biscuit and swallowed a mouthful of coffee. The tension in the kitchen was palpable. Fifteen police officers and station staff had crammed into the room.

'Superintendent Jensen has been summoned to regional head-quarters in Hammerfest, as you know. He's still there, talking to head office and the assembly members. It's taking time. That's the official version, anyway.'

He drank some more coffee, bit into another biscuit.

'Do help yourselves . . .' he ventured, glancing around with a suspicious look.

Brattsen knew he was not liked. He had never understood why. Klemet did, though. The man was a brute: distrustful, crude, bitter, partisan, racist. He could go on. But Brattsen saw himself as a straight-talking, up-front character. Too up front, he readily conceded that, but effective. Capable of taking tough decisions when he had to. In all honesty, he had told Klemet, after one of their rare outbursts (Klemet tried to contain the hostility between them, as a rule), that he failed to understand why people disliked him so much. Beyond his comprehension, Klemet thought, watching him take another biscuit.

'Now, let me give you the real version. Jensen's been temporarily relieved of his duties. Taking a break. Being let go. Bye bye. Time out. Bon voyage. Well-deserved holiday. Ha! Look at you all . . . Don't worry, he'll be back. When this is all over. Get it? This business has been dragging on far too long. Pussy-footing around the chaps out in the tundra. Huh! Who lays down the law around here? Us or them? This still Norway, or what?'

Brattsen taunted Klemet with a hard stare.

'Eh, Klemet? What do you say? Are we still in Norway, or aren't we? Have I missed an episode? Just here for show, are we?'

Klemet boiled with rage. Brattsen was provoking him openly, in front of the whole station. Sitting next to him, Nina fidgeted uneasily. It was she who spoke, breaking the tension.

'You have no right to talk like that, Rolf. We've been working as hard as you on this, making inquiries all over the region. We've covered thousands of kilometres already. But the breeders' world is complicated. Sami culture is very different from ours. We have to respect it. And we're making progress. We have every reason to believe the French geologist is relevant to the investigation, and we're going after him. Plus, he faces a charge of sexual harassment.'

'Sexual harassment. Oh yeah, I saw a report here somewhere. Great stuff. Real open-and-shut case. Some hormonally charged adolescent schoolgirl fantasising about getting touched up. What the fuck is that all about? Good luck there. We're investigating a murder, and the fucking stolen drum, and you bring in a complaint from a fourteen-year-old kid because some guy put his hand on her knee, probably by accident?'

Red with fury, Nina leaped to her feet.

'You cannot say that. You're an unjust man, Rolf, and your behaviour is anything but impartial. That young girl deserves to be taken seriously.'

Brattsen listened, half grinning, clearly delighted to have goaded Nina beyond her usual self-control. Not a good sign, Klemet thought.

Nina went on, 'And the Sami cannot be dismissed as low-life wrongdoers. They're protected by the Constitution and they have specific rights, which we must respect.'

'Very good, Nina. I see you were paying attention in class in Kiruna. Very good. We'll get a long way with all that . . .'

The officers stared at one another around the room. No one could see where Brattsen was going with this. He's spinning it out, Klemet thought, playing cat and mouse, just for fun. He had planned his little presentation for maximum effect. He was plainly enjoying taking centre stage . . . but patience had never been Klemet's strong point. He spoke up.

'We are making progress with the investigation, Rolf,' he said. 'Real progress. But it's raking up events that happened a long time ago, possibly connected with a mine, and–'

'Well, fuck that, for a start!' Brattsen burst in. His expression was furious now. 'We're not here to write a bloody anthropological treatise, or some other fucking nonsense. You can forget all that bollocks about the mine and your geologist, for Christ's sake. You'd have to be blind or stupid not to see this is a straightforward breeders' vendetta. Johann Henrik and Olaf Renson are in it up to here, one way or another. Clear as a mountain spring. So now, listen up, all of you. Hammerfest want fast results. And our elected representatives in Oslo are getting terribly nervous and upset, the poor darlings. So we're going to shake things up a bit, what do you say? Today's Monday. Before Wednesday, I want Johann Henrik and Olaf Renson here at the station for questioning. And the press outside when we bring them in.'

Klemet had heard enough. He stood up and banged his fist on the table.

'You cannot decide to bring people in and hold them just like that, when our investigation is taking us in a completely different direction!'

Brattsen was grinning broadly now. He was enjoying this. He adopted a soothing, honeyed tone.

'Oh, that reminds me. I should have made this clear from the outset, of course. Hammerfest has confirmed the new, interim superintendent. Me. So I'm the one taking the decisions, Klemet. And I've decided that from this moment onwards, the Reindeer Police are off the murder case and the drum investigation. You're clearly out of your depth, so you can get along back to the tundra, counting reindeer. Is that clear? See – I can be quite considerate when I want to. Sparing you the embarrassment of having to arrest your breeder buddies.'

There it is, Klemet thought. He's been building up to this from the start. Klemet was sure Brattsen had even been mulling over the exact form of words in that pernicious mind of his. He eyed his new superior. Rolf had reverted to his habitual hard glare. My fist in that face, just once, Klemet thought. But he fought to retain his self-control. Let nothing show. Give the bastard no satisfaction whatever.

He sensed without looking at her that Nina was horrified, on the brink of another outburst.

The room remained silent. The officers glanced around at one another, and at Klemet. Brattsen had been the Sheriff's official deputy, but that didn't make him his natural successor. The Deputy Superintendent took responsibility for a number of public order issues, that was all. Everyone knew that, logically, Klemet should have been appointed for the interim. He was respected, and he had the experience and ability. Brattsen seized the moment, picking up the tray.

'So, dear colleagues – anyone for a biscuit before you get to work?'

Several officers hesitated before helping themselves on their way out, to Brattsen's intense satisfaction. Klemet stayed behind, alone. Brattsen glared at him, then tipped the rest into the waste-paper basket before leaving.

'Dear God, Klemet, how could you not say anything?' Nina burst out angrily, when he joined her in her office. 'He humiliated us. And took us off the case! And you just took it, saying nothing. Like you were almost grateful!'

'That's enough, Nina.'

'No, listen to me. Since the very beginning of all this, it seems to me you've been taking one step forward and two steps back. As if you were afraid to make a move.'

'That's not fair, Nina. I move forward on the basis of facts. And that takes time. If you want to see some action, go and join forces with Brattsen. He's less thorough than me. Prefers to arrest people first and ask questions later. Me, I tend to do things the other way around.'

'I've always stood by you, Klemet, but I prefer to speak my mind. You seem demotivated. And, to be quite frank, I actually wonder if you aren't happier dealing with ordinary breeders' business after all. Anything for a quiet life.'

He was stunned by Nina's attack. His pleasant, smiling, cheerful colleague was firing poisoned darts now. First Brattsen, now her.

Was he going to have to justify himself to this spoiled kid with her big blue eyes, who understood nothing about life here and was discovering everything for the first time? Who was she to judge him, after more than thirty years in every station in the region, a hardened investigator who had done time on the Palme inquiry?

He turned on his heel and stormed out, slamming the office door.

Central Sápmi

Aslak Gaupsara followed the geologist step by step up the mountain's icy flank. From time to time, the stranger tossed him a numbered shard of rock, and Aslak stowed it away in his backpack. The Frenchman focused all his attention on the stones, striking them hard, swearing under his breath, breathing out clouds of vapour. Often, he lost his temper. He was a tormented man. Aslak had known for many years that outsiders were interested in his country's stones. This stranger was not the first he had accompanied. But he seemed more on edge than the rest. Aslak had been working as a guide for a long time. He knew the other breeders the outsiders sometimes hired, too. The foreigners' talk was all stones, and mineral ores, and mines. And getting rich. They talked a lot about getting rich. They talked about progress, too. Most often, they expected an enthusiastic welcome from the Sami breeders. And they were surprised when they were met with sullen, inscrutable faces. The foreigners didn't understand. Where they saw mining opportunities and what they called progress, the breeders saw something quite different. They saw highways cutting through their pastures, trucks frightening the reindeer, accidents when the animals had to get across to the other side.

The foreigners would shrug their shoulders at all this and talk about money. They said that for every reindeer lost, the herder would get money. Still, most breeders were unresponsive. And then the strangers would get annoyed. Saying the Sami didn't understand their good fortune, that they risked losing everything, that the mines would come no matter what.

Often, when the breeders got together in spring and autumn to round up and sort the reindeer, they would talk about this. Aslak had even been visited by some of them in his tent. Olaf had come, as had Johann Henrik. Mattis came often. He didn't understand the way things were going any more. They all came to see Aslak, when he was perhaps the least affected by it. The others knew that. That was why they came. He had told them, you have too many reindeer. That's why you need such vast expanses of pasture, why there are so many disputes. But they would argue that you needed a lot of reindeer to cover your costs – the snowmobiles, the quad bikes, the cars, the abattoir truck, helicopter hire. You don't understand, Aslak, they would say. You've got barely two hundred reindeer.

And Aslak would look at them, and say: I have two hundred reindeer and I live well. I have two hundred reindeer and I don't need huge areas of pasture. I have two hundred reindeer and I keep watch over them. I'm always with them. I milk the females. They know me. They stay near me when I walk up to them. I don't need to spend days and days looking for them all over the tundra. My skis and dogs are all the equipment I need. Does that make me a bad herder, because I have fewer reindeer, because I don't need a snowmobile?

Often, when he said that, Aslak saw a veil of sorrow darken the other herders' faces. They would fall silent. The older ones would remember that they too had lived like that once. The youngest said they liked their scooters. They liked being able to spend an evening in town on a Saturday, after a hard week's work. And snowmobiles were a good thing, in any case. Aslak would nod. And say nothing. And the young herders would fall silent, too. But sometimes they came back to see him. Just to try to understand how it was before. Some were afraid of him. Still, they came. Not right up to his tent, but Aslak could see them watching him from a distance, when he was out on his skis with the reindeer. They would watch him for hours. Until the cold drove them back.

*

Kautokeino

Someone was knocking on Klemet's office door. Nervously.

'What?' he called out, still in a foul mood.

Nina entered the room and planted herself in front of him, hands on her hips, with a determined frown. She had put on her snow-suit and slung her rucksack over one shoulder. Ready to go out.

'Off to join Brattsen, or are you planning to go round up some reindeer?' he asked drily.

'Get your stuff, Klemet, all of it, we're going on patrol. We don't need to stay here with Brattsen watching our every move. Hurry up. I'll wait for you by the garage.'

She left as suddenly as she had appeared. Klemet rolled his eyes. Out of a need to get back to routine, keep up appearances, he had just started reviewing the latest reports on breeder disputes, neglected since the drum's disappearance and Mattis's death. He had no real desire to go back to all that, but he was undecided. He distrusted Brattsen, but recognised that he had manipulated the situation with some flair. Klemet tapped at his keyboard. Rather too much flair for someone like him, come to think of it. For a moment, he had considered tipping off Johann Henrik and Olaf, but quickly changed his mind. It would only make matters worse for them. For him too. He banged his fists on the desk. There was no point staying here doing nothing. Nina was right. They might as well get out into the field. As ordered.

He collected his things and found her ten minutes later, by the garage. She had wasted no time: filled the water containers, tidied up the back of the patrol car, loaded clean sleeping bags. What was she planning? Nina showed him the passenger seat, without a word. Then she climbed in and gunned the engine, reversing out fast.

The sun had risen. Outside, the light was sharp and bright. He closed his eyes, feeling the icy air stinging his right cheek in a draught from the window, but did nothing to fend off the attack of the cold. He liked Nina's initiative. She was getting him out of Brattsen's way. Their absence would pass unnoticed. The Reindeer

Police were supposed to be out on permanent patrol, far from base. They should have been on leave this week, but the schedules were all over the place. They could very easily set off for a few days, send the odd harmless message back every now and then. Brattsen wouldn't even notice. Too busy on other business.

Nina parked in front of the supermarket and cut the engine. She was thinking exactly the same.

'The key thing is not to tread on the toes of the teams Brattsen will be sending out into the *vidda*,' she said. 'If we do, he's quite capable of putting us in total quarantine.'

'Brattsen's banking on his plan to question Johann and Olaf,' said Klemet. 'I know him. He's like a mad boar, charging on ahead; never bothering to follow up other leads at the same time. And he's been dreaming of getting one over on the Sami. The bastard's in seventh heaven.'

Nina had never heard Klemet talk so freely. This business was weighing heavily on his mind.

'I can't even understand why he's stayed around here for so long, when he can't stand the Sami. Not sure who he hates more, in fact: the Sami or Asian immigrants.'

'That's a bit of an exaggeration, Klemet, isn't it? I know that Sweden has its share of racists, but here in Norway—'

'An exaggeration? The man could be a spokesperson for the Progress Party. And he doesn't even bother to disguise the fact. God knows, they've been setting out their stall in plain sight for years now. Twenty per cent of the seats in parliament, and no one's even bothered any longer. We're swimming in oil money and everyone's fallen asleep.'

Klemet took a deep breath.

'Do you think Tor's reprimand is political?' asked Nina.

'Think? I know it is. But we'll know more about that before long, don't you worry. You're right, Nina, I was sleeping on the job. Too close to retirement, I guess. But I can't let Brattsen tear down everything we've put in place. And we have to see the investigation through to the end.'

He saw Nina's radiant look. She seemed straightforward and easy-going, but she was a fighter at heart.

'We'll need a new base,' he reflected.

'We've got one already,' she said. 'Your tent. And if I remember rightly, you've even stocked up on a few bottles. Courage for the task ahead. If there's any left, that is.'

Her face shone with a broad smile. She held out a hand to him. He shook it firmly, smiling back.

They spent the afternoon preparing field provisions, fetching the trailer, the snowmobiles and supplies of petrol. They left the patrol car and the trailer in front of Klemet's house and headed straight for the tent. He threw some logs on the fire, which caught immediately. It was still cold inside the *lavu*, but Nina felt better already. Klemet had created a really welcoming atmosphere, she thought. She settled herself near the fire and took out the folders. He sat down next to her and took out his own dossiers. The tent was big enough to spread everything out. He pulled some cushions and chests into position, organising their workspace, and plugged his computer into a discreetly hidden extension socket. She smiled. He really had thought of everything.

'Let's start with the GPS readings,' he suggested. They each took out their section of the data. Klemet produced a bundle of 1:50,000 maps from his pack and spread them out between them. The next two hours were spent in silence as the maps filled with red dots and lines. Both officers were absorbed in their task. Being sidelined from the investigation had redoubled their energies. For the first time, they felt united by a shared understanding.

41

Monday 24 January

8.10 p.m., Kautokeino

Klemet felt a shiver run down his spine. Sorting the GPS data had proved more taxing than he could have imagined. Some had been lost when the snowmobile was set alight, partly corrupting the file. But he had established a logical method, and most importantly, a chronological list of readings. After that, transferring the data to the maps had been a relatively speedy process. He had made sure Nina followed the same procedure, and in half an hour they had obtained a rough itinerary – rough but telling. Next, Klemet had entered the data into the police GPS software. After hours of painstaking work, it was deeply moving to picture Mattis in flesh and blood, riding his snowmobile in the last days and hours before his death.

Most of the red lines on the map showed Mattis going about his business in the immediate vicinity of his trailer, doubtless keeping an eye on his reindeer. The massed lines drew waves across the landscape, breaking against the boundaries of his neighbours' pasture, with prolonged spells at the trailer in between.

'For a breeder involved in neighbour disputes, Mattis spent plenty of time back at his trailer,' observed Klemet. 'Too much time. He left his reindeer unattended – in the days prior to his death at least. Not surprising his neighbours had had enough.'

Nina was the first to trace a line that shouldn't have been there. Not at the time indicated for it, at least.

'Didn't Berit say she heard the suspect snowmobile outside the museum at around five in the morning?'

'Yes, about then. The scooter's headlamps lit up her bedroom. The driver was wearing orange site overalls.'

'Yes. And now, look at the date of the last reading.' Nina zoomed in on the GPS map. 'This was at four-twenty-seven in the morning on Monday January tenth. The last time Mattis parked his scooter in front of the trailer,' she noted. 'He must have spent a good part of the night watching the reindeer.'

'True,' said Klemet. 'And he couldn't have been at his trailer at four-twenty-seven that morning and riding away from Juhl's place after stealing the drum at five, given that there's about a two-hour ride between the two.'

'But then, what's this return trip to Kautokeino, on the Sunday evening?'

'The evening or the night of the theft.'

'Yes. Mattis's scooter leaves Kautokeino at one-fifty-two in the morning. So he took two and a half hours to get back to the trailer. Not surprising in the snowstorm that night. Conclusion,' Nina went on, 'he can't have spent the night watching his reindeer, as he told us.'

'Which explains why he was so tired when we saw him.'

The two officers pored over the lines again.

'Perhaps he was telling the truth – and someone else had borrowed his scooter?'

'Someone who had been at the trailer beforehand?'

Klemet frowned.

'After all,' Nina went on, 'we have the tracks of a second scooter, with two people on it. We don't know anything about what time they arrived. Nor what they wanted. Perhaps they were breeders who had come to give Mattis a hand rounding up his reindeer. And they could have got into a fight over something or other.'

'But Mattis said he didn't have any help, remember. He said he'd been working alone all night. Why would he want to hide the fact that he'd had help? It doesn't make sense, Nina. No. I can see only one explanation.'

He looked at her and saw she understood, but couldn't put it into words.

'You mean Berit may have been mistaken as to the time she gave?'

'Mistaken. Or she was lying deliberately.'

'Berit? Lying? Impossible. She might have heard another scooter at five. The thief's scooter.'

'That's one hypothesis,' admitted Klemet. 'But the data shows Mattis's scooter, with or without Mattis driving it, arriving outside Juhl's – and Berit's house – around ten on Sunday night. And it doesn't move during the evening. That raises a lot of questions.'

Suddenly, he looked at his watch.

'It's half past eight. Not too late to pay Berit a call.'

Ten minutes later, Klemet and Nina pulled up outside Berit's home, then sat for a moment in the car. It was pitch dark now, as it had been at 5 a.m. on the day of the theft. The Youth Hostel – scene of a drunken party that same night – was clearly visible across the narrow road.

Berit's small, yellow wooden house stood just a few dozen metres from the entrance to Juhl's museum. Anyone standing at one of her windows had a clear view of its entrance. There were lights on inside the house. Berit went to bed early, but for the moment she was still up. Deep snow lay all around the walls, almost reaching the windowsills, the thick white drifts illuminated in the glow of the street lights. A section of the snow cover on the roof had fallen away. Berit had cleared a path to her front door, but left the rest of the ground around the building untouched. Her car was parked in a small covered space that also sheltered a pile of birch logs.

As they got out of the car, Klemet and Nina saw a silhouette pass slowly behind the kitchen window. Parallel scooter tracks ran into the snow under one window. Their footsteps creaked in the crystal powder. The temperature had dropped again, to almost minus 30°C. Klemet knocked on the door. They heard small noises inside and the door opened.

Berit greeted them with an air of surprise. Then her face creased into a smile, as she recognised Nina.

'Don't stay out there, come into the warm, you'll die of cold.'

The officers stepped inside and took off their shoes. Berit led them straight into the kitchen and invited them to sit at the small pine table. She was wearing a royal blue wool-cloth tunic cut in a pretty, flaring shape. A band of red velvet was sewn around the hem, flounced like a theatre curtain and edged by a fine fillet of gold braid. Around her shoulders and across her chest, she wore a richly coloured scarf in the Sami livery of red, yellow, green and blue, fastened with a brooch. Her red wool headdress was also stitched with strips of gold braid, lighting up her deeply lined face and brown eyes.

Berit remained standing, her hands clasped in front of her, glancing from Klemet to Nina with a questioning look.

'Coffee?'

Without waiting for a reply, she turned and prepared the cafetière. The kitchen was modestly furnished, like the rest of the house, in varnished pine. Klemet guessed there would be two bedrooms upstairs, at the very most. The sitting room would be about the same size as the kitchen, or very slightly bigger. A laundry room would complete the layout, doubtless behind the small door to the left of the antiquated fridge. The floor was covered with brown linoleum. The few visible utensils were tidily arranged in places they had doubtless occupied for years. Apart from a packet of coffee and a small basket containing two apples, there was no food to be seen. The kitchen table was covered with a square of chequered PVC cotton, puckered in places and criss-crossed with cuts.

Nina felt sure her mother would have admired Berit's simple life, although the dim light gave no feeling of cosy intimacy, merely heightening Nina's impression of gloom and loneliness. Berit was a woman to whom life had not been kind. She contented herself with the strict minimum. Her solitude was not the only explanation: her Laestadian faith did not encourage the acquisition or display of material wealth.

Berit smiled again at the officers and took out two cups. Then with a knife she cut the two pieces of fruit into thin slices, which she placed on two plates, one in front of each of them. She lit a small candle and set it in the centre of the table, then poured herself a glass of water. But she did not sit down. Klemet and Nina sat in silence, respecting the solemnity of the moment. They said nothing, but watched the older woman closely, trying to decipher the expression on her kindly, lined face, framed by the glowing colours of her outfit.

Berit was the first to break the silence.

'How can I help? Do you have any news about Mattis's murderer?'

'The investigation is progressing,' said Klemet. 'And I hope you can help us, Berit. In fact, I'm sure you're going to be able to help us.'

Berit smiled, her hands joined in front of her.

'Well, I'll be happy to, God willing.'

Klemet nodded and took a map plotted with the GPS readings from out of his rucksack. Something to back him up. Berit moved forward to take a look.

'You see, Berit, you said you heard the thief's scooter at around five o'clock in the morning, on Monday. But we haven't found any tracks to confirm this. Which is strange. On the other hand – we know that one scooter in particular was here a few hours before that.'

He paused. Berit maintained her slight, attentive smile. But her knuckles whitened, clutching at her glass of water.

'Really, are you sure?'

'You know there was a party going on at the Youth Hostel?' Nina intervened for the first time.

'A party?'

'Do you remember the weather that night?' Klemet added quickly.

Berit looked confused and uncertain now, caught off guard by the quick-fire questions. She placed a hand on the back of the chair in front of her, as if to steady herself.

'A party, the weather . . . I don't understand any of this. Please. I'm not as young as I was. I'm very tired.'

Her eyes half closed and she looked suddenly lost. A figure of pity.

'Berit, you said you were woken up by the sound of a snow-mobile engine,' Klemet persisted. 'Did you hear our car pull up tonight?'

'I . . . Yes . . . No, I don't know. I think I wasn't paying attention. I was tidying up.'

'Berit, there was a storm that night. The wind was blowing very hard. You couldn't have heard the snowmobile driving away from the museum. The gale would have covered the noise. That's the truth.'

Berit gripped the chairback, saying nothing. Her mouth worked in small, strange movements, as if she was biting the inside of her lower lip. But she remained silent. Klemet decided the moment had come to force her hand.

'The thing is, Berit, we know that Mattis's scooter was parked here for a good part of that evening. From ten o'clock on Sunday night until around two-twenty on Monday morning. Does that seem strange to you? Like the scooter tracks in the snowdrift out-side, as if someone had piled into it without stopping in time. Very strange, don't you think?'

'Oh dear God, my God . . .' Berit's voice was shaking. With trembling hands, she placed her glass on the table, spilling a few drops of water.

Nina stood up and took the older woman gently by the shoul-ders. She pulled out a chair and helped her to sit down. Berit let herself be guided. Nina held Berit's right hand in hers.

'Can you tell us, Berit,' she asked, 'did Mattis come to see you here on that Sunday night?'

'Oh dear God, my God, almighty Lord.'

Berit shot a desperate look at Nina, who tried to coax her with an encouraging smile. Berit stared at her, then shifted her gaze to Klemet, who was leaning across the table. She looked back to Nina, who sat watching the Sami woman attentively.

'Oh Lord help me!'

Berit burst out sobbing. She wept freely, invoking almighty God, shaking her head, unaware of her tightening grip on Nina's hand. The young policewoman kneeled close to Berit's chair, clasping her hand in return. Klemet looked for a roll of kitchen paper, but could find only a teatowel. He got to his feet, fetched it and held it out to Berit, who was still crying, nodding and shaking her head, her whole body trembling now. Nina took a corner of the cloth and gently wiped the corners of Berit's eyes. The Sami woman seemed to recover herself. Her tear-soaked face cleared for a brief moment. She smiled sadly, sniffed and placed a trembling hand on Nina's cheek. Then she looked at Klemet.

'Yes, Mattis was here that night. That was the last time I saw him.'

She burst out sobbing again. The police officers exchanged glances. Nina was deeply moved by the older woman's reaction. Her eyes were filling with tears, too. Klemet invited her to speak first, with a jerk of his chin.

'Tell us about it, Berit,' said Nina.

Berit took the teatowel and blew her nose into it at some length.

'Oh Lord, my Lord . . .'

Her voice was calmer now. She shook her head a little.

'Mattis, that poor, poor man. He never had any luck in life. He was desperate that night. And he'd been drinking. God knows, he'd been drinking.'

'What happened?' asked Klemet. 'Why had he been drinking?'

Berit wiped her eyes.

'The drum, Klemet. The drum. He was obsessed with drums, you know that. But it was different with the drum at Juhl's place. That one was genuine. And someone had got it into Mattis's head that he could harness its power and become an even greater shaman

331

than his father. Oh dear God, Klemet, the Lord knows I tried to reason with him. But he had been drinking that night, and . . . he went outside. I saw him come back again not long afterwards. He was carrying something wrapped in a blanket, and he went upstairs to one of the bedrooms. I heard him chanting, grumbling, shouting, then chanting *joïks* again. And he became angry. I heard the sound of a breaking bottle at one point, and then he was crying. He went on like that for perhaps two hours. It was horrible, it went on and on. I started to feel really worried at one point. I went upstairs. I didn't even dare open the bedroom door. I looked through the keyhole. Oh dear Lord, the vision of it! I came straight back downstairs.' Berit looked shaken. 'I sat down here on this same chair, and I prayed. And I prayed.'

Berit drank some water. She seemed calmer now and had stopped crying.

'Finally, he came down. The poor man. He looked so unhappy, so desperate. There was no life in his eyes. I don't think I had ever seen him like that. He came into the kitchen, and he was still crying a little. He cried on my shoulder, weeping like a child. And then, all of a sudden, he straightened up, and he said, "At any rate, it'll cost him if he tries to get it back now." That was all. But he looked thoroughly decided. He collected his things and left.'

Berit pressed the teatowel to her mouth for a moment, unable to speak.

'And I never saw him again.' Her voice sounded choked and she broke down, sobbing all over again.

The two officers let her cry. Nina took her hand once more.

'What time was it when Mattis left?' asked Klemet.

Berit recovered herself.

'It must have been the time you said just now, about two or two-thirty in the morning. I was exhausted.'

'So he went outside for a moment around midnight?' said Klemet. 'Can you say for certain where he went, and what was under the blanket?'

Berit looked at him.

'You know perfectly well, Klemet. He went to the Juhl Centre, and he was the one who took it, the cursed drum whose power he had been told could be his. Oh dear God, that whole night he tried to control the drum. I could see what he was doing. He wanted it to obey him, but it wouldn't – the poor man – of course it wouldn't. And it tore him apart that he was not up to the task.'

'Do you know to whom he was referring when he said, "It'll cost him if he tries to get it back"?'

'No. No, I have no idea. But I do know that's what killed him.'

42

Monday 24 January

9.50 p.m., Kautokeino

Rolf Brattsen's new orders had been carried out with exemplary rapidity. Brattsen had been crystal clear. No hanging about. Action. Fast, effective action. They needed results.

'We're going for it,' he said.

Brattsen would have liked to authorise his men to carry their fire-arms, but he recognised that might be taking things a little too far. According to the information obtained to date, Olaf Renson was still at the Sámediggi in Kiruna. Brattsen saw little point in putting his Swedish colleagues onto the case. It would only complicate things, and he hated bureaucracy almost more than he hated the Lapps and Pakistani immigrants. Might as well wait until Renson came back to Kautokeino. The latest session of the Sami parliament had ended earlier in the afternoon. Brattsen had made discreet inquiries and discovered Renson would be back in town the fol-lowing morning.

Two teams were sent to corner Johann Henrik, before the breeder set out into the *vidda* from his trailer. They would camp as close as possible to his pitch, ready to act in the early hours of the morning. Discretion was vital. In any case, Brattsen didn't expect

the breeders to put up much of a show of resistance. He was counting on the Lapps' natural respect for authority. The only one likely
to cause trouble was Renson. That idiot was capable of rallying the
media and coming over all indignant and horrified, as only he knew
how, all those years ago when he was arrested for planting explosives under the pithead in Sweden.

If all went well, Rolf Brattsen would be the man putting the two
Lapps behind bars, by Tuesday. Even earlier than planned. Fucking
brilliant work, he told himself. Old Olsen was right – his intuition
had paid off. And if everything continued to plan after that – if the
Frenchman and Aslak proved equally effective, out there in the
tundra – he would soon be a rich man.

10.10 p.m., Central Sápmi

Aslak and the geologist turned in for the night after another, even
longer day's work. The Frenchman kept to his own corner of the
tent, examining carefully the rocks he had collected. He made notes
in his book, looked at maps, added symbols, consulted other books,
peered at the stones through a magnifying glass, took measurements,
made more notes, swearing continuously.

Aslak did not know the science of stones like this stranger – who
seemed like a man possessed. But he knew which stones were soft
enough to carve, though he preferred to work with reindeer antlers.
He had learned the art from his grandfather, following the animals
on their migration, when the old man, unable to help him with the
reindeer any more, spent his days in the camps they installed at each
stage of the journey – after long treks or much shorter distances, as
the reindeer saw fit. The family followed this ritual twice a year.
The first was in spring, when the herds left the *vidda* after the birth
of their calves, heading north to the coast and the rich green pastures of the inshore islands. The reindeer fled the summer heat of
the *vidda* and the mosquitoes that tormented them. For the herders
following them, the journey could take up to a month. The return
trip took place in the autumn, when the summer pastures were

exhausted. The reindeer obeyed their instinct, moving back to the *vidda*. Winter feed was meagre. Lichen was made edible only because it was soaked and softened in the snow.

Aslak remembered how the long, slow migrations induced a state he had experienced nowhere else, a state he had never truly recovered since becoming a man. One of the young herders who came to see him sometimes had used the word 'happiness'. Aslak had no idea what he meant. He only knew that, as a child, he had learned everything a man needed to know in life, from his grandfather.

The old man had great difficulty walking. But during the long days waiting at camp, when the herders were out keeping watch over the animals at pasture, from a distance, he would sometimes take short walks. One day, he had taken Aslak to the top of a low mountain, with a flat summit, beyond which other mountains stretched as far as the eye could see. Aslak had learned to love the mountains when his grandfather had told him: 'See, Aslak, they respect one another. None tries to be higher than the other, to cast a shadow over his neighbour, or hide him, or be more beautiful. We can see them all from here. If you go to the top of that mountain over there, it will be the same – you will see the others, all around.' His grandfather had never said such things to him before. His voice was quiet and calm, as always. Melancholy, too. 'Mankind should be like the mountains,' the old man had said. Aslak had looked at his grandfather, and the landscape stretching in every direction. The gentle, sleepy ranges of Sápmi had never looked so beautiful. In the rays of the sun, the endless, billowing swell of heather sparkled and glowed with life – the colours of fire, blood and earth. His grandfather held a reindeer antler he had picked up along the way. He took out his knife and began to carve the bone. They had sat quietly on the summit. Finally, his grandfather had shown him the antler, on which he'd carved their initials and the date. Then he'd wedged it between two big rocks. He was tired, he said. Before walking back down to the camp he had clasped Aslak's hand and told him: 'When I am dead, men will know I came here today with my son's son.'

*

Kautokeino

Klemet and Nina conferred for a moment in the sitting room. They believed Berit's version of events. Mattis's farmstead and his wilderness trailer had been searched already, but the drum had not been found. Fresh coffee and a new candle stood waiting in the kitchen when they returned. Berit had dried her tears but her eyes were swollen. Klemet knew her well enough to understand her tortured feelings. He went over to her and took her gently by the shoulders.

'Berit, why did you give the police a false time? You knew that was wrong.'

She gazed at him with immense sorrow in her eyes.

'Mattis was like a younger brother to me. When I was a very young girl, I helped my mother deliver him. Our families grew up together. When he was living in his trailer, out in the *vidda*, he would come and see me here sometimes, to get something to eat, then sleep in the bedroom upstairs. It was easier for him than going back to his little farmstead, which is a lot further away. I did his laundry. I gave him food. I listened to him. He knew I would never judge him. He found some peace here.'

Klemet nodded.

'Berit, we need to know exactly who Mattis saw in the days leading up to his death. It's very important we try to find the person he was talking about just before he left here.'

Nina spread out the set of photographs she had brought from her desk at the station. She sorted out the pictures of the protagonists in both investigations, which had now, unquestionably, become one. They had identified the thief. But it remained to be seen whether or not Mattis had acted alone. Nina looked at the faces in the pictures. Mattis, Ailo, John, Mikkel. Johann Henrik. Olaf. The pastor. Helmet Juhl. Berit herself. Racagnal. And Aslak. Nina had added one of Mads's daughter Sofia. And completing the line-up, to remind her, pictures of Aslak's wife, and the NRK journalist Tomas Mikkelsen.

Berit looked at the photographs. Klemet and Nina studied her reaction, but she registered nothing but an overwhelming sense of sadness. She touched the picture of Aslak's wife.

'Poor woman . . .'

She shook her head.

'I don't know what to say. Mattis knew everyone. Helmut – he made drums for him sometimes, tourist souvenirs. Drums again. Always drums. He couldn't get away from them, the poor man. It would have helped him if he could. He was in a world of his own. He believed everything was possessed of a soul: the smallest rock, the trees, everything.'

Berit crossed herself. A reflex. She pushed the first photographs to one side and looked again at the rest. Gently, she slid out the photograph of Aslak, gazing at it as she did so. Then she picked up Olaf's portrait.

'Mattis and Olaf weren't close. I think Olaf was suspicious of him, a little. Or found him too . . . too distant. Mattis went to one of Olaf's political meetings once. He was interested in those things, Mattis. Sami history. Independence. Sami values. I think Mattis may even have voted for Olaf in the elections to the Sami parliament. But when Olaf asked Mattis to hand out tracts in the markets, Mattis almost always forgot to go. Olaf grew tired of him. He began to criticise Mattis. Olaf said that Mattis's obsession with the drums reminded him of the politicians who wanted to round the Sami up into a theme park for tourists. I remember his exact words, because I thought that was unpleasant, and harsh.'

She placed Olaf's photograph on top of Aslak's and took the next one. Ailo Finnman. Before she could say anything, Nina stayed her hand.

'Berit, you haven't said anything about Aslak . . . Yet he and Mattis were quite close, weren't they?'

Berit looked like a little girl caught doing something she knew was wrong. Then she narrowed her eyes.

'Oh. Aslak. Yes. That's true. They knew one another. They respected each other. They saw one another out in the *vidda*. That's all.'

338

She picked up Ailo's photograph, as if to cut short her comments on Aslak. Nina was surprised, but let her continue.

'Him. Mattis would have done better to leave him well alone. And the other two as well. Always together. Ailo Finnman. He had his family. They think they can do whatever they want. They threaten everyone out in the *vidda*. They elbow everyone aside to make room for themselves.'

'Mattis spent time with them?'

'A little. Sometimes they did small bits of business between themselves. He gave them a helping hand, too, during the triage. I told Mattis to keep away from them, but he always did as he pleased. The others sold his drums on the black market. And they sold other goods, too. I never wanted to know anything about that. But you must know, Klemet. Small-time trafficking, using the big trucks that drive right across Sápmi, moving between Norway, Sweden and Finland all the time.'

'Do you know if Mattis had been anywhere else before coming to see you on Sunday? According to his GPS readings, he was in Kautokeino from ten o'clock onwards that night. But perhaps he came to you a little later than that?'

'Yes, that's possible. I can't remember the exact time now. If your machine tells you that, then it's probably true. I don't know who else he would have seen. Or if he saw anyone at all. He had definitely been drinking before he arrived, that I do know. That wasn't surprising. He knows I have no alcohol here. And I never allowed him to drink in this house. But dear God, oh, that night, he had drunk and drunk . . .'

Klemet and Nina thanked Berit for her help. She placed the last of the photographs on the top of the pile, then looked across at those Nina had set to one side – the photographs from Henry Mons's 1939 expedition.

'Goodness me, whatever is he doing there?' she said.

The two officers bent over the top photograph, moving it further into the candlelight.

'Who do you mean?' Nina's voice was feverish with excitement.

'Him. The small man with the moustache.'

'Do you know him?' asked Klemet.

'No, but the other day, when I was cleaning upstairs at Olsen's house, for the first time in a long while, I saw the pictures in the old man's bedroom. And there was that face. It might very well be his father.'

Olsen's father. The mystery man on the expedition. He must have been a farmer at the time, perhaps supplying some of the equipment – vehicles, or pack animals. But that did not explain his disappearance from the photographs shortly after Niils Labba had left with Ernst Flüger, the German geologist. The expedition had taken place before Karl Olsen was born, but he might have heard about it from his father.

'We'll pay him a visit,' said Klemet. 'We'll soon see. When is he most likely to be over at the farm?'

'He's there every morning at the moment,' said Berit. 'Mikkel and John are working on the machines. They come over in the morning, and Olsen likes to keep an eye on them. To make sure they do a good job.'

'John and Mikkel? Have they been working for Olsen for long? I thought they were just doing odd jobs at the garage.'

'They get everywhere,' said Berit. 'They've been hanging around Olsen's farm for years. Yes, years. And Mattis would go and find them there too, sometimes. He would work on the machines with them. Mattis borrowed Olsen's tools. They probably discussed their bits of business there.'

Klemet's mobile rang. He looked at the name on the screen. Tor Jensen. Klemet moved into the sitting room and took the call. The conversation lasted just a few minutes. The Sheriff was back in Kautokeino. Not quite incognito, but almost. He had heard about the Reindeer Police being taken off the case and wanted to see Klemet that evening. He meant business – Klemet understood that from his tone. Jensen was back, and Klemet was delighted.

Back in the kitchen, Nina greeted him with a radiant,

knowing smile. An intensely satisfied smile, too. In the middle of the kitchen table, a dark, oval, convex shape had been placed on a blanket. Klemet knew immediately what it was. The drum. The drum stolen by Mattis. The drum that had led to his murder.

43

Monday 24 January

11.30 p.m., Kautokeino

Klemet and Nina drove back to the tent in a state of high excitement. On the way Nina told him that while he was out of the room, it had suddenly occurred to her that they hadn't asked Berit the simplest and most obvious question. Mattis had left the drum in the bedroom, in Berit's care. And Berit had stowed it right there in her kitchen cupboard. Patrol P9 had left immediately, taking the priceless artefact with them. Berit was under strict orders to say nothing about the drum to anyone: the investigation was still ongoing. She was already open to charges of false witness and receiving stolen goods, and had not been difficult to persuade.

'What do we do with the drum now?' Nina voiced both their thoughts. 'We're meant to be out in the tundra checking reindeer herds, not helping the investigation along.'

'Well, let's not spoil the party straightaway,' said Klemet. 'I'm not handing it over to Brattsen. No way.'

'But he's about to arrest Olaf and Johann Henrik.'

'He's arresting them for Mattis's murder, not the theft of the drum. Except he's hoping he can wave his magic wand and catch everything in the same net. He'll have to be extremely convincing now.'

'But how can we keep the drum a secret? The UN conference is just days away.'

'I'm aware of that. But we have to consolidate our position. Find out more about what the drum can tell us. And let Brattsen get bogged down in his own mess, good and deep. Then everything will work out.'

'Well, I don't much like playing games,' said Nina. Concentrating on the icy road ahead, Klemet pictured her scowl from the tone of her voice. 'And what about the Sheriff? Are you planning to tell him?'

Klemet hadn't decided on that yet. Tor was on their side, but Klemet preferred to wait and see what his boss had in mind, now that he was back in Kautokeino.

'We'll out find out shortly, he's coming round to the tent.'

'And what about the drum itself? Shouldn't we be protecting it somehow? Juhl said it had to be treated before it could be exposed to the air and light. If it deteriorates because we don't know how to look after it, there'll be a high price to pay.'

'We'll stop by Uncle Nils Ante's place tomorrow morning first thing. He's sure to know what to do.'

Back at the tent, Klemet and Nina pored over the drum. The fire-light cast strange shadows around the sides of the *lavu*, as if the painted motifs had sprung to life. A line was drawn across the upper section, just as Henri Mons had remembered it, with the stylised reindeer, reminiscent of prehistoric rock art drawings. The central cross was there, too. But the complexity of the motif came as a surprise to Nina. She took out her camera and photographed it, eager to preserve a permanent record of its design. Then she resumed the close study of its taut, crackled skin.

Reindeer appeared in both sections. Fish, too. Two dark birds might represent crows, though the species couldn't be identified with any certainty. There was a snake, huge and thick, to judge by its size compared to the other animals. But Nina quickly reflected that their relative proportions bore no relation to reality here. The birds and fish were the same size as the reindeer. Some of the signs looked rather like Native American motifs, she thought. There were ragged pine trees, a sun, or perhaps a figure standing in the sun. To the bottom left of the cross, Nina saw some sort of boat in a circle. Beneath the dividing line, the design featured a grille-like pattern. And there were lozenge shapes straddling the line. Strange wave-like forms lined the right-hand edge of the drum, smaller at the bottom, but forming bigger, broader curves towards the upper section. Nina was struck by the asymmetry and the finesse of the motifs, convinced their meaning could be deciphered. But how?

She looked again at the central cross. It was broad and wide, drawn in double thickness, with a lozenge motif at the centre. Each branch of the cross supported a different symbol. Another was drawn at the heart of the lozenge shape. Nina glanced at Klemet, hoping to catch some flash of comprehension in her colleague's eyes.

'What do you think?'

He was lost. He wasn't prepared to admit it, yet, but the indecipherable drum forced him to acknowledge the chasm separating him from traditional Sami culture, setting him apart, as it always had. Dozens of academics would have moved heaven and earth to lay hands on this artefact, but Klemet was unable to make sense of it. He had grown up isolated from Sami culture, and this drum – the very heart of that culture, the key to this whole case – was as strange to him as it was to Nina. He remembered his uncle's words. The Sami had been caught up in a holy war, a true war of religion. And they had lost. Klemet himself was the living, breathing proof of that. In the presence of this drum, an object that should have stirred strong, deep-seated emotions in him, he felt helpless.

He studied the design again. The dividing line was placed very high up across the oval surface. The cross was central to the bigger of the two sections and was elaborately decorated. Was that unusual? He had no idea. He could identify the reindeer, fish, birds, what looked like pine trees and mountains, perhaps, or – more likely –

Sami tents. Even then he couldn't be sure. No point playing the art expert, he told himself. Fine Sami you are.

'We must tell Tor,' said Nina.

'True. He should know about this. But tell me, Nina – you're not Sami, you know nothing about the culture, so what do you see in the drum? An untrained eye might spot something new . . .'

Nina had overcome her initial excitement at the discovery. She was scrutinising the symbols now, commtting them to memory.

'Yes, that's true. There are things I think I can see, but I'm being influenced by what I know about the drum's history. I see a cluster of Sami tents. Why? I don't know. And this frontier, this separation. It might be the surface of an expanse of water, dividing the world above from the underwater world. And the lozenges look to me like icebergs. The underwater section is the biggest, the most important. Perhaps a lake concealing something? A drowned village? Some sort of dam project? Klemet, you said you first came to work here when people were protesting in Alta. Wasn't that about a dam project?'

He got to his feet, lifted the drum and turned it over, looking at it from every angle.

'That's an interesting theory. I was focusing on childhood memories, but they're very vague. My uncle's stories about the frontier between the realm of the living and the dead. But a drowned village. Or a flooded mine—'

'Or both!'

'Or both.'

'This grille pattern following the line might be some sort of trackway – branches laid half in and half out of the water.'

'A trackway . . . Why not?'

'Here's a stylised figure of a man holding two crosses: a pastor? And there, you see a cross symbolising the sun, but you can interpret it in other ways too: your kingdom of the dead, perhaps. Or it may have nothing to do with the sun. I see a kind of compass, or a wind-rose. And that circle looks like another compass,' Nina suggested.

'But why two compasses?'

'Why? I don't know. The person who drew the drum may have had a lot to hide.'

'Or a lot to tell,' muttered Klemet. His face darkened.

Ten minutes later, the Sheriff arrived. His air of exhaustion had vanished and he looked ready for action, clad in grey fatigues with patch pockets and a navy blue parka. Klemet hadn't seen Tor in uniform for years. The addiction to liquorice sweets had taken its toll: the outfit was a little tight. But that didn't matter. The Sheriff was out for revenge, thought Klemet. Big-time.

Before he arrived, Klemet had stowed the drum carefully in one of the chests lining the tent. He offered the Sheriff a beer.

'So what happened in Hammerfest?'

'Hammerfest! Bunch of clowns. The entire region is hamstrung. Every interested party has people strategically placed. Either there's a Labour-ite in every cupboard—'

'Like you,' Klemet pointed out, grinning.

'Enough of your cheek . . . Or you've got a Progress Party man pulling the strings and manipulating the Conservatives. That's how it is down in Oslo and, believe me, that's exactly how it is out here in the back end of the Finnmark. Just as many fucking idiots as down there in the capital.'

Nina looked shocked to hear her superintendent talk this way. Tor Jensen was unfazed.

'The Progress Party?' she said.

'Wouldn't surprise me one bit. They're gaining power and influence in the region. Up here, in the Red North! They've got the scooter lobby on their side.'

'The scooter lobby?'

The Sheriff turned to Nina, irritated by her questions.

'You should know all about that, in the Reindeer Police. The scooter lobby, for Chrissakes! Tell her, Klemet. Do your fucking job.'

The Sheriff's temper was clearly up, Klemet thought, with some amusement. He never swore, usually.

'Snowmobile users want the right to go riding around in the mountains on public holidays, like the Easter weekend, which is one of the best weekends of the year around here: still plenty of snow and bright sunshine too. Norwegians from the coast come up for family outings. They spend three or four days in their little log cabins in the tundra, on the riverbanks. With their snowmobiles. But Easter is when the reindeer produce their young, and the herds need to be left undisturbed, or the mothers might abandon their calves, which means big losses for the breeders. Which means a clash of interests. It's not just about the snowmobiles, but that sort of sums up the kind of people you're dealing with.'

'And the fucking snowmobile lobby carries a lot of clout in towns down on the coast,' added the Sheriff. 'Easy pickings for the Progress Party when they're looking for new voters.'

'It's the same on the Swedish side, in Kiruna,' said Klemet. 'There's a powerful scooter lobby there, too. People who don't want rules and regulations governing their free time – family outings, hunting, fishing – for whatever reason.'

'No way I'm letting Brattsen fuck everything up,' the Sheriff added, more to himself than to anyone else.

Klemet sat silent for a moment, watching his boss's furious face in the firelight, then turned to Nina, who was sitting back on her heels. They exchanged a long glance, then she invited Klemet to speak, with a jerk of her chin.

'Good news and bad news this end.'

'Don't play on my nerves, Klemet, this really isn't the time.'

Klemet carried on regardless.

'First the good news: we've reached a major breakthrough in the investigation. A very big breakthrough. Lots of people will heave a huge sigh of relief. Now the bad news: it may bring the whole of the rest of the case to a standstill. Or rather, the people at the top will take advantage of Brattsen's arrests to call a halt there, drawing a line under the whole thing, on the eve of the UN conference.'

'You've found the drum?'

'In the chest behind you.'

347

Tor turned quickly to look.

'Steady,' said Nina. 'It's very fragile.'

The Sheriff lifted out the blanket and opened it carefully. He stared at the drum for several minutes.

'Never seen anything like that before.'

Klemet explained how and where they had recovered it. The Sheriff nodded.

'Well, she's guilty of harbouring stolen goods, whatever you say. Anyone else know about this?'

'No one.'

'Hm.' The Sheriff picked the drum up again. 'So what does it tell us, this damned drum? Any idea?'

The officers' blank looks told him all he needed to know.

'Well now, let's see ... Whole load of animals there. A snake. Something dangerous by the look of it. Seals over here.'

'I thought they might be birds. Crows, perhaps,' said Nina.

The Sheriff frowned.

'Seals, crows, some sort of animal. Birds on the right there. Or mountains. There, over to the left, those are definitely tents, like on the cross. And some kind of sledge pulled by a reindeer. The dots on the sledge, what would they represent? Children? A swarm of mosquitoes. Or, no, what about iron ore? What do you reckon? And the stylised figures look as if they're carrying, well, pistols.' The Sheriff gave a long sigh. 'Got any kind of explanation for all that?'

'No, just a theory of Nina's, for the moment.'

Klemet invited his colleague to elaborate while the Sheriff listened, nodding.

'A flooded mine, or a drowned village. It's possible. Why not? In which case, our next question is whether the drum tells that story and nothing more, or whether it holds clues to the location of the village, or the mine. And what's the link with Mattis's murder?'

'Mattis was after the drum's power. He wasn't interested in its monetary value,' said Klemet.

'He wasn't interested in money if it meant the pittance he earned selling the meat from a handful of reindeer,' said the Sheriff. 'But the prospect of a great deal of money can change a man, Klemet. Even someone with no apparent interest in it, believe me. At any rate, for the moment, the drum is here with you, which is fantastic news. The case isn't completely solved, but the fact that it's been found will calm things down.'

'We weren't planning to hand it back straightaway,' Nina corrected him.

Tor Jensen stared incredulously at the young woman. He glanced at Klemet, who seemed in agreement. The Sheriff realised they meant business.

'Nina's right,' said Klemet. 'If we give the drum back — coupled with the arrest of the breeders — it will effectively close the case. Everyone will be only too pleased to clear up the whole mess on the eve of the conference. But we know that's not the end of the story. We need time. And we need you.'

'For God's sake, Klemet, I'm yesterday's man around here, and you've been taken off the case, dammit. Or have you forgotten that?'

'Double or quits,' Klemet retorted. 'If we lose, we lose just a little bit more than we would have lost anyway. But if we manage to solve the case, you'll get your share of the credit. People will say you did your duty in the toughest of circumstances, that you took brave, risky decisions. And everyone will be so happy with the outcome that all these . . . minor procedural irregularities will be forgotten.'

'Yes, but if we screw up?'

'If we screw up, you're on the next boat to Spitsbergen. Without the remote-postings bonus.'

The Sheriff looked again at the drum, stroked its rim.

'I'm going home. I haven't seen this. And neither have you. You'd better keep Berit on a tight leash. Tomorrow, I'll bring the rest of the dossier I've been compiling for you, about your French geologist. I'll give you three days, Klemet and Nina. Not a minute more.'

44

Tuesday 25 January

Sunrise: 9.18 a.m.; sunset: 1.45 p.m.

4 hours 27 minutes of sunlight

Johann Henrik's trailer, Central Sápmi

Johann Henrik's arrest was carried out smoothly, early in the morning, exactly as Rolf Brattsen had planned. The police had blocked every possible route off the site in case the breeder tried one of his trademark quick getaways, but the strategy had brought unexpected problems of its own. The cold was razor-sharp now, and one of the police officers suffered frostbite, while the others were badly chilled by the long, silent wait. The sky was clear, with just a few scattered clouds, and the thermometer had dropped to around minus 40°C. Johann Henrik wouldn't have got far. In this cold, even Sami herders hesitated to go out. And Henrik could see he was trapped. He had sworn, spat, shouted threats, tried to make sure the police would be held responsible if his herd got mixed up with his neighbours' animals. The officers carried out their instructions to the letter, making no concessions beyond a call to Henrik's son, so that he could make arrangements to watch the herd in his father's absence.

Olaf Renson's arrest would be more complicated. But there, too, Brattsen had shown foresight and knew what to expect. Renson was an experienced media manipulator, with an excellent network capable of mobilising quickly. Brattsen had supervised the operation, but was careful to remain in the background. Old Olsen had advised him not to show his face to start with. 'If it all goes according to plan,' he told the Acting Superintendent, 'you'll have plenty of opportunities to show yourself in the right light. Your friends will know how to show their gratitude.' Really, Olsen thought of everything.

Kautokeino

Renson was eating breakfast at the Thon hotel when the police came for him. One of the officers informed him of the arrest warrant. As predicted, Renson reacted furiously, shouting in protest, calling on the hotel staff and a handful of guests at nearby tables to witness the scene. He cited his status as an elected representative of the Sami people, denouncing the arrest as a scandalous example of bare-faced discrimination. Brattsen had briefed his men: be firm, but use no physical force. And make no comment whatsoever. Don't try to argue with him. The officers had been powerless to stop Renson asking the hotel staff to alert the media. After that, he had dragged out his departure, showing no overt resistance until Mikkelsen, the NRK reporter, arrived with a handful of press colleagues. With the journalists in place, Renson allowed himself to be taken away, remonstrating loudly about miscarriages of justice, accusing the officers of incompetence and racism, castigating them for the absence of genuine Sami police upholding Sami justice in the Sami territories.

'All we get is a few token Sami, collaborating with the Norwegian system. I am the victim of appalling injustice – proof again of our desperate need for enhanced autonomy!'

Brattsen was delighted. Indirectly, Renson was implicating Klemet Nango in his arrest. Old Olsen was right. If the arrest proved unfounded, Nango would be held responsible in the eyes of the populace.

Nina and Klemet listened to Renson's outraged declarations on the radio in Klemet's car – an old red Volvo parked now outside his uncle Nils Ante's house in Suohpatjavri. The two officers, in plain clothes, were keeping a low profile. This time, Miss Chang heard the car pull up and greeted Klemet and Nina on the doorstep, wrapped in a thick fleece blanket.

'Hello, Klemet! This is your girlfriend?'

'My colleague.' Klemet smiled, amused by the young Chinese woman's easy familiarity. 'Is my uncle in?'

'Come, he is finishing his breakfast.'

The three of them moved into the kitchen, from where Klemet heard the beat of music, played on instruments he couldn't identify.

'Chinese instruments. What an extraordinary sound,' exclaimed Nils Ante. 'I'm trying to incorporate them into a *joïk* I'm writing for Miss Chang-Chang's grandmother. Ah, and here is your charming girlfriend, at long last!'

'Nina's my patrol colleague.'

'And you've come patrolling all the way out here?'

'There's something I have to talk to you about.'

'Really. Well, listen to the beginning of my *joïk* first.'

Nils Ante cut the music. A melodious chant rose in his throat. He extended his hands towards his young companion.

The days are long
When I cannot be with she
To whom I have given my heart.

His voice rose and fell with the long, meandering chant, repeating the words over and over, modulating the sound each time. Miss Chang held his hand, brimming with tender affection, drinking in the enchanting sound. The *joïk* went on for three long minutes. Klemet began to lose patience.

352

'That's just the first verse, of course,' said Nils Ante at length. 'So, do you like it?'

'It's very beautiful. As always,' Klemet admitted. 'The last part is rather melancholy, but lovely.'

'And you, Nina, what do you think?'

Nina had sat listening, wide-eyed.

'Umm, I didn't quite get the meaning!' she admitted, laughing. Miss Chang laughed too, quickly joined by Nils Ante.

'Is that *joïk* really for Miss Chang's grandmother, or Miss Chang?' asked Klemet.

Nils Ante responded with a wink.

'Wait for the next bit. Now, to what do I owe this second visit in such a short space of time? More vultures circling lower overhead?'

Klemet signalled to Nina, who placed a blanketed bundle on the kitchen table.

'Can Miss Chang keep a secret?'

'As if my life depended on it. So – what have you got there?'

Nina lifted one fold of the blanket. Nils Ante greeted the sight of the drum with a long whistle. He put on his glasses and took a closer look. Before studying the signs and symbols, he turned the drum over and cast a discerning eye over the curve of the back, its contours and texture. He looked at the stitching and nodded, as an appreciative connoisseur.

'I didn't know you were such a specialist,' said Klemet.

'Why bring it to me, then, uncouth nephew? You're hoping I'll be able to tell you a thing or two about it, aren't you? I can't guarantee its authenticity, if that's what you're after. But it seems to conform to all the usual criteria. You would need expert analysis to determine the exact nature of the materials used. The ink, for example. But it is very beautifully made. I imagine this is the one that disappeared from Juhl's museum?'

Klemet nodded.

'The signs on this drum are quite fascinating,' said Nils Ante. 'I'm no expert. I'm more of a *joïker*, as you know. But I can see two or three things of interest. The upper section is quite simple. You've got a hunting scene, with this man stretching his bow. He's hunting two reindeer and surrounded by quite thick, bushy pine trees. This is a scene showing a good, successful hunt. And the triangles either side of the line, filled with dots—'

'They're icebergs, aren't they, with the submerged part and the visible part?'

'Nonsense. These are Sami tents, of course, and the dots symbolise their inhabitants. The tents are fully occupied. What you see there is a Sami camp with many people in it, and lots of game, and luxuriant pine trees symbolising abundance and plenty. This is a happy scene.'

Nina listened attentively. Klemet was fascinated, too. The drum's hidden meaning was being revealed, bit by bit.

'But you surely notice something else?' Nils Ante went on. 'The happy scene, the harmonious village, is concentrated in a tiny section of the drum, right at the top. This line, as you know, Klemet, separates the realm of the living from the realm of the dead.'

'We thought it might be something else,' said Nina. 'The surface of the sea, perhaps, or a lake. A lake that might have drowned a village, or flooded a mine.'

'—separating the living from the dead, then,' Nils Ante went on as if he hadn't heard. 'And this realm of the dead is vast. Bigger than anything I remember seeing on other drums. But again, I'm no specialist. One thing is very clear, though. In this bottom section, below the tents with the dots representing the people, the same tents are overturned and empty. As if the inhabitants had been evacuated. Or were dead. And the realm of the dead is huge and terrifying here. The shaman would have had his work cut out with this. Times must have been hard indeed for those poor devils.'

'What do you mean?' asked Klemet.

'A magic drum includes a whole host of figures, and through these signs the shaman communicates the philosophy of life and the life of men. And the message here is very dark. This snake, for example, is very disturbing. It must symbolise evil – you know we

354

have no snakes here in Sápmi. And you see these small figures here?'

'The other tents, you mean?' said Klemet.

Nils Ante heaved a sigh.

'Goddesses, O twice-uncouth nephew! But if they're the ones I think they are, their presence is surprising, because mostly they go about in threes, and here there are only two.'

'So?'

'So I'm going to give you the name of someone who will be able to help you. Go and see him, say I sent you. A rather odd character. He has dedicated his life to these drums.'

Nils Ante scribbled a name on piece of paper and searched for a number on his mobile.

'Hurri Manker. If he's still alive, he'll be able to tell you one or two interesting things, I'm sure of that. He lives in Jukkasjärvi.'

'The place with the ice hotel?' Nina recognised the name. Jukkasjärvi was not far from Kiruna, in Swedish Sápmi. Before achieving fame as the site of the ice hotel, the little village had been a vital centre for Sami trade. It was built on the banks of a river, making it ideal for commerce and transport at a time when roads had been non-existent.

'Call him first,' Nils Ante advised. 'He often goes out hiking in the region. And come back and see me afterwards. I may have finished my *joïk* by then.'

They left Nils Ante's house, after a series of hugs from Miss Chang. Klemet called the number straightaway. A quavering voice replied. Briefly, Klemet explained his request, without going into too much detail. Patrol P9 was in luck. Hurri Manker was on a day-long visit to Karesuando, in Swedish Lapland. If they hurried, they could see him that afternoon, before he headed back to Jukkasjärvi.

Klemet and Nina drove due south. The drum still held plenty of secrets. Their visit to Olsen's place, checking the old man's photographs, could wait. Klemet thought about the landscape clues Eva Nilsdotter had given them. Identifying the location, and catching up with Racagnal would be well-nigh impossible.

45

Tuesday 25 January

Central Sápmi

André Racagnal reckoned he had spent enough time at the first site. He'd made some interesting discoveries. He would have to take a detour via Malå to check the data and see what the core samples had to say, if any existed for the places in question. The trouble with gold, as Racagnal well knew, was that it had been sought by mankind for thousands of years. Specialists usually worked on the assumption that every major seam had already been discovered long ago. If a rich seam lay undiscovered in Lapland, it would cause a sensation in the mining industry.

He and his Sami guide had set off early that Tuesday morning. The geologist had explained where he wanted to get to and what sort of faultlines he was looking for. They had ridden for two gruelling hours in near-zero visibility. Incredible as it might seem, that Sami devil in his four-pointed hat had taken him to the exact spot he sought. The snow was a faint blue now, tinged with a lick of fire. The sun would rise at 9.15 a.m., but its flaming rays already flickered along the eastern horizon, in a brutal clash of colour. Racagnal liked the acid contrast of blue and orange. A perfect match for his vision of the world.

He stood facing the flaming light. Everywhere he looked, the horizon was barred by the smooth contours of low, treeless, snow-covered mountains. The sunlight danced from summit to summit. In the same moment, the whole tundra awoke. The terrain beneath his feet was mostly granite. He took out a map. There would be numerous seams of granulite and quartz running west-south-west to east-north-east. Some of the seams identified on the map would be worth observing.

Racagnal checked Olsen's old map. The granite was broken by an irregular but quite clear faultline. What was that hiding? The map's author was meticulous. In places, he had included tiny geological cross-sections relating to specific points. These were highly unorthodox for a geological map. The field book would have provided further, precise detail. This cross-section suggested granulite filled with kaolinitic clay and fragments of various other rocks. Autunite was present, it seemed, in the form of scattered flecks and aggregates. Racagnal was doubtful. This would hardly get him any nearer to his gold seam. The old maps in Malå, and their accompanying field books, would prove vital, he felt sure. But he was a good forty-eight hours' journey from the Geological Institute. An eternity. And time was running desperately short.

Nina was making the journey from Kautokeino to Karesuando in daylight for the first time. They had taken the same road by night, a few days before, to reach the Geological Institute in Malå. This region of Sápmi was desolate and uninhabited. An inhuman place, she thought, gazing out at the landscape. The harsh, magnificent scene prompted thoughts of her father. His uncompromising, innate sense of good and evil sat well with this stark panorama. For the people of the tiny villages dotting the Norwegian fjords, that black-and-white view of the world was part of their DNA. And yet it had never stopped her father from – from what, actually? From making her life and her family's life a misery? Nina refused to ponder the question any further. She shook herself in her seat.

'Tired?' asked Klemet.

'No, just shaking the grey matter up a bit,' she replied, with a sad smile that Klemet missed, staring ahead at the road.

'Yes, it's a strange business. I'm curious to meet this man Hurri.'

They drove on, preoccupied, for a while longer. The cold air crystallised on the car windows, despite the full-on heating. On the road, the sun shot blue rays across the black ice. The studded tyres allowed them to eat up the kilometres without risking their lives on every bend. They had crossed into Finland.

'Aslak told me once that this was where his father went missing, when he was a boy,' said Klemet. 'He'd gone out in search of his reindeer. They'd crossed to the wrong side of the border.'

'He would have incurred a fine if he didn't get them back, was that it?'

'Yes. The national boundaries really screwed things up for the breeders, put it that way,' said Klemet. 'I can't be sure – it was something of a taboo subject at home – but I think that was partly what drove my grandfather to give up reindeer breeding.'

'The national borders?'

'Before, Sápmi was one territory and the Sami lived here alone. But with the borders in place, the Finnish breeders found themselves marooned, unable to cross to the summer pastures on the Norwegian coast, or the winter pastures in what is now northern Sweden. They had no choice but to start feeding their reindeer themselves. Which is how the Finns came to set up reindeer-breeding farms. Stock-breeding there is completely different to how we know it in Norway and Sweden. Their traditional, nomadic way of life was destroyed. And that's why they've always been so hard on Swedish or Norwegian herders who allow their reindeer to stray to the wrong side of the border.'

'How strange.'

'Aslak's father risked his life because he dreaded a fine he would have been unable to pay. So many conflicts have started that way. The frontiers have killed a great many breeders, in my opinion.'

*

3.30 p.m., Karesuando

Hurri Manker was an eccentric character, viewed with scepticism by many. His critics had long since decided he was taking shameful advantage of the local tourists, letting them believe he was a true shaman and serving up a mish-mash of New Age nonsense. They based their evidence on Hurri's publicity flyers and his website promising extraordinary shamanic performances. He took people on excursions to his ancestors' sacred lands, embroidering the outings with horrifying, far-fetched tales and legends. Others claimed he was gifted with genuine powers – of the most mysterious kind, of course – and that he was capable of performing miracles. Even more reason to give him a wide berth, they whispered.

In reality, Hurri Manker was a town-dwelling Sami, one of the first of his people to complete a university education. Using a borrowed family name, he had followed in the footsteps of his uncle, a Swedish ethnologist noted for his systematic study of Sami drums. Hurri Manker held a doctorate and was a member of several learned societies, often invited to speak at conferences. He was a true scholar, widely considered by museum curators and the academy at large as the world's leading living expert on shamanic drums, a reputation he had forged over many years of travel, research and study.

His more colourful local reputation stemmed from his exploits as a young student in the 1970s, when he had thrown himself into the Sami people's first politicised struggle. In this resolutely traditional, conservative milieu, he had earned himself a number of fierce enemies, who readily accused him of every Marxist-Leftist evil under the sun. Cultivating his cynical streak and caustic humour, Hurri delighted in his thoroughly undeserved reputation and did nothing whatever to dispel it. On the contrary, he did everything he could to ensure it became even more exaggerated over time.

Hurri was researching the parish records in Karesuanda. Klemet and Nina found him, as arranged, in the candlelit presbytery of the small church. The wood and stone building was covered in thick hoar frost, the boughs of the surrounding trees weighed down with the burden of snow. Karesuanda's four hundred inhabitants straddled the Swedish/Finnish border in scattered farms paralysed by the cold. Nothing moved, but smoke rose from the chimneys and faint lights flickered here and there at the windows. There were no curtains, of course, in this high place of Laestadianism. The preacher Lars Levi Laestadius had spent several years here, leading his crusade against sin and alcohol, setting out to conquer Sami souls. In this forgotten region, far from anywhere, visitors quickly understood that alcoholism or devout religion were the only alternatives. Karesuando was not a place of subtle nuances. Grey was banished. Black or white. Everyone must choose.

The pastor was out on his rounds, and Hurri Manker greeted Nina and Klemet as if to his own home. He was small and balding, with plain round spectacles, a thick khaki-coloured parka, snow trousers and reindeer-skin boots. He wore a scarf pulled up over his nose, to warm his face. Manker had removed his fox-fur chapka, but quickly pulled it on again once their greetings were over. The pastor had turned down the heating on his way out and the temperature was no more than 10°C indoors. Hurri, who wore thin gloves allowing him to turn the pages of the registers, rubbed his hands vigorously from time to time. He removed his spectacles, peering at the officers with sharp, twinkling eyes.

'The Reindeer Police,' he said, in a lively, lilting voice. 'I've often heard talk about you. And now here you are in the flesh. This is an honour!'

Klemet and Nina had no idea whether he was serious.

'We've come to see you as part of a criminal investigation, and we must ask for your absolute discretion,' said Klemet immediately. 'This is in the strictest confidence.'

'I understand,' Manker reassured them. His breath condensed in clouds of vapour. 'You mentioned a Sami drum in your possession and, as a prelude to our conversation, I should tell you straightaway that I am extremely sceptical. Extremely. I know all the extant Sami drums. If I haven't seen a drum personally, I've studied every document relating to it. None has ever come to light after being passed from hand to hand like that.'

'This is the drum that was stolen from the Juhl Centre,' said Nina.

'And you've found it! Congratulations. But my view is unchanged. I was deeply sceptical about the Kautokeino drum from the outset. It seemed to appear from out of nowhere.'

Manker's uncompromising stance matched his current surroundings.

'But you'll agree to take a look at it, won't you?'

'Of course! And perhaps it'll be Christmas morning all over again, who knows? I'm fascinated by anything to do with a Sami drum, genuine or otherwise. So, show me your treasure.'

Delicately, Nina opened the blanket on the heavy presbytery table. Hurri Manker replaced his spectacles. Klemet and Nina held their breath, looking for all the world like an expectant couple waiting to see their first baby scan. Manker's breath hung in clouds. He peered closely at the drum but said nothing. The silence was unbearable. He took a magnifying glass out of his battered briefcase and studied the signs drawn on the skin, then moistened a finger and passed it over one symbol. Put the finger to his tongue. He touched the skin. He took a fine scalpel and cut a minuscule sliver from the edge. He did the same with a sliver of wood from the frame.

'I'll be back,' he said.

Nina and Klemet stared at one another. Hurri Manker soon reappeared. He placed a small case on the table and took out a portable electronic microscope.

'You're very well equipped,' said Nina. 'That's the model our forensics use.'

'When you work in Sápmi or Siberia, as I do, you can't just pop back to the lab to fetch something you've forgotten. When I set off on a field mission, I take my mobile lab with me, every time. Costs the taxpayer a fortune. Here, hold this lamp, like that, please,' he instructed Nina.

Hurri made another study of the skin, then jotted notes in an exercise book.

'I'll be back.'

He disappeared again. Klemet shook his head, exasperated. Nina said nothing, overawed by the tense, icy atmosphere. Hurri Manker returned almost immediately with another, larger case lined with insulating material. He took out a cotton bud, dipped it in a phial filled with solution and rubbed one of the symbols. The bud coloured faintly. He repeated the operation several times. He prepared several test tubes and soaked the cotton buds in more solutions. He plugged in an electronic device. A series of dials and tiny indicator lights lit up.

'We must wait a few minutes. What would you say to a really hot chocolate and some cinnamon rolls?'

He disappeared again without waiting for their answer. Manker seemed to relish keeping the officers in suspense. He returned with a small tray, set it down on the table, checked the test tubes and the machine.

'Aren't you interested in what the symbols mean?' Klemet's irritation was clear.

Hurri responded with a wicked smile. He was enjoying this.

'Of course I'm interested in them. They'll interest me even more once I've confirmed the drum's authenticity, or otherwise. You might argue that it's still interesting even if it proves to be a fake. But in that case it cannot be analysed in the same way. And we cannot expect the same things from it. So I must know what materials have been used to make it: the wood, the type of skin, the ink. And so on and so forth. Always keep the best till last, no?'

Klemet forced a smile.

'First, the wood. Birch, which is a good start, is it not? The drum has been carved mostly from a knot of birchwood. An elaborate, traditional method indicating expert knowledge. You see, the knot has first been hollowed out into a bowl shape, after which a hooped strip of wood is added, as a stretcher for the skin. It's a very fine skin: de-haired calfskin, from an animal roughly a year old. A female, apparently, in the very best tradition of such things. Whoever crafted this drum was going by the book. I can tell you that it

362

comes from the Lahpoluoppal region, between Kautokeino and Karasjok. Now the ink. Good old-fashioned work here, too. The dark-blood colour, the taste and the results of my initial tests leave little room for doubt: red alder sap mixed with saliva, I'm ninety-five per cent certain. Very traditional. Reindeer blood was sometimes used, too. Whatever was to hand. I would need to carry out more tests, but I'm sure this is traditionally made ink.'

'So the drum is authentic?' Nina demanded to know.

Hurri Manker looked at the young policewoman and her colleague, his expression serious now. He bent over the drum, examining the symbols, then looked up again. Klemet and Nina saw the intense emotion in his face. When he finally spoke, his voice was choked.

'We are in the presence of an authentic antique drum. And no ordinary one at that. Of the hundreds or thousands of drums that existed in Sápmi, only seventy-one remain – seventy-one known drums, documented, catalogued, authenticated. I know each one by heart. Some are in private collections, others are in museums. And still others have disappeared. But we have precise descriptions of them all. So I can assure you,' Hurri spoke slowly now, with due solemnity, 'that we are in the presence of the seventy-second drum.'

Klemet and Nina saw tears in his eyes.

46

Tuesday 25 January

Kautokeino

Kautokeino police station bustled with activity. There were no secure cells standing ready, like those in stations down on the coast. One or two interview rooms were used for party-goers sobering up on a Saturday night, with the duty officers keeping a quiet eye. The last time anyone had been held at the station for questioning was the previous summer, when two tourists – a German and a Finn – had got into a fight over a girl who had found herself unable to choose between them. The station's only real lock-up had to be emptied of jerrycans and piles of firewood. Meanwhile, Olaf Renson and Johann Henrik had been installed in the kitchen. The duty officers dropped in from time to time, for coffee and a chat. Johann Henrik sulked openly, refusing to talk to anyone, while Olaf maintained his state of high outrage, cursing everyone in sight.

A small group had collected outside – just a few hardy souls undeterred by the biting cold. The gathering merited a brazier, nonetheless, and a handful of the Spaniard's supporters took turns in front of the fire. Two hastily scrawled placards read 'Free the breeders' and 'Justice for the Sami'. Other partisans huddled for warmth in the entrance of the Vinmonopolet liquor store next door. People moved between the two at ten-minute intervals, warding off the effects of the cold. Tomas Mikkelsen had already conducted an initial round of interviews and broadcast his first report. Photos were circulating online, too, attracting the usual crop of hate mail in their comment threads.

In the station kitchen, Rolf Brattsen gloated over the two breeders with thinly disguised glee.

'Your room will be ready in just a few minutes, gentlemen,' he said, grinning broadly. 'At last we can offer you some appropriate accommodation. A nice little cell, same as any other self-respecting Norwegian. You wouldn't be wanting any special treatment now, would you? Or perhaps you'd prefer one of those wigwams of yours?'

He guffawed with laughter, watched by the two other officers posting guard at the kitchen door.

'You're making a very big mistake. You'll pay for this,' said Renson. 'You've got nothing on us. The business with the ears is sheer nonsense. Our dispute was resolved a long time ago and everyone knows it.'

'Yeah, yeah – and everyone knows Laplanders' feuds are never-ending, too. Spread like cancer. You think the fire's out and it springs up again somewhere else. But we're going to see to it once and for all, this time. Your pals in the Reindeer Police have been very helpful.'

'They're no friends of ours.'

'Oh, really?' said Brattsen in a tone of innocent surprise. 'Everyone out in the tundra thinks of them as the Lapps' own private security force, don't they?'

'Go to hell, Brattsen. You're all the same. We're going to change all that. You've had it all your own way in the region for far too long.'

'Ooh, I'm trembling in my boots,' said Brattsen, leaving the kitchen. 'Then again, we know all about your unorthodox methods, don't we, Olaf?'

*

Karesuando

Hurri Manker sat in silence for several minutes. Collecting his thoughts, Klemet guessed, as he watched the Sami academic. He seemed to be meditating. At last, he looked up, his expression calm and serene.

'This is the first time an authentic drum has been identified since the Second World War.'

'Are you absolutely certain it's genuine?' asked Nina.

'Yes, absolutely. I reserve my opinion as to its exact date. I don't have the equipment for that here. Either it's very old and beautifully preserved, or it's more recent, but made using traditional materials and techniques.'

'Do you know anyone capable of making a traditional drums like this now?'

'I knew someone, yes. But he was murdered, two weeks ago.'

'Mattis Labba—' stammered Nina.

'Yes, Mattis. A tortured soul, but exceptionally gifted and skilled. I worked with him for a long time, learning the ancestral techniques. But he'd been drinking to excess in recent years. He had beome unreliable.'

'Mattis could have made a drum like this?' Klemet was astounded.

'Not lately, no. His skills had diminished, sadly. But he had once been capable. And his father before him, and his grandfather, and his great-grandfather.'

'What do you mean?'

'I mean that he came from a family whose exceptional knowledge of Sami culture had been handed down from generation to generation. Not only handicraft skills, but the symbolism and power of signs like these. Mattis tended to misinterpret that power. He expected too much of it. He was forced to grow up too soon. His father, Anta, distanced himself from his son. I think he thought that Mattis was not equal to the task. And Mattis suffered greatly because of that. But that's another story. The Labba family tradition reaches back over centuries.'

'So Niils Labba had the gift, too?'

'Mattis's grandfather? Yes, as I said. And for generations back. Their family, and two or three others in Sápmi, took it upon themselves to pass on the knowledge. I'm talking about a very little-known aspect of the Sami tradition. And one that many people would find disturbing, if it was made public. But some families saw themselves as the guardians of traditions that had become secret, due to the campaigns of persecution carried out by the royal Scandinavian armies and the pastors, beginning in the seventeenth century.'

'And this drum?'

'One of the things that was handed down in secret over the generations, I suspect. For its own protection, quite simply.'

'What about the symbols?'

Hurri Manker nodded.

'The separation between the two worlds places great importance on the underworld, the realm of the dead. Very great importance.'

'But with a hunting scene, and village life, with lots of people and healthy, bushy trees as a sign of abundance, up at the top. And the same village, empty, underneath,' said Nina.

'Exactly. You don't need me – you've read it all perfectly yourselves!'

'I'm afraid that's as far as it goes,' said Nina.

'Well, yes, the abandoned village is the first rather disturbing sign, though natural symbols like these others, here, are very common. Sami religion in the pre-Christian era was based on an extensive pantheon – gods of nature and natural phenomena. For the Sami, everything has a soul. Nature itself has a soul, it is a living thing. The power expressed through natural phenomena was the object of a very particular cult. This large cross with a lozenge shape in the centre represents the sun – a classic symbol on many drums, known as the Beaivi. Highly effective for driving out evil spirits and sickness. Now, look at what the sun bears in its branches. At the top, we have a deity.'

'So it's not a tent?'

367

Manker smiled patiently.

'A deity. Like these two here, on the left, but I'll come back to them later. The goddess in the sun is called Madderakka. Very important. She is the origin of all things, the great ancestor, the woman-chief. She receives mortal souls, and she has a particular faculty: she forms unborn infants in her own body. But there's one thing I find very disturbing: these little dots on her head.'

'Are they unusual?'

'No – but they can have only one meaning, sadly. Sorrow. Misfortune. What we see here is a malevolent Madderakka. The dots are an indicator of how dangerous she is. And that casts a very dark shadow over the kingdom of the dead, here. Unsurprising, really, when we read the rest.'

'What in particular?'

'Well, let's look at the two other goddesses I mentioned, these two here on the left. Their positioning varies in different Sami regions and traditions. Most often, there are three of them. They are the daughters of Madderakka, the woman-chief. The Sami believed a person's soul travelled through life in stages, from goddess to goddess. The figure furthest to the right is Sarakka. She is the eldest daughter. She's also said to be the most accomplished of the three. Sarakka is the first to receive the souls presented to her by her mother. Sarakka enables the soul to become an unborn foetus. In bygone days, Sami women gave birth in tents, or peat huts, with an open hearth in the middle.'

'I've seen those,' said Nina.

Hurri was in full flow. He seemed not to hear her and continued with his explanation.

'And Sarakka lived in the hearth, inside the tent. Which is why she was known as the fire-mother. She was the guardian of all Sami women. Even after the Samis' forced Christianisation, children baptised in church were sometimes brought home and baptised again with a new name, in honour of Sarakka.'

'Which goddess takes care of the soul next?' asked Nina.

'You have the goddess to Sarakka's left. She is called Juksakka.

The goddess of the bow, which makes her easily recognisable. I have rather a soft spot for Juksakka, in fact – she turns girls into boys.'

Nina eyes widened in astonishment.

'Yes, the Sami believe all children are girls to begin with, in their mother's belly. Those who become boys do so thanks to the good offices of Juksakka. We owe her a great deal, you and I, officer,' said Hurri, addressing Klemet.

'I'll remember that,' Klemet promised. 'But you mentioned three goddesses.'

'Yes, and in fact, you see the trees surrounding them? You will notice that a large space has been left for the third goddess. Look at the position of the left-hand tree.'

'Exactly.' Nina peered at the drum.

'We're missing a goddess. The third daughter. Her name is Uksakka. Uksakka lives in the entrance to the tent or hut, just under the awning. She is sometimes known as the doorkeeper. And do you know what her role is? She keeps watch over everyone entering and leaving. She protects mothers and their infants after a birth. She guards them against sickness and enables the child to grow. Her presence in the doorway, opposite the fire, is symbolic: she prevents children from falling into the fire. And I can find only one interpretation of her absence here.'

Klemet and Nina listened expectantly.

'Whoever drew these symbols wants us to understand that people were defenceless in the face of danger. If we add Uksakka's absence to the evil manifestation of the woman-chief Madderakka, we have the ingredients of a highly unusual story. This drum is unique in that regard – it does seem to tell a story. Now, let's look at the sun again – the symbols suspended in its branching rays. They are easily read. On the left, you have a soldier, the figure with the bow in each hand. On the right, with two crosses, we have a pastor. And right at the bottom you have the symbol of the king, you see? With his crown. A soldier, a pastor, and a king, all under the sway of the malevolent Madderakka.'

Nina frowned in concentration.

'Would the soldier, the pastor and the king be the bringers of the great catastrophe?'

'Well done, not bad!' Hurri was genuinely impressed. 'I think you have put your finger on a crucially important element. Yes, absolutely. And for Madderakka, the mother-queen, to be so closely connected to the symbols of earthly power, the catastrophe must have been great indeed. And see here, we have two huge crows just above Madderakka, between her and the goddess daughters. Now, look at the rest. We have the empty village. Something has happened – we are clearly meant to read the image as such, because it's right underneath the inhabited village. The contrast is striking and intentional. And to the right of the village, you have the sign that I take to be a doorway of some kind. There's a symbolic aspect to it, though I can't quite pin it down.'

The professor looked up at the two police officers, in search of clues. But nothing was forthcoming.

'Suppose it is indeed a doorway of some kind. Or a building. Or a monument. I'm out of ideas for the moment. Look lower down. These very regular motifs. Strange, aren't they? Even more surprising in that they clearly represent some sort of hallucination. But I'm in the dark again here. Because the hallucination leads on to a series of coffins. Four coffins. Death. Many deaths. We have the explanation for the empty village. Everyone has died. But why the hallucination? Where does it come from?'

Hurri looked concerned.

'Below the coffins, there is even a funeral ship. You see it there? An upturned ship with a cross. And the people next to the ship are upside down, too. Dead, undoubtedly. They're the same people that we see standing upright, to the right of the door, or monument. They have moved from life into death. Who are they?'

'They're all carrying weapons,' said Nina. 'What sort of weapon?'

'Yes, a weapon. An axe. Or a pistol, perhaps?'

'A pistol?' Klemet frowned. 'Not many of those around here. Especially not in the past.'

'In which case, perhaps they're soldiers,' said Nina.

'But the soldiers are represented with bows, aren't they?' Klemet looked questioningly at Hurri.

'True. But there may have been various ways to represent soldiers. Each drum-painter will have depicted them differently, though individual painters tend to be consistent in the use of their particular symbolism. Each painter would always draw soldiers consistently, for example, in their own way.'

Hurri Manker helped himself to another cup of hot chocolate and bit into his cinnamon roll. His nose was red with cold, but he was not complaining. Still chewing, he ran a chilled finger over the right-hand section of the drum.

'A reindeer pulling a sledge. First time I've seen that on a drum. And these dots on the sledge. A sledge as an evil omen? It doesn't make sense.'

'Someone suggested they might be stones,' said Klemet.

'Ah yes, indeed. A sledge for transporting stones.'

Manker nodded slowly. He seemed to be sizing up the different hypotheses, processing the hundreds of symbols he had identified and committed to memory from other drums, finding similarities, connections. He opened his mouth to speak, then seemed to change his mind. He sat deep in thought once again.

'If these people are carrying weapons – it doesn't matter if they're axes, or pistols, or rifles, or something else – something is clearly happening to them, and they die,' said Klemet. 'They are the same people, that seems to fit.'

'Unless the upside-down ones have lost a battle against the people on the other side,' prompted Nina.

Still Hurri Manker said nothing. He seemed not to have heard the officers' suggestions. His eyes narrowed behind his small, round spectacles.

'I'm fascinated by the mind of this drum painter,' he said at last. 'I think the design can be read on several levels. I'm sure he wanted to conceal something, in case the drum fell into the wrong hands. But at the same time, he wanted to deliver an important message.'

'What do you see in the other symbols?' asked Nina.

'A process of elimination is what's required,' said Hurri. 'There, the square with two crosses on top – that's a church. Unquestionably. And we should note that it's positioned directly opposite from the crows, on the other side of the sun. Do we take that as a sign? I have no idea. At the bottom right, there's an area differentiated from the rest. These cone shapes down here. At first, I thought they represented a Sami camp. But now I think they're mountains. And between the two other mountains further to the left, either a high pass, or a sun in the process of rising or setting. And a reindeer, clearly visible, and two fish, and a boat. And in the middle of this section, a cross. Astonishing.'

'A religious cross, or a cross to mark the location of something?' asked Nina.

'You've hit the nail on the head,' said Manker. 'Inspired intuition again, my dear!'

'Brilliant,' said Klemet drily. 'X marks the spot, between two mountains. That narrows it right down, we'll be there in a flash.'

'But there are these fish and the boat,' said Manker. 'A lake with rich stocks of fish.'

'Terrific, that narrows it down again to about a hundred possible places. Easy.'

'And the reindeer indicates pasture, perhaps a migration route,' Hurri went on.

'You think that gets us any further at all?' Klemet remained unconvinced.

Nina widened her eyes at him behind the professor's back. Her partner responded with a deep sigh.

'Setting that to one side,' Hurri continued, 'I believe we're making progress. We still have this circle, to the bottom left of the sun. Very strange, too. And a figure in the middle, and four other smaller figures standing on its rim. Three of them are human, but one has dots above its head.'

'Some kind of malevolent being?' said Nina, softly.

'Yes, most certainly. And the animal next to it is a wolf. A wolf alongside the humans, surrounding this other figure.'

'The Sami sometimes refer to Man as a wolf on two legs,' said Klemet.

'Well,' said Hurri, 'that may be exactly what this drawing means. Men as malevolent as wolves.'

'And the man in the middle?' asked Nina.

'He's wearing skis, as you can see, and carrying a ski stick. The Sami only ever skied with one stick. The ski represents winter and movement. In the other hand, he seems to be carrying the same weapon as everyone else, but upside down.'

'A deserter!' said Nina. 'Or a soldier refusing to shoot. Or to carry out orders, trying to get away.'

Hurri shot another admiring glance at the policewoman.

'I don't know for sure if that's what we see here, but your interpretation is superb. I'll have to borrow you from the police for a few weeks to look at my other drums. Now, there are just two symbols left for us to examine. First, the snake. I'm intrigued by this because, as we know, there are no snakes in Sápmi.'

'Yep,' said Klemet. 'So what?'

'So the absence of snakes in Sápmi does not mean that our drum-painter ignores their existence. The snake may symbolise external intervention. Or perhaps we should pay closer attention to the snake's shape, the direction in which it lies. I would be tempted to interpret it in the context of the drum's function as a kind of map.'

'A map?' said Nina.

'The more we look at it, the more I'm convinced that this drum is indeed authentic and utterly remarkable. Because it does not fulfil the usual functions. I'm absolutely certain – at least, I'm as certain as I can be – that it comprises two drums in one. One telling us a tragic story, and the other pointing to a specific location.'

'Where the catastrophe took place?'

'I'd stake my last flask of hot chocolate on it, yes.'

'The signs down the right-hand edge, these rippling waves,' said Klemet. 'A chain of mountains, perhaps, the Swedish-Norwegian border? That might help us to pinpoint the spot marked by the "X".'

'Yes, but I think the author is consistent in his use of symbols,' said Hurri. 'All his other mountains straddle the rim of the drum. That's no accident. When you talk about rippling waves, you're nearer to the truth than you think—'

'The aurora borealis!' said Nina.

Hurri Manker looked at her with the satisfaction of a schoolmaster who knows his favourite pupil will not disappoint.

'We may wonder why the Lights have been included here,' he said. 'Especially given that they take up so much space around the edge of the design. I don't think they are here merely for decoration. Everything in this design has a meaning. Should we connect them to the hallucination? I don't think so. It's tempting, but the Lights are too remote from it.'

Nina noticed Klemet's faraway look in the candlelight.

'My grandfather told me some extraordinary things about the Lights,' he said. 'He had to ... give up breeding reindeer when I was very small. But he said the breeders used the Lights as a kind of compass during the migration.'

'Now that's interesting,' said Hurri.

'Yes, he said the Lights always unfurled from east to west.'

Hurri raised a hand for silence. He had just had an idea. He closed his eyes, then opened them again.

'The Lights are here to point out a direction. North, quite simply.' And he laughed delightedly at his discovery. 'The cunning of this shaman! We might have taken the drum, held it in front of us and decided that the top was north. But no! To find north, we have to turn it through ninety degrees. Bravo! The aurora tells us how to hold the drum, and the east–west movement tells us how to locate east and west on the drum. And hence north, too. Our map is beginning to take shape. But, of course, it remains altogether too vague for me.'

'Not for us, perhaps,' said Klemet, quietly.

He was remembering the geographical characteristics they had identified, with Eva Nilsdotter's help, at the Nordic Geological Institute. Eva made a great Madderakka, in a funny kind of way.

*

374

Patrol P9 headed north in Klemet's ageing Volvo. The drum had been carefully wrapped in its blanket once again.

'You were thinking the same as me, weren't you?' said Klemet.

'The curse Niils Labba talked about when he handed the drum to Henri Mons in 1939?'

'Yes. It fits the images of death and evil. I wonder if Niils actually made the drum, or one of his ancestors.'

'We'll have to wait for Hurri's other test results.'

'Yes. Though I don't think the drum's exact age is crucial for our purposes. Eva Nilsdotter talked about the legendary seam that had brought bad luck, but which no one had managed to identify.'

'And Flüger's field book. The seam he was looking for: "The entrance is on the drum." And "Niils has the key".'

'Yes. Shame – I rather liked your drowned village. Or the flooded mine.'

'The drum tells the story of the curse. Think about the reindeer transporting the stones on sledges. Mineral ore. People were using reindeer to transport mineral ores.'

'The mine . . .' Klemet thought hard. 'This doorway. It could be the mine entrance, not a building at all. Nina, the doorway represents the mine. That must be it. And the reindeer are transporting the mineral ore through the doorway, with the little figures of men carrying weapons. Guards, perhaps.'

'Or miners. With axes – those aren't weapons, Klemet! Remember what Hurri said: the drum-painter was consistent in his use of symbols. On this drum, the soldier carries two bows, like the symbol on one of the branches of the sun, not axes. I'm sure the other figures are miners. And the upside-down figures are the same miners, but dead. And inside the circle, another miner, trying to escape on skis, but who has been caught.'

Nina's face shone with intense excitement. Klemet had never seen her like this before. She took the drum out of its blanket and held it in front of her, turning it to catch the faint glow from the ceiling light in the car. Klemet concentrated on the dark road ahead, shooting quick, sidelong glances at his colleague.

The rest of the journey was spent in silence. They encountered only three big trucks, looming like monsters from the abyss. Their brightly lit cabins and powerful headlights swept the tundra, revealing strange shadows that disappeared as soon as they had passed. Behind them, they threw up clouds of swirling snow, the tiny flakes dancing in fury at their disturbance.

Nina had fallen asleep. Klemet thought over everything that had happened since the beginning of the affair. What had Mattis got himself into? Everything suggested he had been cruelly manipulated, to get at the drum. His good faith had been abused. His naïvety, too. Was he really the heir to a long line of Sami shamans, their people's secret-keepers? Klemet couldn't picture Mattis – an ordinary, small-time herder – in that role. If Mattis had been aware of his ancestral duty and his failure to live up to it, he had good reason to sink into despair. I'd have done the same, thought Klemet. What would I have done in my grandfather's position, when he took the decision to give up reindeer breeding? I might have hung on. And I would have gone under in the end, like Mattis. Perhaps. He wasn't sure, though. His father hadn't gone under. He had stuck with his peripatetic life, a succession of odd jobs at the farm in the *vidda* and the mine in Kiruna.

In mid-evening, on the approach to Kautokeino, Klemet decided to stop at Suohpatjavri. He hesitated to wake Nina, then left the engine running, turned up the heating, took the drum and walked into his uncle's house without knocking. Closing the door behind him, he heard Nils Ante's melodious voice coming from upstairs.

Chang with her eyes so black, in Suohpatjavri
The treasures of all the world at once
She is young, she is rich, she is beautiful
She has two thousand reindeer who worship her
And the green pastures dance at her sight.

Klemet waited in silence in the doorway. The *joïk* lasted for several long minutes, the same words repeated over and over, to subtly different, guttural melodies. Nils Ante was singing in the middle of the room, under the enchanted, adoring gaze of Miss Chang, seated next to the computer. The screen was turned to face his uncle. Klemet could see Miss Chang's elderly grandmother watching on Skype. He wondered what on earth time of day it was in China. The old lady clapped her hands and spoke at the same time. Miss Chang started and sprang to her feet, ducking around Nils Ante to take Klemet by the hand.

'My grandmother spotted you first, again, and she even recognised you!' she declared, delightedly.

'Better than an alarm system,' said Klemet, grinning and waving to Miss Chang's elderly relative, who waved back, her movements made jerky by the internet connection. 'I see the *joïk*'s taking shape,' he said to his uncle.

'As I told you before, I'm getting to the nub of the matter. It will make a pretty piece. We'll try it out on YouTube, and I shall perform it at the Easter Festival. Let's have some coffee.'

The two men waved in the direction of China and headed downstairs.

'And where is your charming colleague?'

'Sleeping in the warm, in the car. We've just come back from Karesuando. Hurri Manker was there.'

'And so?' Nils Ante was impatient. He reached for the coffee pot, still warming on the stove, and filled two cups.

Klemet told his uncle all about Hurri Manker's scholarly conclusions. Madderakka, the evil mother figure with the dots over her head; Uksakka, notable by her absence; the king, the soldier and the pastor; the hallucination; the deserted village; the transport of the mineral ores; the Lights. He told him about their own theories, too: the miners, perhaps, and a deserter, or a miner trying to run away. Nils Ante sipped his coffee, listening to every word of his nephew's explanation, serving himself two more cups of coffee before Klemet had finished. He made a fresh pot, then examined the drum on its blanket in the midde of the kitchen table, without saying a word. He was clearly moved and thoughtful. Like Hurri, just a few hours earlier.

'Mmm. Do you know what story I think the drum is telling? The story of the colonisation of our land.'

'Go on, then, explain.'

'The Scandinavian kingdoms began to take an interest in Sápmi because of the fur trade, then, little by little, for its natural resources. Wood, water, minerals.'

'Sure. The Spaniard's bored us rigid with all that, time and again. The Sami are victims, their birthright has been looted. Like the Native American tribes.'

'Well, the Spaniard is quite right. But you are apparently unaware of a number of truly tragic episodes in that colonisation process. When it began, in the seventeenth century, there were no roads in Sápmi. It was uncharted territory. Trade followed the rivers, in summer. When the Swedish monarchy began looking for ores to pay for its wars and weapons, it mounted expeditions to explore the region, sent map-makers. There were small mining operations, whose working conditions you can well imagine, here at the edge of the world, far from everything. It must have been appalling. I shudder at the very thought of it.

'The Swedes recruited the Sami by force,' Nils Ante went on, 'to work in the mines. And they used reindeer to transport the ores to the rivers. There's your story. Any Sami who refused was beaten and imprisoned. Behold the foundations of the wealth of your splendid Nordic kingdoms. It didn't last, of course. The small mines all closed, one after the other. Many Sami lost their lives. The Scandinavian countries seized the land for next to nothing, with the blessings of the Crown, delighted to have tamed our country. But all this was still on a small scale. It was another two hundred years before the Swedes returned in force, with the railway this time.'

'And the same on the Finnish and Norwegian sides?'

'It was all the same back then. The frontiers only came to Sápmi much later. Everyone tried to fill their pockets on the backs of Sami labour. The drum tells the story of one of those mines. But not just any one. This business of the dead, and the village emptied of its people, the curse, reminds me of a song that tells a similar story. You know, for centuries *joïks* were our way of passing on our history. Those coffins are quite dreadful. And the crows. And the dead. And this village. Klemet, the drum tells of a Sami village that was exterminated. I had always hoped the legend was not true. But it all makes sense when you look at this drum. The soldiers are not the only cause. This symbolic hallucination is no accident, right here at the entrance to the mine. That's the killer. They were annihilated by a mysterious sickness. You have to find it, Klemet, before it kills again, if the seam is uncovered once more.'

47

Wednesday 26 January

Sunrise: 9.13 a.m.; sunset: 1.50 p.m.
4 hours 37 minutes of sunlight

8.45 a.m., Kautokeino

Kautokeino felt almost springlike. The temperature had softened abruptly, as it often did. The cloud cover maintained a clement minus 17°C, the air could be breathed in comfort and the cold was quite bearable. In front of the police station, the group of protesters had swelled. A dozen Sami had gathered around the brazier. The placards had multiplied, too. The demands were essentially the same, but the tone was harsher now: 'Justice = shame', 'End the witch-hunt NOW'. Renson and Johann Henrik had spent their first night in the cell.

Acting on Klemet's advice, Nina did not stop at the station but drove straight past, stopped to buy copies of the *Finnmark Dagblad* and the other local paper, *Altaposten*, then headed straight for the tent. Her partner had already made the coffee.

No news had reached them on the whereabouts of the French geologist. They would have to set out in search of him. Nina thought about Nils Ante's words of warning, as reported by Klemet when he had accompanied her home the previous evening. They must act fast, before the mysterious seam began killing again. First, though, they had to pay a discreet call on Karl Olsen. See if the old farmer could tell them anything about his father.

The Sheriff's car pulled up in front of Klemet's house at almost exactly the same time as Nina. Tor Jensen was still clad from head to foot in his old fatigues, and even more fired up than before. The cloud cover created a bright, even glare and Jensen was wearing sunglasses, accentuating his martial get-up. He removed them as he bent under the tent flap, tossing two folders onto the reindeer skins.

'More on Racagnal and his outfit. The second folder contains some information about the firm he was working for on his first visit around here.'

Klemet poured him some coffee and opened the first folder. The Frenchman had been working for the SFM for twelve years. He had visited every corner of the globe and over the course of his career, he had served just three companies in total, starting with another French outfit that had eventually folded in the 1990s, according to the dossier. Well before that, Racagnal had moved on to a Chilean firm, Mino Solo, for whom he had carried out missions in Latin America and Europe – the only new piece of information to come to light since the dossier was first compiled. He had been working for Mino Solo on his first extended stay in Lapland, from 1977 to 1983, dividing his time between mining and dam projects.

'So?' asked Nina.

'Nothing red hot,' said Klemet, 'apart from the details on Mino Solo, the outfit he worked for when he last came here. Still, I can't believe it's a coincidence. This guy, a specialist on the region, turns up out of nowhere, the drum disappears just afterwards, and Mattis is found stabbed.'

'Take a look at the second folder,' advised the Sheriff.

Klemet pulled out a few sheets of paper: a police report and some newspaper cuttings. This was all new to them. The documents described Mino Solo and its activities in Lapland between 1975 and 1984, before the company was forced to leave. Two corruption cases. Abuse of power and influence. A series of botched environmental inquiries. Threats. Complaints from the locals. Anonymous damage to property. The police report was harsh, but in most cases there was no conclusive proof. The press articles suggested tensions had been running high; a number of protests had been held. Klemet recognised a very young-looking Olaf Renson in one photograph, brandishing a placard reading: 'Let our river live, Mino Solo OUT'.

Mino Solo was presented as the embodiment of all the ills of industrialisation afflicting the region, responsible for a wave of trouble and unrest. Hundreds of engineers and labourers, both Norwegian and foreign, had poured into small Sami villages, bringing a host of problems. Everyone had heaved a sigh of relief when the sites were closed down.

Klemet replaced the file and stared into space.

'A river!'

Nina and Sheriff eyed him, uncomprehending.

'A river. The snake on the drum, it's a river! Why the hell didn't I see that before?'

The Sheriff still looked lost but Nina understood. Klemet had to be right. She fetched the drum and all three bent over the drawings.

'Of course, the seam lies near a major river leading to the sea. Logical. The ore had to be transported. Even with reindeer, it couldn't be taken very far overland.'

Klemet turned to one of the chests around the edge of the tent and pulled out a set of 1:50,000 maps of the region. He spread them out on the reindeer skins covering the floor, then lit more lamps, adding to the light from the flames.

'Racagnal applied to explore two areas around Kautokeino,' said Klemet. 'One application was lodged last autumn, covering the north-west, but a second one was rushed through last Wednesday, covering three zones within a large area extending east and south-east as far as the Finnish border. Eva Nilsdotter, the director of the Nordic Geological Institute, spotted that the zones he selected had characteristics in common. Which means he must be acting on precise descriptions. He must be out there now, on the trail of a specific seam described in a specific document. We think it's the same seam that the German geologist was looking for in 1939.'

'On what grounds?' asked the Sheriff.

'Just a bunch of coincidences for the moment, nothing concrete, I admit. We're basing our assumptions on a set of photographs from 1939. Eva Nilsdotter eliminated one of the three areas by estimating the distance Flüger had covered on foot back in 1939. All three areas, including the one discounted by Eva, feature a river following roughly the same course – flowing from the north-west, heading south, then turning back east and then down again, to the south-east. And now, look – take the drum, turn it so that north as indicated by the aurora is aligned with north on the map. It's a near-perfect fit. The snake follows the river's path exactly. Now, that's more than a bunch of coincidences, wouldn't you say?'

'Fascinating,' breathed the Sheriff.

'It means,' said Klemet, 'that the French geologist is looking for the seam indicated on this drum—'

'Without ever having seen it.' Nina finished his phrase.

'So the old geological map that Eva was talking about must really exist somewhere. Perhaps Racagnal knew something about it. Eva identified a high plateau with a lake to the south-east, and areas marked by faultlines to the north-east. And if we look at the symbols on the drum, with the mountains, a lake, it more or less fits. Look at this map. Turn it around like this,' Klemet rotated the map, 'and you've got the river flowing in the right direction, a lake here and higher mountainous areas to either side. It's clearly the best fit of the two remaining possibilities. And there,' Klemet declared, pointing at the sheet, 'the seam, marked by a cross on the drum, is within this area. That's where we'll find Racagnal.'

Central Sápmi

André Racagnal dismissed the second area more quickly. But he had taken some samples nonetheless. He was known as the best tracker of boulders in the profession – rocks torn out of a seam by a passing glacier and carried along as the ice advanced. Tracking interesting boulders back upstream along the path of an ancient glacier could lead you to their mother seams. In the early stages of an expedition, when he was setting out to explore an unknown area, trusting to luck, Racagnal's patient observation was his great strength. His older colleagues – the ones who had watched him at work out in the field – called him the Buddha of the Boulders. But they had watched his serene calm disappear, too, when he identified a boulder that might lead to a promising seam. Then, the Buddha became the Bulldog. Hilarious. It kept them entertained, at least. But they were right. Once he fastened onto the trail of a decent boulder, he forgot everything else around him. The second zone he had explored here had demonstrated his Buddha-like qualities to the full. There had been a hint of frustration, too. But he consoled himself that he had time in hand for the third zone, which he was now approaching.

Without the old geological map, he would never have made such rapid progress. He had covered a fair distance since this morning. No need to comply with the scooter regulations now. And if he ran into trouble on that score, the old farmer and his pal, that stupid bastard of a cop, would sort it out. The sky was cloudy, but the light was bright and glaring. Racagnal glanced at the map, then looked at the surrounding landscape. He had entered a twisting valley, bare of vegetation except for a few gnarled bushes huddled low on the ground. The snow cover was thin, and he could see numerous rocky outcrops, like brown stains peppering the rolling swell of white. He observed a good twenty or so rocks. Took quantities of quartz samples, as in the other two areas – some interesting micas, feldspar coloured an evocative, appetising shade of pink. He was in a markedly granitic zone, and that was exactly what he was after. From experience, he could tell that there were large quantities of quartz here, too.

He had been wielding his Swedish hammer all morning, shattering rock after rock. The shards were highly revealing. He got out his magnifying glass from time to time, but even with the naked eye he could identify the quartz slivers, like tiny splinters of glass, gleaming dully in the rock.

At 11.12 a.m., he felt he was making real progress at last, and for the first time. He liked precision and he noted the exact time in his field book. From the outset, Racagnal had been alert to the indications of yellow metal on the map, and old Olsen's gold-mine obsession. In its natural state, it was highly unusual to find significant quantities of gold. Its presence was revealed in tiny splinters and slivers. But at 11.12 a.m., he had found a new boulder, not that large, partly buried in the snow, whose intriguing, blackish colour caught his eye. Its rounded shape indicated that it had been carried in the glacier over a long period. Impervious to the cold now, Racagnal brandished his hammer and shattered the boulder into pieces, revealing brilliant yellow-coloured fragments in the rough surface. Steady now, he told himself, feeling the adrenalin rush, the bulldog straining at the leash. He called the Sami guide, told him to set up the shelter and spread reindeer skins on the ground inside. He breathed deeply, containing his excitement, a feat he managed often enough, and watched the Sami set out the equipment. Racagnal got out the camping stove and set about making coffee. He enjoyed the ritual, just as when he'd cornered one of his little minxes. When you figured you were getting somewhere, that was when you had to slow down. Take your time. Savour the moment. Enjoy the adrenalin flooding your being. Too bad if it was a false alarm. Rocks could disappoint. A little minx could slip from his grasp. So it was important to relish the preliminaries. At last, he took out his magnifying glass, eyeing the intense yellow in the black rock. He even felt like letting the Sami in on the moment.

'Look,' he said, simply.

The Sami came over and looked, his expression a complete blank. The geologist shrugged his shoulders and peered at the intense yellow in the rock. He walked the few paces over to the snowmobile trailer and took out a measuring instrument, an SPP2 scintillometer – a pistol-shaped device, battery-powered, weighing about a kilo. He buckled the leather strap and changed the batteries. In this cold, he got through three times as many batteries as in Africa. The SPP2 began to emit noise, about a hundred shocks a second. But the granite rocks round about pushed it up to three hundred. Natural radiation. Deceptive. Gold was possible in faults like these, running through igneous rock. You had to push on, ignoring the whining from the SPP2.

He had already got through a good thirty or so batteries in almost a week. The SPP2 was picking up normal radioactivity for the region, sometimes up to four hundred shocks a second. On three separate occasions, it had registered minor peaks of almost five hundred shocks a second. Routine stuff for any experienced geologist. But now, it was different. For the first time, the readings were up into the next scale, measuring up to fifteen hundred shocks per second. The SPP2 was whining louder. Over seven hundred shocks per second. Racagnal looked again at the boulder. It wasn't granite, but an altered block, with a fissure running through it. He took a deep breath and gazed around him. The bare, snow-capped hills kept their secret for now, but he would make them talk.

'Stay here,' he told Aslak.

Racagnal unhooked the trailer and climbed aboard the snow-mobile, armed only with his SPP2 and his hammer.

'Go fetch, Bulldog!' he muttered, gunning the engine.

He didn't have to ride far, just a hundred metres along the hill-side, crushing a few dwarf birches in his path. He stopped on the edge of a shallow dip. Several large rocks lay scattered below but one in particular, a little bigger than the first, caught his attention. He took out the SPP2 and switched it on. The device whined so loudly he was forced to switch to the next scale, a second time. Up to five thousand. The reading set his heart racing. The SPP2 registered four thousand shocks a second. Racagnal threw down the machine, grabbed his hammer and smashed it onto the rock, roaring like a lumberjack with the effort. He picked up a piece and saw the same bright gleam of vivid yellow, deep in the black rock.

'Fuck.' His voice came in a slow whisper. 'It *isn't* gold. It's uranium.'

He raised his head and looked around. The Sami was sitting on the reindeer skins, facing him. From this position on the hillside he could see down the valley, stretching into the distance. The sun was bright now, behind a thin veil of cloud. The snow glittered and shimmered, its surface broken here and there by the naked branches of birch trees, forming dark, impressionist touches on the immaculate white. Soft, blue-grey mountains bordered the horizon. He felt an exquisite tremor of excitement.

'That idiot farmer thinks he's looking for gold, and his priceless fucking mineral seam is fucking uranium ore.' Racagnal's voice rose slightly as he spoke.

He smiled faintly.

'Well, that changes everything. Playtime's over now . . .'

And he hollered aloud, the icy air rasping in his throat.

'Fucking idiot! Uranium! Fu-u-uck!'

The Sami herder watched everything from his distant vantage point. He didn't catch everything. But one word, at least, was perfectly clear.

Klemet parked his Volvo in front of Olsen's cowshed. He and Nina had decided he should go alone to ask Olsen about the portrait Berit had mentioned – a joint delegation would be too high-profile, given that the Reindeer Police were officially off the case. Meanwhile, Nina was touring the service stations in Kautokeino, making discreet inquiries as to the types of oil used in snowmobiles in the area, hoping for a match for the oil found on Mattis's reindeer-skin poncho.

Klemet knocked at the farmhouse and heard footsteps. Olsen opened the door, hunched forward, his head lowered slightly. A moment's surprise was quickly concealed and he eyed Klemet with an air of deep suspicion.

'The Reindeer Police. In plain clothes. Well, well, see this!'

'Good morning.' Klemet was politeness itself.

'What do you want?' Olsen snapped back.

'I was wondering if you could take a look at a photograph.' Klemet proceeded with caution.

'Something to do with the drum and Mattis, is it?' Olsen's tone was aggressive.

'I don't think so,' said Klemet, evasively.

'Because I heard you were off the case, see? You wouldn't be coming round here without good reason, against orders, by chance, now would you?' The old farmer's tone was insinuating.

'Absolutely not,' said Klemet. 'This is just out of sheer curiosity. My old uncle thought he recognised someone you might know, on a photograph he found.'

Giving Olsen no time to respond, he took out a close-up of the expedition photograph showing the man with the moustache.

'What about it?' growled Olsen.

Klemet said nothing, but held the picture up for the farmer to inspect.

'It's my father,' said Olsen finally. 'The old man's been gone a while now. Dropped dead, just like that. Aneurysm. Boom. All over. But that's an old photograph. Where'd you find it?'

'Seems he was with a group of people hiking in Lapland just before the war.'

'Dunno. Never heard about that. Nothing to do with all this. Why are you showing it to me now? Why come here?'

'No need to worry, Karl.' Klemet smiled soothingly. 'What did your father do?'

'He was a farmer, fool! What the hell kind of question is that?'

Klemet nodded. 'He never mentioned an expedition with some foreigners right before the war? Nothing about a mine, I suppose?'

'A mine? Guarded by trolls, I suppose? Fairytale nonsense! The old man never said much. Hardly spoke at all, really. He just worked the land. And then, boom, aneurysm. End of story.'

Klemet could see there was no point in insisting. He didn't want to arouse Olsen's suspicions even further. He thanked him with a nod of the head, raised a hand in a gesture of parting and left. Then paused and turned.

'A French geologist has been taking a look around here for a while now. Obtained a permit from the mining affairs committee last week. You wouldn't happen to know if he mentioned anything about an old geological map he might have in his possession?'

'I never met the man,' said Olsen. 'He asked to see me. But I don't know him. Never heard anything about a map like that.'

Klemet thanked him with another nod.

Driving slowly past the house, he saw Olsen in his kitchen, talking into the telephone, gesticulating nervously.

The hours that followed were some of the most hectic Racagnal had known in a long while. He continued his exploration of the zone, checking his old and new maps, covering the pages of his field book with sketches, taking samples, brandishing the scintillometer all over the place, measuring the radioactivity. Progress was slow, and he cursed the rapidly fading daylight. Still, he was convinced.

When the sun had disappeared below the horizon, and the bivouac was installed for the night, he settled himself in front of his radio set. The Sami was boiling reindeer meat – a little treat Racagnal had allowed himself, to celebrate his discovery. Taking the Sami's gun, he had shot a reindeer a few hours earlier, and his guide had taken charge of cutting it up and preparing the meat. The quartered carcass had been placed in the dwarf trees near by, their branches bending under the weight.

First, the geologist called Brattsen. The Acting Superintendent asked him to wait while he found a quiet place to talk, then came back on the line. Racagnal was brief.

'You can tell Olsen I've found something. Perhaps something very big, if what I think is confirmed. But it's not what he thought. Get ready for a big surprise.'

'What then?'

'I can't say more over the radio. I need a few more days. But tell Olsen our fortune may be more than made.'

Brattsen was excited and intrigued, Racagnal could tell. He relished the thought of the two Norwegians waiting impatiently for news. He gave them his current position and outlined his plan for the days ahead.

'Sure you know what you're doing?' said Brattsen.

'No worries on that score. Couldn't handle it without the Sami

389

guide, though, even if I am the best in the business. And rest assured, I'll be discreet.'

He ended the call.

Next, he contacted his company's operational logistics centre. At La Défense on the edge of Paris, in the tower housing the offices of the Société Française des Minerais, a special department was on call 24/7 to dozens of teams scattered across the globe. Racagnal identified himself and explained that he needed to contact the chief duty geologist straightaway. He was put through immediately. The man in question was well used to taking quick-fire decisions. Paradoxical really, thought Racagnal, in the world of geology, dedicated to studying the evolution of the earth itself, measuring time in tens of millions of years, carrying out explorations often for decades at a time. But the mining industry was a slave to the rules of the purest form of capitalism, where the only time that mattered was the timeframe of the trading floor. The announcement of even a minor discovery could have extraordinary or terrifying repercussions for a company's share price. Which meant taking fast, often highly profitable decisions.

The chief geologist had known Racagnal for years. Knew him through and through, including his darkest side. He had decided long ago that it was no concern of his if the man preferred adolescent girls to mature women. He knew when Racagnal was deadly serious about a find, too, even though he stated nothing in plain terms over the radio. Whatever it was, it clearly had huge potential. He gave Racagnal everything he wanted.

'I'll send Brian Kallaway,' said the chief geologist. 'Brilliant kid, the best glaciologist on our books right now. Canadian. And Canadian geology is a perfect match for Lapland, as you well know. He can leave tomorrow morning and be with you in the field during the day. He can carry out the low-level reconnaissance flight for a radiometric survey. What's your preferred method on the ground? Electric, electromagnetic, magnetic? Or a geochemical study?'

'I don't have much time,' said Racagnal, then corrected himself quickly. His deadline with Olsen was irrelevant here. 'There's another licence round in a few days. I need to nail this right away or it might slip from under our noses. There are some Norwegians out here already. Send me this Kallaway, let him do the aerial survey and readings for the zone I indicated just now. But he's got to keep a low profile. Prospecting is ultra-sensitive up here, as you know only too well.'

Racagnal cut the connection. This evening, he was dining on reindeer stew. All that was missing was a little minx. Like that Sofia, the one who wouldn't cooperate. But soon, no one would be able to refuse him much.

Karl Olsen was waiting for Brattsen in the parking area next to their usual reindeer enclosure. The old farmer massaged his neck vigorously. The pain had got steadily worse over the past few days as his excitement rose. Two weeks had passed since their first meeting, and he had made good use of the time, he had to admit. Olsen poured himself a cup of scalding coffee and slurped it noisily. Sidelining Tor Jensen had sparked tension in the locality. The Labour supporters found themselves cornered. The Labour government in Oslo wanted results, and this was precisely the argument the Right had used at the regional level. To save face the Finnmark regional council, controlled by Labour, had announced that Jensen had been temporarily assigned to coordinate security during the UN conference, but no one was fooled. Olsen had made sure of that. He imagined the local Labourites would fight back once the conference was over, but he didn't give a damn about that.

He saw the policeman's car pull up. Brattsen opened his passenger door.

'Got a visit from your cowboy in the Reindeer Police,' said Olsen. 'Asking questions, all innocent-like. With an old photograph of my father that I'd never seen before. I don't like it. Don't like it at all.'

'Nango?' Rolf wore his usual hard, uncomprehending expression. He seemed bothered by the news, though.

'You said on the phone you had something to tell me?' Olsen went on, turning painfully to face the policeman.

'The Frenchman's found something big, apparently.'

'What, already? He's done it?'

'Apparently. Seemed very sure of himself. He's got to get a specialist in from Paris to guarantee his findings.'

'A specialist from Paris. I don't like that either. Reckon the bastard's trying to get one over on us?'

'He's no choirboy.'

'I don't like that one bit,' said Olsen.

'He gave me his position.'

'Ah?'

'About a hundred and fifty Ks from here. To the south-east.'

Olsen massaged his neck and thought carefully. He poured his cold coffee out of the window and helped himself to another cup. He sipped it, then placed it on top of the dashboard.

'We're going to have to get out there ourselves. You can find some pretext. I want that man in my sight from now on.'

'Not sure that's wise,' said Brattsen. 'The two breeders are being held for questioning. I'm expected to do the honours. And some people are surprised Aslak isn't there at the station with Renson and Johann Henrik.'

'All the more reason to go after him and the Frenchman, then. See, it's all falling into place, there's your excuse. And the questioning can wait. We'll have to set off immediately.'

'I can spin things out a little, but not beyond the end of the conference, for sure. I need to question the breeders tomorrow. I can get out to the *vidda* on Friday or Saturday.'

'Well, you see, that's perfect. I'll leave for Alta this afternoon. A couple of days' shopping. And then I'll join you.'

Brattsen nodded. Olsen could see he was out of his depth.

'All over soon, lad,' he said, reassuringly. 'They're handing out the mining licences soon enough, and after that, nothing will stand in our way. We just need to be sure the Frenchman has found our gold seam. And doesn't get up to any tricks. But you'll take care of that, eh? Future head of security at the mine, and all that . . .'

48

Nina had returned from her tour of the service stations in Kautokeino by late afternoon. Under the thick cloud cover, it was already pitch dark. And bitingly cold after the milder daytime temperatures. Or maybe I'm just tired, she told herself. She went straight to Klemet's tent, pushed back the flap and crouched down beside the fire. She took off her gloves and rubbed her hands vigorously. Klemet was sitting on the other side of the hearth, reading through the files.

She spoke first, still rubbing her hands over the flames.

'The oil on Mattis's cape doesn't come from a snowmobile.'

He closed his file, waiting for the rest.

'I've checked the components on the cans sold in the service stations, talked to people filling up and the attendants. No doubt about it. Snowmobiles don't use oil of that type. Nor cars. It's a type is used in tractors, big mechanical diggers, that kind of thing. And heavy-goods vehicles. It wasn't a brand I'd heard of.'

Nina reached deep into her parka and pulled out her notebook.

'Arktisk Olje is the maker's brand. And the oil is called Big Motors Super Winter Oil.'

'It's a special oil for tractors and big farm machinery?'

'Yes, and heavy-goods vehicles.'.

The tent flap was raised, letting in a draught of cold air. The Sheriff took a seat next to Klemet, then unbuttoned his parka and the jacket of his over-tight fatigues, exhaling in relief.

'So, where are you both up to? The patrol car's been parked outside the house for a little too long. You shouldn't hang about here.'

'I know,' Klemet cut in. 'But for pity's sake, Tor, we've been following up a whole set of leads at once, centuries apart, across a vast area. And all in secret, right under Brattsen's nose, in a region where everyone knows everything in the blink of an eye.'

'You've got the drum. You know who took it. That's fantastic work already, Klemet.'

'I stopped by Olsen's place just now. Thought he seemed very suspicious.'

'Olsen, the Progress Party councillor?'

'Yes. Our mysterious moustachioed man, in Henri Mons's photo, is Olsen's father. I could tell he didn't want me to know.'

Nina looked up at the news.

'His father?' said the Sheriff. 'Olsen's father and Mattis's grandfather were together on the 1939 expedition? Now there's a coincidence.'

'Well, not really when you think about it. History repeats itself down the generations. Mattis worked at Olsen's place sometimes,' Klemet reminded them. 'Berit told us he worked with two other herders there, John and Mikkel, but all as mechanics.'

'On the old man's tractors and agricultural machinery,' said Nina, staring straight at her colleague, the realisation dawning as she spoke the words.

Karl Olsen's farm lay in darkness when Klemet's red Volvo rolled slowly into the yard. He had made sure no one saw him turn onto the track leading to the buildings. He would have a hard time justifying his presence here, with no warrant, in plain clothes, when he was supposed to be out in the tundra 'counting reindeer'. A quick call to Berit, ostensibly making sure she was still available for questioning, was all it had taken to discover the old farmer had gone to Alta for a couple of days. John and Mikkel would be coming to do some maintenance work on the small machinery and tools, she said, but not before tomorrow morning. Berit herself would stop by only tomorrow afternoon, to see to the cows.

The Sheriff had been uncomfortable with the idea of the unlawful nocturnal visit. Nina had been more categorical: it was absolutely out of the question. Klemet had muttered something inaudible and the Sheriff had taken the deciding vote, saying he would talk to the examining judge in Tromsø the next day and was practically certain to get everything approved. On this common-sense decision, the trio had separated.

Once his colleagues had left, Klemet had gone to his garage, filled a small bag, checked the street was deserted and driven off. It had taken him fifteen minutes to reach the farm, with a few detours en route. Parking behind the barn, he would have to walk just a hundred metres or so, avoiding the main approach to the house.

He sat in the car with the engine switched off, for two long minutes. He had wound down one window, listening out for suspicious noises. The cold seized him and he cursed his inadequate clothing.

He took out a small torch with only a faint beam and moved slowly towards the barn wall, stopping frequently. He reached its big door, which stood slightly open. Inside, the vast space held two tractors and at least three big machines used in Olsen's arable fields. The walls were all fitted with panels hung with tools and smaller, lightweight equipment, together with shelves and an impressive collection of knives. As a precaution, Klemet slipped on a pair of thin gloves before checking the blades, one after the other. None matched what they knew about the blade that had killed Mattis. But that meant nothing. Any set of farm buildings was full of hiding places. And Klemet hadn't come for that.

He scanned the corners of the barn and found what he was looking for. Several five-litre jerrycans of oil stood lined up next to an old cupboard and a set of battered petrol cans. The jerrycans were from various brands, but two contained Big Motors Super Winter Oil, from Arktisk Olje.

Klemet was satisfied. He retraced his steps, poked his head out of the barn door and looked around. A few hundred metres below, the main road was lined with street lamps, lighting up the few passing cars. He was preparing to leave when he heard a truck approaching along the main drive. Soon, headlights swept the big farmyard. Hastily, Klemet shrank back into the barn.

Who could be coming to Olsen's place while the farmer was away? He pulled the door shut and hid in a dark corner. The truck stopped and the engine died. One of its doors opened shortly after, and Klemet heard something heavy hitting the ground, followed by footsteps. And a whistle. The truck driver was whistling a pop tune. The man seemed to be alone. Klemet tried to look through a crack in the wooden barn wall, but could see very little. He heard the man jumping on the spot, doubtless to keep himself warm, still whistling. Interminable seconds passed. Klemet was surprised to find himself trying to identify the pop song.

Suddenly, the noise was drowned out by another vehicle turning into the main drive. A small diesel van, thought Klemet. Headlights swept the yard before dying when the engine was switched off. Two doors slammed. Klemet heard the three men clap each other on the shoulder. He recognised a voice. Mikkel, one of the herders working for Ailo Finnman and doing occasional maintenance work on Olsen's machines. Great, thought Klemet. He'll be coming into the barn. He looked around in the semi-darkness, searching for a better hiding place. But no footsteps approached the barn door. The three men stayed outside in the yard.

Klemet heard the truck door open again and thought another man had opened the rear door of the smaller van. He heard someone manipulating the truck's hydraulic tailgate. The men grunted with effort. They seemed to be shifting merchandise from one vehicle to the other, apparently from the lorry to the van. Klemet was overcome with cold. Five long minutes went by. He had left his thick gloves in the car, and now his fingers hurt.

Outside, the three men stopped at last, slammed the vehicle doors shut once more and lit cigarettes, talking about the merchandise. Klemet listened hard. His suspicions were confirmed: the three were involved in trafficking. One of the trio – John, it seemed – said he would soon need a new stock of cigarettes. A list was passed around – the man Klemet had identified as John told his colleague the spirits were listed on the paper. The other man, who was Swedish, said he would have to come back in three days. Klemet heard someone whistle and click their fingers. Then the three said their goodbyes. The Swede climbed back into the cabin of his truck, called out, '*Hasta la vista*, guys!' to the other two, and slammed the door.

The van was the first to start up, driving all the way around the yard. For a second, its headlights swept the bigger truck's cabin. Peering through the crack, Klemet caught a flash of the Swedish driver's tattooed arm.

49

Thursday 27 January

Sunrise: 9.08 a.m.; sunset: 1.56 p.m.
4 hours 48 minutes of sunlight

Kautokeino

The crowd outside Kautokeino police station was getting bigger. The protesters had got themselves organised. A small encampment was taking shape, spilling onto part of the market square opposite the council offices. A number of breeders had towed wilderness trailers to the site. Three braziers warmed the thirty or so permanent protesters. Others stopped by early in the morning on their way to work. New placards had appeared.

Brattsen pushed his way through, his face set in a stubborn glare, jostling a breeder carrying a placard with the words 'No to Colonisation' handwritten in large letters. The Acting Superintendent looked particularly bad-tempered today. He would happily have exchanged insults with the character in the blue four-pointed hat. But he forced himself to say nothing. He was Kautokeino's police chief now. He'd been advised to keep on his best behaviour. The role of police chief was a representational one, too. 'The public face of the force.' Well, fuck that for a start. Pen-pushing bureaucrats. Still, Olsen had told him they were closing in on their goal, and he had to watch his step. The old farmer kept talking to him about his father, then reminding him of his future role as head of security at his miraculous mine. With a fat salary. No more kid gloves for the Sami and every other parasite on society then.

Rolf reached the door of the police station, turned and shot a defiant glare at the protesters grouped in a semicircle about ten metres away. A silent stand-off ensued, then he turned and disappeared inside without a word. He poured himself a coffee and went down to the basement. Asked the officer on guard to open the cell. The two Sami breeders had not been let out to freshen up that morning. Brattsen stared at them.

'Well? Jesus, you look rough. Regular pair of criminals!' He grinned. 'So, the three of us are going to have a little chat, aren't we?'

Renson drew himself up to his full height.

'Yeah, yeah. You can keep your arrogant posturing for later, Renson. Won't do you much good here.'

Footsteps sounded in the corridor outside. Brattsen turned around. Tor Jensen stood in the cell doorway, an enigmatic smile on his lips. He was accompanied by a small man in a suit and another police officer.

'Carry on, Brattsen,' said the Sheriff, still smiling. 'The examining judge and myself will be conducting a small search. But don't let us get in the way of your questioning.'

'What the fuck?' Brattsen burst out.

'The examining judge can't spare us much of his time. We'll tell you all about it later, if necessary,' said the Sheriff. 'Least we can do for Kautokeino's big chief of police.' He addressed the examining judge. 'Isn't that right, sir?'

Brattsen swore into his coffee but was certain he'd get no response from the judge, a man he knew to be very nice and cosy with the local Labour Party. He glanced at the two prisoners, jaw clenched, then pushed past the Sheriff and disappeared upstairs, calling over his shoulder, 'I'll talk to you two when you've had a chance to clean up. Make yourselves look halfway decent, if you can!'

*

Nina and Klemet were waiting for the Sheriff and the judge at the entrance to the track leading to Olsen's farm. They were still using Klemet's elderly red Volvo. And they preferred to continue operating in plain clothes. They were about to go after Racagnal, but first, Klemet wanted a clean conscience.

The judge got to work quickly. Two police officers took samples of the motor oil, working meticulously, taking plenty of photographs, then wrapped up the oil cans and placed them in the back of the police van. They seized the knives, too, and carried out a detailed search of the barn.

The examining judge moved on to Olsen's house. One officer opened the door with ease. No one in Kautokeino felt the need to install complicated locks. While the Sheriff and the judge searched the ground floor, Klemet went straight upstairs, followed by Nina. They found old Olsen's bedroom, with its stale, acrid smell. And they had no trouble recognising Karl Olsen's father in the photographs on the wall. These were mostly of family but one or two showed Olsen Senior out in the countryside, or in his fields, sometimes posing with other people – probably farm labourers. In these pictures, he adopted a dominant, paternalistic pose. Often, the workers – a downtrodden lot, thought Klemet – were posed crouching in a line, one knee to the ground, facing the photographer, while Olsen stood lording it behind them, his hand on one of their shoulders.

'There's the interpreter from the expedition,' said Klemet. 'He must have worked for Olsen. The photo's dated 1944.'

'And here's Karl Olsen with his father,' said Nina. 'The only picture where you see them together. Olsen can't be very old there. No more than ten, I'd say, probably less. He hardly even reaches the metal detector his father's wearing across his chest.'

'Looks as if Olsen Senior caught the metal-detecting bug on the 1939 expedition,' said Klemet. 'Must have carried on with it alone, afterwards.'

'He certainly did,' said Nina. 'Look here.'

She had found the door to the tiny storeroom. She looked

400

around inside, saw the old chest, the rolled maps, the yellowing newspapers, the storage boxes. Everything smelled stale and old. She leafed through a handful of papers.

'These must be the maps Olsen's father used. His name was Knut, apparently.'

They looked again at the photographs.

'Berit said that the other pictures had been put up in the attic,' said Klemet. 'Let's see if they can tell us anything.'

They climbed the narrow stairs leading to the attic, clearly very little used. The space was large and tidily arranged except for one corner stacked with a jumble of old storage chests. Klemet found the trunk Berit had mentioned, with pictures of Olsen's wife's family. A stern-looking lot. Like his own Laestadian family. The same accusing looks.

'Klemet, come and see this,' Nina called from the other end of the attic.

She was crouching behind two chests, pointing to two devices lying side by side on the floor. One was the metal detector seen in the photograph on the bedroom wall. She pointed to the second device and its instantly recognisable brand name.

'A Geiger counter. The Geiger counter used in 1939.'

'Yes. Maybe Flüger didn't die in a fall, after all,' she said quietly and indicated the bottom of the device, marked with clearly visible, brownish stains. Faded but unmistakable. Klemet and Nina recognised them immediately. Blood.

Brian Kallaway jumped down from the helicopter that had dropped him next to Racagnal's bivouac. The SFM had laid on the full works, as often when it sensed something really big. The company was more than able to mobilise the required resources. The helicopter also deposited a huge pallet shrouded in netting, suspended from the undercarriage for the flight. The drop contained a snowmobile, jerrycans of petrol and storage chests full of equipment and provisions.

The Frenchman observed the young Canadian, knowing exactly

what he thought about the crack glaciologist the company had sent to help him. A joker. A joker with too many Mickey Mouse degrees, all dressed up for an adventure like fucking Tom Cruise, and as if that wasn't enough, he was wearing a pair of little, round John Lennon glasses. One of the new breed, incapable of working in the field unless they're surrounded with gadgets. Think it makes them look professional. The kid was wearing a heavily pocketed parka with special reflective fabric all over it, boots fit for an expedition to the fucking North Pole, and the latest brand of glacier goggles around his neck. His three-day beard had been carefully trimmed. A special pocket on his sleeve held a miniaturised GPS. He wore his ultra-light Estwing hammer slung around his hips, like a gun. Racagnal counted at least two radiation dosimeters on his snowsuit. He wasn't in the least surprised. Too many young geologists took ridiculous precautions nowadays. Racagnal could remember when guys would carry blocks of uranium in their backpacks and use them to decorate their desks back at the office. No one worried about a bit of radiation back then. But for the past ten years, all radioactive samples had been consigned to special storage. Too dangerous. Everything was too fucking dangerous now.

Kallaway was already unfolding his portable solar chargers, ready to power his armoury of electronic devices. Racagnal grinned openly at the Canadian's panoply of state-of the-art equipment. Kallaway had no idea why his colleague was chuckling to himself. He'd been told Racagnal was a pro of the old school. Something of a hard man, that was all.

'Two-twenty,' he announced, looking at his watch with a satisfied air. 'Don't think we could have done it any quicker than that. Good thing the weather's with us, or the pilot would have refused to take off.'

Racagnal shook his head. The kid even had a Polimaster PM1208 watch with its own miniaturised Geiger counter, for Christ's sake. A Mickey Mouse geologist and no mistake. He waited for the helicopter to take off, heading for Alta, then turned to Kallaway.

402

'Aerial surveys?'

The Canadian looked disappointed at the terse greeting. Not a word of praise for his efficient touchdown in the depths of Lapland, with all the required equipment, less than twenty-four hours after receiving his mission order. Yes, he had completed the aerial surveys.

Under normal circumstances, the early stages of uranium prospecting were carried out by air, covering vast expanses of terrain. The results were still haphazard, of course. If the uranium ore was a metre below ground, or beneath a lake, nothing would show up. But an aerial survey could identify likely areas for further exploration.

Brian Kallaway went to shake Aslak's hand. The Sami returned his firm grasp, saying nothing. Kallaway moved one of his devices over to a folding table he had set up and spread a map next to it.

'This section contains several spots,' he announced. 'Where did you find your boulders?'

Racagnal indicated his finds on the Canadian's map.

'Well,' said Kallaway, 'I'll get to work right away. I'll start by exploring this area, and you carry on over there. After that we'll take this direction and intersect with this axis, following the river upstream. Shouldn't need more than a couple of hours.'

The Sheriff and the judge headed back to the station, while Klemet and Nina returned to Klemet's house. Their equipment and uniforms lay waiting where they had left them several days before.

The old Geiger counter would be sent away for immediate tests on the blood stains. If that was what they were. The examining judge had also ordered DNA samples from Ernst Flüger's remains in the cemetery in Kautokeino. If necessary, he could order an examination of the German geologist's cranium, too.

Klemet and Nina adjusted their uniforms: the grey fatigue trousers and thick navy-blue jackets.

'What I think,' said Klemet after a long silence, 'is that the interpreter, the one Henri Mons told you about, must have talked to

403

Knut Olsen, his employer. Told him what Niils Labba had said to the German geologist. All about the drum, the mine, the map. And that fired Knut's imagination.'

'That would certainly explain why he disappeared so soon after Flüger and Niils Labba left,' said Nina. 'He followed them. Simple as that. And he must have waited for Niils Labba to go off alone, then attacked Flüger. Perhaps he threatened him. Perhaps Flüger tried to defend himself. And so Knut Olsen struck him with the Geiger counter.'

'He didn't find the field book, even so. But perhaps that was how he found the map. The famous map Eva was talking about.'

'Is she on her way?' asked Nina.

Klemet glanced at his watch.

'Should be here in two or three hours.'

'Do you really think the old geological map was in Olsen's store-room?'

'She'll be able to tell us, I hope. I gave her all the clues from the drum, so that she can incorporate them when she examines the other maps at Olsen's place,' said Klemet.

He looked forward to seeing Eva in Kautokeino. And he found himself thinking about the night he'd kissed Nina. He was relieved that Nina seemed to have dismissed the embarrassing incident. She didn't bear a grudge. She said very little about her boyfriend, the fisherman from down south. Lucky guy. Klemet had never met him, of course, but he felt kindly disposed towards him, if only because he had enabled Klemet to cut Fredrik from forensics in Kiruna down to size.

It hadn't escaped Klemet's notice, either, that Nina seemed troubled by her last encounter with Aslak, ten days ago, when she hit the reindeer while driving to the airport, en route for France. Klemet's memory of his own last encounter with Aslak, as he and Nina had ridden across his land, still rankled. The image of Aslak always left him deeply troubled. It always would. And that was something he could never come to terms with.

He looked at Nina, buttoning herself into her navy fatigue jacket,

404

the Reindeer Police badge shining on her sleeve. She patted her uniform, replacing items in the pockets. She took out her note-book, leafed through it and tried to return it to her breast pocket. It didn't quite fit and she searched for whatever was in the way. She pulled out a small pouch, seemed to remember something and red-dened at the thought. Aslak's gift. She saw that Klemet had noticed.

Nina opened the little bag.

'Aslak give this to me after I hit the reindeer. I hadn't even looked at it,' she added, as if to justify herself. But she seemed flustered.

Klemet said nothing. He checked his stuff, collected his bags and went outside to finish loading the patrol car. After two trips, every-thing was ready. He stood waiting on the doorstep. But Nina had sat down at the living-room table, looking preoccupied.

'Let's go, Nina.'

'Just a minute.'

Klemet sighed and headed for the kitchen to pour himself a glass of water. Passing behind Nina's chair, he looked to see what she was doing. She had taken out a piece of paper and was sketching designs.

'Do you have to do that right now?'

Nina slid the paper across the table, with Aslak's gift. Some sort of pendant, strung on a thong of plaited reindeer leather, and almost certainly pewter, which was often used in Sami jewellery. Klemet didn't recognise the design. The forms were rounded, and the whole piece was asymmetrical, with two bead-like shapes at the top. In the lower section, a sort of upright strut on the right-hand side counterbalanced a curved, snake-like shape on the left. The curves were perfectly regular. Klemet was unable to decipher the design but, he had to admit, it had a certain beauty.

Nina pushed the paper further towards him. She had made sev-eral sketches, the last of which included four letters, G, P, S and A. G and P were at the top, S and A underneath.

'Not difficult,' she smiled. 'My father used to doodle things like that when he needed to relax. He'd use our family name, or his first name, or mine, or whatever. He'd take the letters, alter their shapes for artistic effect, almost like a monogram, or a cipher. He designed a ring that way once, with the first letters of his first name and family name, and my mother's. My mother never wore it. I think she disapproved of jewellery. But my father often wore it. You see, Aslak's taken the first and last letters of his composite family name: Gaup and Sara.'

Klemet looked again at the pendant. He could make out the rounded forms now. With a little effort, the letters were plain to see. Nina smiled, pleased with her discovery. She gathered up the pendant and folded the piece of paper.

'Right, let's go,' she said brightly.

He stood rooted to the spot, barring her way. Nina found herself pressed close against her colleague. Her eyes opened wide in surprise. He held out his hand.

'Show me the pendant again, please.'

Nina stepped back, took out the pouch and held it out to Klemet with a faint, uncertain smile. He took it between his fingers and examined it closely. He closed his eyes, opened them again, held the pendant up on the end of the leather thong, watching it turn slowly while Nina looked on in amusement. Finally, he held it upright between his thumb and forefinger.

'The S, Nina, look at the S.'

Nina was still smiling. Then her expression froze. She clapped one hand over her mouth and sat down suddenly on the chair.

'Oh my God,' she cried. 'That shape. Oh my God, Klemet, it's an exact match. One of the marks on Mattis's ear.'

50

Thursday 27 January

Central Sápmi

The Canadian glaciologist worked quickly, drawing on the full gamut of his expertise and equipment. In just two hours, he had identified two more boulders. No doubt about it, their concentrations of uranium were interesting, to say the least. Exceptional, even. From the readings on his SPP2, the boulders were very promising indeed.

'I'm getting spikes at eight thousand shocks a minute, with the presence of yellow material,' he declared.

Kallaway was one of a breed of specialists used only sparingly by men like Racagnal. A matter of pride. But the boulders might have been carried twenty kilometres from their source and it was almost impossible for him to get that far alone. Kallaway was a necessary evil. The kid had jumped for joy when he discovered a more rough-cut, angular block about two and a half kilometres from the first finds. This one hadn't travelled far in the glacier. They were approaching the source.

The glaciologist spent a few hours carrying out initial tests and poring over the maps of the area. Before setting out, the documentary resources department at the SFM had sent all the available reports on the locality to his laptop. Back in the relative shelter of the bivouac, Kallaway entered his data, pushing his glasses up the bridge of his nose and exclaiming with enthusiasm at regular intervals. He had given up trying to communicate with the Sami guide, who sat aloof, distant and inscrutable, just like his French colleague. Kallaway didn't care. They needed him and he was doing a fine job in record time. The company would be very satisfied with his work.

He had to admit, the surly Frenchman had shown remarkable intuition. He found it hard to believe Racagnal's account of the short time he had spent out here in the field. Early in the afternoon, flushed with the success of their initial exploration, he had contacted headquarters by radio, praising his colleague's work.

'The Buddha of the Boulders! Amazing . . .'

But when Kallaway ended the call, Racagnal leaned forward and smacked him hard in the face, half knocking him out.

'Dare to call me that, would you, you little arsehole? And watch what you say over the fucking radio.'

Klemet and Nina had no time to lose. The match for one of the marks on Mattis's ears was a sensational discovery. But it posed new problems, too. Driving into the centre of Kautokeino, Klemet tried to collect his thoughts.

'Mattis was murdered because he was in possession of a drum indicating the location of a fabulous mine. Why? Either because he'd stolen it, or because he refused to hand it over to someone else. Someone took advantage of him, gave him reason to believe he could harness the drum's power. Aslak?'

'Can you really see Aslak wanting to take control of a mining operation?' said Nina.

'No, but perhaps Aslak wanted the drum, for its power?'

'You mean Aslak might be some kind of shaman?'

'A shaman—' Klemet echoed her words, quietly.

'As far as I understand,' Nina went on, 'true shamans don't go around telling everyone about their powers. So why not Aslak? He has his mysterious side. And the Sami seem to respect him.'

Klemet shook his head. Unconsciously, he was driving more slowly now.

'I don't know. It's just – well, it doesn't fit the image I have of him.'

'What image, Klemet?' Nina was suddenly impatient. 'The image that made you back off with some lame excuse when you were supposed to question him? I'd be very interested to know exactly what this "image" consists of. I've been completely open with you. I didn't have to tell you about the pendant, believe me, but I chose to show it to you.'

He said nothing, staring at the road ahead. He opened his mouth to speak, then shut it again. He had been on the point of telling her something, but thought better of it.

'Whoever is after the drum is also looking for the mine,' he said, cautiously. 'They manipulated poor Mattis. Racagnal's looking for the mine indicated on the drum, we know that for sure now. What we need to find out is whether he's been acting alone. What if he attacked Mattis, to get him to reveal the location of the drum?'

'I thought you suspected Mikkel and John?'

'I do, but Johann Henrik says they were out in the tundra with him on the Tuesday Mattis was killed. Not far from the trailer, admittedly – he said they were trying to contain Mattis's herd. And we haven't checked whether the old French ethnologist – Henri Mons – knows Racagnal. They could have been in on this together, after all.'

It was Nina's turn to fall silent.

'No,' she declared, finally. 'Or if they are, Henri Mons is unaware of the fact and has been manipulated in turn. But I don't believe that. Mons had profound respect for Niils Labba. He was genuinely moved when he told me his story. I'm much more intrigued by the role played by Olsen's father Knut.'

'I can't imagine Aslak would have been capable of killing

Mattis in cold blood,' said Klemet. 'Something in their connection to one another escapes me. Johann Henrik might be able to shed some light on that. But we can't talk to him now, thanks to Brattsen.'

'Berit might know something. She seemed highly evasive when we showed her the photograph of Aslak.'

Klemet thought back to the scene in Berit's kitchen: the older woman's distant expression, a troubled look she had tried to conceal. He glanced in the rear-view mirror, flicked the indicator and made a broad about-turn, heading for Juhl's museum. He parked on the street just above the main buildings. A minute later, he was knocking on Berit's door.

Berit answered the knock. She seemed unsurprised at the sight of the police officers and showed them into the kitchen once they had taken off their boots. Her eyes were puffy. She had obviously been crying. Klemet gestured to Nina with a jerk of the chin.

Nina took Berit's hand and glanced at Klemet. He nodded.

'Berit, we have reason to believe that Aslak might ... that he might be the one who stabbed Mattis.' Nina spoke quickly, her words tumbling out. 'Or at least that he was the one who made the marks on the ears.'

Berit started in horror, pulled her hand free and clapped it over her mouth, stifling a cry. She stared wildly at Klemet, who nodded again, saying nothing. Berit burst out crying, her head in her hands.

'Oh dear Lord, no!'

Nina took her gently by the shoulders.

'Berit, we know you were very close to Mattis. We're so sorry. But we must—'

Berit looked up suddenly. Her expression was completely altered. Fiery, tragic and proud.

'I am not weeping for Mattis now!' Her voice was loud and strong. 'But for Aslak. Oh dear God, Aslak. My Aslak.' And she shook her head in anguish, hiding her eyes in her hands.

Klemet and Nina stared at one another in astonishment.

'What do you mean, Berit?' Nina shook her gently, encouraging her to speak.

'It isn't him! It isn't him!' Berit was gasping now, unable to catch her breath. Her expression was one of utter despair, as if the foundations of her world had crumbled.

Brian Kallaway and André Racagnal were getting ready to leave. They would push on and explore a little further, while Aslak stayed behind at the bivouac. Racagnal wasn't worried the Sami would try to slip away. Still, he made sure to send a message back to Brattsen every two hours – nothing too compromising, just giving his location. The threat of reprisals back at Aslak's camp was enough to keep him in check, it seemed.

Except Racagnal wasn't so sure after all. The look in the herder's eye, when he passed him up close, could be disconcerting. No, He wasn't worried, still less scared. The Sami was the one who ought to be scared. But the man let nothing show, nothing at all. He never hurried, never spoke. He just watched Racagnal, hardly ever taking his eyes off him. He ate his own reindeer provisions, slept in his corner, never let himself become dependent on the Frenchman for anything at all. Often, he just lay stretched out, propped against a rolled-up reindeer skin, watching him. Like a wolf watching his prey. A wolf that knows the prey won't escape. That's what that fucking Sami reminds me of, thought Racagnal. And the thought pierced him to the quick. It was obvious: the Sami was a predator with all the time in the world. A wolf certain of success.

'What? What's up with you, you bastard?' Racagnal shouted at the guide. 'Want my fist down your throat, do you?'

Brian Kallaway looked startled by his colleague's sudden outburst, but he dared not speak. He finished gathering up his equipment, pulled on his crash helmet and lowered his eyes when Racagnal turned his furious glare in his direction.

*

Nina stood up as Berit gasped and sobbed. Nina could see Klemet was thinking the same as her. And both of them refused to believe it. Could Berit have done the unthinkable deed? Never. Not her. It made no sense at all, a mad idea.

Nina shook Berit more firmly by the shoulders.

'Berit, you have to tell us. This is too important.'

Berit looked up imploringly at the two police officers.

'Aslak,' she began, struggling to regain her composure. 'Aslak. He was ... Oh dear Lord God ...'

'He was what, Berit?'

She took a deep breath.

'He was the man I loved. The only one.'

Nina and Klemet were stupefied. They had been expecting something big. A confession of some kind, but nothing had prepared them for a secret like this. Berit and Aslak.

Berit blew noisily into a handkerchief. Nina sat down to her right, Klemet pulled up a chair on her left. The candle shivered.

Berit stared at the fragile flame in the middle of the table – the room's only source of light. And she kept staring at it as she talked for the next half-hour, uninterrupted not even once by either of the police officers.

Never, Berit assured them, had anything of a carnal nature ever passed between them. And Aslak knew nothing of Berit's feelings, either. Her flights of passion were fantasies, mere illusions, and she had tried to absolve herself with frenzied prayers. More than once she had hidden, to watch Aslak lead his reindeer along a valley. She had looked on admiringly, so many times, as he threw his lasso, or wrestled a reindeer in the enclosure so that he could mark it, even castrate it with a single bite. So many times, too, she had trembled with violent, unnamed sensations, dazzling and exhausting. And there were the dreams. The restless nights.

Berit was hiding nothing now. She stared at the candle, shrinking now but still bright. The vivid dream had recurred often, so often, in which she, Berit, went on all fours in the midst of the herd, as if she were a reindeer herself. The dream in which Aslak

412

caught her in his lasso. Her silent hopes had evaporated the day Aslak met Aila, the woman who would become his wife.

Aila was so young at the time, barely fifteen years old when she was promised to Aslak. Aslak's father was already dead. Anta Labba, Mattis's father, had arranged the contract. The future bride was a member of his family. Aila was fifteen, delicate and bright, already skilled in the preparation of skins and a capable craftswoman. Berit had no chance. She had wanted to die. But she was needed at home. Her young, handicapped brother had filled her thoughts and deeds. But in her dreams, she belonged to Aslak.

And that was the story of Berit Kutsi's life. On the one hand, the dubious attentions of Pastor Lars Jonsson, who wanted her to experience the sensation of sin, the better to answer the call of the Lord, and, on the other, her silent passion for the man she considered the finest Sami God had ever taken into his protection on this earth. She had chosen the way of prayer and reflection, and dedicated her life to others.

Berit sat in silence for a long while, her hands folded on the table in front of her, her head slightly bowed, gazing dreamily into the tiny flame, in the semi-darkness of the kitchen.

'Do not harm Aslak,' she said finally.

She seemed unburdened. Klemet and Nina waited to hear what she would say next, certain the story did not end there. Klemet knew that he and his colleague were on the same wavelength. The idea pleased him. They were unafraid of the silence. Seconds passed. Berit seemed to be in the grip of some inner struggle. But Klemet knew the hardest confession was over. They had only to wait now, for the rest. The candle flickered and dimmed. Berit stared at it. The darkness closed in around them.

'God knows our religion acknowledges no saints,' she began. 'But if there were to be one, it would be Aslak. All he has done for his wife ...'

'What do you mean?' said Nina.

'Have you ever met Aila?'

Nina nodded.

'So you have seen that she is robbed of her reason, in part. I told you she was quite beautiful. When they met, she was fifteen years old. He was twenty-five. And Mattis, dear God, Mattis was twenty. It was in 1983. Troubled times in the *vidda*. This was a few years after the business of the dam on the river Alta, the one people wanted to stop being built. Perhaps you remember, Klemet. People were bitter.'

Nina thought of the newspaper cuttings describing the protests. She pictured the photograph of Olaf Renson as a young militant objector.

'Aslak was beyond all that. He was never interested in politics. He lived in a different world. Some people reproached him for it, but that was how it was. He showed such integrity. Eventually, people left him in peace. Some even respected him for it. And the dam was built anyway. Perhaps you remember, Klemet, or perhaps you had already left by then, or was it just before you came back? I don't remember. But the region was overrun by hundreds of foreign workers. And . . . things happened. In that year, 1983, one of the foreigners went after Aslak's young fiancée. It happened in one of the tunnels serving the dam. One evening, when everyone had left. She was raped, there in the tunnel. Did you know that, Klemet?'

Berit turned to look at him for the first time since the beginning of her story. Klemet shook his head. No, he hadn't known that. He felt overcome with emotion, and the image of Aslak. He nodded for Berit to go on.

'Almost no one knew. And those who did know, did nothing. What was a poor Lapp girl worth compared to the foreigners working on the dam? One policeman knew. He did nothing. He's dead now. I prayed for his soul. Aila was raped. She was fifteen. She was betrothed to Aslak. They were to be married when she turned eighteen. She knew she was promised to Aslak. She didn't want to disappoint her uncle, Anta Labba. Above all, she didn't want to lose Aslak. She was in despair. She did not know I was in love with him. She came to see me one day. Dear Lord, she was so beautiful. But oh God, her misery. She placed her hands on her belly and I understood. She begged me to help her, on her knees. Dear God, she begged me to help her extinguish the child.'

Berit covered her face with her hands. Her chest heaved, but she kept control.

'I could not do it. I could not. Aila went away. She was in such despair, she wept, like a child who does not understand. Oh Lord, the tears, and the wailing. I can see her now, in front of me, wailing and crying.'

Berit's throat tightened. She burst into tears again, sobbing and shaking, her features contorted. She buried her face in her arms on the table.

Nina and Klemet stared at the dying flame, waiting for Berit to continue. She sat up straight, but her voice was distant now, and altered, as if someone else was speaking through her. She did not look at the candle, but gazed into the distance, through the frost-framed window. She spoke very slowly.

'I found out later. The child was born much too soon. A boy. Aila delivered it all alone. Then she took it up above the dam, which had been opened by then. And she ... she saw the baby's body bounce off the rocks. And after that, she lost her reason.'

Berit fell silent again. The flame was sputtering.

'Aila was never the same after that. Sometimes she would cry out, "*Lapset, lapset*", "child, child", liked a wounded animal. And she would throw her hands up in the air over her head. Like she was trying to catch something. She never spoke again.'

The candle flame died, leaving a tiny swirl of smoke. A shaft of moonlight shone through the window, its pale gleam lighting up the faces of the three people sitting at the table.

'How do you know this?' asked Nina.

'From Aslak. He knew she was with child, and he stood by her. He knew what she had planned to do when the time came. It was the last time we spoke to one another. I never dared speak to him again after that. But Aslak never forsook Aila. He took care of her, like a saint.'

Nina saw Klemet nodding in the darkness. He understands, she thought.

Berit stayed sitting in her darkened kitchen when the police officers got up to leave. They had reached the door when they heard her voice, faint and almost unrecognisable, speaking out of the darkness.

'Do not harm Aslak.'

51

Thursday 27 January

Central Sápmi

André Racagnal was keeping an eye on Brian Kallaway. Mickey Mouse hadn't tried calling him the 'Buddha of the Boulders' a second time. Racagnal was still suspicious, though. He stood close by whenever the kid put a call through on the radio, listening in.

Kallaway was unnerved, and not just because knew he was being watched. After several hours coaxing the rocks to give up their secret, taking measurements with the SPP2, searching the maps, situating their finds on the old geological map, he pushed one of the maps across to Racagnal, with trembling hands.

'It's there . . . ' he stammered. 'We'll be over it tomorrow morning. Dead certain. I recorded spikes at eight thousand shocks with yellow material. Incredible. We're heading towards something huge.'

'So that's what the guy drew on his map,' said Racagnal, as if talking to himself. 'Probably had no idea what he'd found. Saw yellow in the rocks. Thought it was gold. Didn't understand he'd found uranium.'

'You're right, I'm sure. This map looks pretty old. Uranium wasn't of much interest prior to the Second World War. But it's a different kettle of fish now! This is an incredible find, do you realise?

417

We'll need a whole lot more readings and some exploratory drilling. But if the seam delivers the goods, the SFM could become the world leader in uranium. This is massive!'

'Yeah. You said it. But remember, kid. For the moment, you keep your mouth shut. Is that clear?'

'Sure. Of course.' Kallaway had hoped his colleague would relent slightly, on the brink of such a massive breakthrough. He hesitated a moment, then went on, 'One thing's bothering me, all the same.'

'Oh yeah?'

'Well, I'm not worried as such. Just a niggling detail.'

'Go on, let's have it.'

'OK. According to my calculations and projections, and the findings we situated on the old map, the comparisons I've made, and—'

'Spit it out, for fuck's sake!'

'This huge uranium deposit could be right next to the Alta river. Mining it, if it's commercially viable, will be extremely tricky. Very little room for manoeuvre. We'd need maximum security – the risks are huge. Not a problem for us, I don't think, we have the expertise. But imagine if a smaller outfit got there before us. The consequences could be appalling. Imagine tons of radioactive residue pumping straight into the Alta. I don't need to spell it out to you. An entire region contaminated, every town downstream evacuated. And the end of reindeer breeding at the same time. Thank God we know how to avoid all that. It'll be expensive. But worth it, in my view.'

'Class over?' said Racagnal. 'May we continue? We're going to pack everything up, transfer the bivouac so we're ready to start at first light tomorrow. Everything has to be done tomorrow, get it? That's the deadline for lodging the licence applications ahead of the decision round on February first. Our last chance. Yours, too, if you want any kind of future in this business, do you get me? You've got your work cut out, kid.'

Racagnal turned around, feeling the Sami's eyes on his back. He pointed at the guide. The man hadn't understood a word, but Racagnal knew he had been watching him all the time.

'And you! Get this bivouac packed. We're leaving in an hour.'

Racagnal was wrong on one point. Aslak sat chewing quietly on a thin piece of reindeer bone, but he wasn't looking directly at Racagnal. Instead, he was staring hard at the tag on Racagnal's silver wrist-chain, as he had done before in his tent. The tag Aslak's wife had recognised.

Eva Nilsdotter had just arrived from Malå. The director of the Nordic Geological Institute found Patrol P9 installed back at the police station. Rolf Brattsen hadn't been seen for a while. He had finished questioning the two Sami breeders and had left shortly afterwards, saying he had to check some facts out in the field. No one dared asked what. He had seemed tightly wound, aggressive and excited all at once. No one knew when he would be back.

The protesters were still outside in force. The custody of the two Sami men, both of whom were politically active, had sparked a chain reaction. Some factions in the Norwegian parliament had started expressing concern about what was going on in the Far North. All the more so because according to reports on the NRK television news, banners demanding 'Sápmi for the Sami' had begun to make their appearance.

Eva found Klemet and Nina in the latter's office, studying a map. The geologist seemed to be thinking hard.

'My dears, you've hooked a monster, if you only knew it. First thing, none of the old maps in your farmer's attic correlate with Flüger's field book. But we know he was extremely interested in something. On the other hand, I've been giving a little more thought to your case and the clues on the drum, trying to put the two together, with some help from my teams. Remember Flüger mentioned yellow minerals and blocks of altered black rock. We cross-checked it all with some aerial survey records, and here,' she pointed to a spot on the map, 'we have a radioactive zone with granite, and graphitic schists – the kind that can be used to produce uranium. Stop looking at me like a couple of boggle-eyed fish – it means that, potentially, you have a uranium deposit somewhere in this vicinity. If it gets into the hands of some small-fry operation, if they feel at all tempted to use explosives to get at some samples deeper down without waiting for the proper boring equipment, it will lead to contamination and a major ecological catastrophe, with the river flowing so close by. Not to mention the risks from radon gas. I mentioned that to you before. It's never a problem in a properly installed uranium mine – with employees properly equipped, the right ventilation, you can get on with the job. But without that, radon is a one-way ticket to lung cancer, practically guaranteed. And if you smoke, too, you're a dead man walking. Radon's an absolute bugger. I wonder if that isn't what did for the population on your drum. Show me the photograph of it.'

Klemet took out an enlargement.

'See here. This motif leads straight from the mine to the coffins – your "hallucination" or some such. A clear link. I don't know when your drum dates from, but the miners may well have succumbed to radon gas, which is odourless. It's still present in some mines even today, in Africa and elsewhere, where the men are never warned about the dangers. And if the miners smoke, they die very quickly. Radon is insidious stuff. I'm quite sure the Sami were all raging tobacco fiends back in the day. Big drinkers too, of course. The Swedes lured them in with booze and smokes – the usual tricks when you're trying to tame the noble savage anywhere on this earth.

'No one knew anything about uranium when the drum was made, or the mine was first exploited, obviously. People were interested in the yellow pigment because it was used by the royal courts of the day to decorate porcelain and glassware. If the mineral carted off on the sledge is indeed uranium, you can be sure it will have wreaked havoc with the labourers in a poxy little mine with no ventilation whatsoever. Guaranteed.'

Rolf Brattsen and Karl Olsen met on the outskirts of the town of Maze, on Highway 93, halfway between Alta and Kautokeino. The Acting Superintendent looked thoroughly bad-tempered, as usual.

He had left his car discreetly parked and driven to meet the old farmer in his pick-up.

The latest message from the French geologist had been urgent and hurried. Olsen didn't trust the man. The more he thought about it, the more he worried that the Frenchman was planning to get ahead of him. Because if the deposits were that spectacular, he might be tempted to go ahead and declare the find behind Olsen's back, despite all the checks and balances he had arranged. And he, Karl Olsen, who had pursued his old father's dream his whole life, would be left high and dry. There could be no question of that.

He turned awkwardly to face Brattsen, wincing from the shooting pains in his neck. Brattsen had not brought good news. His lenient attitude to the French geologist's sexual harassment charge had aroused suspicion among his colleagues back at the station. People were getting angry.

'Thanks to those two bloody Sami detainees and their networks. Bad as the Commies, the lot of them. Proper shit stirrers.'

Brattsen's new-found promotion was in the balance.

Olsen knew he couldn't count on Brattsen. The man was a stubborn, bone-headed ass. But he glimpsed a solution, nonetheless. It was just possible he could save Brattsen's skin – he would need him in the future, after all – and secure the gold seam, all at the same time.

'Have we got the Frenchman's position?' Olsen asked, narrowing his eyes.

'Yeah, that's one thing we do have. He's in a completely deserted area. No pasture anywhere near. No one ever goes there, it's miles from anywhere.'

'Simple, in that case. Don't you worry, lad, everything will work out. We'll pay a call on our French friend, keep an eye on him from a distance, then move in close. And when we're sure he's found what he's looking for, we pounce. Understand? You'll be the one who brings him in, under arrest. The others won't be able to say a thing. Do you see that, lad?'

'Yeah, fine. But his company might still submit the application for the drilling licence.'

Olsen said nothing. He knew the answer to that, but he wanted Brattsen to come to the obvious conclusion himself.

'Well yes, of course. And there's a risk he'll talk under arrest, too.' The old man sighed in mock disappointment.

'Yeah, a risk he'll tell everyone he was out prospecting on your behalf,' said Brattsen, crossly.

'Oh, I wasn't even thinking of that,' said Olsen. 'I was thinking that he might tell everyone how you delivered young Ulrika into his clutches, remember? The little fifteen-year-old barmaid?'

He watched with satisfaction as Brattsen's expression changed, abruptly.

52

Friday 28 January

Sunrise: 9.02 a.m.; sunset: 2.02 p.m.
5 hours of daylight

7.30 a.m., Central Sápmi

Racagnal and Kallaway set off very early after a short, cold and rest-less night. Kallaway found the tense atmosphere exhausting. He chewed his breakfast, explaining to Racagnal precisely what had to be done next. Thanks to the boulders, he had identified the path followed by the ancient glacier. The ice had probably advanced about a metre a day. By tracing the line back and studying the geo-logical maps, they were getting close to the mother seam. And after looking at the old geological map that Racagnal had come by (though he refused to say how), Kallaway was in no doubt: accord-ing to his calculations, they were less than three hundred metres from a hugely important uranium deposit.

'Can we go now?' Racagnal cut him short, leaning on his long Swedish hammer.

The sun had not yet appeared over the horizon, but the glare reflecting off the snow would soon give adequate light. There was no time to lose. The drilling licence had to be registered with the

Administration on Monday at the latest, for approval by the mining affairs committee meeting in Kautokeino, on Tuesday 1 February.

Kallaway had loaded his snowmobile and checked the radio. He pictured himself announcing the news to Paris. This would be huge. He smiled to himself, unaware that Racagnal was watching him, and raised his hand in a discreet gesture to the Sami guide. Kallaway was in a cheery mood now. Followed by the Frenchman, he quickly covered the few hundred metres between the camp and the mountainside. Never had he experienced such a feverish sense of excitement. For the last leg, he fastened on a pair of ultra-light snow shoes. They moved forward until they were close to the crest of a ridge rising steeply above them.

When Kallaway was almost at the top, he stopped. Just over the flat summit, a section of the mountain fell away abruptly in a kind of ramp. Kallaway moved forward again along the crest, to get a better view. His expression froze. In the middle of the slope – impossible to see if you were not standing directly over it – he saw a shadow. Or perhaps just a strangely shaped piece of fallen rock. He took out his powerful field light and shone the beam down onto the spot. The shadow disappeared, leaving a small dip in its place. He made his way carefully down the slope towards it.

'Racagnal!' he yelled. 'Down here, quick!'

The Frenchman was following close behind. Leaning forward on his hammer, he saw straightaway. 'The entrance to an old mineshaft.'

Kallaway moved further forward. The mine entrance was tiny. A man would have to bend double to get inside. He shone his torch down the passage. His throat felt dry and tight. He turned back and felt the blast of Racagnal's breath on his face.

'Carry on,' said the Frenchman. 'I'm right behind you.'

Kallaway felt desperately uneasy. Bent double, he made his way along the narrow passage, trying not to slip. About two metres inside the opening, it turned a corner. They emerged into a small chamber about five metres by three. The ceiling was barely a metre and a half above the rock floor. The rough walls showed signs of irregular blows from hammers and picks. Some sections of the rock

424

had been hollowed out more deeply than others, showing the veins the miners had pursued.

Kallaway whistled.

'Can you imagine? Guys came all the way out here in search of ore.'

He took his Estwing hammer and struck the rock wall. It looked for all the world like pitchblende, natural uranium ore.

'When does it date from, this mine, do you reckon?'

'No idea,' said Racagnal. 'I know people were prospecting here in Lapland in the 1600s. Might be a mine from back then. We're not here for a history lesson. Get your torch over here.'

Kallaway shone the beam in the direction indicated. Racagnal switched on his SPP2, setting the scale to fifteen hundred shocks. The whine shot up to the maximum immediately. In the narrow chamber, the noise was unbearable. Kallaway covered his ears. Racagnal didn't react. He turned the knob to five thousand. The whine reached maximum intensity in a quarter of a second. Kallway had lowered his hands but pressed them to his ears again immediately, grimacing. Racagnal showed signs of nervousness. He set the device to fifteen thousand. Only twice in his career had he needed to set the SPP2 so high: a few days ago, on a boulder, and once on a mission to Cigar Lake mine in Canada, with the highest concentrations of uranium recorded anywhere in the world: two hundred and ten kilos of uranium per tonne of ore. Two hundred times more than almost any other deposit on the planet. Again, the whine rose quickly to the maximum. Fifteen thousand shocks a second.

Kallaway stared at Racagnal, eyes wide behind his small round glasses. Cigar Lake had just been outclassed.

9 a.m., Kautokeino

Patrol P9 was just about to set out on Racagnal's trail when Klemet saw his uncle Nils Ante walking towards the entrance to Kautokeino police station. Klemet was astounded. This had to be the first time he had seen his uncle come anywhere near a police station – one of the places he generally kept well away from, the other being church. Klemet waved. To his equal surprise, Hurri Manker had come along too. What was the drum specialist doing this far from Jukkasjärvi? What were the two of them doing here together?

Klemet cursed under his breath. Racagnal had to be stopped before disaster struck. Added to which, there was still some doubt over the exact spot they were heading for. He would have to collect evidence and keep a record of tracks encountered along the way, too. The weather was on their side, fortunately. Tracks were much harder to conceal in winter, in the snow. He could have done without this extra worry.

His uncle walked over. Klemet glanced anxiously at the sky. Just at that moment, the sun rose, working its usual magic. But Klemet saw worrying signs, too. By mid-afternoon, the weather could turn stormy. And bye-bye to tracks in the snow, then.

'Greetings, nephew! Back in uniform? Doesn't suit you, you know ... I have a couple of things for you. Are we staying out here in the cold, or going back to your house? My friend Hurri, whom I haven't seen for years, was quite overcome by your business with the drum. He absolutely insisted on coming to see me to talk about it. He's come all this way, especially.'

'Nina,' said Klemet, addressing his colleague who had already seated herself in the patrol car, 'let's go into the garage for five minutes. After that, we really have to go, Uncle.'

The little group entered the police garage, its door still standing open. Klemet indicated a space to the side, where two old sofas had been installed facing one another. Between them, a rickety wooden chair supported two half-full ashtrays. The station's smoking area. Everyone took a seat except Nils Ante. Klemet could hardly believe his ears when his uncle began singing a *joïk*. Police officers walking past the garage entrance stopped and stared. Seeing Nina and Klemet sitting with the *joïker*, they shrugged their shoulders and went about their business.

'That *joïk* reminds me of something,' said Nina.

But Klemet got to his feet, glaring at his uncle in exasperation.

'Is that what you've come wasting my time for?' he burst out. 'To sing me the final version of the *joïk* for your Chinese girlfriend? Come on, Nina, we're going.'

He took two paces forward, then spotted Hurri Manker's wicked look. Manker grabbed his sleeve.

'Listen to your uncle. You may learn something.'

'That's not Miss Chang's *joïk*,' said Nils Ante, crossly. 'Really, you hardly listened when I sang it before. And I would ask you to show her a little more respect, Klemet. She's not "my Chinese girlfriend", she is my precious Miss Chang-Chang.'

Klemet gave an exasperated sigh. 'So?'

'The *joïk*, there was a *joïk*,' explained Manker. 'I paid no attention to the symbol at first. The rest was so richly allusive. But it's prominently displayed, in fact, right in the middle of the sun – you know, the cross, supporting the figures of Madderakka, the king, the soldier and the pastor. I couldn't be sure if it was of any significance, but I wanted to be certain. We did some research, your uncle and I. He's a remarkable man, with a remarkable, encyclopaedic memory for *joïks*. And your uncle's stroke of genius was to make the connection with Mattis. And one of Mattis's *joïks*.'

'The *joïk* you were singing, Nils Ante! It's the same one Mattis sang when we visited him, just before he was killed,' said Nina.

'And Mattis was singing his father's *joïk*, which was his father's *joïk* before him,' said Nils Ante, delighted to have stopped his nephew in his tracks. 'I found it among my old recordings. If you listen to it out of context, without the drum, it seems like one more *joïk* among many. A dark *joïk*. Very dark, in fact, but there are plenty like that. But it talks about a very precise location. A mountain stream flowing into a lake, and the shore of the lake describing the shape of a bear's head, and an islet in the lake.'

'I think,' said Hurri, 'that the *joïk* gives precise directions to the place indicated on the drum. I truly believe so. And the *joïk* says that the story should never be forgotten, from generation to generation. It's a warning from beyond the grave. The maker of the drum –

which dates from the late seventeenth century, I'm certain of that now – had to ensure the message was passed on. As you know, at the time the Sami had no written language. This man knew how to make drums, and he was a *joïker*. We shall never know what became of him, sadly. But thanks to his *joïk*, he could be certain that, one day, someone would discover the drum, and the secret it held. And the song says: "Andtsek made coffee on the western slope. The sun rose. Their herds mixed on both sides of the valley. The other Jouna was on the other side of the valley." We think that this is the information missing from the drum. You said you wanted confirmation as to which of the two remaining zones to search in?'

Klemet took out both maps from the patch pockets on his fatigue trousers and spread them over his knees. His uncle peered at the contour lines.

'A valley with two fords and two pastures. Here.' Nils Ante pointed to a precise spot on one of the maps.

53

Friday 28 January

Intersection of Highways 93 and 92

The P9 patrol car drove fast along Highway 93, heading north. Racagnal must have passed that way to reach the territory he planned to explore. The quick succession of events in recent days, from the discovery of the drum to its successful decoding, had left Klemet feeling something close to euphoria. For a time. But the more he steeped himself in the background to the case, the darker his mood became. Was the tragedy that had decimated Sami villages in the seventeenth century poised to repeat itself today? The mobilisation of Sami politicos like Olaf Renson, in the 1980s, against companies like Mino Solo, showed that things were different now. To an extent. The Sami hadn't had to stage a full-scale revolt, as they had back in the mid-nineteenth century, for example. But recent events showed that progress could be reversed only too quickly. Would the region be able to resist the lure of a rich uranium mine, even if the risks were huge?

Klemet indicated and parked in front of the Renlycka cafeteria, run by Johann Henrik's wife. Henrik was still being held for questioning, but the examining judge – who had remained in Kautokeino for the time being – had told Klemet that he and his fellow detainee

Renson would be released that evening. With a gala reception due to open the UN conference on Sunday evening, everyone agreed that the freeing of the two Sami herders was an excellent idea. The judge wanted to hold them just a little longer, all the same, until Mikkel and John could be brought in for questioning instead. The arrest of two more Sami could easily pass for harassment, but the oil stains provided tangible evidence, in this case at least.

Two heavy-goods vehicles stood parked outside the cafeteria, one Russian, one Swedish. Klemet and Nina went inside. Johann Henrik's wife was installed behind the cash register, as usual. A man sat alone at a table in one corner. He nodded a greeting to the two police officers, who nodded back. Klemet and Nina approached the counter and ordered coffee. Johann Henrik's wife did not seem overjoyed to see them.

'Have you seen this man?' asked Klemet, showing her a photograph of Racagnal.

'Yes.' Her response was immediate. 'He was sitting in the same place as the Russian truck driver, over there in the corner, with all sorts of maps. He spent a long time here.'

'Can you remember when? Which day?'

She thought for a moment. A cheerful whistle sounded from the toilets, accompanied by a flush.

'It must have been a Friday, or a Tuesday. I remember because the truck driver whistling in the toilet stops here every Tuesday and Friday. This is his regular route. And I remember he had words with the man in your photograph.'

'And do you know where he was going?'

'All I know is that he wanted to go to Aslak's camp. He didn't say anything else.'

'Has he been back since?'

'No.'

Klemet paid for the coffees. He and Nina took a seat just as the toilet door opened. The driver of the Swedish truck emerged, whistling and clicking his fingers.

'Get my sandwiches ready, darlin', I'll be back in five minutes.

430

Gotta get off after that. *Hej*, Igor – hands off my sexy Sami while I'm out of the room!'

The Russian trucker laughed and raised a hand. The driver left the café, still whistling. Klemet recognised him as the Swedish trucker with the tattoos, the small-time trafficker. He whispered in Nina's ear. The two police officers watched the Swede leave. Outside, he pulled on a fur-lined work overall and opened a metal box fixed underneath his trailer. Klemet put down his coffee cup. The driver had just taken out an oil can. Brand name Arktisk Olje. The same as the cans in Olsen's garage. Nina spotted it, too.

The driver emptied the can using a funnel and carried it over to a skip on the parking lot. Then he came back to the cafeteria, whistling and wiping his hands energetically on his filthy overalls.

Brian Kallaway had never felt such excitement in his life. Success! The deposit he had just discovered, or rediscovered, would put his company at the top of the global game. And he, Kallaway, had tracked the boulders to the mother seam! Though the discovery was also thanks to Racagnal's hunter instincts, he had to admit. Kallaway was overjoyed. He and Racagnal had returned to their snow-mobiles. He felt as if he was walking on air. Euphoric. He had even forgotten all about Racagnal's evil moods. He clapped the Frenchman on the shoulder, laughing out loud. He was delighted. Absolutely delighted.

The Canadian set up the radio in the snowmobile trunk and put a call through to headquarters in La Défense. He simply had to share this fabulous discovery. He turned to Racagnal, all smiles.

'No offence, André, but I see now why the guys call you the Bulldog. You've done a great job.'

He turned back to the radio, adjusting the frequency, ready to make the call. Kallaway didn't hear Racagnal quietly asking him what he intended to say over the airwaves. Full of the thrill of his announcement, Kallaway didn't hear either when Racagnal said he shouldn't have called him the Bulldog. The last thing he saw was the swift movement of a long, thin shadow in the ground on front of him. He barely had time to feel the explosion of pain when the Frenchman's rock hammer shattered his skull.

Questioning the Swedish trucker had proved a lively business. The young man put up a fight, yelling loudly and insulting the two officers. Finally, Klemet forced him to the floor and straddled him while Nina fastened the handcuffs behind his back. With his overalls pulled tight across his chest, he was unable to cry out. The Swede calmed down eventually, but he continued to shower the police officers with insults and obscenities. Klemet left him inside the café with Nina, who called the station. The Sheriff promised reinforcements within fifteen minutes.

Outside, Klemet pulled on a pair of thin gloves and opened the truck's passenger door. He climbed into the cabin, settled himself in the seat and looked around before making a careful, systematic search of the bunk and cupboards. He turned everything over, leafed through the porn and mechanics magazines, checked the cigarette cartons and half-empty bottles of vodka. At last, he found what he was looking for.

The Swede hadn't made much of an effort, really. The heavy dagger, in its holster, was fixed to a wide leather belt hanging in a small fitted storage space behind the driver's seat. Klemet lifted it carefully and withdrew the blade, examined it closely then pushed it back into the holster and carried it to the cafeteria. The Swede was still lying face down at Nina's feet. She was taking the Russian driver's details and photographing his papers before letting him go. Klemet showed Nina the knife and thrust it under the Swedish driver's nose. The man's face turned ugly. He spat.

'Perhaps you have something to tell us, before things get really nasty for you,' suggested Klemet.

Sirens sounded in the distance. Brattsen would have made some joke about the charge of the Light Brigade. Shortly, the reinforcements from Kautokeino filled the small parking lot outside the cafeteria. Johann Henrik's wife sat impassively behind her cash register, smoothing her small Sami pinafore.

'So?' said Klemet, brandishing the dagger under the driver's nose a second time.

'You of all people should know a fucking Lapp dagger when you see one.' The Swede leered cockily now, determined to keep up the repartee. Then his face drained white. The Renlycka's door had opened to admit the Sheriff and five officers from Kautokeino bringing in two Sami herders. The young men hung their heads, avoiding eye-contact. Mikkel and John.

John looked utterly broken.

'It was the first time we'd met in front of Olsen's barn, Klemet. I promise. What you saw, it was the first time. It was stupid. Just a bit of booze and fags, that's all. Nothing to get worked up about.'

'I'm not interested in that. I want to talk to you about Mattis's death.'

John's eyes opened wide in horror. He stared wildly at the Swede, then at Mikkel, who looked fit to explode.

'It wasn't me!' Mikkel's voice was raucous and much too loud. 'Not me! We were just supposed to get the drum back, that's all. That's all! I swear it wasn't me!'

'Who for?' Klemet was shouting now, right in Mikkel's face.

'For Olsen!' Mikkel squeaked in terror. 'And Mattis hadn't got it. He was pissed, Mattis was, pissed as a rat. But I wouldn't have hurt him, never. I didn't want to go out there on my own. It wasn't me. It wasn't me, I swear. I didn't even have a knife. It wasn't me,' he said, breaking down in sobs. 'I just set fire to the scooter. That was all I did. Like Olsen said – destroy the GPS, so no one could see where Mattis had been on Sunday night.'

'And what was Aslak doing there with you?' Klemet hollered again.

'Aslak? Aslak? There was no Aslak. He wasn't there, not Aslak,' wailed Mikkel. 'It was just me and . . .'

Across the room, on the floor, the Swede had fallen silent. He turned his head and spat in Mikkel's direction.

54

Friday 28 January

Central Sápmi

Aslak saw the Frenchman return to the bivouac alone. His clothes were stained, his face expressionless, apart from one thing. His pupils were fully dilated. He was carrying his hammer, covered in blood, and made no attempt to conceal it. He took the radio set and spoke to someone in Swedish, in a dull monotone, giving his position.

'Not far from the deposits. Come quickly before the storm closes in. You won't be disappointed.'

He ended the call. Aslak watched him, never once taking his eyes off the man. Evil itself. He thought of his wife. What was she doing now? He had been gone too long. She would have no food left. How would she cope? Aslak had to leave. If the men on the radio came here, perhaps there would be no one back there to threaten Aila. Aslak's knife was still tucked inside his reindeer-skin boot. It never left him. The man with the hammer thought Aslak had accepted his authority. But a man like Aslak would never accept evil.

He pictured the sign his wife had drawn in the dust. He had understood there and then that he had to act. Perhaps his wife would find peace at last. Perhaps not her reason, but peace of a kind. She had known too much misery to hope she could ever know happiness again. She was misery itself. And suffering. And shrieking.

Aslak saw the man with the bloodstained hammer and understood. The sky was obscured now by heavy, dark grey cloud. The storm was approaching. Like the day his grandfather had left. He had set out alone one night, during a winter storm; like all old people who had become a burden to the clan. They would set out alone across the tundra and were never seen again. Aslak scanned the clouds. A storm like the one when he was seven years old, at the boarding school in Kautokeino. On the same day his grandfather had left, Aslak had left, too. At seven years old, he had leaped from a window in the school building, out into the storm, never to return.

He thought of his herd and his dogs. He had failed. A good herder never abandoned his animals. He looked at the Frenchman, standing motionless, ten metres away. And he thought of Mattis. He thought of Mattis's body as he had discovered it, alerted by the smoke from the snowmobile. He remembered what he had told the Reindeer Police. Mattis had been killed by the laws of men. Their rules. Their insatiable greed. People like the man facing him now had wrought the downfall of herders like Aslak. Mino Solo had brought evil and sorrow. And he, the man with the hammer, had brought evil and sorrow twice over. He would pay.

Johann Henrik's wife missed nothing from her vantage point behind the cash register. She saw how Mikkel had betrayed the Swedish driver. She approached Klemet.

'Olsen came by here this morning. Very early. He came in to fill his thermos with coffee. Your colleague was with him, in his car. The Sami-hunter. And they went that way.'

She pointed along Highway 92, to the north-east, in the direction of the gathering clouds.

Klemet and Nina set off immediately, followed by an extra patrol from Kautokeino. The Sheriff called the judge back at headquarters, asking him to search Olsen's safe. They were likely to make some interesting finds.

The patrol cars drove to a fork in the road and parked. The officers worked quickly. Everyone knew exactly what they had to do. A few minutes later, four snowmobiles had been unloaded from the trailers and began threading along a rift marking the bottom of a small hill, the hard, glittering flank of snow covered with twisted, skeletal scrub. The four scooters turned onto a frozen river, winding for a few kilometres, then turned again to make the climb to the high plateau. Klemet could see Aslak's camp in the distance. The quiet was unnerving. He couldn't see any smoke. He accelerated. What had driven Aslak to commit an act like that on Mattis's body? Aslak was capable of extraordinary things, as Klemet well knew. Acts no one else would dare attempt.

The four scooters slowed on the approach to Aslak's tents. Everyone drew their weapons: the Sheriff had brought them from the safe back at the station in Kautokeino. The gun felt strange to the touch, thought Klemet. This was the first time he had gone armed since joining the Reindeer Police. The other two officers made their way around the outside of the tents. There was no noise from inside. Klemet signalled to Nina to lift the flap on the main *lavu*. His gun trembled slightly in his hand. Nina pulled the canvas back sharply and Klemet dived inside but stopped instantly. Nina followed and saw why. Klemet stood with his gun held loosely against his thigh, gazing down at Aila's body. Nina kneeled beside her. Aila's face was tinged with blue. She had been dead for several days, it seemed. The fire was completely cold. She lay on her back, her arms held up, as if trying to catch something beyond her grasp.

Nina stayed kneeling on the floor, pointing out something to Klemet. He followed her gaze. Near the hearth, someone had written two letters with their finger on a smooth patch of earth. MS. For Mino Solo.

'The other marks on the ears,' he said, quietly.

55

Friday 28 January

Central Sápmi

André Racagnal watched the Sami guide. The guy had been watching him, too, from the start. He was still watching him now from under his four-pointed hat, with his lasso slung across his chest. Except Racagnal didn't need him any more. Now, everything would work out. He'd make sure the farmer kept his side of the deal, the old bastard. Everything would work out fine. He'd exploit the fucking mine, with the world at his fucking feet, and he'd have himself a fine brace of little minxes when he got back.

The wind had risen and thin flakes of snow whirled around him. Fuck, it was cold! He rubbed his face with his livid, red-stained hand. He felt hot. And that bastard's looking at me still. He picked up his hammer and moved towards the Sami. The bastard wasn't moving. Racagnal didn't need him now. All over for him. He'd served his purpose. He could toss him aside. He stepped forward again. The other man stared straight at him. Fuck him. Racagnal moved slowly. Finally, Aslak got to his feet. Racagnal saw his eyes, his clenched jaw, his wrinkled nose. The wolf was biding his time.

'Get on with it,' he said. 'We're breaking camp. Moving on to the next valley. The kid's waiting for us there. We're almost done. Then you can get off back home to your wife. And you'll get your dogs.'

He moved forward again, held out his SPP2.

'Here, put this in its case.' He placed the device on the small folding table.

The Sami was forced to turn slightly to reach for the SPP2. For a quarter of a second, Racagnal would be out of his field of vision. The guide straightened up and reached out carefully, feeling for the device but keeping his eyes on the Frenchman.

He was barely a metre away now. Racagnal acted with brutal force. The Swedish hammer swung through the air and hit home hard with a hideous cracking sound. But that Sami bastard had anticipated his move. Racagnal had caught him on the shoulder, probably shattered his clavicle. Surprised to have missed the Sami's skull, he was caught off guard for two or three seconds. That was enough. The Sami pulled a large dagger out of his boot, its handle oiled and gleaming. Everything seemed to happen in slow motion after that. Despite his wrecked shoulder, the man flung himself at Racagnal, who, too close to lift the hammer for a second strike, tried to push the Sami away with his free hand.

The Frenchman could hardly comprehend what happened next. The guide opened his huge jaw wide and bit Racagnal's hand. Racagnal roared, but the man's teeth clenched tighter than a trap. In the next instant, with no time for anything but the cold inrush of fear, he saw the Sami slice at his wrist with a powerful swipe of the dagger. Racagnal released the hammer and clutched the source of the spurting blood. Yelling with pain, he saw the snow turn red. The Sami was threatening him with the knife now, but didn't seem ready to kill him. Aslak crouched down, keeping his eyes fixed on his opponent, who was dancing now in agony. The guide reached for Racagnal's severed hand, lying in the snow. No, not the hand, but the silver wrist-chain and tag, that had slipped free. The Sami rose to his full height.

'Mino Solo,' he said. 'Mino Solo.'

*

When the officers called back to the station to report the discovery of Aila's body, the Sheriff dispatched a team straightaway. The judge had made a detailed search of Olsen's place, including opening the old man's safe, in which they had found papers linking Olsen to the French geologist, a draft employment contract for Brattsen as head of security at a mine somewhere in the region, and a statement by Ulrika, a fifteen-year-old girl from Kautokeino, detailing how she had been raped. By Racagnal.

The four officers set off again. The sky was increasingly overcast. Visibility was still good, but the weather would turn bad very soon. Nina was worried. How would they find the exact spot in a snow-storm? Despite the cloud cover, it was turning much colder, fast. They should have turned back, continued the chase later.

Klemet reassured her. He knew these mountains. He felt more at home here now than ever before. He had committed everything to memory – the details of the drum, the *joïk*, the maps. They drove on, Klemet in the lead, keeping up a steady pace. Nina was right, they had very little time. Only the most experienced rider could find a way across the tundra in weather like this. The wind was blowing the first flakes of snow almost horizontally now. Nina's helmet covered her head completely, but she felt thin fingers of cold stealing over her left temple. Like someone working the point of a knife into her skin. She wanted to cover the chink in her helmet with her glove, to stop the pain, just for a minute, but she daren't let go of the handlebar, dreading she might lose control of her heavy machine. Worse conditions lay ahead, she could see that. The sun was still above the horizon, but hidden now behind thick bars of black cloud.

Klemet made the going even tougher by choosing a short cut though a steep valley. Most of the breeders avoided going that way. Klemet rode into it without a second thought, aware that he was saving precious time. The others followed bravely. At last, he emerged at the far end, riding down a gentle slope to a small, wind-ing river. Rounding a bend, Klemet almost collided with a man on his knees in the middle of the frozen surface. The man stared in horror at the snowmobile pulling up sharply just a couple metres away. His face was gashed and bleeding. Olsen.

The old man flung his arms wide and pointed to a crashed scooter on the nearby bank, half buried in powdery snow. He hadn't seen a rock, concealed beneath the drift. A body lay stretched out a little further away. Motionless.

'Oh, thank God you're here,' declared Olsen, his face a picture of relief, then wincing suddenly at the sharp pain from his neck. 'The lad's worse than useless. A hopeless rider. I was guiding him on the trail of a dangerous villain. He—'

His confident tone faltered as Klemet shoved him aside and turned Brattsen over. He was unconscious but otherwise unhurt. Klemet left the two reinforcements to take statements and deal with the pair, then rode on, followed by Nina, racing ahead into the storm.

Racagnal shook his head, in pain and incomprehension. He was trembling all over. But the other man seemed in no hurry to kill him. He felt a glimmer of hope when the Sami untied his lasso and bound him tight. Very tight. But now he was pulling him; pulling him and forcing Racagnal to walk, following his scooter tracks in the snow.

They walked for what seemed like an eternity. Racagnal stumbled, sinking deep into the snow, howling with pain at every fall. The cold bit at the stump of his wrist. The pain was unbearable. The Frenchman sweated as the cold closed in around them. The storm had risen now, making earth and sky almost indistinguishable. The wind blew hard, sweeping everything in its path. They walked on through snowflakes swirling in all directions. Racagnal hollered and yelled, cursing the Sami guide. But the man jerked him forward, pulling him on, impervious to the storm and his own steadily increasing pain.

Before long, the wind seemed to die down. Racagnal recognised the steep slope leading down to the mine. The Sami had followed their tracks this far. The guide tugged at the rope again, with brutal force. Racagnal fell forward, roaring and cursing.

Then they were at the mine entrance. Aslak tugged again, forcing Racagnal to crouch down. The Sami pitched him forward into the middle of the chamber, in almost total darkness, then dragged him almost to his feet under the low ceiling. He could feel the man doing something, but he had no idea what. Then he realised, too late. Another rope was bound tight around his shoulders, pinning his arms closer to his sides, and binding his legs. He fell, unable to move. He could no longer clutch his wrist, to try to staunch the bleeding. He shrieked liked a madman, in rage, pain and terror. He was going to die here. Then he felt the Sami stuffing something into his mouth. He struggled, but he was powerless to resist. The rock choked his voice. Pitchblende. His mouth was filled the filthy stuff. The Sami untied Racagnal's scarf from around his neck and knotted it tightly over his mouth. By the faint light from the tunnel entrance Racagnal watched, exhausted, defeated, as the man's silhouette loomed over him, then moved away.

'Mino Solo. For Aila.'

Klemet recognised the valley immediately, though he had never been there before. He and Nina found the abandoned bivouac. The snowmobile. The blood-soaked hammer. The storm had scattered objects and papers all around. A folding table had blown away. The wind was sweeping everything in its path.

Klemet and Nina didn't speak. The sky was almost dark now, though it was barely 2 p.m. Nina pointed to faint traces on the ground, leading into the storm. They could see no more than ten metres or so. The horizon was a blank. They climbed back aboard their scooters and followed the tracks, neither too slowly, to avoid sinking into the snow, nor too fast, so as not to hit any unseen obstacles.

Klemet was afraid now. He would never admit it, but he was afraid. All his life, he had struggled with his fear of the terrifying storms that battered the tundra. He thought he had conquered it by sheer force of will, stepping out alone from the Reindeer Police huts into the freezing dark. But the fear returned when Aslak was around, he knew that. And Aslak had done a terrible thing. He would have to pay. Klemet would have to arrest him, if he was still alive.

Slowly, they moved forward. The tracks were more, and difficult to follow. The snow swirled angrily, closing in on them. Twice, Klemet had spotted traces of red in the beam of his headlights.

This storm. It was the same. Exactly the same. He shut out the image, but it forced its way back. His childhood self, seven years old. On a window ledge at the boarding school in Kautokeino. Clutching a small bag of provisions, collected carefully over several days. Provisions for two people. Enough to get back to his farm. To run away from school, where he and his friend had been beaten for speaking Sami. He had stood on the window ledge in the freezing night, preparing to travel thirty kilometres in the pitch dark, at minus 30°C. At seven years of age. And this was the very same storm, he knew that now, its breath blasting his ears. He forced himself to go on.

The wind made light of his snowsuit, insinuating itself through the slightest chink, into the furthest corners of his memory. The same storm, the same dread. He came to a place on the mountain where the tracks headed in two directions. To the left, they led down a steep slope, a kind of narrow ramp. But he could see nothing beyond that. Klemet turned his snowmobile in the other direction, up towards the summit. The tracks were fainter than ever now, of a man alone. Klemet looked up ahead, his face creased with tension. He followed the beam of the headlights, searching the snow, blown horizontally by the screaming wind. Higher up, almost obliterated by the gusts of flakes, he saw the silhouette of a man, one shoulder drooping forward, wearing a four-pointed hat. Aslak was waiting for him.

Klemet took a deep breath. He turned to Nina. Through the tumult, he glimpsed his colleague's exhausted, heart-stopping expression.

'Wait for me here,' he yelled, hoarse with the effort.

Klemet rode forward. He knew the confrontation was inevitable. Even Nina had understood that. He stopped in front of Aslak. The herder's features were hollow with exhaustion. His reindeer-skin cloak was soaked with blood at the shoulder. He was suffering, but

442

gave no sign of it. His hands were empty, his fists clenched. Klemet breathed deeply. He would have to speak first.

'Why, Aslak? Why Mattis?' he shouted over the storm.

Aslak's face had lost its hard, inscrutable expression. Pain and exhaustion were written there now. His eyelids drooped. He shook his head, holding back a shudder of pain. The wind and snow whipped at his face. His eyelashes and beard were white with frost.

'Mattis was dead when I arrived,' he shouted back. 'I wept for him, Klemet. I cried tears for the first time in my life.'

Klemet could see Aslak was sincere. Saw, too, that the admission cost him nothing.

'When I was a child, I never cried. For Aila, with the baby, I never cried. Mattis was a victim of men. And rules. The Reindeer Administration. And business. Mino Solo was the worst. You know that. All guilty. The council. The people handing out licences. They knew about Aila. They did nothing for her. That was why I cut and marked the ears. That was why I left them in the town. So that people would know.'

'Why didn't you come and see me?' Klemet shouted, narrowing his eyes against the ice crystals stinging his face.

'I don't believe in your justice, Klemet.'

'The blood? Around Mattis's eyes?'

'For our elders. On the first day of the return of the sun after the long night, a wooden ring would be dipped in blood. They looked through it to watch the sun rise, to give courage to those who had lost heart.'

Aslak fell silent, his eyes half closed. It seemed to Klemet that he saw a spark of humanity in them, for the first time in his life.

'Mattis had lost heart.' Aslak spoke loud and clear over the storm. 'I helped him to see through the ring of blood. He died the day the sun was reborn. But he will find new courage in the afterlife. He is at peace.'

Aslak held out his fist and opened his hand. He was holding Racagnal's bloodstained bracelet.

'Aslak . . .'

Klemet shook his head. Tears mingled with the snow in his eyes.

He could no longer feel the wind whipping him. He shouted over the gale.

'Aslak – Aila is dead. We found her just now.'

Klemet saw Aslak close his eyes for a moment. His fists, tightly balled until now, were unclenched. As if he had taken a decision and felt calmer as a result.

His silhouette was barely visible through the veil of snow. The sky was as black as night. Aslak moved forward into the beam of the headlights, close enough to reach out and touch Klemet. His voice was barely raised.

'Klemet, make sure my herd does not suffer.'

The two men looked at one another. Klemet struggled to fight down his terror of the darkness closing in all around. There was something he had to say, but he felt paralysed. Aslak began to turn away.

'Aslak!' Klemet shouted out again. 'Where is the Frenchman? Aslak, I have to arrest you!'

Aslak turned and looked back.

'I shall accept the justice of the mountains.' His voice rang out. Then he came closer to Klemet, speaking quietly again.

'Are you afraid?' And for the first time, his face looked wonderfully kind.

Klemet said nothing, overcome with emotion.

'You are wrong to feel afraid,' said Aslak, gently.

'You don't know what I'm thinking!' Klemet burst out.

'I know what you're thinking.'

'What do you know?' Klemet was yelling now, tears stinging his eyes. 'We were seven years old. Dear God, Aslak! Seven years old!'

'But we were supposed to go together, Klemet. It was our pact.'

Klemet could hold back no longer. He slumped forward over the bars of his scooter, crying in the dark like the child he no longer was.

Nina watched helplessly from below. She saw Aslak turn and walk away, saw her colleague's shoulders shaking. But she made no move.

When Klemet raised his head, Aslak had disappeared into the Arctic night.

Author's Note

When I arrived in Sweden in 1994, I knew absolutely nothing about life in Scandinavia, nothing about the culture or the history. I was there because I had met a Swedish woman, and she was the only thing that interested me! But, as a journalist, I quickly realised that my ignorance was an advantage, because I had no preconceived ideas whatsoever. Absolutely everything was new to me, and I absorbed it all like a sponge, discovering all the wonderful aspects of Scandinavian culture.

Not long after my arrival in Sweden, one of the first elections was held for the Sametinget, the Sami parliament of Sweden. A voting office was installed at the Stockholm city hall for the Sami who lived there.

I was curious about it, so I went to interview the voters. I met a young Sami student who told me that she was voting for a certain party because of their stance on land rights for the ancestral Sami territory. She came from a family of reindeer herders who used the land as pasture, but they were struggling against a mining company that wanted to prospect there. She invited me to visit her family in Sápmi so that I could see it all for myself. This was my first contact with the Sami.

It was at this time that I discovered a darker side of Nordic society, one in which certain injustices had continued for decades, thanks to an implicit racism and imperialist attitude – something that one could scarcely imagine surviving in this forward-thinking country. This new awareness influenced my understanding of the Sami from that moment on. I've never viewed them as an exotic folk culture, the way they're often depicted in magazines, but rather as a people at war, equipped with insufficient weapons, and battling for their very existence against a more powerful foe. And in the light of their struggle for survival, it's exasperating for them when they're represented merely as the token indigenous people, wearing brightly coloured costumes, tending to Santa's reindeer. Now that I had a deeper insight into their plight, I wanted to share it with the world – although I hadn't yet figured out the best way to do that.

Several years later, I learned for the first time about the 'reindeer police', a special unit in northern Norway tasked with settling conflicts that arise from reindeer herding. I realised that, by following these special police units, I could show the way of life in Sápmi from a unique, accessible perspective. I wrote several articles about the reindeer police for *Le Monde*, and later produced a television documentary about them. For two months, I followed these police officers on their patrols, on snowmobiles during the snowy winter, spring, and autumn weeks, learning everything I could about their lives and their work with the reindeer herders. At the same time, I was doing intensive research into the culture of this region of the remote north, writing articles about different aspects of the community and the economy there. I listened to stories that I never would have heard in Stockholm or Oslo, stories that showed me an entirely different side of Scandinavia.

And, finally, after all the people I had met, and all the stories I had seen and heard, I was left with no choice but to write it all down.

Olivier Truc, 2014

Olivier Truc was born in France in 1964. He has worked as a journalist since 1986, and has been based in Stockholm since 1994, where he is currently the Nordic and Baltic correspondent for *Le Monde* and *Le Point*. As a reporter, Olivier Truc covers subjects from politics and economics to social issues like immigration and minorities. He has also produced TV documentaries, including one that portrays a group of Norwegian policemen in Lapland. This is his debut novel.